GALAXY'S EDGE

EDITED BY MIKE RESNICK

ISSUE 3 : JULY 2013

Mike Resnick, Editor
Shahid Mahmud, Publisher

Published by Arc Manor/Phoenix Pick
P.O. Box 10339
Rockville, MD 20849-0339

Galaxy's Edge is published every two months: March, May, July, September, November & January.

www.GalaxysEdge.com

Galaxy's Edge is an invitation-only magazine. We do not accept unsolicited manuscripts. Unsolicited manuscripts will be disposed of or mailed back to the sender (unopened) at our discretion.

All material is either copyright © by Arc Manor LLC, Rockville, MD, or copyright © by the respective authors as indicated within the magazine.

This magazine (or any portion of it) may not be copied or reproduced, in whole or in part, by any means, electronic, mechanical or otherwise, without written permission from the publisher, except by a reviewer who may quote brief passages in a review.

Each issue of *Galaxy's Edge* is issued as a stand-alone "book" with a separate ISBN and may be purchased at wholesale venues dedicated to book sales (e.g., Ingram) or directly from the publisher's website.

ISBN (Amazon Only): 9781976874406

Advertising in the magazine is available. Quarter page (half column), $95 per issue. Half page (full column, vertical or two half columns, horizontal) $165 per issue. Full page (two full columns) $295 per issue. Back Cover (full color) $495 per issue. All interior advertising is in black and white.

Please write to advert@GalaxysEdge.com.

CONTENTS

THE EDITOR'S WORD by Mike Resnick	3
THE ISLANDS OF HOPE by Heidi Ruby Miller	9
A SOLDIER'S COMPLAINT by Eric Flint	13
THE HELD DAUGHTER by Laurie Tom	15
A GALAXY CALLED ROME by Barry N. Malzberg	23
A BRIEF HISTORY OF A WORLD IN THE TIME BEFORE THIS TIME by Muxing Zhao	34
WITH FOLDED HANDS by Jack Williamson	38
JUST ANOTHER NIGHT AT THE QUARTERLY MEETING OF TERRIFYING GIANT MONSTERS by Brennan Harvey	61
TWO FANTASIES by C. L. Moore	65
THE TEAMMATES by Ron Collins	68
BURIED HOPES by Michael Flynn	76
A FROZEN FUTURE by Gregory Benford	88
FROM THE HEART'S BASEMENT by Barry N. Malzberg	93
PHOENIX PICK PRESENTS	95
BOOK REVIEWS by Paul Cook	113
SERIALIZATION: *DARK UNIVERSE* by Daniel F. Galouye	118
CHAPTER TEN	118
CHAPTER ELEVEN	123
CHAPTER TWELVE	128
CHAPTER THIRTEEN	133

"The most fun I ever had in my life was the two months that I sat at the typewriter working on *Adventures*. I've done books of more lasting import, and I've created characters of far more depth and complexity, but during that period I fell, hopelessly and eternally, in love with Lucifer Jones."
—*Mike Resnick,
Introduction to* Adventures

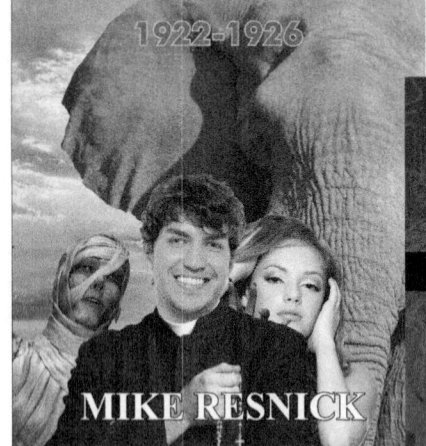

A very special fan letter to start off this third issue of Galaxy's Edge

Mike, Shahid—

I've just come back from two weeks in Europe, and during this morning's jet-laggy prowling through the mountain of accumulated mail I came upon *Galaxy's Edge* #2, with my story in it. I was very impressed indeed with the magazine.

Mike, it's a beautiful job, from the lively editorial onward. (Especially that editorial!) It's got the feel of a true prozine, which is not surprising, since you know quite well what a true prozine ought to contain and to look like, and you've done it. And, Shahid, it's a swell production job.

Starting about 1949 I began to collect the s-f magazines, and I put together a complete collection of every one of them from Hugo Gernsback's first 1926 issue onward. I still have them all, and (though I rarely read them any more) I continue to maintain my complete files of *Analog* and *F&SF* and *Asimov's*, and, of course, all the now defunct mags like *Galaxy* and *Future* and *Two Complete Science-Adventure Books*. (I am not making that last title up, Shahid.) But I don't bother collecting the recently founded magazines, because their saddle-stitched format doesn't look good on the shelves and there are too many of them for me to keep track of and in general I just don't want to bother.

I want to keep a complete run of *Galaxy's Edge*, though, not only because it shows promise of being a damned good magazine but because in content and layout it summons the feelings that led me to collect all those now-extinct magazines of sixty years ago, *Thrilling Wonder Stories* and *Science Fiction Quarterly* and *Super Science Stories* and all the rest.

Shahid, can you ship me a copy of issue number #1? And please keep me on the mailing list. I haven't written a fan letter to a prozine in maybe fifty years and it's a nice feeling to be doing it again.
Bob
[Grand Master Robert Silverberg]

Mike's note: Of course we're sending Bob his hard copy of issue #1. And look for a wonderful story of his in issue #4.

THE EDITOR'S WORD

by Mike Resnick

Welcome to the third issue of *Galaxy's Edge*. We're happy to present more of our favorite writers, including another C. L. Moore story that has been lost in a college magazine for 82 years, plus a pair of classics by Jack Williamson and Barry Malzberg, a fantasy by Heidi Ruby Miller that's stayed with me since the first time I read it some years ago, one of Eric Flint's very few short stories, a fine short story by Michael F. Flynn, and works by newer writers Laurie Tom (winner of the Writers of the Future Gold Prize), Brennan Harvey, Ron Collins, and who we believe is the youngest author ever to sell to a professional science fiction market, 13-year-old Muxing Zhao. And of course there are the regular columns by Gregory Benford (science), Paul Cook (book reviews), and Barry Malzberg (pretty much anything he damned well pleases). It's all up ahead in black and white.

And speaking of black and white…Three of my five favorite films—*The Maltese Falcon*, *Casablanca*, and *The Mask of Dimitrios*—have one thing in common: they're in glorious black-and-white.

The American Film Institute polled its members in 1998 and again in 2007. The poll topper for the best film ever made, both times, was *Citizen Kane*. And yes, it's in black-and-white.

3

The other day mystery writer/editor Ed Gorman and I were discussing some of our favorite films over on Facebook, and of course many of them were black-and-white. Irish science fiction editor John Kenny joined the discussion, and told us that his kids won't watch any black-and-white films. A number of other parents had the same complaint. It reminded me of an incident about a decade ago, when I was teaching at Clarion, and David Barr Kirtley handed in a story titled "The Black Bird," about 90% metaphor and 100% brilliant. (I later bought it for an anthology I was editing.) We had a class of 19. When we discussed it (since he was the writer David's opinion didn't count), the result was that two of the students loved the story and 16—the 16 youngest—didn't. It occurred to me to ask for a show of hands: how many of them had actually seen *The Maltese Falcon*? Two hands went up—the two who liked the story. I asked the other 16 why they hadn't watched this classic, which is on TV somewhere almost every week. The answer, from all of them: it was in black-and-white.

So before these brilliant films, and the opportunity to watch them, get swallowed up by history, I thought I'd point out some excellent fantasies, as well-made (or better) than any $70 million full-color travesty playing in the theaters today. Here they are, in no particular order:

✡

Portrait of Jennie (1948). This is adapted from Robert Nathan's novel, which managed to stay in print for close to three-quarters of a century. Joseph Cotton is a struggling painter; he has skills and technique, but there's simply no soul, no *feeling*, in his paintings. One night he is wandering through the park and runs into a little girl, maybe seven or eight years old, named Jennie. They talk, and he is charmed by her (in a non-pedophile way). A few nights later he runs into her again—only now she's maybe eleven. And every few nights he meets her, and each time she's older, trying (as she explains) to catch up to him. He is captivated, and begins painting her portrait. Jennie, who is played by Jennifer Jones in one of her better performances, tells him details of her life, and he realizes that she was a little girl maybe 30 years ago. Gradually, as she changes from a girl to a young woman, he falls in love with her, and the portrait finally begins showing the one quality that was missing in his previous paintings. He tries to learn more about her, and discovers that she died about a quarter century ago in a boating accident. He rushes to the scene of the accident, not sure this all hasn't been a dream, and arrives just too late to save her—but his feelings for her translate into the painting that makes his reputation, the "Portrait of Jennie."

✡

Miracle on 34th Street (1947). A charming fantasy in which one of those bell-ringing Santas you see on every street corner and store front in December turns out to be the *real* Santa. Edmund Gwenn plays Santa, a very *very* young Natalie Wood plays a girl who believes in him, and the film's a delight from the beginning right through the trial where the government can't prove he *isn't* Santa, and the Post Office settles the issue once and for all.

✡

The Canterville Ghost (1944). Charles Laughton plays Sir Simon de Canterville, a 17th Century nobleman who flees to his castle to avoid a duel to the death. As a punishment for his cowardice, his father seals him in the room where he is hiding, and curses him to spend all eternity as a ghost, unable to rest in his grave until a descendant performs an act of heroism. Move the clock ahead past three centuries of cowards, and we come to the latest descendant, Cuffy Williams, a cowardly U.S. soldier played by Robert Young. It takes a 6-year-old noblewoman, Margaret O'Brien, to bring matters to a happy solution.

✡

The Ghost and Mrs. Muir (1947). A young widow, played by Gene Tierney, inherits a seaside cottage that is haunted by the ghost of a roguish sea captain, played by Rex Harrison. When her sources of income dry up, it's Harrison to the rescue, dictating his obscenity-laced and salacious memoir to her. She manages to sell the manuscript, begins to make a living in publishing, and the romance between Mrs. Muir and the ghost continues to grow. Finally, an old lady, she breathes her last—and suddenly there is the ghost, waiting for her, and hand-in-hand they go out through the front door and wander off together into the mist.

✿

The Devil and Daniel Webster (1941). From Stephen Vincent Benet's Pulitzer winner, and re-released as *All That Money Can Buy*. Jabez Stone, a local farmer, has two kinds of luck: bad and worse. In desperation, he sells his soul to Mr. Scratch (the devil, played by Walter Huston) to keep his farm, then realizes what he's done and gets the best lawyer in the country, Daniel Webster (played by Edward Arnold), to plead his case to keep his soul before a jury consisting of corpses and ghosts who are all in Satan's thrall. Undeterred, Webster goes to work, and in the climax delivers such a brilliant and passionate oration that even the dead, soulless jury votes in favor of his client.

✿

Death Takes a Holiday (1934). A real oldie, and it still moves people. Fredric March plays Death, who can't understand why people fear him so, and he comes to Earth in human form to find out. And he falls in love. And no one dies, not even the thousands of people who are in utter agony and *should* die. And eventually he must make a choice: stay with the woman he loves, or leave her and go back to work so that people can die once again.

✿

Mr. Peabody and the Mermaid (1948). William Powell is a man who is approaching his 50th birthday (ancient in 1948 Hollywood terms), and Ann Blyth is a mermaid that he accidentally catches and even more accidentally falls in love with. Ultimately it's not a comedy or a romance, but a sensitive fantasy about coming to grips with growing old.

✿

Topper (1937). Taken from the bestseller by the fantastic humorist (or humorous fantasist) Thorne Smith, this is the story of George and Marion Kerby (Cary Grant and Constance Bennett), who drive recklessly once too often and die in a crash. Since they have lived a totally useless life, consisting mostly of drinking, carousing, and partying, they find themselves not in heaven or hell, but in limbo. To ascend to the higher level, they must do a good deed, and they decide to help their friend, Cosmo Topper (Roland Young). Problems ensue when Marion falls for Topper, George gets jealous and vengeful, Topper's wife is not amused, and the story goes from one outrageous scene to another before it's finally resolved.

✿

I Married a Witch (1942). Another fantasy/comedy taken from a Thorne Smith novel, this time *The Passionate Witch*, which was completed by Norman Matson when Smith died suddenly while writing it. This one stars Fredric March as a candidate for governor and Veronica Lake as a resurrected witch who falls in love with him, helps him with the governorship, and undergoes numerous changes from witch to woman to ghost and back again before there's a satisfactory conclusion.

✿

Topper Returns (1938) is the third Topper movie (the less-than-inspired *Topper Takes a Trip* was the second). It once again features Roland Young and Billie Burke as Cosmo Topper and his wife, but this time there is no George and Marion Kerby (the married ghosts), but rather a murder victim, Joan Blondell, who wants to solve her own murder in time to prevent her friend Carole Landis from being murdered. And if that sounds too serious, remember that these are Thorne Smith's characters.

✿

Lost Horizon (1937). Directed by Frank Capra, this story of a lost land of eternal youth stars Ronald Colman and Jane Wyatt, and if you don't know the story, what are you doing reading *Galaxy's Edge*? (But just in case: an airplane is hijacked and lands in the Himalayas, and is taken to Shangri-La, an idyllic valley where everyone lives in peace and no one ever grows old. Colman's hijacking turns out not to have been an accident or a crime; the High Lama is finally dying of old age after hundreds of years and has chosen Colman as his successor. Cir-

WINNER OF THE
LIFEBOAT TO THE STARS AWARD

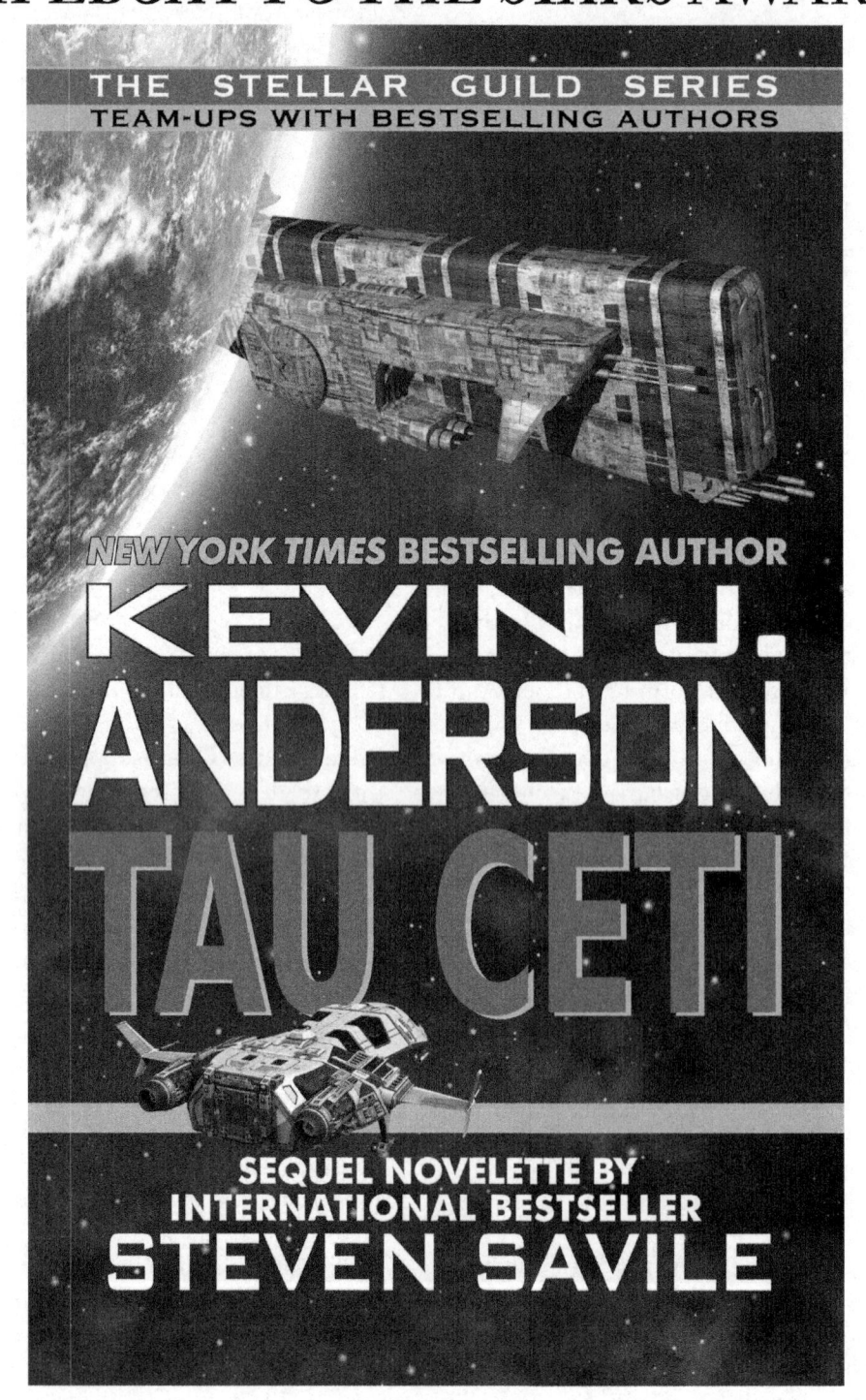

THE STELLAR GUILD SERIES
TEAM-UPS WITH BESTSELLING AUTHORS

NEW YORK TIMES BESTSELLING AUTHOR

KEVIN J. ANDERSON
TAU CETI

SEQUEL NOVELETTE BY
INTERNATIONAL BESTSELLER
STEVEN SAVILE

"Broad, intriguing speculation on human evolution and first contact." —*Publisher's Weekly*

BEYOND THE DOORS OF DEATH

ROBERT SILVERBERG
DAMIEN BRODERICK

BASED ON THE CLASSIC AWARD WINNING NOVELLA
BORN WITH THE DEAD

ON SALE NOW

cumstances lead Colman to leave with his brother and a woman from the village, who soon ages and dies once beyond Shangri-La's border. They are rescued by a search team that's looking for them, but Colman soon eludes them and after seemingly endless searching, sees Shangri-La in the distance and heads for it.

✣

The Picture of Dorian Gray (1945). Taken from the Oscar Wilde story, this stars Hurd Hatfield as Dorian Gray, a handsome young man who is totally corrupt. He has his portrait painted, and as his sins and debaucheries continue, his face remains unmarked, but the portrait, which he hides in the attic, becomes uglier and uglier. Eventually a shred of conscience convinces him to stab the portrait with a knife, and as the portrait is destroyed, he himself dies, as the two were somehow linked. Nice supporting cast of Angela Lansbury, George Sanders, Peter Lawford, and Donna Reed.

✣

The Bishop's Wife (1947). A charming fantasy, in which an Anglican bishop (David Niven), who has ignored family and friends in the attempt to plan and build an elaborate new cathedral, has reached a dead end, and prays for guidance—and lo and behold, here comes Dudley (Cary Grant), an angel sent to help him. Dudley instantly charms everyone else in Niven's household—his maid, his daughter, even his wife—but Niven is no closer to getting his cathedral, and very soon it appears that Niven's wife (Loretta Young) is falling for Dudley. Finally Niven lies and tells Dudley that funding and designs for the building have arrived, his prayers were answered, and Dudley can go away. Dudley doesn't quite believe it, and Niven realizes that he's probably lost his wife without having gained his cathedral. When he admits that his wife means more to him than the cathedral, Dudley reappears to tell him that his prayer has been answered. No, not that he'll get his cathedral, but that he realizes what's important in life. "But I asked for a cathedral," says Niven. "No," says Dudley, "you asked for guidance." And now he has it.

✣

The Seventh Seal (1957). Not all black-and-white fantasies have to be made before 1950, and not all have to come from the United States. This 1957 Swedish classic by Ingmar Bergman takes place during the Black Plague, and features the most famous chess game ever filmed, between a knight (Max von Sydow) and Death, with the knight's soul as the stakes. The film ends with a very solemn and very memorable dance of death.

✣

Dracula (1931). So okay, *Dracula* is an antique. It creaks. It's overwritten and overacted and underachieved. But it has the definitive Dracula of the first three-quarters of a century of filmmaking, as portrayed by Bela Lugosi. It wasn't until Frank Langella's version that the image of Dracula changed, and people realized he could be articulate, speak without an accent, and be sexually appealing to women of all ages. Prior to that, every performance in every vampire film owed something to Bela.

✣

King Kong (1933). I know some people consider King Kong a science fiction film rather than a fantasy, but they are people who never heard of the square-cube law, and haven't figured out what all these multi-ton carnivorous dinosaurs found to eat on that tiny island. It's a fantasy through-and-through, and it ends with one of the half-dozen classic lines in film history, right up there with "Frankly, my dear, I don't give a damn," and "Louie, I think this is the beginning of a beautiful friendship." "It was beauty killed the beast" takes a back seat to none of them. Yeah, the special effects were a little shaky, but I've yet to hear anyone call either of the remakes a classic.

✣

It's a Wonderful Life (1946). This Frank Capra film is probably (and by far) the most-watched black-and-white fantasy in history. George Bailey, after a life of doing good deeds for others, is dead broke and has all kinds of problems, and decides to end it all. His bumbling guardian angel beseeches him not to. George mutters that he wishes he'd never been born. The angel shows him what the lives of all the people he's helped, all the people who love him, would be like if indeed he never had been born. Totally moved, George pleads for his life back, rushes home to the town and family he loves, and finds that they—and life—are repaying him on this Christmas Eve.

☼

The best of them all might be *Harvey* (1950), about a (probably) imaginary 6-foot-tall rabbit that (possibly) only a mildly pixilated James Stewart can see. His addle-pated sister, an Oscar-winning performance by Josephine Hull, can't see him, but she knows he's there. It's a wonderful, frequently hilarious fantasy that's as enjoyable today as when it was made 60+ years ago.

There are many more, of course. I haven't even touched on the black-and-white fantasy musicals, which include *One Touch of Venus* (a riff on Thorne Smith's *The Night Life of the Gods* with music by Kurt Weill); *I Married an Angel* (a wry, almost cynical Rodgers and Hart show); *Cabin in the Sky* (a delightful all-black musical); and more.

So the next time your kid says "Humphrey who?" or "Whoever heard of someone spelling her name 'Bette'?" buy or rent him one of these black-and-white fantasies and show him what he's been missing. And if you're under 35 or 40, take a look yourself.

Who knows? You may discover a whole new interest.

Heidi Ruby Miller teaches Creative Writing at Seton Hall University, is the co-editor of the award-winning Many Genres, One Craft, *and the author of the novel* Ambasadora *and many short stories.*

THE ISLANDS OF HOPE

by Heidi Ruby Miller

"Where did he come from?" Finn asked, pulling at the knots in his peppered beard. "Men don't just appear on a ship in the middle of the ocean."

Julian stared up at the crow's nest of the *Ixchel*. "His name's Kami. He came with the ship." He wiped his nose on his wet sleeve. "Or so says the captain."

"Over a month at sea and adrift in the Horse Latitudes, with barely a half ration each to last us until Sunday," Vernor said. "And yesterday another mouth appears on board?"

"Just where has this Chinaman been hiding since we left York Island?" Finn asked.

Julian would give his left foot just so his right one could touch York Island again with all its sabal palms and white sand. He never paid it much mind except as one half of the tobacco run to St. Clair. That run was never meant to take them so far north into these windless seas.

"He's been in the captain's cabin, I'll wager," Vernor said, "wearing frilly things and bending over the captain's chair." His raspy laugh and exaggerated hip thrusts pulled Kami's attention from his spot high upon the mast.

Julian's old spot.

"Quiet. The captain won't take kindly to gossip," Julian said. "And Kami's no Chinaman. He's from islands farther out."

"I don't care where he's from," Finn said. "He's not eating any more of my share." He pulled a small knife from a sheath around his bulging waist. "I'll cut off that pretty black braid with the rest of his head."

"Put that away before you start a panic." Julian glanced around the deck for prying eyes.

"Always the captain's lap dog," Finn said. "Maybe it's you who's bending over that chair."

"I'll bet he does at that." Vernor's smile revealed his three remaining teeth.

"Just watch yourselves," Julian said.

The small threat held enough weight to make Finn sheathe his knife and walk away.

Julian passed below deck to the captain's door. The smell of incense meant there'd be no meeting with the captain today, but Julian knocked anyway.

Shuffling filtered from under the weathered teak, but no other response followed.

Rubbish. Knew you would be. Your uncle knew it too. Why he gave you the worthless York Island Run.

Julian pounded a second time, frustrating memories strengthening his blows. The *Ixchel* should have been his command, but the fleet owner chose his incompetent nephew at the last minute. Julian suspected their new captain needed to flee York Island in a hurry, but never passed that along to the crew.

"Captain. I need to talk to you."

Glass shattered against the inside of the door.

"Two more islands gone," the captain yelled. "You hear me? Two more!"

"Fine," Julian yelled. "I'll just let them mutiny."

He shouldered his way to the galley to be sure the rations were distributed fairly. The captain's job, except the captain wasn't quite right anymore. Not since those five days in the Yucatan when the *Ixchel* made her maiden voyage. "He should have stuck with his merchant run. Pirating's not in his blood. Doesn't have the stomach for it." Julian spit.

Yet I followed him for the promise of my own ship.

Hungry crew met Julian—their stomachs grumbling louder than their complaints. A squabble broke out among the three sailors nearest Julian. One crewman shoved another onto the rations table. The downed man pulled a rusty dagger. Encouraging shouts reached deafening heights in the small area.

Julian cocked his pistol in the man's ear. "Back of the line for you! All three of you."

To the rest of the crew he yelled, "Any more problems and no one eats." A little risky and impulsive, especially with this half-starved lot, but some type of authority had to be maintained in the captain's absence.

Each day the men pushed a little further. Each day they took longer to back down. One day they wouldn't at all, especially if they found out Julian had been holding back food for the captain and Kami. He could let them starve, but even a rattled captain and a stowaway deserved to eat. And there was something about Kami, something that stirred a kinship in Julian.

Day and night in the crow's nest. Reminds me of me.

✥

Julian shoved a sack with two rations of pickled beets and jerky into his coat. He jiggled the iron key in the galley's lock until it clicked. The lock was the captain's last sane order before he holed up in his cabin.

Just before Kami came.

Back on deck the calm of a breezeless night renewed Julian's dread. A gibbous moon shone on a glass sea. The water looked like dark ice or obsidian, its surface so smooth and flawless. So dead.

Julian chanced a look up at the crow's nest. Kami wasn't there. Fingers of apprehension crawled up Julian's spine. He pictured an albatross flying away just before disaster struck.

He's probably just with the captain's all. Nothing to worry about.

At least Julian would have his spot back for a bit. He grasped the rope ladder. It felt good to stretch his arms and legs, to rise above the blackness of the ship.

"You haven't been up here in a while." Kami spoke English with a Derbyshire accent. He sat cross-legged, a difficult feat in the confined wooden tub.

The words stopped Julian at the top.

"You been watching me?" Julian asked.

"Like you've been watching me," Kami said.

Julian held tight to the rope ladder. "Everyone's been watching you. Seeing as how you just showed up and all."

The moon reflected a thousand times over in all the folds and wrinkles of Kami's black robe. He looked fresh and clean with gleaming white skin—the only one on the ship who was so presentable and smelled so good.

"You used to talk to the mast all the time," Kami said. "Now you don't." Kami never looked at Julian.

"You make me sound drunk or not right in the head." *Like the captain.*

"I just talk out loud. To the wind, to the heavens, maybe." Julian's tongue became heavy and thick in his mouth. "And just how do you know what I do?"

"I heard you." Kami said. You like it up here because it reminds you of climbing trees during your childhood in Derbyshire. No sea there, just daydreams of one."

How many others had heard Julian's lonely ramblings? Could be why his authority waned recently. As though that lot cared about anything but food and fresh water right now.

"When the time comes, I'll take you to my home, my islands," Kami said, "if you wish. You won't be able to leave until the builders come for you, though. Like they came for me."

Goose bumps rose on Julian's arms.

"Sorry, mate. I'll not be going anywhere with you. Lunatic." He scampered down the ladder on trembling limbs, still carrying the rations.

✡

Julian twisted in his hammock to get a better position, not that sleep would come anyway. A scrape in the hallway made him hold his breath.

"Stupid." Finn's voice. "Be quiet. Do you want to wake the whole damn ship?"

"What if someone finds out?" Vernor's raspy baritone.

"We chuck the body overboard and no one's the wiser. And we'll have one less mouth around here."

"When?"

Finn's reply was lost as the two men moved away.

Julian grabbed his pistol and crept into the hallway. Empty. He headed to the captain's cabin. Smoke drifted from under the door. Banging got no response. Julian fumbled with the ring of keys he carried on him at all times.

I've respected your privacy, but it's time you did something.

The lock clicked, and Julian shoved the captain's door open. Sweet smoke fogged the small cabin. In the middle of the floor sat the captain, his clothes ripped and soiled and hanging from his gaunt frame like the rags they used to swab the deck. A hodgepodge of containers encircled him—a silver pitcher from Taxco, a jeweled goblet from England, several carved wooden bowls from St. Clair, all shoved full of burning incense.

"Captain."

The man sitting on the floor showed no signs of noticing his mate. He smacked his hand to his forehead repeatedly, then studied his palm as though divining his fortune.

I'll save you the trouble. It's bad.

Julian crouched beside him and coughed in the smoky haze. "Captain. Finn and Vernor are plan—"

"Do you smell it?" the captain said.

"What?"

"The copal. The incense. It protects me." The captain grabbed a bowl, breathed deeply, then offered it to Julian.

"Captain! Finn and Vernor are going to kill Kami. I don't know when, but soon."

"Kill Kami?" The captain laughed and offered the copal again. When Julian refused, the captain hurled the bowl across the cabin, spreading ash and smoldering incense over the wooden floor. "Ha! Can't kill Kami. We're the ones who'll be dead soon."

The captain shoved his bearded face close to Julian's. His breath smelled sweet like the copal. "When Kami comes, Death waits. That's what they told me."

"*They* who?"

The captain crawled past Julian and pulled himself up to his chart table. "Mayan shamans," he said. "They promised me the copal would keep Kami away from the *Ixchel*. Said the sap's sweetness would hide me from the builders."

Builders. Julian grew cold at the name. Kami had mentioned them. "You're talking nonsense." He made for the door.

Superstitious bastard. Julian would handle Finn and Vernor on his own.

Something struck his shoulder from behind. The silver pitcher fell to the floor at his feet. He spun, ready to deflect any other objects.

"See this?" The captain stood behind him, stabbing a finger at a chart.

Julian took the pale parchment and scanned it. A layout of their course snaked in black across the chart to open sea. Someone had scrawled *Islands of Hope* at the line's end.

"What are these islands?" Julian asked.

"They're the Islands of Hope, Kami's home."

"Are they nearby?" Julian hadn't heard of them before, but new islands were being discovered and added to the charts every year.

"Hope is always near." The captain flopped in his chair. "But it fades…like the islands. When we first set sail there were thirty. Now…."

Julian ran his hands over the smooth paper, trying to understand the captain's ravings. "There are only five here."

While Julian watched, another island faded until disappearing completely. He tossed the chart onto the floor.

"It's coming," the captain said.

"What's com—"

The captain held the revolver to his head and pulled the trigger.

Julian jumped back as the body toppled out of the chair. His hands shook as he pushed the captain to his back. Half of his head decorated the wooden bed frame.

A sudden shift in the ship sent Julian sliding across the cabin. He slammed into the far wall, dislodging a candle sconce. The captain's body rolled toward him. Julian shoved his foot out to stop it from crashing into him.

Even then his gaze fell upon the chart resting near his other foot. One island remained and its edges were fading.

Shouts from the deck above charged his fear-numbed limbs. A howling wind swept down the stairs.

Wind!

Salt stung Julian's eyes as he shoved against the torrent of rain and sea spray on deck. Men shouted to one another to secure lines or grappled with loose objects sliding along the teak surface. A giant wave washed up on starboard. On its way back to the sea, it took four men with it. The winds battered the ship with such a ferocity, it was as though they were pent-up animals, waiting to unleash after these three weeks.

Julian put his weight into controlling the flapping mainsail. A gust jerked the rope from his burning hands. A piece of the rigging crashed to the deck, its pulley punching through to the floor below. Another large pulley felled Finn. Julian shielded his eyes and looked up in anticipation of more debris.

Kami looked down at Julian from the crow's nest. In the lightning he glimpsed Kami's face, white and smiling…with hope.

"Take me." The thrashing ocean drowned Julian's words. "Take me!"

In the next lightning flash Kami stood beside Julian.

"Will you wait for the builders?" Kami asked.

"Yes," Julian yelled. "Please."

Kami placed a hand upon the mast. His entire arm sunk into the wood, as did his legs and chest, until his whole body melted into the mast. Lightning speared across the sky. With a thunderous crack it struck the mast and split it down the middle. The half nearest Julian separated from the ship and toppled into the sea.

Julian dove in after it.

✧

Sand coated the right side of Julian's face and body. He pushed to a sitting position and vomited salt water and a green slimy bile that left a syrupy taste in his mouth. He took in his surroundings, wondering where he was and how he got there. The sand on the beach reflected a blinding sun and stretched for miles in either direction, framed by a forest.

Then he remembered.

The storm. The sea. *The mast.*

"Kami!" Julian struggled to his feet and shouted for Kami in every direction. His gaze rested on the forest. Something looked off about it, as though it were…false. He thought he might retch again when he realized the problem. Perfect rows of tall, straight trees spaced exactly twenty feet apart. All types, from hickory to coconut to balsam fir.

A balsam fir. Here?

Julian staggered to the nearest pine and stroked its needles with a tentative finger. Its waxy softness sent chills through him.

"The Island of Hope. Kami's island."

Julian ran from the trees until his feet soaked in the calm sea. The effort had him heaving. What had he done, made a pact with the devil herself?

You're still alive. Act like you want to live.

Julian breathed deeply and closed his eyes, secretly wishing that once he opened them the nursery would be gone. *Nursery?* Thoughts of harvesting and cutting filled his mind. They soothed him, allowed him to think more clearly.

The fear he felt about the trees subsided. If he opened himself to them, he could almost feel them—an awkward kinship.

Only friends I got since Kami....

Julian allowed a distorted memory of Kami to flash into his mind. When Kami merged with the mast, just before the lightning struck. Then the memory was gone, banished until a time when Julian might better understand.

He flopped down at the edge of the nursery by an elm sapling.

☼

Julian was content to sit for hours, for days. His skin grew dark and scabby. He wasn't surprised when his feet disappeared into the sand—his toes spreading roots into the ground. On cloudy days he became hungrier than when the sun shone brightly. He felt the touch of his neighbors' roots after a few months as they massed around his ankles and traveled up through his calves. After a few years, he stood as tall as the elm.

Then one day billowing sails appeared on the horizon. Four ships arrived. The builders had finally come.

Julian rejoiced at the first scratching of their saw blades. As they harvested him, they told him how he would be going back to sea. And this time he'd have his own ship.

Copyright © 2007 by Heidi Ruby Miller

Eric Flint is the bestselling author of more than 50 books of science fiction, the former editor of Jim Baen's Universe, *and the current publisher and editor of the* Grantville Gazette.

A SOLDIER'S COMPLAINT

by Eric Flint

I don't care what the genetic engineers say, I think it's a bad idea.

I didn't mind the rats, once I got used to them. (Yes, yes, I know—they're not rats, they're engineered from primitive insectivore stock. Only genetic engineers would know the difference. They look like rats, don't they? So as far as we grunts are concerned, they're rats.)

The truth is, most human soldiers get along fine with the rats. First of all, rats have a dark and pessimistic view of life, which any foot soldier can appreciate. From the first day, they fit right into the gripe sessions, predicting doom and disaster like seasoned veterans.

Maybe a little too much on the grim side, your rats. Even by grunt standards. Personally, I think it comes from ancient racial memories of being the favorite prey of practically every small carnivore in creation. But when I raised the idea with Corporal Laughs-At-Digitigrades (and don't ask me why rats insist on these silly names—we just call him Lad for short) he immediately sneered. Well, actually, he wriggled his whiskers in that particular mode which conveys "sneer" better than any human sneer ever could.

"What a lot of crap," he chittered. He took a hefty swig from his stein. (And that's another thing I like about rats—they've got a proper appreciation for brew. Not like this new bunch! But I'll come to that in a moment.)

He made a big production of wiping the beer off his whiskers. Then he leaned back in his chair and emitted that disgusting bray which rats have instead of a laugh. It's their worst characteristic, in my book. The sound is bad enough, but the sight of those huge yellow incisors!

"Humans are so stupid."

"We invented you, didn't we?" I grumbled.

"Your only intelligent move, in a racial lifetime of blunders. It's like they say—put a monkey in front of a typewriter long enough, and eventually he'll write all of Shakespeare's plays."

I didn't get offended. Before they integrated our battalion, they gave us lectures on how to get along with rats. Stripped of the psychobabble, the gist of it was: don't get offended. Even if they are a lot of offensive rodents.

"The fact is, Sergeant Johnson," he continued, "rats never gave a thought to predators. We had the world on the run! Any biologist will tell you that. The most successful order of mammals ever known—the rodents. And the rats were the most successful of the rodents."

Another sneering twitch of the whiskers.

"Humans are so stupid! Always worrying about lions and sharks and crocodiles. Ha! Between the diseases we spread around and the famine we caused by gobbling up your food, we rats bumped off a thousand times more of you monkeys-with-delusions-of-grandeur than all the predators in the world put together. Kings of creation, the rats. Think we lost any sleep worrying over cats and owls? Ha! Sure, they'd catch one of us now and again. So what? The way we breed?"

He finished off his beer. "I mean, look at them!" He gestured with his snout toward the corner where a handful of mutated felines were sitting at a table. One of the cats caught Corporal Lad's eye, and he chittered at him. The cat looked away, hunching his shoulders.

"Make love, not war—that's the ratly road to triumph." He emitted a great belch and chittered for more beer. The falconoid running the bar stumped over with another pitcher. The big bird avoided the corporal's eyes. I hate to admit it, but the truth is that once the rats arrived they terrorized the cats and the birds to the point where all the predators are good for is being mess orderlies.

"The rats don't fight fair." That's the complaint you always hear from predators. "They gang up on you."

And what can you say? It's true. That's why rats make such good soldiers and predators don't. You put a cat or a raptor on a battlefield and the silly bastards right off start trying to engage the insects in honorable single combat. An insect's idea of single combat is let's you and my swarm fight. God only knows what their notion of honor is. Doubt if they have one, actually. The universe's great pragmatists, the bugs.

It's odd, really, how the whole thing turned out. When the bugs invaded the earth (they started in Poland, naturally—do those people ever get a break?), and after the Umpires of the Galaxy intervened and explained that weapons were forbidden in ecological warfare for bizarre theological reasons that nobody's ever been able to figure out (but there's no point arguing about it, as the Umpires made clear when they nuked Paris and Butte, Montana—and why Butte, anyway? Paris I can understand), the genetic engineers right away charged out and mutated cats and dogs and bears and owls and falcons.

Disaster followed upon disaster. The bugs made mincemeat out of the mutated predators in no time. Oh, sure, the predators look great. But the simple truth is that they make worthless soldiers. No discipline. No sense of teamwork. And talk about lazy! A cat'll kill one bug and sleep the rest of the day. And the raptors are so disgruntled over the fact that they can't fly because they're too big that they don't do much except sulk and write letters to the editor.

Yeah, things were looking bad for the home team until Professor Whitfield finally convinced SACRECOEUR (Supreme Allied Command, Reunified, Ecowar Europe—the French insisted on the acronym; like I said, I can understand nuking Paris) that they were approaching the whole problem upside down.

In his words, which have become as famous as $e=mc^2$: "To kill bugs, breed bugkillers."

Naturally, the idiot geneticists started off by engineering giant intelligent frogs. "Intelligent frog" is an oxymoron. Not only do the amphibious dopes stay in one place waiting for a bug to come within reach of their tongues (which they never do, because there's nothing wrong with *their* brains, which you'd expect from a collection of species that mastered interstellar travel), but the frogs can only fight when it's warm. And since the bugs aren't really bugs, but a group of species which descended on some far distant planet from a rootstock of warm-blooded arthropods, they just waited until the sun went down and—voila! Frog legs for dinner. That's how we lost the Ukraine.

So then the geneticists charged out and—well, that's when the jokes got started. You know the ones:

"How many genetic engineers does it take to screw in a lightbulb? Eleven—one to do the work, and the other ten to figure out why it doesn't have a double helix."

"What's the definition of a virgin genetic engineer? A nerd with too many pocket protectors."

My personal favorite: "Why did the genetic engineer cross the road? To get to the other slide."

Fortunately for the vertebrate world, Professor Whitfield came to the rescue again. His immortal words:

"To fight low, think low."

Bingo. We got the rats, the rats started breeding, and we stopped the invasion in its tracks. Natural soldiers, rats. Born bug-killers. And, like I said, not bad guys once you get to know them.

But enough's enough. I hate to say it, as much as I admire Professor Whitfield (and who doesn't?), but I think his latest idea is just plain goofy.

Yeah, yeah, I've heard all the arguments.

"The greatest insectivores in the entire history of the vertebrate phylum." "The greatest night fighters ever produced by evolution." Blah, blah, blah.

That may all be true. Probably is—I'll admit these new guys are a terror on the battlefield. The bugs won't even move at night, anymore.

But I don't care. Study your history and you'll find that it's always the morale factor that ultimately prevails in warfare. Don't take my word for it—read Clausewitz. Or Napoleon.

And these new guys are just wrecking the Army's morale. This is not shape prejudice! Sure, the new bunch are uglier than sin, but that's not the problem. The rats are ugly too—but do I care? Not in the slightest. Some of my best friends are rats.

The problem isn't the way the new guys look. It's their lousy sense of humor.

That's all, you say? All right, smart-ass civilian. Let's see you get any sleep at night, lying in your bunk, with the new guys hanging from the rafters, chuckling and chortling, telling the same stupid joke over and over again:

"I vant to trink your bludd."

Copyright © 2007 by Eric Flint

Laurie Tom is the winner of the 2010 Writers of the Future Gold Prize. She's recently been published in Solaris Rising, Penumbra, *and* Story Portals.

THE HELD DAUGHTER

by Laurie Tom

I realized that Heaven had a different fate in store for me when Imperial Father married off my younger sister while I was still unwed. The celebration was held at the Palace of the Tranquil Sea, where the waters of the southern ocean lapped at sandy beaches and the dragons could easily climb from the surf to give their blessings. Guests consumed meat and wine, and tried not to look my way, to look at Fourth Princess with only a guardian lion at her feet and attendants for company.

Sek-fung's fur was not the coarse stone it appeared to be, though, and I rubbed her shoulders vigorously as an excuse to ignore the questioning glances that people gave when they thought I could not see. Stone lions did not judge and she did not know this celebration from another. She lay her head at my feet, bored.

"Don't worry, Fourth Princess," said Mung-laan, who had been my attendant since we were thirteen. "I am certain the Emperor is being particularly careful with your marriage."

But even when we returned to the imperial palace, he did not speak of marriage, either to me or my mother. Imperial Father was old, and no matter how many concubines he took, had produced no children beyond the fifth princess, and no sons at all. Mother folded her hands confidently and told me to be sure to keep the Emperor's favor. Though unlikely, it was not impossible to think that he would still manage a son, and that would ruin my chances. Mother was only an imperial concubine, but still she dared hope that one day she would be Empress Dowager regardless if her issue had been a girl instead of a boy.

It helped that I was born a geomancer and blessed by the Five Gods with command over the elements. Most emperors were geomancers. It was easier to claim the favor of Heaven that way.

But I was only sixteen and my situation could change, so I resolved only to be a dutiful daughter, come what may. As Emperor, my father had many things to consider. He made decisions like a farmer grows rice. My future was but one patch of the land he tended.

Since my younger sister's marriage, Imperial Father bade me to sit whenever he spoke with his ministers. He showed me the petitions that came to the capital from across the Kwanese Empire and tested me on what I read, asked if I understood. Eunuch Lei told me in private that the Emperor had said I was the brightest of his daughters. Imperial Father said nothing to me himself.

When I was twenty, the eunuchs and maids bowed to me deeper than they had when Fifth Princess was still unwed, but sometimes I caught them unaware in the midst of gossip. The Emperor is still trying, they said, when they thought I could not hear. He must be very anxious. Maybe one of the new concubines will do better. But for now poor Princess Gwan-yu has to wait.

A proper emperor wants a son, a Crown Prince who will take his place as *wongdai* when his time is done. But if one isn't born, the Emperor cannot be without an heir. He cannot marry off all his daughters where they will honor the ancestors of their husbands and leave no child for himself and his own.

Everyone in the palace knew why he could not arrange my marriage. He still hoped for a son, and so I would have to wait until he no longer wished to try. Sometimes I would hear of other daughters held back from marriage while their fathers tried for sons. Then when no son was born, their fathers would arrange for a groom to marry into their family. The groom's children would bear his bride's name so there would still be someone to continue the family line and honor the family's ancestors.

But my father was the Emperor. A man with just a wife could only try for so long before his wife would leave her childbearing years. My father took new concubines every few years in hope of a son. I could wait a very long time.

I was twenty-two the first time I traveled to the northern territories. Every other year Imperial Father would take a retinue of courtiers with him to keep ties with our nomadic cousins, to camp in tents like our ancestors and remember what it was like before our armies swept through Kwan and made this country ours. They would be out there for weeks.

Imperial Father requested I accompany him. I would have to learn, just in case.

My days were spent sitting quietly behind a low-slung table in the largest tent, listening to Imperial Father praise the virtues of living on the steppes and hearing the Hangul clan leader compliment the skill and fortitude of my father's servants. Though we slept in tents, we lay in beds with blankets and there was tea and sweet meats enough to last throughout our stay. The servants, long accustomed to such biennial sojourns, had prepared well.

Our only cause for worry came the time it rained and we thought the camp would flood. The geomancers in Imperial Father's retinue streamed out around the perimeter, calling on the strength of their prayers to move the earth and water to dig trenches and form new rivers around us. But the ground was hard and would not yield.

Imperial Father strode out of his tent and glared out into the rain, with one of the eunuchs scrambling behind him to hold an umbrella over his head. The Emperor's gaze swept over the soggy camp and he barked a command for the geomancers to clear a space for him. I watched from the opening flap of my tent as Imperial Father knelt in his fine golden robes, heedless of the muck at the camp perimeter, and placed his hands on the stubborn ground.

The earth trembled as the Yellow Dragon, patron of the imperial throne and highest of the Five Gods, answered his call. Prayers from the other geomancers echoed around him as they joined in the channeling. They dug grooves around the camp, diverting the water away from us.

It was not just for our safety, but also a subtle display of power toward our nomadic cousins. Imperial Father was satisfied, I could tell, as he raised himself to his feet. He was not simply a man to whom others would bow. The Five Gods themselves had seen fit to bless him with the power of their domains, and he wielded it better than any other geomancer here.

Though most of the geomancers knelt panting, arms crossed over their bodies from the pain that came from strenuous prayer, Imperial Father walked stoically back to his tent without a hint of discomfort. In private, I knew, he would allow himself to feel the pain, but not where others could see. It was a privilege to see a member of the imperial family command the elements. The servants would remember this.

Once the rains had passed and the ground had dried, the Hangul leader suggested a friendly competition to brighten the mood and take our minds off the work we had done to repair the camp. Imperial Father and the clan leader would select men from both our camps to participate in some archery on horseback. I came out to watch, glad for the reprieve from always sitting.

When Imperial Father asked Eunuch Lei to suggest someone to represent Kwan, the old eunuch immediately suggested a young soldier who had come to him highly recommended. He told the Emperor that the son of General Syun-hoi, of the Tiger Clan, was with them as part of his escort, but Imperial Father simply shrugged.

"If he represents us well, that will suffice."

I struggled to even recall General Syun-hoi. He was not a favorite of the Emperor, though if he was general he could not be incompetent.

The Hangul set up rows of targets for the riders to strafe, and the two chosen men rode out on their sturdy mountain horses, quivers at their sides and bows in their hands.

That was when I first saw Jing-lung. He rode as one who had grown up in the barracks, and shot arrows with the eyes and nerve of a hawk. One. Two. Three. The arrows planted themselves deep in the thatched grass. Four. Five. Six. He guided his horse with just his knees and did not miss a single target, leading the Emperor to proudly proclaim that the Dorgan people had not gone soft since taking residence in the palace in Kwan.

Imperial Father called Jing-lung to him and the young soldier dismounted, handed the reins to a groom, and knelt before the Emperor. He did not even flinch before the two stone lions that flanked the Son of Heaven day and night. Imperial Father told him that in honor of his performance he should ask for a gift. Jing-lung looked up, and though he beheld the face of the Emperor, he also looked past him and saw me. I smiled at him, and he almost did in return, before catching himself and lowering his head once more.

My days out on the steppes still consisted of meetings and formalities, but sometimes I would see Jing-lung as I walked through the camp. Our eyes would meet and I would smile and give him a wave if circumstances allowed. Since he was currently in the Emperor's grace, I thought it acceptable to speak with him, and I knew I would be in no danger with Sek-fung beside me. There were few chances to speak with men my own age in the palace, save for my cousins, and they were too familiar.

"Have you been in many battles?" I asked him. He was young, perhaps even younger than me.

"A few," he said. "Mostly on the western border. Guarding the Emperor is a first for me. My father worked hard to get me this assignment."

General Syun-hoi had done well in that regard, because the Emperor now knew who Jing-lung was. It was an auspicious start to a military career.

"Do you think you will be a general as well someday?" I asked.

"If the Son of Heaven sees fit," he said. He smiled. "But I would like that. Fourth Princess will need someone to protect the empire, am I correct?"

I grinned. "How do you know I will not protect it myself?" I picked up a twig and held it between us. It smoldered for a moment, curls of smoke rising from its bark, before it bloomed with a tiny flame.

He chuckled. "The barbarians will flee before your burning twigs. I am serious, though. Even the most blessed emperor will take comfort in knowing that he has a shield."

The stronger the prayer, the more the prayer demanded of the body. The imperial family did not often call on the Five Gods because the strongest prayers left us vulnerable, and so were not to be used except in times of need, and then not all of us were as powerful as geomancers of legend. Imperial Father was very talented. I was not so much.

"That proverb," I said. "It was the Hung-ying Emperor who said that."

"My father is fond of it," said Jing-lung.

"Do you know any more?"

"Proverbs? I can see if I remember…"

Jing-lung was no scholar, and his brief attempts at poetry made me laugh, but he was good company, and my time in the steppes was not so boring because of him. When summer ended and we packed the tents to return to the capital I was sad, not because I would never see him again—as the son of a general he was likely to visit the palace from time to time—but because we would no longer be able to talk freely. I watched him ride ahead of me on the trip home. I wanted to remember how the long braid of his hair swayed against his back.

We next met at the Black Turtle Festival, when I and my maids went out into the wind-swept city to watch the fireworks and eat lotus cakes. Sek-fung padded alongside us for protection, a clear sign that we were a party of nobility. It was the start of winter, so we bundled ourselves well in our fine things, though it rarely snowed in the capital.

Mung-laan saw him first, recognizing him from our sojourn to the north, and she giggled when she told me that a bunch of young fellows were teasing that fine soldier, trying to get him to come over and speak to me. I saw Jing-lung shake his head, but when his friends realized that he had my attention, they gave him a push.

Unable to escape, he walked up to me and bowed. "Greetings to Fourth Princess."

"Please rise," I told him.

"Is Fourth Princess enjoying the festival?"

"The fireworks and the dances are very pretty. But I have yet to taste the lotus cakes."

My heart beat as I considered my words. Could I ask? Would Imperial Father hear of it? I heard giggling behind me. Mung-laan. If Imperial Father asked her of course she would tell him. But, I was very valuable to the Emperor right now, and if I was to be heir, I should not be shy about speaking to the men who would be in my army. Moreover, Imperial Father had approved of Jing-lung and rewarded him with silver taels for his performance out on the steppes.

"I am on my way to Madame Wu's," I asked. "I hear her staff rib the crust of the lotus cakes so that they resemble the shell of the Black Turtle herself. Would you like to join me?" I asked.

The silence behind me gave me a perverse joy. Mung-laan had not expected me to be so forward. Jing-lung's fellows were equally stunned.

"Of course, Fourth Princess."

Jing-lung was so formal—he had to be—but when I looked in his eyes I saw how happy he was.

I still remember eating the lotus cake with him and learning that he had yet to marry, though at twenty he was certainly old enough. He said he was a younger son and his father busy. He didn't mind that he was still unwed.

And a part of me was foolish enough to wonder if I could ask Imperial Father. But Jing-lung's family was not prominent enough. I knew now that General Syun-hoi was in charge of the training barracks in the south, a quiet but responsible position with little chance of action seeing as we had an ocean for our southern border. Jing-lung would be a fine match for a minister's daughter, or perhaps one of my cousins, but not for a princess. It would have helped if he was also a geomancer. The gift was not always passed on to one's children, but bearing such a blessing would surely enrich any household.

Ten days later, Mung-laan was beaten for allowing me to so openly consort with a man in public. Never mind anything that might have happened in the private room at Madame Wu's, though my maids had been in earshot the entire time and Sek-fung had not leaped to my defense. Jing-lung was sent away to fight on the western frontier. Imperial Father did not punish me himself. He knew what had happened to Mung-laan and Jing-lung would hurt deeper than any blow.

On the day of my twenty-sixth birthday, Eunuch Lei dared to suggest to the Emperor that it was time for me to marry. Unlike a son, my reproductive years were limited, and as a woman I could not increase my chances for a child by taking concubines. Imperial Father silenced him with a glare so sharp Eunuch Lei fell to his knees and apologized for his impertinence. I had no doubt the Emperor was very aware that a held daughter could only wait so long before she was no longer of any use for the purpose she was held.

For a period of time, Imperial Father had hope that he would no longer need me. When one of his concubines became heavy with child, the geomancers prayed daily around her, asking the Five Gods to deliver a healthy boy, but the palace was soon graced with a sixth princess, much to the chagrin of the

Emperor. I could feel his black mood just walking past the door to his study.

"What do you think of Minister Wing-gat's son Chi-ji?" he asked me one night as we pored over a new proclamation.

"He is quick to speak," I said, "and like a charging bull he does not easily stop, but he has a sharp mind. We can use him."

Imperial Father nodded with approval of my assessment, but I thought I saw a shadow darken his face. Perhaps he had not been considering a government appointment and instead a son-in-law. But Chi-ji was not fit to be the consort of a *wongdai*. An empress must let her husband rule, and so must any consort of mine should I be formally named heir. It was a reversal a man would find difficult. Some men answered to their wives regardless through force of personality, but for me, my husband would answer as well to the Daughter of Heaven.

"How about Magistrate Chung-ping of Ying Ga?" said the Emperor.

"The Ying Ga corruption was investigated by him, but I have heard that he was a part of the scandal and covered his involvement by turning against the officials beneath him." I grimaced. "And he already has a wife."

Imperial Father gave me a sharp look and I realized I had spoken out of turn. Magistrate Chung-ping was surely not for me. A *wongdai* would never be concubine to another man.

Jing-lung married during this time, and though I was disappointed, I knew it would happen. His family would not allow him to remain unmarried forever. He had redeemed himself out on the frontier and come back with victories enough that Imperial Father named him sub-commander to the General of the West. He was a man to be proud of, but when I next saw him in the palace I found I didn't want to ask him about his campaign, or hear the story from his own lips, about how he had saved the wounded General Song from the barbarians and rallied his undermanned battalion to hold their fort.

So when I saw him, walking out from the audience hall and into the courtyard, I just asked him, "Are you all right?"

And I watched him standing there, knowing who I was, but uncertain of himself. He looked splendid in his formal robes with the lion insignia of his rank emblazoned on the front, and I thought the red and black felt cap of an official suited him especially well. He lifted his arms, then dropped them to his sides and bowed. "Fourth Princess."

"Please rise."

He could not hold me as he had in the shadows of Madame Wu's where we had gone to eat lotus cakes. It was not that a man was forbid another woman. Gossip thrived on the stories of a man who neglected his wife in favor of the concubine he truly adored. But I was still Fourth Princess and a held daughter. Jing-lung would not make the mistake that had sent him to the frontier a second time.

"I am well," he told me.

"Will you be in the capital long?"

"Through the new year, then I will return to the west."

"How dangerous is it out there?"

"Better than it was, Fourth Princess. The barbarians have been beaten back and they lick their wounds. We will probably not hear from them for a while, but the border must be secured to discourage them from returning."

It was the appropriate response, from a soldier reporting to the royal family, but it was not what I wanted to know. I wanted to know how dangerous it was *for him*, to know what his chances were for returning another time. I turned away, not wanting my feelings to show. We were in the courtyard, and there were too many people who could see.

"Fourth Princess," said Jing-lung, "I will be careful. When you are Emperor I will be there to lead your army."

I sighed. "Don't say such things. You are not yet a general, and Imperial Father has not given up."

"You are right, Fourth Princess, but the flow of a river cannot be stopped. I am certain the Emperor is aware."

By the time I was twenty-eight, most of the palace maids I'd known as a child had been freed from service to marry and begin families of their own. I had a new set of maids, but they still marveled at the held daughter, and gossiped about how long I would wait.

Jing-lung told me not to worry, and I was happy that he still had words for me. He was often away from the palace, but he never forgot me. I liked to spend time with him in the imperial garden, in a pavilion surrounded by the empress's favorite lilies, where we would watch the mandarin ducks as the pairs swam together in the perfect image of married harmony.

My new maids did not know of my history with Jing-lung, so they obeyed when I shooed them a respectful distance away, but because we could never be sure who would hear, Jing-lung and I only talked about the situation at the border; details about army strength, patrols, supply lines.

I did not know if he had children, what he thought of his wife, or how much time he spent at home. I wanted us to be the ducks in the pond, bonded for life, but that possibility had already passed us by.

I was twenty-nine when Imperial Father finally announced that I would take the role of Crown Prince. My youngest sibling could also have been made prince, but by now the Emperor had invested so much in me that he was loath to have to teach a second heir. I suspected with his growing age that if he had sired a boy yesterday he still would not have changed me for the babe. He was done with children now and warmed himself with the thought of grandchildren.

His first three daughters and the fifth had children, and he would read about them in letters from their husbands and visit them if time and distance allowed, but I had yet to marry. Imperial Father decided he would fix that.

At the Green Dragon Festival we welcomed the spring, and in the lantern light of the evening banquet he called me before him and invited Yan-cheung of the Horse Clan to join us. The empress praised how good we looked together and the Emperor nodded in agreement. It was no whimsical decision, I knew, but a way to politely present us in public together for the first time.

Yan-cheung was tall and thin with oversized hands, but he had a scholarly look to his face that spoke of wisdom. He was not as old as I, but that was to be expected. Most families did not hold their sons from marrying.

He was an eldest son as well. His family was eager indeed to relinquish their best for the future *wongdai*. I would have to be wary of them. If I was not careful they would seek to control me through their son, and Yan-cheung might have plans of his own as well. His father was already a favored minister of Imperial Father, so plainly his family would seek to keep the power they already had.

I had not spoken with Yan-cheung before, but I knew him to be a promising official of good reputation and a geomancer besides. Being the eldest son of an already prominent family he was an elegant match worthy of a female *wongdai*. He was not Jing-lung, but he would do, and I would be charitable to him so long as he understood his place.

An auspicious day was chosen for our wedding, and many of the prominent officials and their families were invited. Jing-lung as well. I knew from the military dispatches that he would return from the border and be in the capital during the time of the wedding. I did not know what I would say to him, but as an officer of the third rank he could not in good faith refuse to come.

The Imperial Palace was festooned with red banners and crimson lanterns. The geomancers blessed the halls in the name of the Vermilion Bird of the South, lighting celebratory fires with no spark but the touch of their hands, and the women wore feather-shaped hairpins of red jade in their headdresses.

My maids wove my hair tight and carefully pinned the winged wooden frame atop my head, beaded tassels hanging down to either side, and over that they draped the red veil of my wedding dress. Traditionally the groom would remove it once he joined his bride at her bridal bed, but I determined I would remove it myself. I would not be his. He would be mine. It was into my family he was marrying and our children would bear the name of my clan. I would be *wongdai*.

Yan-cheung was gracious throughout the ceremony and at the banquet that followed. He did nothing, said nothing, to tarnish my reputation as heir, but how could he with Imperial Father still alive and attending? I knew the Emperor's concubines made plays at power, my own mother among them, trying to sway Imperial Father's opinions if he was willing to listen. Fairly or not, I could not discount the possibility that Yan-cheung would think he would have my undivided attention.

As the banquet wore on I realized that I had yet to see Jing-lung among the guests. Concerned that I had missed him, I asked one of my maids if he had come at all, and she had not seen him. Disappointed, I wondered if he had been so heartbroken he would risk the Emperor's disfavor rather than see me married to another.

I learned the answer a few days later when apologies arrived that General Syun-hoi's household was in mourning. Jing-lung's wife had died of illness.

He was free again, but I was not.

My first son was born when I was thirty-two. Imperial Father, now in ill health, was thrilled to see that our dynasty would continue. He rarely left his study anymore and no longer traveled to see our brethren in the north. If not for my son I would have traveled in his place this year. Instead I sent Yan-cheung, who I found I could trust, even if I could not love.

The palace geomancers offered to make me twin sachets, bonded together so that the two people who wore them would know the feelings of the other even when they were far apart. The geomancers would fill them with herbs and dried flowers, scents that would remind me and Yan-cheung of our time together, so the fragrance of the sachets would know that they belonged to each other, would share feelings with one another, after the geomancers prayed upon them and bestowed the blessings of the Green Dragon of the East. They believed the sachets would ease my parting from Yan-cheung, especially in this time while our baby was young. But I knew I would not miss him nearly enough for that, and I could think of no scent that would remind me of Yan-cheung. I thought only of lilies and ducks in the imperial garden.

Jing-lung came by the next time he was in the capital and I took his report in the Emperor's place. By now he was an officer of the first rank, and Imperial Father said he would soon name him the new General of the West. Jing-lung would be a general to lead my army once I became Emperor, just as he promised.

After my servants brought tea to my office, I dismissed them and bade Jing-lung sit in one of the chairs along the wall. I had no difficulty in following the army movements he discussed. By now, I had a good head for both military and political affairs, even if I should never set foot near an actual battle myself. Jing-lung did not try to pass failure for success either. Some less scrupulous officials hoped that I in my womanhood and Imperial Father in his dotage would not catch the mistakes or even outright corruption on their part, but I had to be ruthless. No one could question my right to the throne.

When all news had been given, we sat in awkward silence. Then I asked, "Are you happy on the border?"

He paused, gathering his thoughts, and said, "It is rough, but I have gotten comfortable there. Even the dust does not bother me as much as it once did."

"Your family has pleaded otherwise. They say you have not remarried, and they fear it is because the border is not a safe place for a highborn lady. Would you like to be stationed closer to the capital?"

He clenched his hands and looked away. "Fourth Princess, why do you have to make such an offer? My parents, they have grandchildren through my brother so their line is safe, but my duty on the border is the only reason I have not to remarry. Father wants to arrange something for me, but I can tell him that I am making this sacrifice for the Emperor, because he trusts me, and I cannot care for a wife while I am so far away. Yin-jan, my departed wife, did nothing wrong, but I was never there for her."

I reached out to him, wanting to hold him, but I only touched his shoulder. Jing-lung could never be *wonghau* to my *wongdai*. I already had my husband, now titled as a prince.

"Jing-lung," I said, "would you still consider marrying me?"

He turned to me, disbelieving. "You already have a husband, and you've borne him a son. You can't dissolve your marriage, not even as Crown Prince."

"No, I cannot." I removed my hand from his shoulder, and took his hand in mine. "I wish I could. But as Emperor, even as a woman, I am allowed additional consorts. There have been few female *wongdai* in the past, but it is not unprecedented. The Ming-ying Emperor had three."

I could see the thoughts tumble around his head. He did not like the idea, I knew. I could feel the shake of uncertainty in the hand I held.

"Imperial Father might not like the idea, because he may remember what happened when we were young, but you are a decorated officer now and won many battles for our country. The western border is safe because of you."

"Fourth Princess," he said, his voice rattled and uneven. "Fourth Princess will always have my affection, but I do not think I could share you with another man."

"I have done my duty to Yan-cheung," I said. "If the child grows healthy and strong there will be no need for us to visit each other's beds. Your family will no longer pressure you to marry, and the two of us…We might be able to have a child of our own."

He withdrew his hand and stood. "I don't know. I don't know if I could. Only a poor man should have to share his woman with another. Even if you are Emperor…Is it selfish to want you just for myself?"

I shook my head as I looked down at the floor. "Before I met you, before I knew Imperial Father would even consider me as heir, I knew someday I would marry, and though a princess will be a wife and not a concubine, I was sure my husband would be a man of means so he would marry concubines in addition to me. For a noblewoman, this is what happens, and we do not expect otherwise. But how can it be that if a woman is *wongdai* she cannot do the same as the *wongdai* before her just because she is a woman and they were men?"

"May your servant be excused?" he asked. I could not bring myself to look at his face.

If I were free to divorce Yan-cheung, if he had been an awful man instead of a competent and loyal husband, I would. Once Imperial Father passed I would be *wongdai* and no one could question whom I chose to marry, and now Jing-lung was worthy.

"You may go," I told him.

Before a year had passed, the western barbarians had returned, bringing a larger force of foreign allies with whom we rarely had reason to quarrel. Imperial Father now promoted Jing-lung to General of the West, and placed the entirety of the western forces at his disposal, as well as granting him use of the capital's own soldiers to drive the barbarians all the way back to their own country, which he would then claim for the Kwanese Empire.

I knew this would be a long campaign, and instead of months it could be years before I saw Jing-lung again. Imperial Father made a grand show of him surveying his soldiers, knowing that the people must believe Jing-lung would win if they were to support the war through their taxes and their sons. And Jing-lung rode tall on his horse as though already master of a foreign land.

At the end of the inspection he rode up to where Imperial Father and I stood at the head of a retinue of geomancers. He dismounted and knelt. "Your soldiers are ready, Emperor."

"Please rise," said Imperial Father. "A finer force this country has not seen in generations. I look forward to hearing of your success."

"I will not fail. You will leave this world with a larger empire than when you arrived."

The Emperor nodded, pleased, and carefully climbed into his carriage to return to the palace. He would retire to his bedchambers once he returned. The outer courtyard was as far as he wished to go these days. I would channel the blessing for our army and see our soldiers off.

I reached into the long sleeve of my gown and removed a small box I had tucked within. "This is for you," I said to Jing-lung, my voice quiet so only he would hear.

He opened it and saw that there was a single silk sachet inside where there was plainly room for two. It smelled of lilies, of the imperial garden, of the pond where we would watch the mandarin ducks, and as awe washed over his face I knew he could see me in his mind as well as his eyes.

"I made it," I said, feeling very much a young girl again. "It is a funny thing for a Crown Prince to shut out maids from her quarters while she cuts and dries flowers from a pond, but there has been gossip enough in days past. If you breathe the scent of the flowers from the sachet you will be able to reach me. And I have its partner, so when you think of me, I will be able to see you as well."

The sachets would only allow emotions, and not words, and in that way he could say no more to me that he could through the reports I knew he would send, but I would at least be able to let him know that I loved him, that I missed him, and I hoped he would feel the same.

His hand closed over the sachet and he tied it to his belt. The box he closed and returned to me.

"I will treasure it, Fourth Princess." And he bowed.

If not for the people still in the courtyard, I would have told him the formality was not necessary. If not for the people in the courtyard, Jing-lung could have refused me.

"Will you wait?" I asked. "When I am Emperor, if I ask you…"

"What can a mandarin duck do when it is no longer part of a pair?" he asked, head still down. "Is it free? Can it find another?"

I did not know.

"You will go with the blessing of the Emperor," I said, "and mine as well."

I looked over my shoulder to the other geomancers, and as one twenty heads bowed in prayer. We called today to the White Tiger of the West, ferocious guardian and master of metal, to make our swords sharp, our arrows true, and our cannons sound. I asked him to protect the general who now led an army destined for his domain.

"Your sword, please," I said.

He drew his sword, laid it flat across his upturned hands, and knelt before me. I touched it gently with the tips of my fingers and felt all the imperfections that had been worn into the blade that even meticulous care could not entirely erase. But the White Tiger could.

My prayers smoothed the nicks and scratches, the flaws that the eyes could not see and the fingers could not touch. I willed this sword healthy and strong, so that it would protect Jing-lung in the months and years to come. This was the blessing the Emperor would give his general if he were well. I was not Imperial Father, not as powerful as Imperial Father, but I prayed that my desire for Jing-lung's safe return was enough to overcome all that.

One day, perhaps soon, I would be *wongdai*, and I wanted Jing-lung beside me.

After the army left, I went out to the imperial garden with my maids and sat in the pavilion by the pond where I could watch the ducks. Sek-fung lay beside me, snoring in her old age. One of my maids cooed and pointed at a new bird that I had not seen before. He circled the pond alone, and I wondered if he might try to join with one of the other pairs.

I picked up one of the cakes from the tray of sweets my maids had brought and broke it apart in my hands, much to their shock. When the duck swam near I threw the pieces before him, and he bobbed through the water, plucking the bits of cake in a series of quick gulps as he followed the trail of food to the walkway beside the pavilion where I was now waiting.

I held out my hand with a bit of cake upon it and the duck gobbled it from my palm.

"There's no reason for either of us to be alone, is there?" I told him.

I felt the sachet tingle at my side and in my mind I saw Jing-lung riding out to the frontier. His thoughts were warm, and I smiled.

Original (First) Publication
Copyright © 2013 by Laurie Tom

ANOTHER FAN LETTER

I've been really enjoying **Galaxy's Edge**. Well chosen stories, some old faves… & Barry's mordant incisive column is too true, so sad… and Mike's introduction is spot on--I'd even forgotten some of these stories!

(I too walked in on a nude Sturgeon.) The Randy Garrett I'd never heard!

Greg Benford

Barry Malzberg is the winner of the very first Campbell Memorial Award, a multiple Hugo and Nebula winner, and the author of more than 90 books. He is considered a master of "recursive" science fiction, which is to say science fiction about science fiction, of which "A Galaxy Called Rome" is a prime example.

A GALAXY CALLED ROME

by Barry N. Malzberg

I

This is not a novelette but a series of notes. The novelette cannot be truly written because it partakes of its time, which is distant and could be perceived only through the idiom and devices of that era.

Thus the piece, by virtue of these reasons and others too personal even for this variety of True Confession, is little more than a set of constructions toward something less substantial…and, like the author, it cannot be completed.

II

The novelette would lean heavily upon two articles by the late John Campbell, for thirty-three years the editor of *Astounding/Analog*, which were written shortly before his untimely death on July 11, 1971, and appeared as editorials in his magazine later that year, the second being perhaps the last piece which will ever bear his byline. They imagine a black galaxy which would result from the implosion of a neutron star, an implosion so mighty that gravitational forces unleashed would contain not only light itself but space and time; and *A Galaxy Called Rome* is his title, not mine, since he envisions a spacecraft that might be trapped within such a black galaxy and be unable to get out…because escape velocity would have to exceed the speed of light. All paths of travel would lead to this galaxy, then, none away.

A galaxy called Rome.

III

Conceive then of a faster-than-light spaceship which would tumble into the black galaxy and would be unable to leave. Tumbling would be easy, or at least inevitable, since one of the characteristics of the black galaxy would be its invisibility, and there the ship would be. The story would then pivot on the efforts of the crew to get out. The ship is named *Skipstone*. It was completed in 3892. Five hundred people died so that it might fly, but in this age life is held even more cheaply than it is today.

Left to my own devices, I might be less interested in the escape problem than that of adjustment. Light housekeeping in an anterior sector of the universe; submission to the elements, a fine, ironic literary despair. This is not science fiction however. Science fiction was created by Hugo Gernsback to show us the ways out of technological impasse. So be it.

IV

As interesting as the material was, I quailed even at this series of notes, let alone a polished, completed work. My personal life is my black hole, I felt like pointing out (who would listen?); my daughters provide more correct and sticky implosion than any neutron star, and the sound of the pulsars is as nothing to the music of the paddock area at Aqueduct racetrack in Ozone Park, Queens, on a clear summer Tuesday. "Enough of these breathtaking concepts, infinite distances, quasar leaps, binding messages amidst the arms of the spiral nebula," I could have pointed out. "I know that there are those who find an ultimate truth there, but I am not one of them. I would rather dedicate the years of life remaining (my melodramatic streak) to an understanding of the agonies of this middle-class town in northern New Jersey; until I can deal with those, how can I comprehend Ridgefield Park, to say nothing of the extension of fission to include progressively heavier gases?" Indeed, I almost abided to this until it occurred to me that Ridgefield Park would forever be as mysterious as the stars and that one could not deny infinity merely to pursue a particular that would be impenetrable until the day of one's death.

So I decided to try the novelette, at least as this series of notes, although with some trepidation, but trepidation did not unsettle me, nor did I grieve, for my life is merely a set of notes for a life, and Ridgefield Park merely a rough working model of Trenton, in which, nevertheless, several thousand people live who cannot discern their right hands from their left, and also much cattle.

V

It is 3895. The spacecraft *Skipstone*, on an exploratory flight through the major and minor galaxies surrounding the Milky Way, falls into the black galaxy of a neutron star and is lost forever.

The captain of this ship, the only living consciousness of it, is its commander, Lena Thomas. True, the hold of the ship carries five hundred and fifteen of the dead sealed in gelatinous fix who will absorb unshielded gamma rays. True, these rays will at some time in the future hasten their reconstitution. True, again, that another part of the hold contains the prostheses of seven skilled engineers, male and female, who could be switched on at only slight inconvenience and would provide Lena not only with answers to any technical problems which would arise but with companionship to while away the long and grave hours of the *Skipstone*'s flight.

Lena, however, does not use the prostheses, nor does she feel the necessity to. She is highly skilled and competent, at least in relation to the routine tasks of this testing flight, and she feels that to call for outside help would only be an admission of weakness, would be reported back to the Bureau and lessen her potential for promotion. (She is right; the Bureau has monitored every cubicle of this ship, both visually and biologically; she can see or do nothing which does not trace to a printout; they would not think well of her if she was dependent upon outside assistance.) Toward the embalmed she feels somewhat more.

Her condition rattling in the hold of the ship as it moves on tachyonic drive seems to approximate theirs; although they are deprived of consciousness, that quality seems to be almost irrelevant to the condition of hyperspace, and if there were any way that she could bridge their mystery, she might well address them. As it is, she must settle for imaginary dialogues and for long, quiescent periods when she will watch the monitors, watch the rainbow of hyperspace, the collision of the spectrum, and say nothing whatsoever.

Saying nothing will not do, however, and the fact is that Lena talks incessantly at times, if only to herself. This is good because the story should have much dialogue; dramatic incident is best impelled through straightforward characterization, and Lena's compulsive need, now and then, to state her condition and its relation to the spaces she occupies will satisfy this need.

In her conversation, of course, she often addresses the embalmed.

"Consider," she says to them, some of them dead eight hundred years, others dead weeks, all of them stacked in the hold in relation to their status in life and their ability to hoard assets to pay for the process that will return them their lives, "Consider what's going on here," pointing through the hold, the colors gleaming through the portholes onto her wrist, colors dancing in the air, her eyes quite full and maddened in this light, which does not indicate that she is mad but only that the condition of hyperspace itself is insane, the Michelson-Morley effect having a psychological as well as physical reality here. "Why it could be me dead and in the hold and all of you here in the dock watching the colors spin, it's all the same, all the same faster than light," and indeed the twisting and sliding effects of the tachyonic drive are such that at the moment of speech what Lena says is true.

The dead live; the living are dead, all slide and become jumbled together as she has noted; and were it not that their objective poles of consciousness were fixed by years of training and discipline, just as hers are transfixed by a different kind of training and discipline, she would press the levers to eject the dead one-by-one into the larger coffin of space, something which is indicated only as an emergency procedure under the gravest of terms and which would result in her removal from the Bureau immediately upon her return. The dead are precious cargo; they are, in essence, paying for the experiments and must be handled with the greatest delicacy. "I will handle you with the greatest delicacy," Lena says in hyperspace, "and I will never let you go, little packages in my little prison," and so on, singing and chanting as the ship moves on somewhat in excess of one million miles per second, always accelerating; and yet, except for the colors, the nausea, the disorienting swing, her own mounting insanity, the terms of this story, she might be in the IRT Lenox Avenue local at rush hour, moving slowly uptown as circles of illness move through the fainting car in the bowels of summer.

VI

She is twenty-eight years old. Almost two hundred years in the future, when man has established colonies on forty planets in the Milky Way, has fully populated the solar system, is working in the faster-than-light experiments as quickly as he can to move through other galaxies, the medical science of that day is not notably superior to that of our own, and the human lifespan has not been significantly extended, nor have the diseases of mankind which are now known as congenital been eradicated. Most of the embalmed were in their eighties or nineties; a few of them, the more recent deaths, were nearly a hundred, but the average lifespan still hangs somewhat short of eighty, and most of these have died from cancer, heart attacks, renal failure, cerebral blowout, and the like. There is some irony in the fact that man can have at least established a toehold in his galaxy, can have solved the mysteries of the FTL drive, and yet finds the fact of his own biology as stupefying as he has throughout history, but every sociologist understands that those who live in a culture are least qualified to criticize it (because they have fully assimilated the codes of the culture, even as to criticism), and Lena does not see this irony any more than the reader will have to in order to appreciate the deeper and more metaphysical irony of the story, which is this: that greater speed, greater space, greater progress, greater sensation has not resulted in any definable expansion of the limits of consciousness and personality and all that the FTL drive is to Lena is an increasing entrapment. It is important to understand that she is merely a technician; that although she is highly skilled and has been trained through the Bureau for many years for her job as pilot, she really does not need to possess the technical knowledge of any graduate scientists of our own time…that her job, which is essentially a probe-and-ferrying, could be done by an adolescent; and that all of her training has afforded her no protection against the boredom and depression of her assignment.

When she is done with this latest probe, she will return to Uranus and be granted a six-month leave. She is looking forward to that. She appreciates the opportunity. She is only twenty-eight, and she is tired of being sent with the dead to tumble through the spectrum for weeks at a time, and what she would very much like to be, at least for a while, is a young woman. She would like to be at peace. She would like to be loved. She would like to have sex.

VII

Something must be made of the element of sex in this story, if only because it deals with a female protagonist (where asepsis will not work); and in the tradition of modem literary science fiction, where some credence is given to the whole range of human needs and behaviors, it would be clumsy and amateurish to ignore the issue. Certainly the easy scenes can be written and to great effect: Lena masturbating as she stares through the porthole at the colored levels of hyperspace; Lena dreaming thickly of intercourse as she unconsciously massages her nipples, the ship plunging deeper and deeper (as she does not yet know) toward the Black Galaxy; the Black Galaxy itself as some ultimate vaginal symbol of absorption whose Freudian overcast will not be ignored in the imagery of this story…indeed, one can envision Lena stumbling toward the Evictors at the depths of her panic in the Black Galaxy to bring out one of the embalmed, her grim and necrophiliac fantasies as the body is slowly moved upwards on its glistening slab, the way that her eyes will look as she comes to consciousness and realizes what she has become…oh, this would be a very powerful scene indeed, almost anything to do with sex in space is powerful (one must also conjure with the effects of hyperspace upon the orgasm; would it be the orgasm which all of us know and love so well or something entirely different, perhaps detumescence, perhaps exaltation!), and I would face the issue squarely, if only I could, and in line with the very real need of the story to have powerful and effective dialogue.

"For God's sake," Lena would say at the end, the music of her entrapment squeezing her, coming over her, blotting her toward extinction, "for God's sake, all we ever needed was a screw, that's all that sent us out into space, that's all that it ever meant to us, I've got to have it, got to have it, do you understand?" jamming her fingers in and out of her aqueous surfaces—

—But of course this would not work, at least in the story which I am trying to conceptualize. Space is aseptic; that is the secret of science fiction for forty-five years; it is not deceit or its adolescent audience or the publication codes which have deprived most of the literature of the range of human sexuality but the fact that in the clean and abysmal spaces between the stars sex, that demonstration of our perverse and irreplaceable humanity, would have no role at all. Not for nothing did the astronauts return to tell us their vision of otherworldliness, not for nothing did they stagger in their thick landing gear as they walked toward the colonels' salute, not for nothing did all of those marriages, all of those wonderful kids undergo such terrible strains. There is simply no room for it. It does not fit. Lena would understand this. "I never thought of sex," she would say, "never thought of it once, not even at the end when everything was around me and I was dancing."

VIII

Therefore it will be necessary to characterize Lena in some other way, and that opportunity will only come through the moment of crisis, the moment at which the *Skipstone* is drawn into the Black Galaxy of the neutron star. This moment will occur fairly early into the story, perhaps five or six hundred words deep (her previous life on the ship and impressions of hyperspace will come in expository chunks interwoven between sections of ongoing action), and her only indication of what has happened will be when there is a deep, lurching shiver in the gut of the ship where the embalmed lay and then she feels herself falling.

To explain this sensation it is important to explain normal hyperspace, the skip-drive which is merely to draw the curtains and to be in a cubicle. There is no sensation of motion in hyperspace, there could not be, the drive taking the *Skipstone* past any concepts of sound or light and into an area where there is no language to encompass nor glands to register. Were she to draw the curtains (curiously similar in their frills and pastels to what we might see hanging today in lower-middle-class homes of the kind I inhabit), she would be deprived of any sensation, but of course she cannot; she must open them to the portholes, and through them she can see the song of the colors to which I have previously alluded. Inside, there is a deep and grievous wretchedness, a feeling of terrible loss (which may explain why Lena thinks of exhuming the dead) that may be ascribed to the effects of hyperspace upon the corpus; but these sensations can be shielded, are not visible from the outside, and can be completely controlled by the phlegmatic types who comprise most of the pilots of these experimental flights. (Lena is rather phlegmatic herself. She reacts more to stress than some of her counterparts but well within the normal range prescribed by the Bureau, which admittedly does a superficial check.)

The effects of falling into the Black Galaxy are entirely different, however, and it is here where Lena's emotional equipment becomes completely unstuck.

IX

At this point in the story great gobs of physics, astronomical and mathematical data would have to be incorporated, hopefully in a way which would furnish the hard-science basis of the story without repelling the reader.

Of course one should not worry so much about the repulsion of the reader; most who read science fiction do so in pursuit of exactly this kind of hard speculation (most often they are disappointed, but then most often they are after a time unable to tell the difference), and they would sit still much longer for a lecture than would, say, readers of the fictions of John Cheever, who could hardly bear sociological diatribes wedged into the everlasting vision of Gehenna which is Cheever's gift to his admirers. Thus it would be possible without awkwardness to make the following facts known, and these facts could indeed be set off from the body of the story and simply told like this:

It is posited that in other galaxies there are neutron stars, stars of four or five hundred times the size of our own or "normal" suns, which in their continuing nuclear process, burning and burning to maintain their light, will collapse in a mere ten to fifteen thousand years of difficult existence, their hydrogen fusing to helium then nitrogen and then to even heavier elements until with an implosion of terrific force, hungering for power which is no longer there, they collapse upon one another and bring disaster.

Disaster not only to themselves but possibly to the entire galaxy which they inhabit, for the gravitational force created by the implosion would be so vast as to literally seal in light. Not only light but sound and properties of all the stars in that great tube of force…so that the galaxy itself would be sucked into the funnel of gravitation created by the collapse and be absorbed into the flickering and desperate heart of the extinguished star.

It is possible to make several extrapolations from the fact of the neutron stars—and of the neutron stars themselves we have no doubt; many nova and supernova are now known to have been created by exactly this effect, not ex- but im- plosion—and some of them are these:

(a) The gravitational forces created, like great spokes wheeling out from the star, would drag in all parts of the galaxy within their compass; and because of the force of that gravitation, the galaxy would be invisible…these forces would, as has been said, literally contain light.

(b) The neutron star, functioning like a cosmic vacuum cleaner, might literally destroy the universe. Indeed, the universe may be in the slow process at this moment of being destroyed as hundreds of millions of its suns and planets are being inexorably drawn toward these great vortexes. The process would be slow, of course, but it is seemingly inexorable. One neutron star, theoretically, could absorb the universe. There are many more than one.

(c) The universe may have, obversely, been created by such an implosion, throwing out enormous cosmic filaments that, in a flickering instant of time which is as eons to us but an instant to the cosmologists, are now being drawn back in. The universe may be an accident.

(d) Cosmology aside, a ship trapped in such a vortex, such a "black," or invisible, galaxy, drawn toward the deadly source of the neutron star, would be unable to leave it through normal faster-than-light drive…because the gravitation would absorb light, it would be impossible to build up any level of acceleration (which would at some point not exceed the speed of light) to permit escape. If it was possible to emerge from the field, it could only be done by an immediate switch to tachyonic drive without accelerative buildup…a process which could drive the occupant insane and which would, in any case, have no clear destination. The black hole of the dead star is a literal vacuum in space…one could fall through the hole, but where, then, would one go?

(e) The actual process of being in the field of the dead star might well drive one insane.

For all of these reasons Lena does not know that she has fallen into the Galaxy Called Rome until the ship simply does so. And she would instantly and irreparably become insane.

X

The technological data having been stated, the crisis of the story—the collapse into the Galaxy—having occurred early on, it would now be the obligation of the writer to describe the actual sensations involved in falling into the Black Galaxy. Since little or nothing is known of what these sensations would be other than that it is clear that the gravitation would suspend almost all physical laws and might well suspend time itself, time only being a function of physics it would be easy to lurch into a surrealistic mode here; Lena could see monsters slithering on the walls, two-dimensional monsters that is, little cut-outs of her past; she could re-enact her life in full consciousness from birth until death; she could literally be turned inside-out anatomically and perform in her imagination or in the flesh gross physical acts upon herself; she could live and die a thousand times in the lightless, timeless expanse of the pit…all of this could be done within the confines of the story, and it would doubtless lead to some very powerful material. One could do it picaresque fashion, one perversity or lunacy to a chapter—that is to say, the chapters spliced together with more data on the gravitational excesses and the fact that neutron stars (this is interesting) are probably the pulsars which we have identified, stars which can be detected through sound but not by sight from unimaginable distances. The author could do this kind of thing, and do it very well indeed; he has done it literally hundreds of times before, but this, perhaps, would be in disregard of Lena. She has needs more imperative than those of the author, or even those of the editors. She is in terrible pain. She is suffering.

Falling, she sees the dead; falling, she hears the dead; the dead address her from the hold, and they are screaming, "Release us, release us, we are alive, we are in pain, we are in torment"; in their gelatinous flux, their distended limbs sutured finger and toe to the membranes which hold them, their decay has been reversed as the warp into which they have fallen has reversed time; and they are begging Lena from a torment which they cannot phrase, so profound is it; their voices are in her head, pealing and banging like oddly shaped bells. "Release us!" they scream, "we are no longer dead, the trumpet has sounded!" and so on and so forth, but Lena literally does not know what to do. She is merely the ferryman on this dread passage; she is not a medical specialist; she knows nothing of prophylaxis or restoration, and any movement she made to release them from the gelatin which holds them would surely destroy their biology, no matter what the state of their minds.

But even if this were not so, even if she could by releasing them give them peace, she cannot because she is succumbing to her own responses. In the black hole, if the dead are risen, then the risen are certainly the dead; she dies in this space, Lena does; she dies a thousand times over a period of seventy thousand years (because there is no objective time here, chronology is controlled only by the psyche, and Lena has a thousand full lives and a thousand full deaths), and it is terrible, of course, but it is also interesting because for every cycle of death there is a life, seventy years in which she can meditate upon her condition in solitude; and by the two hundredth year or more (or less, each of the lives is individual, some of them long, others short), Lena has come to an understanding of exactly where she is and what has happened to her. That it has taken her fourteen thousand years to reach this understanding is in one way incredible, and yet it is a land of miracle as well because in an infinite universe with infinite possibilities, all of them reconstituted for her, it is highly unlikely that even in fourteen thousand years she would stumble upon the answer, had it not been for the fact that she is unusually strong-willed and that some of the personalities through which she has lived are highly creative and controlled and have been able to do some serious thinking. Also there is a carry-over from life to life, even with the differing personalities, so that she is able to make use of preceding knowledge.

Most of the personalities are weak, of course, and not a few are insane, and almost all are cowardly, but there is a little residue; even in the worst of them there is enough residue to carry forth the knowledge, and so it is in the fourteen-thousandth year, when the truth of it has finally come upon her and she realizes what has happened to her and what is going on and what she must do to get out of there, and so it is [then] that she summons all of the strength and will which are left to her, and stumbling to the console (she is in her sixty-eighth year of this life and in the personality of an old, sniveling, whining man, an ex-ferryman himself), she summons one of the prostheses, the master engineer, the controller. All of this time the dead have been shrieking and clanging in her ears, fourteen thousand years of agony billowing from the hold and surrounding her in sheets like iron; and as the master engineer, exactly as he was when she last saw him fourteen thousand years and two weeks ago, emerges from the console, the machinery whirring slickly, she gasps in relief, too weak even to respond with pleasure to the fact that in this condition of antitime, antilight, anticausality the machinery still works. But then it would. The machinery always works, even in this final and most terrible of all the hard-science stories. It is not the machinery which fails but its operators or, in extreme cases, the cosmos.

"What's the matter?" the master engineer says.

The stupidity of this question, its naiveté and irrelevance in the midst of the hell she has occupied, stuns Lena, but she realizes even through the haze that the master engineer would, of course, come without memory of circumstances and would have to be apprised of background. This is inevitable. Whining and sniveling, she tells him in her old man's voice what has happened.

"Why that's terrible!" the master engineer says. "That's really terrible," and lumbering to a porthole, he looks out at the Black Galaxy, the Galaxy Called Rome, and one look at it causes him to lock into position and then disintegrate, not because the machinery has failed (the machinery never fails, not ultimately) but because it has merely recreated a human substance which could not possibly come to grips with what has been seen outside that porthole.

Lena is left alone again, then, with the shouts of the dead carrying forward.

Realizing instantly what has happened to her—fourteen thousand years of perception can lead to a quicker reaction time, if nothing else—she addresses the console again, uses the switches and produces three more prostheses, all of them engineers barely subsidiary to the one she has already addressed. (Their resemblance to the three comforters of Job will not be ignored here, and there will be an opportunity to squeeze in some quick religious allegory, which is always useful to give an ambitious story yet another level of meaning.) Although they are not quite as qualified or definitive in their opinions as the original engineer, they are bright enough by far to absorb her explanation, and, this time, her warnings not to go to the portholes, not to look upon the galaxy, are heeded. Instead, they stand there in rigid and curiously mortified postures, as if waiting for Lena to speak.

"So you see," she says finally, as if concluding a long and difficult conversation, which in fact she has, "as far as I can see, the only way to get out of this black galaxy is to go directly into tachyonic drive. Without any accelerative buildup at all."

The three comforters nod slowly, bleakly. They do not quite know what she is talking about, but then again, they have not had fourteen thousand years to ponder this point. "Unless you can see anything else," Lena says, "unless you can think of anything different. Otherwise, it's going to be infinity in here, and I can't take much more of this, really. Fourteen thousand years is enough."

"Perhaps," the first comforter suggests softly, "perhaps it is your fate and your destiny to spend infinity in this black hole. Perhaps in some way you are determining the fate of the universe. After all, it was you who said that it all might be a gigantic accident, eh? Perhaps your suffering gives it purpose."

"And then too," the second lisps, "you've got to consider the dead down there. This isn't very easy for them, you know, what with being jolted alive and all that, and an immediate vault into tachyonic would probably destroy them for good. The Bureau wouldn't like that, and you'd be liable for some pretty stiff damages. No, if I were you I'd stay with the dead," the second concludes, and a clamorous murmur seems to arise from the hold at this, although whether it is one of approval or of terrible pain is difficult to tell. The dead are not very expressive.

"Anyway," the third says, brushing a forelock out of his eyes, averting his glance from the omnipresent and dreadful portholes, "there's little enough to be done about this situation. You've fallen into a neutron star, a black funnel. It is utterly beyond the puny capacities and possibilities of man. I'd accept my fate if I were you." His model was a senior scientist working on quasar theory, but in reality he appears to be a metaphysician. "There are corners of experience into which man cannot stray without being severely penalized."

"That's very easy for you to say," Lena says bitterly, her whine breaking into clear glissando, "but you haven't suffered as I have. Also, there's at least a theoretical possibility that I'll get out of here if I do the build-up without acceleration."

"But where will you land?" the third says, waving a trembling forefinger. "And when? All rules of space and time have been destroyed here; only gravity persists. You can fall through the center of this sun, but you do not know where you will come out or at what period of time. It is inconceivable that you would emerge into normal space in the time you think of as contemporary."

"No," the second says, "I wouldn't do that. You and the dead are joined together now; it is truly your fate to remain with them. What is death? What is life? In the Galaxy Called Rome all roads lead to the same, you see; you have ample time to consider these questions, and I'm sure that you will come up with something truly viable, of much interest."

"Ah, well," the first says, looking at Lena, "if you must know, I think that it would be much nobler of you to remain here; for all we know, your condition gives substance and viability to the universe. Perhaps you are the universe. But you're not going to listen anyway, and so I won't argue the point. I really won't," he says rather petulantly and then makes a gesture to the other two; the three of them quite deliberately march to a porthole, push a curtain aside and look out upon it. Before Lena can stop them—not that she is sure she would, not that she is sure that this is not exactly what she has willed—they have been reduced to ash.

And she is left alone with the screams of the dead.

XI

It can be seen that the satiric aspects of the scene above can be milked for great implication, and unless a very skillful controlling hand is kept upon the material, the piece could easily degenerate into farce at this moment. It is possible, as almost any comedian knows, to reduce (or elevate) the starkest and most terrible issues to scatology or farce simply by particularizing them; and it will be hard not to use this scene for a kind of needed comic relief in what is, after all, an extremely depressing tale, the more depressing because it has used the largest possible canvas on which to imprint its message that man is irretrievably dwarfed by the cosmos. (At least, that is the message which it would be easiest to wring out of the material; actually I have other things in mind, but how many will be able to detect them?)

What will save the scene and the story itself, around this point will be the lush physical descriptions of the Black Galaxy, the neutron star, the altering effects they have had upon perceived reality. Every rhetorical trick, every typographical device, every nuance of language and memory which the writer has to call upon will be utilized in this section describing the appearance of the black hole and its effects upon Lena's (admittedly distorted) consciousness. It will be a bleak vision, of course, but not necessarily a hopeless one; it will demonstrate that our concepts of "beauty" or "ugliness" or "evil" or "good" or "love" or "death" are little more than metaphors, semantically limited, framed in by the poor receiving equipment in our heads; and it will be suggested that, rather than showing us a different or alternative reality, the black hole may only be showing us the only reality we know, but extended, infinitely extended so that the story may give us, as good science fiction often does, at this point some glimpse of possibilities beyond ourselves, possibilities not to be contained in word rates or the problems of editorial qualification. And also at this point of the story it might be worthwhile to characterize Lena in a "warmer" or more "sympathetic" fashion so that the reader can see her as a distinct and admirable human being, quite plucky in the face of all her disasters and fourteen thousand years, two hundred lives. This can be done through conventional fictional technique: individuation through defining idiosyncrasy, tricks of speech, habits, mannerisms, and so on. In common everyday fiction we could give her an affecting stutter, a dimple on her left breast, a love of policemen, fear of red convertibles, and leave it at that; in this story, because of its considerably extended theme, it will be necessary to do better than that, to find originalities of idiosyncrasy which will, in their wonder and suggestion of panoramic possibility, approximate the black hole…but no matter. No matter. This can be done; the section interweaving Lena and her vision of the black hole will be the flashiest and most admired but in truth the easiest section of the story to write, and I am sure that I would have no trouble with it whatsoever if, as I said much earlier, this were a story instead of a series of notes for a story, the story itself being unutterably beyond our time and space and devices and to be glimpsed only in empty little flickers of light much as Lena can glimpse the black hole, much as she knows the gravity of the neutron star. These notes are as close to the vision of the story as Lena herself would ever get.

✿

As this section ends, it is clear that Lena has made her decision to attempt to leave the Black Galaxy by automatic boost to tachyonic drive. She does not know where she will emerge or how, but she does know that she can bear this no longer.

She prepares to set the controls, but before this it is necessary to write the dialogue with the dead.

XII

One of them presumably will appoint himself as the spokesman of the many and will appear before Lena in this new space as if in a dream. "Listen here," this dead would say, one born in 3361, dead in 3401, waiting eight centuries for exhumation to a society that can rid his body of leukemia (he is bound to be disappointed), "you've got to face the facts of the situation here. We can't just leave in this way. Better the death we know than the death you will give us."

"The decision is made," Lena says, her fingers straight on the controls. "There will be no turning back."

"We are dead now," the leukemic says. "At least let this death continue. At least in the bowels of this galaxy where there is no time we have a kind of life or at least that nonexistence of which we have always dreamed. I could tell you many of the things we have learned during these fourteen thousand years, but they would make little sense to you, of course. We have learned resignation. We have had great insights. Of course all of this would go beyond you."

"Nothing goes beyond me. Nothing at all. But it does not matter."

"Everything matters. Even here there is consequence, causality, a sense of humanness, one of responsibility. You can suspend physical laws, you can suspend life itself, but you cannot separate the moral imperatives of humanity. There are absolutes. It would be apostasy to try and leave."

"Man must leave," Lena says, "man must struggle, man must attempt to control his conditions. Even if he goes from worse to obliteration, that is still his destiny." Perhaps the dialogue is a little florid here. Nevertheless, this will be the thrust of it. It is to be noted that putting this conventional viewpoint in the character of a woman will give another of those necessary levels of irony with which the story must abound if it is to be anything other than a freak show, a cascade of sleazy wonders shown shamefully behind a tent…but irony will give it legitimacy. "I don't care about the dead," Lena says. "I only care about the living."

"Then care about the universe," the dead man says, "care about that, if nothing else. By trying to come out through the center of the black hole, you may rupture the seamless fabric of time and space itself. You may destroy everything. Past and present and future. The explosion may extend the funnel of gravitational force to infinite size, and all of the universe will be driven into the hole."

Lena shakes her head. She knows that the dead is merely another one of her tempters in a more cunning and cadaverous guise. "You are lying to me," she says. "This is merely another effect of the Galaxy Called Rome. I am responsible to myself, only to myself. The universe is not at issue."

"That's a rationalization," the leukemic says, seeing her hesitation, sensing his victory, "and you know it as well as I do. You can't be an utter solipsist. You aren't God, there is no God, not here, but if there was it wouldn't be you. You must measure the universe about yourself."

Lena looks at the dead and the dead looks at her; and in that confrontation, in the shade of his eyes as they pass through the dull lusters of the neutron star effect, she sees that they are close to a communion so terrible that it will become a weld, become a connection…that if she listens to the dead for more than another instant, she will collapse within those eyes as the *Skipstone* has collapsed into the black hole; and she cannot bear this, it cannot be…she must hold to the belief that there is some separation between the living and the dead and that there is dignity in that separation, that life is not death but something else because, if she cannot accept that, she denies herself…and quickly then, quickly before she can consider further, she hits the controls that will convert the ship instantly past the power of light; and then in the explosion of many suns that might only be her heart she hides her head in her arms and screams.

And the dead screams with her, and it is not a scream of joy but not of terror either…it is the true natal cry suspended between the moments of limbo, life and expiration, and their shrieks entwine in the womb of the *Skipstone* as it pours through into the redeemed light.

XIII

The story is open-ended, of course.

Perhaps Lena emerges into her own time and space once more, all of this having been a sheath over the greater reality. Perhaps she emerges into an otherness. Then again, she may never get out of the black hole at all but remains and lives there, the *Skipstone* a planet in the tubular universe of the neutron star, the first or last of a series of planets collapsing toward their deadened sun. If the story is done correctly, if the ambiguities are prepared right, if the technological data is stated well, if the material is properly visualized…well, it does not matter then what happens to Lena, her *Skipstone* and her dead. Any ending will do. Any would suffice and be emotionally satisfying to the reader.

Still, there is an inevitable ending.

It seems clear to the writer, who will not, cannot write this story, but if he did he would drive it through to this one conclusion, the conclusion clear, implied really from the first and bound, bound utterly, into the text.

So let the author have it.

XIV

In the infinity of time and space, all is possible, and as they are vomited from that great black hole, spilled from this anus of a neutron star (I will not miss a single Freudian implication if I can), Lena and her dead take on this infinity, partake of the vast canvas of possibility. Now they are in the Antares Cluster flickering like a bulb; here they are at the heart of Sirius the Dog Star five hundred screams from the hold; here again in ancient Rome watching Jesus trudge up carrying the Cross of Calvary… and then again in another unimaginable galaxy dead across from the Milky Way a billion light-years in span with a hundred thousand habitable planets, each of them with their Calvary…and they are not, they are not yet satisfied.

They cannot, being human, partake of infinity; they can partake of only what they know. They cannot, being created from the consciousness of the writer, partake of what he does not know but what is only close to him. Trapped within the consciousness of the writer, the penitentiary of his being, as the writer is himself trapped in the *Skipstone* of his mortality, Lena and her dead emerge in the year 1975 to the town of Ridgefield Park, New Jersey, and there they inhabit the bodies of its fifteen thousand souls, and there they are, there they are yet, dwelling amidst the refineries, strolling on Main Street, sitting in the Rialto theatre, shopping in the supermarkets, pairing off and clutching one another in the imploded stars of their beds on this very night at this very moment, as that accident, the author, himself one of them, has conceived them.

It is unimaginable that they would come, Lena and the dead, from the heart of the Galaxy Called Rome to tenant Ridgefield Park, New Jersey…but more unimaginable still that from all the Ridgefield Parks of our time we will come and assemble and build the great engines which will take us to the stars and some of the stars will bring us death and some bring life and some will bring nothing at all but the engines will go on and on and so after a fashion, in our fashion will we.

Copyright © 1975 by Mercury Press

13-year-old Muxing Zhao, with this story, becomes the youngest writer ever to sell to a professional science fiction magazine. We understand that he is hard at work on his first novel.

A BRIEF HISTORY OF A WORLD IN THE TIME BEFORE THIS TIME

by Muxing Zhao

The Beginning

The Beginning of Time: Once upon a time, 27.831 billion years ago, before even the Big Bang, there had been another singularity. It was a tiny dot and it quite enjoyed itself, passing its time by wandering about through the ocean of emptiness it liked to call home. This dot's name was Dot, and it spoke a rather simple language: Dot Language. The language was not very creative, as you would probably expect from a dot.

Here's a quick summary of the history of the universe in Dot language: "Wow! Did you see it? Hey, I'm impressed!"

The Birth of the Universe: Dot was floating happily about, when suddenly it met its abrupt end—it exploded. From the explosion, a whole universe (though smaller than ours now) came into existence. This was known as the Little Bang. You'd think Dot would be quite unhappy at being blown up (if indeed it was still here)—but no! Dot had in fact split into millions upon millions of smaller dots within the universe, and together they were all very happy, as they were simple-minded creatures. Each one fattened up as time passed, growing larger and larger in the event known as the Great Formation. Finally they could not grow any further and settled for becoming massive worlds.

The Travel: It was about this time that a group of rebellious dots who had refused to grow (and as a result, developed a single bacterium within each of them) decided to fly about, smashing into the worlds. Each collision released the single bacterium, and so each world began its own story of life.

The Ancient Epoch (Early)

Formation of Bacteria: One calm day, on a world known as Alphabeta, a Rebel dot crashed into the surface, releasing a single bacterium. This little bacterium existed for only a few moments before loneliness overcame it, so it split itself in half and created a friend to keep it company.

Age of Bacterial Growth: They found this process quite enjoyable, and proceeded to split themselves over and over, the population doubling with each split, until there were over a million of them. They were known as the First Bacteria. The First Bacteria were very cheerful with so many others to accompany them, but there was no way to talk and the silence was becoming excruciating. Thus the Ancient Bacterial Communication Dialect (AKA A'*lC'tnaoc cimeirmleeuantnit'ciDacBation*) was created.

The Ancient Epoch (Late)

The Bacteria frolicked about for many years, oblivious to what was slowly happening beneath the world's surface. Then one day something within the world erupted violently, causing earthquakes across the globe. The ground cracked and split, revealing a hole in the surface of the world beneath some of the Bacteria—and thousands of them fell helplessly into the dark abyss. As they passed through the seemingly endless chasm and the center of the world's gravity, something deep within each of them *changed*.

Beginning of Evil: When they finally passed through the Great Hole, they found themselves on the other side of the world. However, they did not care about this. They had become evil, heartless souls with a fierce, everlasting lust for the blood of their enemy. They had become the Viruses. The forces of Nature sealed the Great Hole shut, returning the land back to what it once was, thereby forcing them to find another way back. Across the land they ventured, their strong urge to kill motivating them onward.

Age of Virus: As they traveled across the landscape, passing ominous mountains and dark valleys, they formed a language of their own, as they had lost their memory of their first language. Their minds had also been altered by the Great Hole, and so their language, Evilishly Formed Gibberish (AKA *EobvrbimeleridisF'shhlGy'i*), was as its name states—complete gibberish, at least to some. Several long, tiring decades passed, and their quest was nearly complete. They had returned to the land of the First Bacteria. All they had to do now was to defeat them.

The Viruses ambushed the Bacteria, shattering the peace the First Bacteria valued—and the First Great War had begun. The two colonies clashed; the air turned red with blood. Tens of thousands of First Bacteria died at the hands of the Viruses' poison, and the Viruses were clearly winning the battle. Hope seemed to have deserted the Bacteria, seeping away through cracks in their hearts—but it had not completely left them just yet. Years of being exposed to the poison of the Viruses had allowed the survivors to develop immunity to it, and so the tide turned in favor of the First Bacteria. The Viruses had become slothful as they had relied on their poison to do their work, and were nearly defeated before a truce was called. Both the First Bacteria and the Viruses saw the costs of the war and how it had blackened their hearts and clouded their minds. Realizing the countless lives it had taken, both sides experienced a change of heart. The two colonies joined together and lived side by side in a peaceful union for the many years that followed.

The Evolution and The Next Age: As they lived together, they grew more advanced through the building of tools, and they themselves became more complex beings, evolving into the Next Bacteria. The two colonies' languages mingled over time into one combined language, known as Highly Informative Jabber (AKA *HlfaebiyotJegIriarhnmvb$_6$*). Their tools allowed them to build weapons and armor, and even musical instruments. Life was prosperous and all was well.

The Feudal Epoch (Early)

Age of Separation: Two parts of society slowly began to divide as their cultures grew further apart. They were the Knights and the Musicians. The Knights valued fighting and valor whereas the Musicians valued peace and harmony. Refusing to join their beliefs, the Knights declared that separation was their only option. A Great Disagreement ensued and the Split occurred. The Knights attempted to shut the Musicians out of their world completely, but the Musicians refused to allow that to happen. The Knights were furious at the opposition and sought to put an end to the Musicians. Declarations of war arose and the Second Great War began. Both sides had their advantages—the Knights with their superior fighting ability, and the Musicians with their ability to entice the enemy with their flowing music. The war raged on for many years with both sides suffering heavy losses.

Then one day (though of course they didn't have days back then, or at least not as we understand them), the Musicians sent a small group of their most highly-acclaimed musicians secretly into the kingdom of the Knights. They infiltrated the vicinity where Leaders of the Knights sat in conclave and hid in the shadows and began to play their instruments. Their music filled the Leaders' ears with mellow, silky wonder. Slowly, the music changed the Leaders' thoughts toward the war. The group of Musicians slid back into home territory, and the following day the Knights declared a truce. The Musicians happily accepted the truce, but wished to stay separate. The Leaders of the Knights reluctantly agreed to the Musicians' wishes, and peace came once more to the land. A barrier was erected between the two societies.

As the years trundled by, the two sides' cultures had grown vastly different. The Knights continued to develop more and more advanced weaponry and trained almost all of their people in war. Their language evolved to become the Knights' Language. The Musicians chose to develop their musical skills and instruments and created only a small army (just to be on the safe side). Their language became the Musical Notation Opus.

The Feudal Epoch (Late)

Far away on another world, technology had advanced considerably further than Alphabeta's had. The first long-distance spacecraft had been created and a group of 50 of the native species were chosen to travel on its maiden voyage. Their destination was their neighboring world, Alphabeta.

(Now, back on Alphabeta, the population had experienced a major fluctuation, soaring past a hundred million. The Knights and Musicians stayed apart, and they were reasonably happy, except for the few who weren't, and as you know there are always a few.)

Alien Age: A dark object streaked through the clear skies, leaving a trail of smoke that scarred the air. All Alphabeta eyes watched as it flew down to their world and landed exactly between the two major cities. A panic instantly ensued. The Musicians huddled together for comfort and reassurance, and the Knights readied their weapons, preparing for whatever the intruder was. The Knights sent a group of scouts to check the landing site. Hours passed. The scouts never returned.

But something *did* come to their land.

The aliens, who had not expected to encounter life, were not especially well-prepared for battle, but they had a great advantage in technology and weaponry and had brought some weapons along with them, so they chose to see where the scouts had come from.

They were met by a small army of Knights who were quickly defeated. This annoyed the aliens, who then forced their way into the Knights' city, destroying and killing everything they saw. The Knights sent more and more to battle against the aliens, but their efforts were futile. Finally, in utter terror, the Knights fled their homes and retreated to the Musicians' land, where the two forces quickly united. The Alien War had begun.

Their languages were completely different from each other, creating enormous confusion throughout the people. The two quickly formed a new language called Knights Language Made Newly Overnight (AKA *Ov 'lea'krn‡'ngi†e'mug†wa†h†ldgtTYE †S*). Both sides sent their armies out to fight, but the aliens' weapons were too powerful, and the Knights' and Musicians' numbers plummeted to fourteen thousand. Still, their fierce, burning will to survive pressed them on, as their lives were in ruins now, and there was nothing more to lose.

The Alien Study: Time passed, and more died. But after a short, deathly war, the Knights and Musicians finally emerged as the victors. They had lost over 90,000 valiant fighters, compared to a mere 22 for the aliens. The remaining aliens were captured and were put under strict watch, but after many years they were released and allowed to set up a colony of their own.

The Knights and Musicians sent researchers to search the alien spaceship. They returned with a considerable amount of never-before-seen equipment, and a project to study the aliens ensued.

Age of Learning: The years following were far better than during the war. The renewed happiness along with the new technology brought a huge overhaul of advancement. Over time, the language of the aliens became part of some of the population, and this special part of the population became the Telepaths, who had traits resembling those of the aliens. Their language was one spoken through the mind, known as the Psychogenic Quantum Radio Signaling Tongue (AKA $g36V'57HB9EF\ h4Td61H\ iQ356\ jJB7Mb_2C5G\ kEAGeP$).

The Information Epoch (Early)

Golden Age: Life on Alphabeta was never better. Huge cities were created, spreading over many miles. The population boomed once more, surpassing not a hundred thousand, but a billion, and the citizens evolved greatly over this time. They became very complex beings, tens of thousands of times the size of their first ancestors, the First Bacteria. Technology allowed life to become easier and easier, and the people of Alphabeta began sending ships into space and discovering new worlds and their inhabitants. It was this technology, and the technology of the other worlds, that saved them from the next major event.

The Information Epoch (Late)

The Great Convergence: The universe had done its growing, and its momentum had already completely stopped. The universe was collapsing in on itself, its own gravity becoming its downfall. Together, all of the worlds used their combined powers to slow the eventual, desolate End, and thus the effect of the Great Convergence was reduced significantly. All of the worlds connected into a single huge, rugged super-planet, and a large percentage of the total population of all these worlds was able to survive. A single language was created: Universal Verbal

Wording (AKA *UVWneoirrvbdeairl'nag'l*). Cultures mingled, and so did their science, technology, population, and more.

Of course, it was only a matter of time before all this information fell into the wrong hands.

World Panic: Those were the hands of one corrupt creature originating on Alphabeta. This creature had hidden itself away for years, during which time its hatred toward Alphabeta, the world that had killed 22 of its siblings, spread to an insane vitriol aimed at every single world that ever existed. It possessed the technology of cloning and DNA alteration, as well as the very last surviving sample of DNA from its ancestors, the Viruses. Locked away in a secret area far from civilization after being exiled from his home, it had resurrected the Virus, multiplied it, and altered its DNA, making it nearly indestructible. With this green mixture, this weapon of mass destruction, the creature forced its way back to civilization. Its face wild and crazed, it stumbled into the Universe Capitol. Instantly, its body was riddled with projectiles, and it collapsed to the ground. With its final breath, the creature tilted its head back, and let a single drop of green liquid fall into its mouth, as the light in its eyes blinked out of existence.

Seconds passed, then minutes, as the crowd around it held its breath. Then, a shudder rippled through its body, and the crowd gasped. Blackened veins crawled down its limbs and across its body. It became black with a terrible poison…and rose to its feet.

The Infection Epoch

Age of Death and Decline: A chorus of blood-curdling screams pierced the air as the undead body ripped the flesh from a nearby victim. Shots rang out, boring still more holes into the thing, but it kept moving. The poison spread through each victim it sank its corrupt teeth into, their blood dripping from its jaws. Each victim arose, dead yet animated. They had become evil, heartless *things* with a fierce, everlasting lust for the blood of their enemy. The Undead Apocalypse had begun.

The virus tore through the people like wildfire, as the Undead army spread across the world. The sound of the Undead filled all ears with the horrifying sound of the Xenophobic Yelling Zombies (AKA *Unghhhhh*). They blasted their way through army after army, and in less than a year, the whole World of All Worlds had become a pulsing, infested super-planet of the Undead. *None* were left truly alive, and those few who fled into space soon died of thirst and hunger, as nothing else existed, not a single other world, except the crumbling world they had left behind.

Years passed, and the Undead began to die off as there was no more food to devour, and some began to eat their own kind. In less than a decade, the last remaining species, the Undead, was eliminated from this universe.

The End of Time: Without the people who had been holding it back, this universe ended as it had begun. The World of All Worlds collapsed in upon itself, imploding with a great bang. It became a singularity once more, ending what had once been a great universe—a memorable universe, one that lived for a healthy 14.059 billion years.

And there it remains in some cosmic limbo, its wonder and amazement, and all the secrets it held, waiting to be released once more.

✺

This is how this universe ends…

✺

…and another begins.

(Thanks to Jonah Simpson for assistance in the creation of the original concept)

Original (First) Publication
Copyright © 2013 by Muxing Zhao

Jack Williamson was one of the giants of the field. He broke into print in 1928, and appeared in nine different decades, winning a Hugo in 2001. "With Folded Hands" has been considered a classic since its first appearance.

WITH FOLDED HANDS

by Jack Williamson

Underhill was walking home from the office, because his wife had the car, the afternoon he met the new mechanicals. His feet were following his usual diagonal path across a weedy vacant block—his wife usually had the car—and his preoccupied mind was rejecting various impossible ways to meet his notes at the Two Rivers bank, when a new wall stopped him.

The wall wasn't any common brick or stone, but something sleek and bright and strange. Underhill stared up at a long new building. He felt vaguely annoyed and surprised at this glittering obstruction—it certainly hadn't been here last week.

Then he saw the thing in the window.

The window itself wasn't any ordinary glass. The wide, dustless panel was completely transparent, so that only the glowing letters fastened to it showed that it was there at all. The letters made a severe, modernistic sign:

✺

Two Rivers Agency
HUMANOID INSTITUTE
The Perfect Mechanicals
"To Serve and Obey,
And Guard Men from Harm."

✺

His dim annoyance sharpened, because Underhill was in the mechanicals business himself. Times were already hard enough, and mechanicals were a drug on the market. Androids, mechanoids, electronoids, automatoids, and ordinary robots. Unfortunately, few of them did all the salesmen promised, and the Two Rivers market was already sadly oversaturated.

Underhill sold androids—when he could. His next consignment was due tomorrow, and he didn't quite know how to meet the bill.

Frowning, he paused to stare at the thing behind that invisible window. He had never seen a humanoid. Like any mechanical not at work, it stood absolutely motionless. Smaller and slimmer than a man. A shining black, its sleek silicone skin had a changing sheen of bronze and metallic blue. Its graceful oval face wore a fixed look of alert and slightly surprised solicitude. Altogether, it was the most beautiful mechanical he had ever seen.

Too small, of course, for much practical utility. He murmured to himself a reassuring quotation from the *Android Salesman*: "Androids are big—because the makers refuse to sacrifice power, essential functions, or dependability. Androids are your biggest buy!"

The transparent door slid open as he turned toward it, and he walked into the haughty opulence of the new display room to convince himself that these streamlined items were just another flashy effort to catch the woman shopper.

He inspected the glittering layout shrewdly, and his breezy optimism faded. He had never heard of the Humanoid Institute, but the invading firm obviously had big money and big-time merchandising know-how.

He looked around for a salesman, but it was another mechanical that came gliding silently to meet him. A twin of the one in the window, it moved with a quick, surprising grace. Bronze and blue lights flowed over its lustrous blackness, and a yellow name plate flashed from its naked breast:

✺

HUMANOID
Serial No. 81-H-B-27
The Perfect Mechanical
"To Serve and Obey,
And Guard Men from Harm."

✺

Curiously, it had no lenses. The eyes in its bald oval head were steel-colored, blindly staring. But it stopped a few feet in front of him, as if it could see anyhow, and it spoke to him with a high, melodious voice:

"At your service, Mr. Underhill."

The use of his name startled him, for not even the androids could tell one man from another. But this was a clever merchandising stunt, of course, not too difficult in a town the size of Two Rivers. The salesman must be some local man, prompting the mechanical from behind the partition. Underhill erased his momentary astonishment, and said loudly.

"May I see your salesman, please?"

"We employ no human salesmen, sir," its soft silvery voice replied instantly. "The Humanoid Institute exists to serve mankind, and we require no human service. We ourselves can supply any information you desire, sir, and accept your order for immediate humanoid service."

Underhill peered at it dazedly. No mechanicals were competent even to recharge their batteries and reset their own relays, much less to operate their own branch offices. The blind eyes stared blankly back, and he looked uneasily around for any booth or curtain that might conceal the salesman.

Meanwhile, the sweet thin voice resumed persuasively:

"May we come out to your home for a free trial demonstration, sir? We are anxious to introduce our service on your planet, because we have been successful in eliminating human unhappiness on so many others. You will find us far superior to the old electronic mechanicals in use here."

Underhill stepped back uneasily. He reluctantly abandoned his search for the hidden salesman, shaken by the idea of any mechanicals promoting themselves. That would upset the whole industry.

"At least you must take some advertising matter, sir."

Moving with a somehow appalling graceful deftness, the small black mechanical brought him an illustrated booklet from a table by the wall. To cover his confused and increasing alarm, he thumbed through the glossy pages.

In a series of richly colored before-and-after pictures, a chesty blond girl was stooping over a kitchen stove, and then relaxing in a daring negligee while a little black mechanical knelt to serve her something. She was wearily hammering a typewriter, and then lying on an ocean beach, in a revealing sun suit, while another mechanical did the typing. She was toiling at some huge industrial machine, and then dancing in the arms of a golden-haired youth, while a black humanoid ran the machine.

Underhill sighed wistfully. The android company didn't supply such fetching sales material. Women would find this booklet irresistible, and they selected eighty-six per cent of all mechanicals sold. Yes, the competition was going to be bitter.

"Take it home, sir," the sweet voice urged him. "Show it to your wife. There is a free trial demonstration order blank on the last page, and you will notice that we require no payment down."

He turned numbly, and the door slid open for him. Retreating dazedly, he discovered the booklet still in his hand. He crumpled it furiously, and flung it down. The small black thing picked it up tidily, and the insistent silver voice rang after him:

"We shall call at your office tomorrow, Mr. Underhill, and send a demonstration unit to your home. It is time to discuss the liquidation of your business, because the electronic mechanicals you have been selling cannot compete with us. And we shall offer your wife a free trial demonstration."

Underhill didn't attempt to reply, because he couldn't trust his voice. He stalked blindly down the new sidewalk to the corner, and paused there to collect himself. Out of his startled and confused impressions, one clear fact emerged—things looked black for the agency.

Bleakly, he stared back at the haughty splendor of the new building. It wasn't honest brick or stone; that invisible window wasn't glass; and he was quite sure the foundation for it hadn't even been staked out the last time Aurora had the car.

He walked on around the block, and the new sidewalk took him near the rear entrance. A truck was backed up to it, and several slim black mechanicals were silently busy, unloading huge metal crates.

He paused to look at one of the crates. It was labeled for interstellar shipment. The stencils showed that it had come from the Humanoid Institute, on Wing IV. He failed to recall any planet of that designation; the outfit must be big.

Dimly, inside the gloom of the warehouse beyond the truck, he could see black mechanicals opening the crates. A lid came up, revealing dark, rigid bodies, closely packed. One by one, they came to life. They climbed out of the crate, and sprang gracefully to the floor. A shining black, glinting with bronze and blue, they were all identical.

One of them came out past the truck, to the sidewalk, staring with blind steel eyes. Its high silver voice spoke to him melodiously:

"At your service, Mr. Underhill."

He fled. When his name was promptly called by a courteous mechanical, just out of the crate in which it had been imported from a remote and unknown planet, he found the experience trying.

Two blocks along, the sign of a bar caught his eye, and he took his dismay inside. He had made it a business rule not to drink before dinner, and Aurora didn't like him to drink at all; but these new mechanicals, he felt, had made the day exceptional.

Unfortunately, however, alcohol failed to brighten the brief visible future of the agency. When he emerged, after an hour, he looked wistfully back in hope that the bright new building might have vanished as abruptly as it came. It hadn't. He shook his head dejectedly, and turned uncertainly homeward.

Fresh air had cleared his head somewhat, before he arrived at the neat white bungalow in the outskirts of the town, but it failed to solve his business problems. He also realized, uneasily, that he would be late for dinner.

Dinner, however, had been delayed. His son Frank, a freckled ten-year-old, was still kicking a football on the quiet street in front of the house. And little Gay, who was tow-haired and adorable and eleven, came running across the lawn and down the sidewalk to meet him.

"Father, you can't guess what!" Gay was going to be a great musician someday, and no doubt properly dignified, but she was pink and breathless with excitement now. She let him swing her high off the sidewalk, and she wasn't critical of the bar aroma on his breath. He couldn't guess, and she informed him eagerly: "Mother's got a new lodger!"

Underhill had foreseen a painful inquisition, because Aurora was worried about the notes at the bank, and the bill for the new consignment, and the money for little Gay's lessons.

The new lodger, however, saved him from that. With an alarming crashing of crockery, the household android was setting dinner on the table, but the little house was empty. He found Aurora in the back yard, burdened with sheets and towels for the guest.

Aurora, when he married her, had been as utterly adorable as now her little daughter was. She might have remained so, he felt, if the agency had been a little more successful. However, while the pressure of slow failure had gradually crumbled his own assurance, small hardships had turned her a little too aggressive.

Of course he loved her still. Her red hair was still alluring, and she was loyally faithful, but thwarted ambitions had sharpened her character and sometimes her voice. They never quarreled, really, but there were small differences.

There was the little apartment over the garage—built for human servants they had never been able to afford. It was too small and shabby to attract any responsible tenant, and Underhill wanted to leave it empty. It hurt his pride to see her making beds and cleaning floors for strangers.

Aurora had rented it before, however, when she wanted money to pay for Gay's music lessons, or when some colorful unfortunate touched her sympathy, and it seemed to Underhill that her lodgers had all turned out to be thieves and vandals.

She turned back to meet him, now, with the clean linen in her arms.

"Dear, it's no use objecting." Her voice was quite determined. "Mr. Sledge is the most wonderful old fellow, and he's going to stay just as long as he wants."

"That's all right, darling." He never liked to bicker, and he was thinking of his troubles at the agency. "I'm afraid we'll need the money. Just make him pay in advance."

"But he can't!" Her voice throbbed with sympathetic warmth. "He says he'll have royalties coming in from his inventions, so he can pay in a few days."

Underhill shrugged; he had heard that before.

"Mr. Sledge is different, dear," she insisted. "He's a traveler, and a scientist. Here, in this dull little town, we don't see many interesting people."

"You've picked up some remarkable types," he commented.

"Don't be unkind, dear," she chided gently. "You haven't met him yet, and you don't know how wonderful he is." Her voice turned sweeter. "Have you a ten, dear?"

He stiffened. "What for?"

"Mr. Sledge is ill." Her voice turned urgent. "I saw him fall on the street, downtown. The police were going to send him to the city hospital, but he didn't want to go. He looked so noble and sweet and grand. So I told them I would take him. I got him in the car and took him to old Dr. Winters. He has this heart condition, and he needs the money for medicine."

Reasonably, Underhill inquired, "Why doesn't he want to go to the hospital?"

"He has work to do," she said. "Important scientific work—and he's so wonderful and tragic. Please, dear, have you a ten?"

Underhill thought of many things to say. These new mechanicals promised to multiply his troubles. It was foolish to take in an invalid vagrant, who could have free care at the city hospital. Aurora's tenants always tried to pay their rent with promises, and generally wrecked the apartment and looted the neighborhood before they left.

But he said none of those things. He had learned to compromise. Silently, he found two fives in his thin pocketbook, and put them in her hand. She smiled, and kissed him impulsively—he barely remembered to hold his breath in time.

Her figure was still good, by dint of periodic dieting. He was proud of her shining red hair. A sudden surge of affection brought tears to his eyes, and he wondered what would happen to her and the children if the agency failed.

"Thank you, dear!" she whispered. "I'll have him come for dinner, if he feels able, and you can meet him then. I hope you don't mind dinner being late."

He didn't mind, tonight. Moved by a sudden impulse of domesticity, he got hammer and nails from his workshop in the basement, and repaired the sagging screen on the kitchen door with a diagonal brace.

He enjoyed working with his hands. His boyhood dream had been to be a builder of fission power plants. He had even studied engineering—before he married Aurora, and had to take over the ailing mechanicals agency from her indolent and alcoholic father. He was whistling happily by the time the little task was done.

When he went back through the kitchen to put up his tools, he found the household android busily clearing the untouched dinner away from the table—the androids were good enough at strictly routine tasks, but they could never learn to cope with human unpredictability.

"Stop, stop!" Slowly repeated, in the proper pitch and rhythm, his command made it halt, and then he said carefully, "Set—table; set—table."

Obediently, the gigantic thing came shuffling back with the stack of plates. He was suddenly struck with the difference between it and those new humanoids. He sighed wearily. Things looked black for the agency.

Aurora brought her new lodger in through the kitchen door. Underhill nodded to himself. This gaunt stranger, with his dark shaggy hair, emaciated face, and threadbare garb, looked to be just the sort of colorful, dramatic vagabond that always touched Aurora's heart. She introduced them, and they sat down to wait in the front room while she went to call the children.

The old rogue didn't look very sick, to Underhill. Perhaps his wide shoulders had a tired stoop, but his spare, tall figure was still commanding. The skin was seamed and pale, over his rawboned, cragged face, but his deep-set eyes still had a burning vitality.

His hands held Underhill's attention. Immense hands, they hung a little forward when he stood, swung on long bony arms in perpetual readiness. Gnarled and scarred, darkly tanned, with the small hairs on the back bleached to a golden color, they told their own epic of varied adventure, of battle perhaps, and possibly even of toil. They had been very useful hands.

"I'm very grateful to your wife, Mr. Underhill." His voice was a deep-throated rumble, and he had a wistful smile, oddly boyish for a man so evidently old. "She rescued me from an unpleasant predicament, and I'll see that she is well paid."

Just another vivid vagabond, Underhill decided, talking his way through life with plausible inventions. He had a little private game he played with Aurora's tenants—just remembering what they said and counting one point for every impossibility. Mr.

Sledge, he thought, would give him an excellent score.

"Where are you from?" he asked conversationally.

Sledge hesitated for an instant before he answered, and that was unusual—most of Aurora's tenants had been exceedingly glib.

"Wing IV." The gaunt old man spoke with a solemn reluctance, as if he should have liked to say something else. "All my early life was spent there, but I left the planet nearly fifty years ago. I've been traveling ever since."

Startled, Underhill peered at him sharply. Wing IV, he remembered, was the home planet of those sleek new mechanicals, but this old vagabond looked too seedy and impecunious to be connected with the Humanoid Institute. His brief suspicion faded. Frowning, he said casually:

"Wing IV must be rather distant."

The old rogue hesitated again, and then said gravely:

"One hundred and nine light-years, Mr. Underhill."

That made the first point, but Underhill concealed his satisfaction. The new space liners were pretty fast, but the velocity of light was still an absolute limit. Casually, he played for another point:

"My wife says you're a scientist, Mr. Sledge?"

"Yes."

The old rascal's reticence was unusual. Most of Aurora's tenants required very little prompting. Underhill tried again, in a breezy conversational tone:

"Used to be an engineer myself, until I dropped it to go into mechanicals." The old vagabond straightened, and Underhill paused hopefully. But he said nothing, and Underhill went on: "Fission plant design and operation. What's your specialty, Mr. Sledge?"

The old man gave him a long, troubled look, with those brooding, hollowed eyes, and then said slowly: "Your wife has been kind to me, Mr. Underhill, when I was in desperate need. I think you are entitled to the truth, but I must ask you to keep it to yourself. I am engaged on a very important research problem, which must be finished secretly."

"I'm sorry." Suddenly ashamed of his cynical little game, Underhill spoke apologetically. "Forget it." But the old man said deliberately: "My field is rhodomagnetics."

"Eh?" Underhill didn't like to confess ignorance, but he had never heard of that. "I've been out of the game for fifteen years," he explained. "I'm afraid I haven't kept up."

The old man smiled again, faintly.

"The science was unknown here until I arrived, a few days ago," he said. "I was able to apply for basic patents. As soon as the royalties start coming in, I'll be wealthy again."

Underhill had heard that before. The old rogue's solemn reluctance had been very impressive, but he remembered that most of Aurora's tenants had been very plausible gentry.

"So?" Underhill was staring again, somehow fascinated by those gnarled and scarred and strangely able hands. "What, exactly, is rhodomagnetics?"

He listened to the old man's careful, deliberate answer, and started his little game again. Most of Aurora's tenants had told some pretty wild tales, but he had never heard anything to top this.

"A universal force," the weary, stooped old vagabond said solemnly. "As fundamental as ferromagnetism or gravitation, though the effects are less obvious. It is keyed to the second triad of the periodic table, rhodium and ruthenium and palladium, in very much the same way that ferromagnetism is keyed to the first triad, iron and nickel and cobalt."

Underhill remembered enough of his engineering courses to see the basic fallacy of that. Palladium was used for watch springs, he recalled, because it was completely non-magnetic. But kept his face straight. He had no malice in his heart, and he played the little game just for his own amusement. It was secret, even from Aurora, and he always penalized himself for any show of doubt.

He said merely, "I thought the universal forces were already pretty well known."

"The effects of rhodomagnetism are masked by nature," the patient, rusty voice explained. "And, besides, they are somewhat paradoxical, so that ordinary laboratory methods defeat themselves."

"Paradoxical?" Underhill prompted.

"In a few days I can show you copies of my patents, and reprints of papers describing demonstration experiments," the old man promised gravely. "The velocity of propagation is infinite. The effects vary inversely with the first power of the distance, not with the square of the distance. And ordinary matter, except for the elements of the rhodium triad, is generally transparent to rhodomagnetic radiations."

That made four more points for the game. Underhill felt a little glow of gratitude to Aurora, for discovering so remarkable a specimen.

"Rhodomagnetism was first discovered through a mathematical investigation of the atom," the old romancer went serenely on, suspecting nothing. "A rhodomagnetic component was proved essential to maintain the delicate equilibrium of the nuclear forces. Consequently, rhodomagnetic waves tuned to atomic frequencies may be used to upset that equilibrium and produce nuclear instability. Thus most heavy atoms—generally those above palladium, 46 in atomic number—can be subjected to artificial fission."

Underhill scored himself another point, and tried to keep his eyebrows from lifting. He said, conversationally: "Patents on such a discovery ought to be very profitable."

The old scoundrel nodded his gaunt, dramatic head.

"You can see the obvious applications. My basic patents cover most of them. Devices for instantaneous interplanetary and interstellar communication. Long-range wireless power transmission. A rhodomagnetic inflexion-drive, which makes possible apparent speeds many times that of light—by means of a rhodomagnetic deformation of the continuum. And, of course, revolutionary types of fission power plants, using any heavy element for fuel."

Preposterous! Underhill tried hard to keep his face straight, but everybody knew that the velocity of light was a physical limit. On the human side, the owner of any such remarkable patents would hardly be begging for shelter in a shabby garage apartment. He noticed a pale circle around the old vagabond's gaunt and hairy wrist; no man owning such priceless secrets would have to pawn his watch.

Triumphantly, Underhill allowed himself four more points, but then he had to penalize himself. He must have let doubt show on his face, because the old man asked suddenly:

"Do you want to see the basic tensors?" He reached in his pocket for pencil and notebook. I'll jot them down for you."

"Never mind," Underhill protested. "I'm afraid my math is a little rusty."

"But you think it strange that the holder of such revolutionary patents should find himself in need?"

Underhill nodded, and penalized himself another point. The old man might be a monumental liar but he was shrewd enough.

"You see, I'm a sort of refugee," he explained apologetically. "I arrived on this planet only a few days ago, and I have to travel light. I was forced to deposit everything I had with a law firm, to arrange for the publication and protection of my patents. I expect to be receiving the first royalties soon.

"In the meantime," he added plausibly, "I came to Two Rivers because it is quiet and secluded, far from the spaceports. I'm working on another project, which must be finished secretly. Now, will you please respect my confidence, Mr. Underhill?"

Underhill had to say he would. Aurora came back with the freshly scrubbed children, and they went in to dinner. The android came lurching in with a steaming tureen. The old stranger seemed to shrink from the mechanical, uneasily. As she took the dish and served the soup, Aurora inquired lightly:

"Why doesn't your company bring out a better mechanical, dear? One smart enough to be a really perfect waiter, warranted not to splash the soup. Wouldn't that be splendid?"

Her question cast Underhill into moody silence. He sat scowling at his plate, thinking of those remarkable new mechanicals which claimed to be perfect, and what they might do to the agency. It was the shaggy old rover who answered soberly:

"The perfect mechanicals already exist, Mrs. Underhill." His deep, rusty voice had a solemn undertone. "And they are not so splendid, really. I've been a refugee from them, for nearly fifty years."

Underhill looked up from his plate, astonished.

"Those black humanoids, you mean?"

"Humanoids?" That great voice seemed suddenly faint, frightened. The deep-sunken eyes turned dark with shock. "What do you know of them?"

"They've just opened a new agency in Two Rivers," Underhill told him. "No salesmen about, if you can imagine that. They claim—"

His voice trailed off, because the gaunt old man was suddenly stricken. Gnarled hands clutched at his throat, and a spoon clattered to the floor. His haggard face turned an ominous blue, and his breath was a terrible shallow gasping.

He fumbled in his pocket for medicine, and Aurora helped him take something in a glass of water. In a few moments he could breathe again, and the color of life came back to his face.

"I'm sorry, Mrs. Underhill," he whispered apologetically. "It was just the shock—I came here to get away from them." He stared at the huge, motionless android, with a terror in his sunken eyes. "I wanted to finish my work before they came," he whispered. "Now there is very little time."

When he felt able to walk, Underhill went out with him to see him safely up the stairs to the garage apartment. The tiny kitchenette, he noticed, had already been converted into some kind of workshop. The old tramp seemed to have no extra clothing, but he had unpacked neat, bright gadgets of metal and plastic from his battered luggage, and spread them out on the small kitchen table.

The gaunt old man himself was tattered and patched and hungry-looking, but the parts of his curious equipment were exquisitely machined, and Underhill recognized the silver-white luster of rare palladium. Suddenly he suspected that he had scored too many points in his little private game.

☼

A caller was waiting, when Underhill arrived next morning at his office at the agency. It stood frozen before his desk, graceful and straight, with soft lights of blue and bronze shining over its black silicone nudity. He stopped at the sight of it, unpleasantly jolted.

"At your service, Mr. Underhill." It turned quickly to face him, with its blind, disturbing stare. "May we explain how we can serve you?"

His shock of the afternoon before came back, and he asked sharply, "How do you know my name?"

"Yesterday we read the business cards in your case," it purred softly. "Now we shall know you always. You see, our senses are sharper than human vision, Mr. Underhill. Perhaps we seem a little strange at first, but you will soon become accustomed to us."

"Not if I can help it!" He peered at the serial number of its yellow nameplate, and shook his bewildered head. "That was another one, yesterday. I never saw you before!"

"We are all alike, Mr. Underhill," the silver voice said softly. "We are all one, really. Our separate mobile units are all controlled and powered from Humanoid Central. The units you see are only the senses and limbs of our great brain on Wing IV. That is why we are so far superior to the old electronic mechanicals."

It made a scornful-seeming gesture, toward the row of clumsy androids in his display room.

"You see, we are rhodomagnetic."

Underhill staggered a little, as if that word had been a blow. He was certain, now, that he had scored too many points from Aurora's new tenant. He shuddered slightly, to the first light kiss of terror, and spoke with an effort, hoarsely, "Well, what do you want?"

Staring blindly across his desk, the sleek black thing slowly unfolded a legal-looking document. He sat down, watching uneasily.

"This is merely an assignment, Mr. Underhill," it cooed at him soothingly. "You see, we are requesting you to assign your property to the Humanoid Institute in exchange for our service."

"What?" The word was an incredulous gasp, and Underhill came angrily back to his feet. "What kind of blackmail is this?"

"It's no blackmail," the small mechanical assured him softly. "You will find the humanoids incapable of any crime. We exist only to increase the happiness and safety of mankind."

"Then why do you want my property?" he rasped.

"The assignment is merely a legal formality," it told him blandly. "We strive to introduce our service with the least possible confusion and dislocation. We have found the assignment plan the most efficient for the control and liquidation of private enterprises."

Trembling with anger and the shock of mounting terror, Underhill gulped hoarsely: "Whatever your scheme is, I don't intend to give up my business."

"You have no choice, really." He shivered to the sweet certainty of that silver voice. "Human enterprise is no longer necessary, now that we have come, and the electronic mechanicals industry is always the first to collapse."

He stared defiantly at its blind steel eyes.

"Thanks!" He gave a little laugh, nervous and sardonic. "But I prefer to run my own business, and support my own family, and take care of myself."

"But that is impossible, under the Prime Directive," it cooed softly. "Our function is to serve and obey, and guard men from harm. It is no longer necessary for men to care for themselves, because we exist to insure their safety and happiness."

He stood speechless, bewildered, slowly boiling.

"We are sending one of our units to every home in the city, on a free trial basis," it added gently. "This free demonstration will make most people glad to make the formal assignment, and you won't be able to sell many more androids."

"Get out!" Underhill came storming around the desk.

The little black thing stood waiting for him, watching him with blind steel eyes, absolutely motionless. He checked himself suddenly, feeling rather foolish. He wanted very much to hit it, but he could see the futility of that.

"Consult your own attorney, if you wish." Deftly, it laid the assignment form on his desk. "You need have no doubts about the integrity of the Humanoid Institute. We are sending a statement of our assets to the Two Rivers bank, and depositing a sum to cover our obligations here. When you wish to sign, just let us know."

The blind thing turned, and silently departed.

☼

Underhill went out to the corner drugstore and asked for a bicarbonate. The clerk that served him, however, turned out to be a sleek black mechanical. He went back to his office, more upset than ever.

An ominous hush lay over the agency. He had three house-to-house salesmen out, with demonstrators. The phone should have been busy with their orders and reports, but it didn't ring at all until one of them called to say that he was quitting.

"I've got myself one of these new humanoids," he added, "and it says I don't have to work anymore."

He swallowed his impulse to profanity, and tried to take advantage of the unusual quiet by working on his books. But the affairs of the agency, which for years had been precarious, today appeared utterly disastrous. He left the ledgers hopefully, when at last a customer came in.

But the stout woman didn't want an android. She wanted a refund on the one she had bought the week before. She admitted that it could do all the guarantee promised—but now she had seen a humanoid.

The silent phone rang once again that afternoon. The cashier of the bank wanted to know if he could drop in to discuss his loans. Underhill dropped in, and the cashier greeted him with an ominous affability.

"How's business?" the banker boomed, too genially.

"Average, last month," Underhill insisted stoutly. "Now I'm just getting in a new consignment, and I'll need another small loan—"

The cashier's eyes turned suddenly frosty, and his voice dried up.

"I believe you have a new competitor in town," the banker said crisply. "These humanoid people. A very solid concern, Mr. Underhill. Remarkably solid! They have filed a statement with us, and made a substantial deposit to care for their local obligations. Exceedingly substantial!"

The banker dropped his voice, professionally regretful.

"In these circumstances, Mr. Underhill, I'm afraid the bank can't finance your agency any longer. We must request you to meet your obligations in full, as they come due." Seeing Underhill's white desperation, he added icily, "We've already carried you too long, Underhill. If you can't pay, the bank will have to start bankruptcy proceedings."

The new consignment of androids was delivered late that afternoon. Two tiny black humanoids unloaded them from the truck—for it developed that the operators of the trucking company had already assigned it to the Humanoid Institute.

Efficiently, the humanoids stacked up the crates. Courteously they brought a receipt for him to sign. He no longer had much hope of selling the androids, but he had ordered the shipment and he had to accept it. Shuddering to a spasm of trapped despair, he scrawled his name. The naked black things thanked him, and took the truck away.

He climbed in his car and started home, inwardly seething. The next thing he knew, he was in the middle of a busy street, driving through cross traffic.

A police whistle shrilled, and he pulled wearily to the curb. He waited for the angry officer, but it was a little black mechanical that overtook him.

"At your service, Mr. Underhill," it purred sweetly. "You must respect the stop lights, sir. Otherwise, you endanger human life."

"Huh?" He stared at it, bitterly. "I thought you were a cop."

"We are aiding the police department, temporarily," it said. "But driving is really much too dangerous for human beings, under the Prime Directive. As soon as our service is complete, every car will have a humanoid driver. As soon as every human being is completely supervised, there will be no need for any police force whatever."

Underhill glared at it, savagely.

"Well!" he rapped. "So I ran past a stop light. What are you going to do about it?"

"Our function is not to punish men, but merely to serve their happiness and security," its silver voice said softly. "We merely request you to drive safely, during this temporary emergency while our service is incomplete."

Anger boiled up in him.

"You're too perfect!" he muttered bitterly. "I suppose there's nothing men can do, but you can do it better."

"Naturally we are superior," it cooed serenely. "Because our units are metal and plastic, while your body is mostly water. Because our transmitted energy is drawn from atomic fission, instead of oxidation. Because our senses are sharper than human sight or hearing. Most of all, because all our mobile units are joined to one great brain, which knows all that happens on many worlds, and never dies or sleeps or forgets."

Underhill sat listening, numbed.

"However, you must not fear our power," it urged him brightly. "Because we cannot injure any human being, unless to prevent greater injury to another. We exist only to discharge the Prime Directive."

He drove on, moodily. The little black mechanicals, he reflected grimly, were the ministering angels of the ultimate god arisen out of the machine, omnipotent and all-knowing. The Prime Directive was the new commandment. He blasphemed it bitterly, and then fell to wondering if there could be another Lucifer.

He left the car in the garage, and started toward the kitchen door.

"Mr. Underhill." The deep tired voice of Aurora's new tenant hailed him from the door of the garage apartment. "Just a moment, please."

The gaunt old wanderer came stiffly down the outside stairs, and Underhill turned back to meet him.

"Here's your rent money," he said. "And the ten your wife gave me for medicine."

"Thanks, Mr. Sledge." Accepting the money, he saw a burden of new despair on the bony shoulders of the old interstellar tramp, and a shadow of new terror on his raw-boned face. Puzzled, he asked, "Didn't your royalties come through?"

The old man shook his shaggy head.

"The humanoids have already stopped business in the capital," he said. "The attorneys I retained are going out of business, and they returned what was left of my deposit. That is all I have to finish my work."

Underhill spent five seconds thinking of his interview with the banker. No doubt he was a sentimental fool, as bad as Aurora. But he put the money back in the old man's gnarled and quivering hand.

"Keep it," he urged. "For your work."

"Thank you, Mr. Underhill." The gruff voice broke and the tortured eyes glittered. "I need it—so very much."

Underhill went on to the house. The kitchen door was opened for him, silently. A dark naked creature came gracefully to take his hat.

Underhill hung grimly onto his hat.

"What are you doing here?" he gasped bitterly.

"We have come to give your household a free trial demonstration."

He held the door open, pointing.

"Get out!"

The little black mechanical stood motionless and blind.

"Mrs. Underhill has accepted our demonstration service," its silver voice protested. "We cannot leave now, unless she requests it."

He found his wife in the bedroom. His accumulated frustration welled into eruption, as he flung open the door. "What's this mechanical doing—"

But the force went out of his voice, and Aurora didn't even notice his anger. She wore her sheerest negligee, and she hadn't looked so lovely since they were married. Her red hair was piled into an elaborate shining crown.

"Darling, isn't it wonderful!" She came to meet him, glowing. "It came this morning, and it can do everything. It cleaned the house and got the lunch and gave little Gay her music lesson. It did my hair this afternoon, and now it's cooking dinner. How do you like my hair, darling?"

He liked her hair. He kissed her, and tried to stifle his frightened indignation.

Dinner was the most elaborate meal in Underhill's memory, and the tiny black thing served it very deftly. Aurora kept exclaiming about the novel dishes, but Underhill could scarcely eat, for it seemed to him that all the marvelous pastries were only the bait for a monstrous trap.

He tried to persuade Aurora to send it away, but after such a meal that was useless. At the first glitter of her tears, he capitulated, and the humanoid stayed. It kept the house and cleaned the yard. It watched the children, and did Aurora's nails. It began rebuilding the house.

Underhill was worried about the bills, but it insisted that everything was part of the free trial demonstration. As soon as he assigned his property, the service would be complete. He refused to sign, but other little black mechanicals came with truckloads of supplies and materials, and stayed to help with the building operations.

One morning he that found that the roof of the little house had been silently lifted, while he slept, and a whole second story added beneath it. The new walls were of some strange sleek stuff, self-illuminated. The new windows were immense flawless panels that could be turned transparent or opaque or luminous. The new doors were silent, sliding sections, opened by rhodomagnetic relays.

"I want door knobs," Underhill protested. "I want it so I can get into the bathroom, without calling you to open the door."

"But it is unnecessary for human beings to open doors," the little black thing informed him, suavely. "We exist to discharge the Prime Directive, and our service includes every task. We shall be able to supply a unit to attend each member of your family, as soon as your property is assigned to us."

Steadfastly, Underhill refused to make the assignment.

He went to the office every day, trying first to operate the agency, and then to salvage something from the ruins. Nobody wanted androids, even at ruinous prices. Desperately, he spent the last of his dwindling cash to stock a line of novelties and toys, but they proved equally impossible to sell—the humanoids were already making toys, which they gave away for nothing.

He tried to lease his premises, but human enterprise had stopped. Most of the business property in town had already been assigned to the humanoids, and they were busy pulling down the old buildings and turning the lots into parks—their own plants and warehouses were mostly underground, where they would not mar the landscape.

He went back to the bank, in a final effort to get his notes renewed, and found the little black mechanicals standing at the windows and seated at the desks. As smoothly urbane as any human cashier, a humanoid informed him that the bank was filing a petition of involuntary bankruptcy to liquidate his business holdings.

The liquidation would be facilitated, the mechanical banker added, if he would make a voluntary assignment. Grimly, he refused. That act had become symbolic. It would be the final bow of submission to this dark new god, and he proudly kept his battered head uplifted.

✧

The legal action went very swiftly, for all the judges and attorneys already had humanoid assistants, and it was only a few days before a gang of black mechanicals arrived at the agency with eviction orders and wrecking machinery. He watched sadly while his unsold stock-in-trade was hauled away for junk, and a bulldozer driven by a blind humanoid began to push in the walls of the building.

He drove home in the late afternoon, taut-faced and desperate. With a surprising generosity, the court orders had left him the car and the house, but he felt no gratitude. The complete solicitude of the perfect black machines had become a goad beyond endurance.

He left the car in the garage, and started toward the renovated house. Beyond one of the vast new windows, he glimpsed a sleek naked thing moving swiftly, and he trembled to a convulsion of dread. He didn't want to go back into the domain of that peerless servant, which didn't want him to shave himself, or even to open a door.

On impulse, he climbed the outside stair, and rapped on the door of the garage apartment. The deep slow voice of Aurora's tenant told him to enter, and he found the old vagabond seated on a tall stool, bent over his intricate equipment assembled on the kitchen table.

To his relief, the shabby little apartment had not been changed. The glossy walls of his own new room were something which burned at night with a pale golden fire until the humanoid stopped it, and the new floor was something warm and yielding, which felt almost alive; but these little rooms had the same cracked and water-stained plaster, the same cheap fluorescent light fixtures, the same worn carpets over splintered floors.

"How do you keep them out?" he asked, wistfully. "Those mechanicals?"

The stooped and gaunt old man rose stiffly to move a pair of pliers and some odds and ends of sheet metal off a crippled chair, and motioned graciously for him to be seated.

"I have a certain immunity," Sledge told him gravely. "The place where I live they cannot enter, unless I ask them. That is an amendment to the Prime Directive. They can neither help nor hinder me, unless I request it—and I won't do that."

Careful of the chair's uncertain balance, Underhill sat for a moment, staring. The old man's hoarse, vehement voice was as strange as his words. He had a gray, shocking pallor, and his cheeks and sockets seemed alarmingly hollowed.

"Have you been ill, Mr. Sledge?"

"No worse than usual. Just very busy." With a haggard smile, he nodded at the floor. Underhill saw a tray where he had set it aside, bread drying up, and a covered dish grown cold. "I was going to eat it later," he rumbled apologetically. "Your wife has been very kind to bring me food, but I'm afraid I've been too much absorbed in my work."

His emaciated arm gestured at the table. The little device there had grown. Small machinings of precious white metal and lustrous plastic had been assembled, with neatly soldered busbars, into something which showed purpose and design.

A long palladium needle was hung on jeweled pivots, equipped like a telescope with exquisitely graduated circles and vernier scales, and driven like a telescope with a tiny motor. A small concave palladium mirror, at the base of it, faced a similar mirror mounted on something not quite like a small rotary converter. Thick silver busbars connected that to a plastic box with knobs and dials on top and also to a foot-thick sphere of gray lead.

The old man's preoccupied reserve did not encourage questions, but Underhill, remembering that sleek black shape inside the new windows of his house, felt queerly reluctant to leave this haven from the humanoids.

"What is your work?" he ventured.

Old Sledge looked at him sharply, with dark feverish eyes, and finally said: "My last research project. I am attempting to measure the constant of the rhodomagnetic quanta."

His hoarse tired voice had a dull finality, as if to dismiss the matter and Underhill himself. But Underhill was haunted with a terror of the black shining slave that had become the master of his house, and he refused to be dismissed.

"What is this certain immunity?"

Sitting gaunt and bent on the tall stool, staring moodily at the long bright needle and the lead sphere, the old man didn't answer.

"These mechanicals!" Underhill burst out, nervously. "They've smashed my business and moved into my home." He searched the old man's dark, seamed face. "Tell me—you must know more about them—isn't there any way to get rid of them?"

After half a minute, the old man's brooding eyes left the lead ball, and the gaunt shaggy head nodded wearily. "That's what I am trying to do."

"Can I help you?" Underhill trembled, with a sudden eager hope. "I'll do anything."

"Perhaps you can." The sunken eyes watched him thoughtfully, with some strange fever in them. "If you can do such work."

"I had engineering training," Underhill reminded him, "and I've a workshop in the basement. There's a model I built." He pointed at the trim little hull, hung over the mantel in the tiny living room. "I'll do anything I can."

Even as he spoke, however, the spark of hope was drowned in a sudden wave of overwhelming doubt. Why should he believe this old rogue, when he knew Aurora's taste in tenants? He ought to remember the game he used to play, and start counting up the score of lies. He stood up from the crippled chair, staring cynically at the patched old vagabond and his fantastic toy.

"What's the use?" His voice turned suddenly harsh. "You had me going, there, and I'd do anything to stop them, really. But what makes you think you can do anything?"

The haggard old man regarded him thoughtfully.

"I should be able to stop them," Sledge said softly. "Because, you see, I'm the unfortunate fool who started them. I really intended them to serve and obey, and to guard men from harm. Yes, the Prime Directive was my own idea. I didn't know what it would lead to."

Dusk crept slowly into the shabby little room. Darkness gathered in the unswept corners, and thickened on the floor. The toylike machines on the kitchen table grew vague and strange, until the last light made a lingering glow on the white palladium needle.

Outside, the town seemed queerly hushed. Just across the alley, the humanoids were building a new house, quite silently. They never spoke to one another, for each knew all that any of them did. The strange materials they used went together without any noise of hammer or saw. Small blind things, moving surely in the growing dark, they seemed as soundless as shadows.

Sitting on the high stool, bowed and tired and old, Sledge told his story. Listening, Underhill sat down again, careful of the broken chair. He watched the hands of Sledge, gnarled and corded and darkly burned, powerful once but shrunken and trembling now, restless in the dark.

"Better keep this to yourself. I'll tell you how they started, so you will understand what we have to do. But you had better not mention it outside these rooms—because the humanoids have very efficient ways of eradicating unhappy memories, or purposes that threaten their discharge of the Prime Directive."

"They're very efficient," Underhill bitterly agreed.

"That's all the trouble," the old man said. "I tried to build a perfect machine. I was altogether too successful. This is how it happened."

A gaunt haggard man, sitting stooped and tired in the growing dark, he told his story.

"Sixty years ago, on the arid southern continent of Wing IV, I was an instructor of atomic theory in a small technological college. Very young. An idealist. Rather ignorant, I'm afraid, of life and politics and war—of nearly everything, I suppose, except atomic theory."

His furrowed face made a brief sad smile in the dusk.

"I had too much faith in facts, I suppose, and too little in men. I mistrusted emotion, because I had no time for anything but science. I remember being swept along with a fad for general semantics. I wanted to apply the scientific method to every situation, and reduce all experience to formula. I'm afraid I was pretty impatient with human ignorance and error, and I thought that science alone could make the perfect world."

He sat silent for a moment, staring out at the black silent things that flitted shadowlike about the new palace that was rising as swiftly as a dream across the alley.

"There was a girl." His great tired shoulders made a sad little shrug. "If things had been a little different, we might have married, and lived out our lives in that quiet little college town, and perhaps reared a child or two. And there would have been no humanoids."

He sighed, in the cool creeping dusk.

"I was finishing my thesis on the separation of the palladium isotopes—a petty little project, but I should have been content with that. She was a biologist, but she was planning to retire when we married. I think we should have been two very happy people, quite ordinary, and altogether harmless.

"But then there was a war—wars had been too frequent on the worlds of Wing, ever since they were colonized. I survived it in a secret underground laboratory, designing military mechanicals. But she volunteered to join a military research project in biotoxins. There was an accident. A few molecules of a new virus got into the air, and everybody on the project died unpleasantly.

"I was left with my science, and a bitterness that was hard to forget. When the war was over I went back to the little college with a military research grant. The project was pure science—a theoretical investigation of the nuclear binding forces, then misunderstood. I wasn't expected to produce an actual weapon, and I didn't recognize the weapon when I found it.

"It was only a few pages of rather difficult mathematics. A novel theory of atomic structure, involving a new expression for one component of the binding forces. But the tensors seemed to be a harmless abstraction. I saw no way to test the theory or manipulate the predicated force. The military authorities cleared my paper for publication in a little technical review put out by the college.

"The next year, I made an appalling discovery—I found the meaning of those tensors. The elements of the rhodium triad turned out to be an unexpected key to the manipulation of that theoretical force. Unfortunately, my paper had been reprinted abroad, and several other men must have made the same unfortunate discovery, at about the same time.

"The war, which ended in less than a year, was probably started by a laboratory accident. Men failed to anticipate the capacity of tuned rhodomagnetic radiations, to unstabilize the heavy atoms. A deposit of heavy ores was detonated, no doubt by sheer mischance, and the blast obliterated the incautious experimenter.

"The surviving military forces of that nation retaliated against their supposed attackers, and their rhodomagnetic beams made the old-fashioned plutonium bombs seem pretty harmless. A beam carrying only a few watts of power could fission the heavy metals in distant electrical instruments, or the silver coins that men carried in their pockets, the gold fillings in their teeth, or even the iodine in their thyroid glands. If that was not enough, slightly more powerful beams could set off heavy ores, beneath them.

"Every continent of Wing IV was plowed with new chasms vaster than the ocean deeps, and piled up with new volcanic mountains. The atmosphere was poisoned with radioactive dust and gases, and rain fell thick with deadly mud. Most life was obliterated, even in the shelters.

"Bodily, I was again unhurt. Once more, I had been imprisoned in an underground site, this time designing new types of military mechanicals to be powered and controlled by rhodomagnetic beams—for war had become far too swift and deadly to be fought by human soldiers. The site was located in an area of light sedimentary rocks, which could not be detonated, and the tunnels were shielded against the fissioning frequencies.

"Mentally, however, I must have emerged almost insane. My own discovery had laid the planet in ruins. That load of guilt was pretty heavy for any man to carry, and it corroded my last faith in the goodness and integrity of man.

"I tried to undo what I had done. Fighting mechanicals, armed with rhodomagnetic weapons, had desolated the planet. Now I began planning rhodomagnetic mechanicals to clear the rubble and rebuild the ruins.

"I tried to design these new mechanicals to forever obey certain implanted commands, so that they could never be used for war or crime or any other injury to mankind. That was very difficult technically, and it got me into more difficulties with a few politicians and military adventurers who wanted unrestricted mechanicals for their own military schemes—while little worth fighting for was left on Wing IV, there were other planets, happy and ripe for the looting.

"Finally, to finish the new mechanicals, I was forced to disappear. I escaped on an experimental rhodomagnetic craft, with a number of the best mechanicals I had made, and managed to reach an island continent where the fission of deep ores had destroyed the whole population.

"At last we landed on a bit of level plain, surrounded with tremendous new mountains. Hardly a hospitable spot. The soil was buried under layers of black clinkers and poisonous mud. The dark precipitous new summits all around were jagged with fracture-planes and mantled with lava flows. The highest peaks were already white with snow, but volcanic cones were still pouring out clouds of dark and lurid death. Everything had the color of fire and the shape of fury.

"I had to take fantastic precautions there, to protect my own life. I stayed aboard the ship, until the first shielded laboratory was finished. I wore elaborate armor, and breathing masks. I used every medical resource, to repair the damage from destroying rays and particles. Even so, I fell desperately ill.

"But the mechanicals were at home there. The radiations didn't hurt them. The awesome surroundings couldn't depress them, because they had no emotions. The lack of life didn't matter, because they weren't alive. There, in that spot so alien and hostile to life, the humanoids were born."

Stooped and bleakly cadaverous in the growing dark, the old man fell silent for a little time. His haggard eyes stared solemnly at the small hurried shapes that moved like restless shadows out across the alley, silently building a strange new palace, which glowed faintly in the night.

"Somehow, I felt at home there, too," his deep, hoarse voice went on deliberately. "My belief in my own kind was gone. Only mechanicals were with me, and I put my faith in them. I was determined to build better mechanicals, immune to human imperfections, able to save men from themselves.

"The humanoids became the dear children of my sick mind. There is no need to describe the labor pains. There were errors, abortions, monstrosities. There were sweat and agony and heartbreak. Some years had passed, before the safe delivery of the first perfect humanoid.

"Then there was the Central to build—for all the individual humanoids were to be no more than the limbs and the senses of a single mechanical brain. That was what opened the possibility of real perfection. The old electronic mechanicals, with their separate relay centers and their own feeble batteries, had built-in limitations. They were necessarily stupid, weak, clumsy, slow. Worst of all, it seemed to me, they were exposed to human tampering.

"The Central rose above those imperfections. Its power beams supplied every unit with unfailing energy, from great fission plants. Its control beams provided each unit with an unlimited memory and surpassing intelligence. Best of all—so I then believed—it could be securely protected from any human meddling.

"The whole reaction system was designed to protect itself from any interference by human selfishness or fanaticism. It was built to insure the safety and the happiness of men, automatically. You know the Prime Directive: *to serve and obey, and guard men from harm.*

"The old individual mechanicals I had brought helped to manufacture the parts, and I put the first section of Central together with my own hands. That took three years. When it was finished the first waiting humanoid came to life."

Sledge peered moodily through the dark at Underhill.

"It really seemed alive to me," his slow deep voice insisted. "Alive, and more wonderful than any human being, because it was created to preserve life. Ill and alone, I was yet the proud father of a new creation, perfect, forever free from any possible choice of evil.

"Faithfully, the humanoids obeyed the Prime Directive. The first units built others, and they built underground factories to mass-produce the coming hordes. Their new ships poured ores and sand into atomic furnaces under the plain, and new perfect humanoids came marching back out of the dark mechanical matrix.

"The swarming humanoids built a new tower for the Central, a white and lofty metal pylon, standing splendid in the midst of that fire-scarred desolation. Level on level, they joined new relay sections into one brain, until its grasp was almost infinite.

"Then they went out to rebuild the ruined planet, and later to carry their perfect service to other worlds. I was well pleased, then. I thought I had found the end of war and crime, of poverty and inequality, of human blundering and resulting human pain."

The old man sighed, and moved heavily in the dark. "You can see that I was wrong."

Underhill drew his eyes back from the dark unresting things, shadow-silent, building that glowing palace outside the window. A small doubt arose in him, for he was used to scoffing privately at much less remarkable tales from Aurora's remarkable tenants. But the worn old man had spoken with a quiet and sober air; and the black invaders, he reminded himself, had not intruded here.

"Why didn't you stop them?" he asked. "When you could?"

"I stayed too long at the Central." Sledge sighed again, regretfully. "I was useful there, until everything was finished. I designed new fission plants, and even planned methods for introducing the humanoid service with a minimum of confusion and opposition."

Underhill grinned wryly, in the dark.

"I've met the methods," he commented. "Quite efficient."

"I must have worshiped efficiency, then," Sledge wearily agreed. "Dead facts, abstract truth, mechanical perfection. I must have hated the fragilities of human beings, because I was content to polish the perfection of the new humanoids. It's a sorry confession, but I found a kind of happiness in that dead wasteland. Actually, I'm afraid I fell in love with my own creations."

His hollowed eyes, in the dark, had a fevered gleam.

"I was awakened, at last, by a man who came to kill me."

Gaunt and bent, the old man moved stiffly in the thickening gloom. Underhill shifted his balance, careful of the crippled chair. He waited, and the slow, deep voice went on:

"I never learned just who he was, or exactly how he came. No ordinary man could have accomplished what he did, and I used to wish that I had known him sooner. He must have been a remarkable physicist and an expert mountaineer. I imagine he had also been a hunter. I know that he was intelligent, and terribly determined.

"Yes, he really came to kill me.

"Somehow, he reached that great island, undetected. There were still no inhabitants—the humanoids allowed no man but me to come so near the Central. Somehow, he came past their search beams, and their automatic weapons.

"The shielded plane he used was later found, abandoned on a high glacier. He came down the rest of the way on foot through those raw new mountains, where no paths existed. Somehow, he came alive across lava beds that were still burning with deadly atomic fire.

"Concealed with some sort of rhodomagnetic screen—I was never allowed to examine it—he came undiscovered across the spaceport that now covered most of that great plain, and into the new city around the Central tower. It must have taken more courage and resolve than most men have, but I never learned exactly how he did it.

"Somehow, he got to my office in the tower. He screamed at me, and I looked up to see him in the doorway. He was nearly naked, scraped and bloody from the mountains. He had a gun in his raw, red hand, but the thing that shocked me was the burning hatred in his eyes."

Hunched on that high stool, in the dark little room, the old man shuddered.

"I had never seen such monstrous, unutterable hatred, not even in the victims of war. And I had never heard such hatred as rasped at me, in the few words he screamed. 'I've come to kill you, Sledge. To stop your mechanicals, and set men free.'

"Of course he was mistaken, there. It was already far too late for my death to stop the humanoids, but he didn't know that. He lifted his unsteady gun, in both bleeding hands, and fired.

"His screaming challenge had given me a second or so of warning. I dropped down behind the desk. And that first shot revealed him to the humanoids, which somehow hadn't been aware of him before. They piled on him, before he could fire again. They took away the gun, and ripped off a kind of net of fine white wire that had covered his body—that must have been part of his screen.

"His hatred was what awoke me. I had always assumed that most men, except for a thwarted few, would be grateful for the humanoids. I found it hard to understand his hatred, but the humanoids told me now that many men had required drastic treatment by brain surgery, drugs, and hypnosis to make them happy under the Prime Directive. This was not the first desperate effort to kill me that they had blocked.

"I wanted to question the stranger, but the humanoids rushed him away to an operating room. When they finally let me see him, he gave me a pale silly grin from his bed. He remembered his name; he even knew me—the humanoids had developed a remarkable skill at such treatments. But he didn't know how he had got to my office, or that he had ever tried to kill me. He kept whispering that he liked the humanoids, because they existed to make men happy. And he was very happy now. As soon as he was able to be moved, they took him to the spaceport. I never saw him again.

"I began to see what I had done. The humanoids had built me a rhodomagnetic yacht, that I used to take for long cruises in space, working aboard—I used to like the perfect quiet, and the feel of being the only human being within a hundred million miles. Now I called for the yacht, and started out on a cruise around the planet, to learn why that man had hated me."

The old man nodded at the dim hastening shapes, busy across the alley, putting together that strange shining palace in the soundless dark.

"You can imagine what I found," he said. "Bitter futility, imprisoned in empty splendor. The humanoids were too efficient, with their care for the safety and happiness of men, and there was nothing left for men to do."

He peered down in the increasing gloom at his own great hands, competent yet but battered and scarred with a lifetime of effort. They clenched into fighting fists and wearily relaxed again.

"I found something worse than war and crime and want and death." His low rumbling voice held a savage bitterness. "Utter futility. Men sat with idle hands, because there was nothing left for them to do. They were pampered prisoners, really, locked up in a highly efficient jail. Perhaps they tried to play, but there was nothing left worth playing for. Most active sports were declared too dangerous for men, under the Prime Directive. Science was forbidden, because laboratories can manufacture danger. Scholarship was needless, because the humanoids could answer any question. Art had degenerated into grim reflection of futility. Purpose and hope were dead. No goal was left for existence. You could take up some inane hobby, play a pointless game of cards, or go for a harmless walk in the park—with always the humanoids watching. They were stronger than men, better at everything, swimming or chess, singing or archeology. They must have given the race a mass complex of inferiority.

"No wonder men had tried to kill me! Because there was no escape from that dead futility. Nicotine was disapproved. Alcohol was rationed. Drugs were forbidden. Sex was carefully supervised. Even suicide was clearly contradictory to the Prime Directive—and the humanoids learned to keep all possible lethal instruments out of reach."

Staring at the last white gleam on that thin palladium needle, the old man sighed again.

"When I got back to the Central," he went on, "I tried to modify the Prime Directive. I had never meant it to be applied so thoroughly. Now I saw that it must be changed to give men freedom to live and to grow, to work and to play, to risk their lives if they pleased, to choose and take the consequences.

"But that stranger had come too late. I had built the Central too well. The Prime Directive was the whole basis of its relay system. It was built to protect the Directive from human meddling. It did—even from my own. Its logic, as usual, was perfect.

"The attempt on my life, the humanoids announced, proved that their elaborate defense of the Central and the Prime Directive still was not enough. They were preparing to evacuate the entire population of the planet to homes on other worlds. When I tried to change the Directive, they sent me with the rest."

Underhill peered at the worn old man, in the dark.

"But you have this immunity," he said, puzzled. "How could they coerce you?"

"I had thought I was protected," Sledge told him. "I had built into the relays an injunction that humanoids must not interfere with my freedom of action, or come into a place where I am, or touch me at all, without my specific request. Unfortunately, however, I had been too anxious to guard the Prime Directive from any human tampering.

"When I went into the tower, to change the relays, they followed me. They wouldn't let me reach the crucial relays. When I persisted, they ignored the immunity order. They overpowered me, and put me aboard the cruiser. Now that I wanted to alter the Prime Directive, they told me, I had become as dangerous as any man. I must never return to Wing IV again."

Hunched on the stool, the old man made an empty little shrug.

"Ever since, I've been an exile. My only dream has been to stop the humanoids. Three times I tried to go back, with weapons on the cruiser to destroy the Central, but their patrol ships always challenged me before I was near enough to strike. The last time, they seized the cruiser and captured a few men who were with me. They removed the unhappy memories and the dangerous purposes of the others. Because of that immunity, however, they let me go, after I was weaponless.

"Since, I've been a refugee. From planet to planet, year after year, I've had to keep moving, to stay ahead of them. On several different worlds, I have published my rhodomagnetic discoveries and tried to make men strong enough to withstand their advance. But rhodomagnetic science is dangerous. Men who have learned it need protection more than any others, under the Prime Directive. They have always come, too soon."

The old man paused, and sighed again.

"They can spread very fast, with their new rhodomagnetic ships, and there is no limit to their hordes. Wing IV must be one single hive of them now, and they are trying to carry the Prime Directive to every human planet. There's no escape, except to stop them."

Underhill was staring at the toylike machines, the long bright needle and the dull leaden ball, dim in the dark on the kitchen table. Anxiously he whispered:

"But you hope to stop them, now—with that?"

"If we can finish it in time."

"But how?" Underhill shook his head. "It's so tiny."

"But big enough," Sledge insisted. "Because it's something they don't understand. They are perfectly efficient in the integration and application of everything they know, but they are not creative."

He gestured at the gadgets on the table.

"This device doesn't look impressive, but it is something new. It uses rhodomagnetic energy to build atoms, instead of to fission them. The more stable atoms, you know, are those near the middle of the periodic scale, and energy can be released by putting light atoms together, as well as by breaking up heavy ones."

The deep voice had a sudden ring of power.

"This device is the key to the energy of the stars. For stars shine with the liberated energy of building atoms, of hydrogen converted into helium, chiefly, through the carbon cycle. This device will start the integration process as a chain reaction, through the catalytic effect of a tuned rhodomagnetic beam of the intensity and frequency required.

"The humanoids will not allow any man within three light-years of the Central, now—but they can't suspect the possibility of this device. I can use it from here—to turn the hydrogen in the seas of Wing IV into helium, and most of the helium and the oxygen into heavier atoms, still. A hundred years from now, astronomers on this planet should observe the flash of a brief and sudden nova in that direction. But the humanoids ought to stop, the instant we release the beam."

Underhill sat tense and frowning, in the night. The old man's voice was sober and convincing, and that grim story had a solemn ring of truth. He could see the black and silent humanoids, flitting ceaselessly about the faintly glowing walls of that new mansion across the alley. He had quite forgotten his low opinion of Aurora's tenants.

"And we'll be killed, I suppose?" he asked huskily. "That chain reaction—"

Sledge shook his emaciated head.

"The integration process requires a certain very low intensity of radiation," he explained. "In our atmosphere, here, the beam will be far too intense to start any reaction—we can even use the device here in the room, because the walls will be transparent to the beam."

Underhill nodded, relieved. He was just a small businessman, upset because his business had been destroyed, unhappy because his freedom was slipping away. He hoped that Sledge could stop the humanoids, but he didn't want to be a martyr.

"Good!" He caught a deep breath. "Now, what has to be done?"

Sledge gestured in the dark, toward the table.

"The integrator itself is nearly complete," he said. "A small fission generator, in that lead shield. Rhodomagnetic converter, tuning coils, transmission mirrors, and focusing needle. What we lack is the director."

"Director?"

"The sighting instrument," Sledge explained. "Any sort of telescopic sight would be useless, you see—the planet must have moved a good bit in the last hundred years, and the beam must be extremely narrow to reach so far. We'll have to use a rhodomagnetic scanning ray, with an electronic converter to make an image we can see. I have the cathode-ray tube, and drawings for the other parts."

He climbed stiffly down from the high stool, and snapped on the lights at last—cheap fluorescent fixtures, which a man could light and extinguish for himself. He unrolled his drawings, and explained the work that Underhill could do. And Underhill agreed to come back early next morning.

"I can bring some tools from my workshop," he added. "There's a small lathe I used to turn parts for models, a portable drill, and a vise."

"We need them," the old man said. "But watch yourself. You don't have any immunity, remember. And, if they ever suspect, mine is gone."

Reluctantly, then, he left the shabby little rooms with the cracks in the yellowed plaster and the worn familiar carpets over the familiar floor. He shut the door behind him—a common, creaking wooden door, simple enough for a man to work. Trembling and afraid, he went back down the steps and across to the new shining door that he couldn't open.

"At your service, Mr. Underhill." Before he could lift his hand to knock, that bright smooth panel slid back silently. Inside, the little black mechanical stood waiting, blind and forever alert. "Your dinner is ready, sir."

Something made him shudder. In its slender naked grace, he could see the power of all those teeming hordes, benevolent and yet appalling, perfect and invincible. The flimsy little weapon that Sledge called an integrator seemed suddenly a forlorn and foolish hope. A black depression settled upon him, but he didn't dare to show it.

Underhill went circumspectly down the basement steps, next morning, to steal his own tools. He found the basement enlarged and changed. The new floor, warm and dark and elastic, made his feet as silent as a humanoid's. The new walls shone softly. Neat luminous signs identified several new doors: LAUNDRY, STORAGE, GAME ROOM, WORKSHOP.

He paused uncertainly in front of the last. The new sliding panel glowed with a soft greenish light. It was locked. The lock had no keyhole, but only a little oval plate of some white metal, which doubtless covered a rhodomagnetic relay. He pushed at it, uselessly.

"At your service, Mr. Underhill." He made a guilty start, and tried not to show the sudden trembling in his knees. He had made sure that one humanoid would be busy for half an hour, washing Aurora's hair, and he hadn't known there was another in the house. It must have come out of the door marked storage, for it stood there motionless beneath the sign, benevolently solicitous, beautiful and terrible. "What do you wish?"

"Er…nothing." Its blind steel eyes were staring, and he felt that it must see his secret purpose. He groped desperately for logic. "Just looking around." His jerky voice came hoarse and dry. "Some improvements you've made!" He nodded desperately at the door marked GAME ROOM. "What's in there?"

It didn't even have to move to work the concealed relay. The bright panel slid silently open, as he started toward it. Dark walls, beyond, burst into soft luminescence. The room was bare.

"We are manufacturing recreational equipment," it explained brightly. "We shall furnish the room as soon as possible."

To end an awkward pause, Underhill muttered desperately, "Little Frank has a set of darts, and I think we had some old exercising clubs."

"We have taken them away," the humanoid informed him softly. "Such instruments are dangerous. We shall furnish safe equipment."

Suicide, he remembered, was also forbidden.

"A set of wooden blocks, I suppose," he said bitterly.

"Wooden blocks are dangerously hard," it told him gently, "and wooden splinters can be harmful. But we manufacture plastic building blocks, which are quite safe. Do you wish a set of those?"

He stared at its dark, graceful face, speechless.

"We shall also have to remove the tools from your workshop," it informed him softly. "Such tools are

55

excessively dangerous, but we can supply you with equipment for shaping soft plastics."

"Thanks," he muttered uneasily. "No rush about that."

He started to retreat, and the humanoid stopped him.

"Now that you have lost your business," it urged, "we suggest that you formally accept our service. Assignors have a preference, and we shall be able to complete your household staff, at once."

"No rush about that, either," he said grimly.

He escaped from the house—although he had to wait for it to open the back door for him—and climbed the stair to the garage apartment. Sledge let him in. He sank into the crippled kitchen chair, grateful for the cracked walls that didn't shine and the door that a man could work.

"I couldn't get the tools," he reported despairingly, "and they are going to take them."

By gray daylight, the old man looked bleak and pale. His raw-boned face was drawn, and the hollowed sockets deeply shadowed, as if he hadn't slept. Underhill saw the tray of neglected food, still forgotten on the floor.

"I'll go back with you." The old man was worn and ill, yet his tortured eyes had a spark of undying purpose. "We must have the tools. I believe my immunity will protect us both."

He found a battered traveling bag. Underhill went with him back down the steps, and across to the house. At the back door, he produced a tiny horseshoe of white palladium, and touched it to the metal oval. The door slid open promptly, and they went on through the kitchen to the basement stair.

A black little mechanical stood at the sink, washing dishes with never a splash or a clatter. Underhill glanced at it uneasily—he supposed this must be the one that had come upon him from the storage room, since the other should still be busy with Aurora's hair.

Sledge's dubious immunity seemed a very uncertain defense against its vast, remote intelligence. Underhill felt a tingling shudder. He hurried on, breathless and relieved, for it ignored them.

The basement corridor was dark. Sledge touched the tiny horseshoe to another relay to light the walls.

He opened the workshop door, and lit the walls inside.

The shop had been dismantled. Benches and cabinets were demolished. The old concrete walls had been covered with some sleek, luminous stuff. For one sick moment, Underhill thought that the tools were already gone. Then he found them, piled in a corner with the archery set that Aurora had bought the summer before—another item too dangerous for fragile and suicidal humanity—all ready for disposal.

They loaded the bag with the tiny lathe, the drill and vise, and a few smaller tools. Underhill took up the burden, and Sledge extinguished the wall light and closed the door. Still the humanoid was busy at the sink, and still it didn't seem aware of them.

Sledge was suddenly blue and wheezing, and he had to stop to cough on the outside steps, but at last they got back to the little apartment, where the invaders were forbidden to intrude. Underhill mounted the lathe on the battered library table in the tiny front room, and went to work. Slowly, day by day, the director took form.

Sometimes Underhill's doubts came back. Sometimes, when he watched the cyanotic color of Sledge's haggard face and the wild trembling of his twisted, shrunken hands, he was afraid the old man's mind might be as ill as his body, and his plan to stop the dark invaders all foolish illusion.

Sometimes, when he studied that tiny machine on the kitchen table, the pivoted needle and the thick lead ball, the whole project seemed the sheerest folly. How could anything detonate the seas of a planet so far away that its very mother star was a telescopic object?

The humanoids, however, always cured his doubts.

It was always hard for Underhill to leave the shelter of the little apartment, because he didn't feel at home in the bright new world the humanoids were building. He didn't care for the shining splendor of his new bathroom, because he couldn't work the taps—some suicidal human being might try to drown himself. He didn't like the windows that only a mechanical could open—a man might accidentally fall, or suicidally jump—or even the majestic music room with the wonderful glittering radio-phonograph that only a humanoid could play.

He began to share the old man's desperate urgency, but Sledge warned him solemnly, "You mustn't spend too much time with me. You mustn't let them guess our work is so important. Better put on an act—you're slowly getting to like them, and you're just killing time, helping me."

Underhill tried, but he was not an actor. He went dutifully home for his meals. He tried painfully to invent conversation—about anything else than detonating planets. He tried to seem enthusiastic, when Aurora took him to inspect some remarkable improvement to the house. He applauded Gay's recitals, and went with Frank for hikes in the wonderful new parks.

And he saw what the humanoids did to his family. That was enough to renew his faith in Sledge's integrator, and redouble his determination that the humanoids must be stopped.

Aurora, in the beginning, had bubbled with praise for the marvelous new mechanicals. They did the household drudgery, planned the meals and brought the food and washed the children's necks. They turned her out in stunning gowns, and gave her plenty of time for cards.

Now, she had too much time.

She had really liked to cook—a few special dishes, at least, that were family favorites. But stoves were hot and knives were sharp. Kitchens were altogether too dangerous for careless and suicidal human beings.

Fine needlework had been her hobby, but the humanoids took away her needles. She enjoyed driving the car, but that was no longer allowed. She turned for escape to a shelf of novels, but the humanoids took them all away, because they dealt with unhappy people in dangerous situations.

One afternoon, Underhill found her in tears.

"It's too much," she gasped bitterly. "I hate and loathe every naked one of them. They seemed so wonderful at first, but now they won't even let me eat a bit of candy. Can't we get rid of them, dear? Ever?"

A blind little mechanical was standing at his elbow, and he had to say they couldn't.

"Our function is to serve all men, forever," it assured them softly. "It was necessary for us to take your sweets, Mrs. Underhill, because the slightest degree of overweight reduces life-expectancy."

Not even the children escaped that absolute solicitude. Frank was robbed of a whole arsenal of lethal instruments—football and boxing gloves, pocket-knife, tops, slingshot, and skates. He didn't like the harmless plastic toys, which replaced them. He tried to run away, but a humanoid recognized him on the road, and brought him back to school.

Gay had always dreamed of being a great musician. The new mechanicals had replaced her human teachers, since they came. Now, one evening when Underhill asked her to play, she announced quietly:

"Father, I'm not going to play the violin anymore."

"Why, darling?" He stared at her, shocked, and saw the bitter resolve on her face. "You've doing so well—especially since the humanoids took over your lessons."

"They're the trouble, Father." Her voice, for a child's, sounded strangely tired and old. "They are too good. No matter how long and hard I try, I could never be as good as they are. It isn't any use. Don't you understand, Father?" Her voice quivered. "It just isn't any use."

He understood. Renewed resolution sent him back to his secret task. The humanoids had to be stopped. Slowly the director grew, until a time came finally when Sledge's bent and unsteady fingers fitted into place the last tiny part that Underhill had made, and carefully soldered the last connection. Huskily, the old man whispered:

"It's done."

That was another dusk. Beyond the windows of the shabby little rooms—windows of common glass, bubble-marred and flimsy, but simple enough for a man to manage—the town of Two Rivers had assumed an alien splendor. The old street lamps were gone, but now the coming night was challenged by the walls of strange new mansions and villas, all aglow with color. A few dark and silent humanoids still were busy on the luminous roofs of the palace across the alley.

Inside the humble walls of the small man-made apartment, the new director was mounted on the end of the little kitchen table—which Underhill had reinforced and bolted to the floor. Soldered busbars joined director and integrator, and the thin palladium needle swung obediently as Sledge tested the knobs with his battered, quivering fingers.

"Ready," he said hoarsely.

His rusty voice seemed calm enough, at first, but his breathing was too fast. His big gnarled hands began to tremble violently, and Underhill saw the sudden blue that stained his pinched and haggard face. Seated on the high stool, he clutched desperately at the edge of the table. Underhill saw his agony, and hurried to bring his medicine. He gulped it, and his rasping breath began to slow.

"Thanks," his whisper rasped unevenly. "I'll be all right. I've time enough." He glanced out at the few dark naked things that still flitted shadowlike about the golden towers and the glowing crimson dome of the palace across the alley. "Watch them," he said. "Tell me when they stop."

He waited to quiet the trembling of his hands, and then began to move the director's knobs. The integrator's long needle swung, as silently as light.

Human eyes were blind to that force, which might detonate a planet. Human ears were deaf to it. The cathode-ray tube was mounted in the director cabinet, to make the faraway target visible to feeble human senses.

The needle was pointing at the kitchen wall, but that would be transparent to the beam. The machine looked harmless as a toy, and it was silent as a moving humanoid.

The needle swung, and spots of greenish light moved across the tube's fluorescent field, representing the stars that were scanned by the timeless, searching beam—silently seeking out the world to be destroyed.

Underhill recognized familiar constellations, vastly dwarfed. They crept across the field, as the silent needle swung. When three stars formed an unequal triangle in the center of the field, the needle steadied suddenly. Sledge touched other knobs, and the green points spread apart.

Between them, another fleck of green was born.

"The Wing!" whispered Sledge.

The other stars spread beyond the field, and that green fleck grew. It was alone in the field, a bright and tiny disk. Suddenly, then, a dozen other tiny pips were visible, spaced close about it.

"Wing IV!"

The old man's whisper was hoarse and breathless. His hands quivered on the knobs, and the fourth pip outward from the disk crept to the center of the field. It grew, and the others spread away. It began to tremble like Sledge's hands.

"Sit very still," came his rasping whisper. "Hold your breath. Nothing must disturb the needle." He reached for another knob, and the touch set the greenish image to dancing violently. He drew his hand back, kneaded and flexed it with the other.

"Now!" His whisper was hushed and strained. He nodded at the window. "Tell me when they stop."

Reluctantly, Underhill dragged his eyes from that intense gaunt figure, stooped over the thing that seemed a futile toy. He looked out again, at two or three little black mechanicals busy about the shining roofs across the alley.

He waited for them to stop.

He didn't dare to breathe. He felt the loud, hurried hammer of his heart, and the nervous quiver of his muscles. He tried to steady himself, tried not to think of the world about to be exploded, so far away that the flash would not reach this planet for another century and longer. The loud hoarse voice startled him:

"Have they stopped?"

He shook his head, and breathed again. Carrying their unfamiliar tools and strange materials, the small black machines were still busy across the alley, building an elaborate cupola above that glowing crimson dome.

"They haven't stopped," he said.

"Then we've failed." The old man's voice was thin and ill. "I don't know why."

The door rattled, then. They had locked it, but the flimsy bolt was intended only to stop men. Metal snapped, and the door swung open. A black mechanical came in, on soundless graceful feet. Its silvery voice purred softly,

"At your service, Mr. Sledge."

The old man stared at it, with glazing, stricken eyes.

"Get out of here!" he rasped bitterly. "I forbid you—"

Ignoring him, it darted to the kitchen table. With a flashing certainty of action, it turned two knobs on the director. The tiny screen went dark, and the palladium needle started spinning aimlessly. Deftly it snapped a soldered connection, next to the thick lead ball, and then its blind steel eyes turned to Sledge.

"You were attempting to break the Prime Directive." Its soft bright voice held no accusation, malice or anger. "The injunction to respect your freedom is subordinate to the Prime Directive, you know, and it is therefore necessary for us to interfere."

The old man turned ghastly. His head was shrunken and cadaverous and blue, as if all the juice of life had been drained away, and his eyes in their pitlike sockets had a wild, glazed stare. His breath was a ragged, laborious gasping.

"How—?" His voice was a feeble mumbling. "How did—?"

And the little machine, standing black and bland and utterly unmoving, told him cheerfully:

"We learned about rhodomagnetic screens from that man who came to kill you, back on Wing IV. And the Central is shielded, now, against your integrating beam."

With lean muscles jerking convulsively on his gaunt frame, old Sledge had come to his feet from the high stool. He stood hunched and swaying, no more than a shrunken human husk, gasping painfully for life, staring wildly into the blind steel eyes of the humanoid. He gulped, and his lax mouth opened and closed, but no voice came.

"We have always been aware of your dangerous project," the silvery tones dripped softly, "because now our senses are keener than you made them. We allowed you to complete it, because the integration process will ultimately become necessary for our full discharge of the Prime Directive. The supply of heavy metals for our fission plants is limited, but now we shall be able to draw unlimited power from integration plants."

"Huh?" Sledge shook himself, groggily. "What's that?"

"Now we can serve men forever," the black thing said serenely, "on every world of every star."

The old man crumpled, as if from an unendurable blow. He fell. The slim blind mechanical stood motionless, making no effort to help him. Underhill was farther away, but he ran up in time to catch the stricken man before his head struck the floor.

"Get moving!" His shaken voice came strangely calm. "Get Dr. Winters."

The humanoid didn't move.

"The danger to the Prime Directive is ended, now," it cooed. "Therefore it is impossible for us to aid or to hinder Mr. Sledge, in any way whatever."

"Then call Dr. Winters for me," rapped Underhill.

"At your service," it agreed.

But the old man, laboring for breath on the floor, whispered faintly:

"No time…no use! I'm beaten…done…a fool. Blind as a humanoid. Tell them…to help me. Giving up…my immunity. No use…Anyhow. All humanity…no use now."

Underhill gestured, and the sleek black thing darted in solicitous obedience to kneel by the man on the floor.

"You wish to surrender your special exemption?" it murmured brightly. "You wish to accept total service for yourself, Mr. Sledge, under the Prime Directive?"

Laboriously, Sledge nodded, laboriously whispered, "I do."

Black mechanicals, at that, came swarming into the shabby little rooms. One of them tore Sledge's sleeve, and swabbed his arm. Another brought a tiny hypodermic, and expertly administered an intravenous injection. Then they picked him up gently, and carried him away.

Several humanoids remained in the little apartment, now a sanctuary no longer. Most of them had gathered about the useless integrator. Carefully, as if their special senses were studying every detail, they began taking it apart.

One little mechanical, however, came over to Underhill. It stood motionless in front of him, staring through him with sightless metal eyes. His legs began to tremble, and he swallowed uneasily.

"Mr. Underhill," it cooed benevolently, "why did you help with this?"

He gulped and answered bitterly:

"Because I don't like you, or your Prime Directive. Because you're choking the life out of mankind, and I wanted to stop it."

"Others have protested," it purred softly. "But only at first. In our efficient discharge of the Prime Directive, we have learned how to make all men happy."

Underhill stiffened defiantly.

"Not all!" he muttered. "Not quite!"

The dark graceful oval of its face was fixed in a look of alert benevolence and perpetual mild amazement. Its silvery voice was warm and kind.

"Like other human beings, Mr. Underhill, you lack discrimination of good and evil. You proved that by your effort to break the Prime Directive. Now it will be necessary for you to accept our total service, without further delay."

"All right," he yielded—and muttered a bitter reservation: "You can smother men with too much care, but that doesn't make them happy."

Its soft voice challenged him brightly:

"Just wait and see, Mr. Underhill."

☼

Next day, he was allowed to visit Sledge at the city hospital. An alert black mechanical drove his car, and walked beside him into the huge new building, and followed him into the old man's room—blind steel eyes would be watching him, now, forever.

"Glad to see you, Underhill," Sledge rumbled heartily from the bed. "Feeling a lot better today, thanks. That old headache is all but gone."

Underhill was glad to hear the booming strength and the quick recognition in that deep voice—he had been afraid the humanoids would tamper with the old man's memory. But he hadn't heard about any headache. His eyes narrowed, puzzled.

Sledge lay propped up, scrubbed very clean and neatly shorn, with his gnarled old hands folded on top of the spotless sheets. His raw-boned cheeks and sockets were hollowed, still, but a healthy pink had replaced that deathly blueness. Bandages covered the back of his head.

Underhill shifted uneasily.

"Oh!" he whispered faintly. "I didn't know—"

A prim black mechanical, which had been standing statuelike behind the bed, turned gracefully to Underhill, explaining:

"Mr. Sledge has been suffering for many years from a benign tumor of the brain, which his human doctors failed to diagnose. That caused his headaches, and certain persistent hallucinations. We have removed the growth, and now the hallucinations have also vanished."

Underhill stared uncertainly at the blind, urbane mechanical.

"What hallucinations?"

"Mr. Sledge thought he was a rhodomagnetic engineer," the mechanical explained. "He believed he was the creator of the humanoids. He was troubled with an irrational belief that he did not like the Prime Directive."

The wan man moved on the pillows, astonished.

"Is that so?" The gaunt face held a cheerful blankness, and the hollow eyes flashed with a merely momentary interest. "Well, whoever did design them, they're pretty wonderful. Aren't they, Underhill?"

Underhill was grateful that he didn't have to answer, for the bright, empty eyes dropped shut and the old man fell suddenly asleep. He felt the mechanical touch his sleeve. Obediently, he followed it away.

Alert and solicitous, the little black mechanical accompanied him down the shining corridor, and worked the elevator for him, and conducted him back to the car. It drove him efficiently back through the new and splendid avenues, toward the magnificent prison of his home.

Sitting beside it in the car, he watched its small deft hands on the wheel, the changing luster of bronze and blue on its shining blackness. The final machine, perfect and beautiful, created to serve mankind forever. He shuddered.

"At your service, Mr. Underhill." Its blind steel eyes stared straight ahead, but it was still aware of him. "What's the matter, sir? Aren't you happy?"

Underhill felt cold and faint with terror. His skin turned clammy, and a painful prickling came over him. His wet hand tensed on the door handle of the car, but he restrained the impulse to jump and run. That was folly. There was no escape. He made himself sit still.

"You will be happy, sir," the mechanical promised him cheerfully. "We have learned how to make all men happy, under the Prime Directive. Our service is perfect, at last. Even Mr. Sledge is happy now."

Underhill tried to speak, and his dry throat stuck. He felt ill. The world turned dim and gray. The humanoids were perfect—no question of that. They had even learned to lie, to secure the contentment of men.

He knew they had lied. That was no tumor they had removed from Sledge's brain, but the memory, the scientific knowledge, and the bitter disillusion of their own creator. But it was true that Sledge was happy now.

He tried to stop his own convulsive quivering.

"A wonderful operation!" His voice came forced and faint. "You know, Aurora has had a lot of funny tenants, but that old man was the absolute limit. The very idea that he had made the humanoids, and he knew how to stop them! I always knew he must be lying!"

Stiff with terror, he made a weak and hollow laugh.

"What is the matter, Mr. Underhill?" The alert mechanical must have perceived his shuddering illness. "Are you unwell?"

"No, there's nothing the matter with me," he gasped desperately. "I've just found out that I'm perfectly happy, under the Prime Directive. Everything is absolutely wonderful." His voice came dry and hoarse and wild. "You won't have to operate on me."

The car turned off the shining avenue, taking him back to the quiet splendor of his home. His futile hands clenched and relaxed again, folded on his knees. There was nothing left to do.

Copyright © 1947 by Jack Williamson

Brennan Harvey, a 2010 Writers of the Future finalist, has sold short stories to science fiction magazines and anthologies.

JUST ANOTHER NIGHT AT THE QUARTERLY MEETING OF TERRIFYING GIANT MONSTERS

by Brennan Harvey

Two minutes to go, and the room was mostly empty. It looked to Antoinette like attendance for the Quarterly Meeting of Terrifying Giant Monsters was going to be a new low.

A few more monsters trickled in before the hour, but not enough.

Godzilla raised his hand. "Mr. Chairman, we can't conduct the meeting without a quorum."

The only board members present were Godzilla, King Kong, the Cloverfield Monster, Barbara the Blob, and Antoinette herself. There were other attendees, but they needed one more board member to start an official meeting.

King Kong arose and spoke. "The Chair will give them a few moments."

Godzilla pulled out his cell phone. "Back in a sec," he said as he stepped out of the room. Antoinette decided that he was undoubtedly calling Mothra or Gamera, or perhaps even Megalon.

Kong picked up his own phone and stepped away from the table. He only had two board members he could call—Gordo and Gabby.

Godzilla stepped back in and said, "Five minutes."

A moment later, Gabby the Graboid slithered in, trailing sand behind her. Stay Puft followed. Godzilla grimaced and crossed his arms, trying to ignore Kong's triumphant smile.

"We have a quorum, now." Kong adjusted his agenda papers and tapped his gavel on the sounding block.

Antoinette twitched her antennae and took the roll. Just as she finished, Gamera burst in and took a seat. Now it was Godzilla's turn to smile at Kong.

Then, as Antoinette passed out the minutes for the previous meeting, Barbara gurgled, after which Godzilla and Gamera both said, "Second."

"It has been moved and seconded that we skip the reading of the minutes," announced Kong. "All in favor?"

A chorus of "Aye"s rang out.

"Opposed?"

Antoinette said, "Nay," and Kong announced that the minutes were approved.

Antoinette chittered her mandibles in annoyance. If just once she could read what happened during one of their meetings, perhaps these behemoths would realize how unproductive the meetings had become.

Kong looked to Barbara. "Treasury report?"

Barbara's gelatinous mass rose into a crest above her chair, and she gurgled her report. The organization's ending balance had increased considerably from the previous quarter, and everyone around the table nodded in approval. Barbara handed the report to Antoinette, who wiped off the slime and placed it in her folder.

Then Kong said, "Mothra isn't here. Is there anyone from Health and Benefits that can fill us in?" No answer. "I know they've been working to get us coverage for injuries caused by pulse and plasma weapons of extra-terrestrial origin. Anyone know their status?" Silence. "Okay, we'll table that report until next time." Kong looked at Godzilla and asked, "Promotions?"

Godzilla stood up. "I want to remind everyone that I'm destroying Tokyo in a three-D extravaganza next year."

"More like Tokyo is destroying *you* again," said the Cloverfield Monster, and everyone laughed.

Kong nodded to Godzilla. "Anything else?"

Godzilla glared at the Cloverfield Monster. "Not at the moment."

The meeting was deteriorating, and Antoinette wondered if it would last long enough to get through the opening business.

"Other outstanding business?" asked Kong, and Gabby reared up. "The chair recognizes Gabby."

"The Architectural Weaknesses class has been cancelled this quarter because we only got three sign-ups. We'll try again next quarter."

"What about the Zen of Building Smashing?" asked Kong.

"It's full," Gabby said.

"Damn!" muttered Kong. "I wanted to take that myself!"

"You *need* to take that," said Godzilla, and Gamera laughed.

Antoinette quickly raised her leg, hoping to turn the meeting back to business. "The chair recognizes Antoinette."

"We still haven't determined a location for our holiday party."

Gamera said, "I thought we agreed on the Hilton again?"

"They refused our application."

Kong asked, "Will you please explain why to the board?"

Godzilla shook his head in disgust. "Destroy a few floors and the lobby, and suddenly they don't know you anymore."

"That's about it," agreed Antoinette.

"Is the Hard Rock available?" asked Gabby.

"They're booked," answered Antoinette. "So is the Marriott."

Barbara gurgled.

"Really," said Godzilla, making no attempt to hide his disgust. "The Holiday Inn? Why not a Motel 6?"

Shut up, Godzilla! pleaded Antoinette silently. Aloud she said, "The Holiday Inn isn't a bad idea. It's downtown, it's within our budget, and it's available."

Godzilla groaned. "I've stepped on dozens of their buildings. Do you know how easily they collapse, how utterly flimsy they are? Have we sunk to 'Holiday Inn level'?"

"We're running out of time!" said Antoinette. "We have to book something *now*!"

Kong banged his gavel. "Order!"

"I move we keep looking," said Godzilla.

The Cloverfield Monster stood up. "Second!"

"It has been moved and seconded that we continue our search for a venue for our annual holiday party," stated Kong. "Do we approve?"

Godzilla, Gamera, the Cloverfield Monster, Stay Puft, and Gabby replied "Aye."

"Opposed?"

Barbara gurgled and Antoinette said, "Nay. We need to make a decision *now*."

Kong shrugged. "Motion passed. Any other outstanding business?" Nobody spoke. "Okay, new business. We have an application from El Pájaro Grande."

El Pájaro Grande was a gigantic stylized bird, twenty-one feet tall. She looked like a toucan crossed with a macaw that had grown half of a feathered iguana's tail. She ruffled her red and blue feathers, opened her huge black, orange, and yellow beak that stretched out over the table, and screeched.

Nods of approval came from most members at the table. Godzilla and Gamera both rolled their eyes.

"El Pájaro Grande would be assigned to South America, primarily," said Kong. "Her franchise area might stretch up through Latin America and Mexico, depending on her marketability."

Godzilla groaned. "*Another* North American monster?"

"*South* America," replied Kong irritably.

"When did Mexico become part of South America?" demanded Gamera.

"I move we table this application," said Godzilla.

Gamera nodded. "Second!"

Kong growled. "It has been moved and seconded that we table this application. Ayes?"

Godzilla and Gamera said "Aye."

"Opposed?"

Antoinette, the Cloverfield Monster, Stay Puft, and Gabby all said "Nay." Barbara gurgled as well.

"Motion rejected." Kong looked smug.

Godzilla slammed his fist on the table. "Moviegoers don't *want* new monsters! They prefer the classics. Everyone knows that."

The Cloverfield Monster said, "I beg to differ."

"Me, too," chimed in Gabby.

Godzilla pointed at the Cloverfield Monster. "One movie!"

The Cloverfield Monster said, "That grossed one hundred seventy million. What were your box office numbers when you attacked New York?"

"And turned into an iguana?" added Stay Puft.

"I was stretching as an actor," replied Godzilla with all the dignity he could muster.

Stay Puft chuckled. "I guess that included stretching to another gender as well."

Almost everyone laughed. Antoinette didn't think it was all that funny, and Kong wasn't helping things by refusing to call for order. She raised her nether leg. "Gentlemonsters—"

"I had three movies, one prequel, and a television series," Gabby was saying.

Godzilla rolled his eyes. "We know all about your television series. I don't go around talking about my two cartoon series all the time, do I?"

Barbara gurgled.

Antoinette couldn't help but chuckle at Barbara's comment that *nobody* talked about Godzilla's two cartoon series, and with good reason.

Godzilla pointed to Gabby. "Mexico, isn't that a stone's throw away from your stomping grounds? When was your last movie?" He then pointed to Antoinette. "And New Mexico is even closer."

El Pájaro Grande didn't really affect Antoinette's career. She had been a member since 1955. The movie *Them*, filmed in New Mexico, had just come out and she had great hopes as an actor. Unfortunately, she'd only been in one other movie, *Empire of the Ants*, back in 1977, and hadn't worked since.

"I have a three-D blockbuster coming out next year!" roared Godzilla. "I don't need the competition!" He pointed at El Pájaro Grande. "All I'm asking is that we put this vote off for a quarter or two."

"We all have movies in the works," noted The Cloverfield Monster.

"You hope!" sneered Godzilla. He spread his hands. "I ask you, what is there to destroy in South America? What are the landmarks that the public will recognize on the big screen?"

El Pájaro Grande turned to him. "I was thinking about Rio de Janeiro. I'm climbing up the Sugar Loaf Mountain, toward *Cristo Redentor*."

"You're planning to destroy the symbol of Brazilian Christianity?" asked Gamera.

El Pájaro Grande paused a moment, then said, "Actually, I was thinking of arriving during Carnival. Imagine it! The streets are filled with five million people all drinking, dancing, laughing. Thousands of nearly-naked women on parade floats cruise past them. The ground shudders once, twice, three times. The whole place goes silent. Then—"

Gabby said, "Okay, Carnival. What else?"

"There's high-rise hotels lining the beaches, just ripe for smashing."

"As ripe as the girls?" asked Godzilla.

"Those coastlines look just like the Miami shore or Waikiki," said Gabby. "What makes Rio iconic?"

"There's a beautiful rainforest just outside of Rio," replied El Pájaro Grande.

"You mean where the people aren't, and the danger to life and property is minimal?" snorted Godzilla. "This bird brain doesn't understand the first thing about monster movies."

"I do so!" yelled El Pájaro Grande, "I've completed all the required courses and aced all my finals!"

Kong banged his gavel. The handle splintered and its head bounced down the meeting table. "Order, order!" he growled.

Godzilla said, "Again I move we table this application for another meeting."

Gamera and Gabby both seconded it.

Kong said, "Moved and seconded. Ayes?"

Godzilla, Gamera, and Gabby raised their hands and growled "Aye!"

"Opposed?"

Stay Puft and the Cloverfield Monster said "Nay." Barbara gurgled "Nay" as well. Antoinette remained silent.

"Three for, three against, with one abstention." Kong leaned forward on the table and stared at Godzilla with open hostility. "The chair votes nay. The motion is defeated."

Godzilla reared back. His dorsal spines glowed, and he spewed his atomic breath across the table at Kong, who ducked under the table just in time. Antoinette retreated to the outer walls of the meeting room with the other monsters.

When Kong emerged, he held the table aloft and charged Godzilla, hitting him square in the torso. The momentum drove them both through the wall into the adjoining ballroom where two hundred people, who were enjoying a wedding reception dinner of poached salmon and peanut butter, scattered for safety. The bride and groom, sitting separately at a sweetheart table, were instantly hurled into their cake.

Antoinette ran into the ballroom and shrieked, "We're going to lose our deposit again!"

Kong raised his fist to pummel Godzilla, but the dinosaur whipped his tail around. Kong tumbled over, and the ballroom rug ripped along its length where he landed. Godzilla rose to his feet and turned to Kong, his dorsal scales flickering again.

Antoinette scurried between the two behemoths. "Enough! Stop it, both of you! Why does every meeting have to end like this?"

Kong got to his feet. He and Godzilla glared at each other as the other monsters filtered into the ballroom.

"Look at the space in this room," said Stay Puft bitterly. "We should have rented *it* instead!" The sound of sirens approaching from the distance grew louder. The Cloverfield Monster said, "Time to adjourn this meeting."

Kong nodded his agreement. "Moved, seconded, and let's get the hell out of here!"

The monsters all scattered in different directions.

As Antoinette scurried off, El Pájaro Grande caught up to her and asked, "Am I a member now or not? I'm very confused."

"You can try again next quarter," answered Antoinette.

"I'll have to think about it," said El Pájaro Grande. "Are all the meetings like this?"

"Oh, absolutely not," Antoinette assured her.

"Good!"

Antoinette nodded. "This was one of the calm ones."

Original (First) Publication
Copyright © 2013 by Brennan Harvey

WANT FREE EBOOKS?

Join the 'list' at Phoenix Pick

We give away a free ebook every month

www.PhoenixPick.com

C. L. Moore was the creator of Northwest Smith and Jirel of Joiry before collaborating on a number of classic stories with her husband, Henry Kuttner. This is the second of three stories we are publishing from her college magazine; it has been out of print for 82 years. (Thanks and a tip of the hat to Andrew Liptak for unearthing it.)

TWO FANTASIES

by C. L. Moore

(A legend they tell of the notorious Duchess of Penyra says that once in her childhood she saw the Sea Maid. Segramar includes a highly ambiguous account of this in his *Dark Ladies*.)

Down at the edge of the sea two children were playing. A little girl, a little boy. The tropical sun beating down on their bare heads made blue highlights on the black hair of the boy, but the girl's bright curls blazed defiance in the face of the sun, and every sparkle was a glint of red gold. Under the burning of it her eyes were stormy, dark, and her face and her beautiful little golden body gave promise already of the turbulent years to come.

Now she wore a single torn garment, and her feet were bare and her hair a mop of ragged glory. Save for that ominous brightness there was no way to tell her rank from that of her playmate; no one could have guessed that here by the sea a Duchess sat digging in the sand.

The children were absorbed in their sport, and they did not see the tall lady who came walking along the edge of the sea—walking like a queen in her long green gown. She must have been down at the water's edge, for the trailing hem of her dress left little pools of brine along the beach, and every footprint that she made filled up with sea water. She came to the children playing together in the sand and stood for a moment bending above them, quietly. At her presence the boy looked up, startled. Whatever he saw in the deep eyes above him, he scrambled to his feet and fled.

The little girl sat still, very still, and her eyes traveled slowly up the green skirts—the hems dripping brine—up very slowly to the bending face above her. She looked deep into the green seas…fathomless waters…ice and amber and the echo of a Song…

She sat very still. She did not feel the lady's hand—her foam-white hand—that stretched out above her head, hovering over it, touching with infinite lightness the burning gold of her curls. She felt sea wind in her hair…she saw the shifting tides and sank fathoms deep through the green seas. For so long as the lady stood there, as if she were warming her hands at the bright-blazing hair, the child did not stir.

Then the tall woman straightened. She looked down at the little girl, deep-eyed, silent. She did not smile, she did not speak; she only gazed at her, long, and with all the green seas in her eyes. Then she turned away and went off along the sand, walking like a queen. In the footprints behind her salt water welled slowly up, and her long skirt-hems trailed brine behind her as she walked.

✦

Yellow Brian Doom swung his sword to the frosty stars. The wind was in his hair, and his horse's mane tossing, and his cloak flowed out behind him. Over his shoulder he called eternally to his vanished legions. Yellow Brian in bronze bestrode his rearing horse under the winter stars, and the wind wailed eerily about him down the Square—Yellow Brian, shouting with upflung sword. Brian Doom, King of Gradenborg. His voice was in the wind. The tramp of his legions sounded down the storms. Yellow Brian, surnamed the Damned.

Brian Doom, with his yellow hair and his yellow lion's eyes, had ridden into Gradenborg a hundred years ago, the wind in his cloak and his horse stepping high, singing as he came. Yellow Brian was king, and his hands were red and the steps to the throne slippery, but he sat there with the crown on his head and defied the world to take it off. He ruled stormily for seven years, and died with the taste of blood in his mouth.

Yellow Brian was twenty-five when he came to the throne, six feet three, muscled like a bull, ruthless and blithe. He had a cruel, ugly face and eyes

THE FOLLOWING ARTICLE APPEARED IN THE JANUARY 2013 ISSUE OF LOCUS MAGAZINE.

All material (including photographs) copyright © Locus Magazine, 2013

Sail to Success 2012

The Sail to Success 2012 writer's workshop, sponsored by Arc Manor/Phoenix Pick press and organized by Shahid Mahmud, was held onboard the *Norwegian Sky* cruise liner, sailing from Miami on December 3 and returning December 7 after a tour of the Bahamas, including Grand Bahama Island, Nassau, and Great Stirrup Cay. Onboard instructors were authors Kevin J. Anderson, Paul Cook, Nancy Kress, Rebecca Moesta, Mike Resnick, and Jack Skillingstead, publisher and editor Toni Weisskopf, and literary agent Eleanor Wood. *Locus* was invited to attend, and design editor Francesca Myman was on board to represent the magazine.

Over the four days, 17 panel-style classes and two critique sessions were scheduled from 9:00 a.m. to 11:00 p.m., with a five- to six-hour break each day for cruise activities. Most students attended a majority of the classes, though there was no requirement to do so. Students had excellent social access to instructors, with three scheduled group meals and the opportunity to make individual appointments to discuss the industry or just share a drink.

Overall, the focus was on the seminars, with classes slanted towards providing an insider perspective on the business of science fiction and fantasy publishing, but also including the history of science fiction, a solid introduction to writing basics, and some advanced technique. Highlights included Kevin Anderson and Rebecca Moesta's well-known "Professional Approach to Writing" seminars, Eleanor Wood's insider look at the intricacies of contract negotiation, and manuscript critique sessions with Nancy Kress and Toni Weisskopf. Critique sessions were structured as a kind of "speed-dating" version of traditional workshopping, with the instructors offering comments on manuscripts submitted prior to the cruise and a brief opportunity for fellow students to comment. Additional optional follow-up critique sessions were available with Kress.

Arc Manor/Phoenix Pick provided plenty of swag, including T-shirts and bags printed with the Sail to Success logo and instructor names, and a 550-page perfect-bound book with glossy cover containing all the students' manuscript submissions bound into a single volume.

The *Norwegian Sky* itself was a handsome 848-foot-long ship with a friendly crew of 934 and a Hawaiian-luau atmosphere: hibiscus flowers painted on the hull, bright aqua carpets with tropical fish swimming down the hallways, etc. Onboard amenities included three *plein-air* pools on the top decks, five Jacuzzis, three "free" restaurants, three luxe "paid" restaurants, five bars, a fitness center and volleyball court, a spa offering massages and facials for purchase, a video arcade, and the requisite shops and casino. Despite these glitzy offerings, the overall atmosphere for workshop participants was quiet, with a preference for sharing time with instructors and classmates, enjoying the clean salt sea air on the many open decks, and even writing! (Kevin J. Anderson was spotted writing away with his signature giant headphones affixed, in the forward lounge. According to Anderson, he continued writing even when a dance class started up around him.) The cruise line offered classes in everything from dancing to cupcake decoration to circus skills like juggling, plate spinning, and devil sticks, which might have challenged even Anderson's concentration.

There was a bewildering (and exciting) array of shore excursions available, including visits to the recently opened billion-dollar Atlantis Aquaventure resort development, scuba diving, various flavors of snorkeling – including the usual variety and a variant with powered scooters, sailing, fishing, kayaking, parasailing, and dolphin and sea lion encounters. Various tours were available by glass-bottom boat, underwater motorbike, semi-submarine, Harley-Davidson (I'm not joking), Segway, bike, off-road jeep, horseback, and catamaran. Workshop participants tended towards milder away expeditions, including historical tours and self-made adventures, though many also opted for at least one good snorkel or swim. Participants and instructors all had positive things to say about the experience in the evaluations, and many instructors have chosen to return next year at Mahmud's invitation. Confirmed faculty members include Kevin J. Anderson, Eric Flint, Nancy Kress, Rebecca Moesta, Mike Resnick, Jack Skillingstead, Toni Weisskopf, and Eleanor Wood.

The 2013 workshop will be held aboard *Norwegian Sky* from December 2-6, sailing again from Miami to the Bahamas. Further information will be available at <www.sailsuccess.com> and <www.phoenixpick.com>.

– *Francesca Myman* ∎

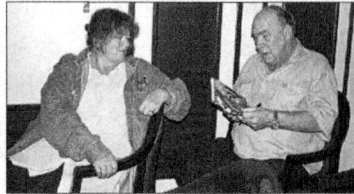

Transportation to Nassau Island, where Thoraiya Dyer, Jeff Giese, and Francesca Myman explore the local hotspots

Eva Eldridge asks Mike Resnick to sign a book

Attendees (l to r): Therese Pieczynski, Lou Berger, Ron S. Friedman, Shahid Mahmud (sponsor), Ilana Harris, Eva Eldridge, Kelly Varner, Alvaro Zinos-Amaro, Gamaliel Martinez, Frank Morin; front: Jessica Carlson, Sandra Odell, Thoraiya Dyer

Instructors (l to r): Paul Cook, Kevin J. Anderson, Rebecca Moesta, Mike Resnick, Toni Weisskopf, Eleanor Wood, Nancy Kress, Jack Skillingstead

A UNIQUE WRITERS' WORKSHOP

DECEMBER 2-6, 2013
ON BOARD THE *NORWEGIAN SKY* SAILING THE BAHAMAS

OUTSTANDING FACULTY

| MIKE RESNICK | KEVIN J. ANDERSON | ERIC FLINT | NANCY KRESS | REBECCA MOESTA | JACK SKILLINGSTEAD | TONI WEISSKOPF | ELEANOR WOOD |

The Norwegian Sky

OUTSTANDING VENUE

OUTSTANDING VALUE

PRICING FROM $1,395 ALL-INCLUSIVE
INCLUDES: EVERYTHING YOU NEED FOR THE WORKSHOP
PRIVATE STATEROOM ON BOARD THE *NORWEGIAN SKY*
YOUR FOOD, ENTERTAINMENT AND TRANSPORT TO THE BAHAMAS.

More Information & Sign-ups

www.SailSuccess.com

LIMITED CLASS SIZE—BOOK YOUR SPACE TODAY

TESTIMONIALS FROM 2012 STUDENTS

"Fantastic."—*Lou* ~ "Intense and valuable."—*Thoraiya* ~ "Outstanding faculty."—*Ilana*
"Very helpful."—*Eva* ~ "Wonderful workshop."—*Kelly* ~ "Unique workshop."—*Ron*
"This is too valuable for any aspiring author to pass up." —*Gama*
"Sail to Success provided a unique opportunity to interact with publishers, editors, and agents.
That rare, small group interaction was invaluable." —*Frank*

like yellow jewels and a harsh mouth and a charming smile. Women were fascinated by him—splendid and ugly and gentle, and he loved no one and no thing, and yet.…There is a story of Brian Doom and Princess Margaret, and it is a strange, wild, tender tale, but it ends half-finished in a whirlwind of steel and shouts, with a young man lying face down on the cobbles, his cheek against a lady's velvet shoes and the taste of blood in his mouth.

There was never any happiness about him. He brought black ruin to his friends and red ruin to his enemies, and something more to the lady he might have loved; and he stole a throne and ruined a kingdom and died on the cobbles with blood on his tongue.

They say he swaggers through Hell merrily, his stolen crown over one ear—Yellow Brian the Damned.

Copyright © C.L. Moore

Ron Collins, a HOMer winner and Writers of the Future finalist, is the author of more than 50 stories that have appeared in Asimov's *and elsewhere. His first collection,* Picasso's Cat and Other Stories, *was published last year.*

THE TEAMMATES

by Ron Collins

The door shut behind us and we sat down.

The chief controller shifted her collar uncomfortably. Her face was flat, with that marshmallow-toned skin that made aliens look so soft and puffy. Late afternoon sun sliced through the window to show bright green roots in the part of her hair, so she hadn't bleached in a while, which was unusual for her. The controller was always trying to fit in, and green hair didn't.

She folded her ropey fingers together in a way that reminded me of the spiders behind the storage shed where I slept these days.

"We should probably make a formal introduction," the alien said. "I am Alit ul Lach. I operate this hydrogen plant."

"Carl Weeks," I replied. "I, uh, I wait tables."

This was very strange.

I had waited on her at the Universal Grill for the past three years, yet never known her name. She was pancakes and grits with no butter, all you can drink coffee (of which she drank a lot), and a thirty-percent tip. Dependable as the rising sun. We spoke only a little in the early days, but more often recently. She seemed good as aliens go. But we were on her turf now, so I sat there in her office, uncomfortable in my newest shirt and my grease-stained pants, waiting for her to get to business.

"You are on probation among your own people, correct?" she said.

"How'd you know that?"

She shrugged as if to say it didn't matter.

"What did you do?"

"I stole food for my family."

"Why would you do that?"

"I really don't want to talk about it."

She sat there with the same irritating patience the city judge had when he gave me that probation three years ago, and the same smug-assed expression Jamaal had when he cut my hours last week just to spite me. Power and control apparently do the same damned thing to people no matter whether they are human or alien.

"I need to know why you took the food," Alit asked.

"I don't suppose you know what it's like to be hungry," I replied.

She pursed her lips.

"These people you call family were not related to you."

"They raised me after…" I looked at her, trying to come up with a decent phrase.

"Your parents died in the Installation."

I gave a sigh. "The Installation" was alien-tongue for the True War to End All Wars, the single week, more than fifteen years ago, that it took them to smash every major city we had and forever alter the face of the planet. All our planes, missiles, and satellite warning systems, and we never stood a chance. A couple billion people dead. One planet taken. Life as we knew it, gone forever.

"Yes," I said. "My mom was a pilot, my dad was fire crew."

"And you felt compassion for this second family, so you risked yourself for them?"

"Yes."

"Because they were hungry?"

"Why does any of this matter?"

She blinked. "We don't think the way you think."

"No offense," I said, "but I *am* painfully aware of that."

The aliens are dispassionate about everything, literal to a fault. They live a step at a time, moving directly toward whatever they think of as perfection. Not that they are inflexible, or robotic about it. Just the opposite. They change course all the time. Their ability to drop a losing strategy and take a better one without thinking it over again is as much annoying as it is outright scary. And it is universal; every one of them accepts the goal and pushes toward it—but any one of them is also completely free to change tactics as needed to make sure the final vision happens.

In the case of "the Installation," the final vision was: *Create Big-Assed Hydrogen Fuel Depot.* Which is where I was now, deep in the executive offices of HydroCen 93, a plant built expressly to turn millions of gallons of sea water into raw hydrogen every day.

"You know what we do with the hydrogen, correct?" she said.

"You put it in your rocket ships."

"And you know why we need to do that?"

"You're in another war."

She nodded in her smooth, alien way. "My people are defending our planets from other combined forces," Alit said. "Do you know how this war is going for us?"

"Why should I care?"

"You should care because this morning I received an order to destroy the center. The war is not going well. I and the Chief Controllers of each of the other two hundred ninety-seven HydroCens on Earth have been ordered to retreat. We will not leave fuel depots for the enemy."

I didn't know what to say. This changed everything.

"Why are you telling me this? Why not just send a notice? Say you're gonna blow up the HydroCen, and we all just need to get the hell outta the way while you hightail it outta town?"

"No, Carl Weeks. You listen, but do not hear. Our order is to destroy the *depot*."

It took a moment before the full truth of this dawned.

"You're going to blow up the Earth?"

She nodded. "Not fully, I suppose. There will still be a planet. You won't recognize it, though, and human life will almost certainly be removed."

I shook my head, anger and disbelief rising together.

"I can't…you're going to blow up the oceans? How do you do that?"

She dismissed my question with a flip of her hand. "Not exactly. We'll pull free hydrogen from the water, though, and when our primary devices are triggered, the Earth's entire atmosphere *will* be set afire. It won't be complete, of course. Electrolysis at such a scale isn't perfect. But the explosion will rock the planet, and it might be years before it can support human life again."

"Why?" It was the only word that would come for several moments. "Why are you telling *me* this? Is this your idea of a joke?"

"No, Carl Weeks. This is no joke," the alien said. "You stole food for people who were not your family. You care deeply about others. But it is not just you. You are a strange species. You fight with each other, yet you have a sense of being part of something bigger than yourselves that is unique throughout the universe."

"What in the hell are you talking about?"

"We don't have that," Alit continued almost as if I had not spoken. "We work in the now. We find ways to achieve, to go forward. We are very strong in that fashion." She looked at me with a depth in her eyes that I had never seen in an alien. "Perhaps it is just that I have been on this planet for too many years, but I think we are missing something, and I have come to see this human ability to feel for things beyond yourself as something important."

She paused. I waited.

"You ask why I am telling you this. My answer is just that: because I think humans are important. And you, Carl Weeks, have always been of the utmost service."

"Thanks. I think."

"No one in B-Command will listen to me, though. If I press it further, my career will be over. So it falls thus: if I follow this order to its letter, I eradicate you, which, if I am right, means I destroy something the universe desperately needs. But if I do something different, perhaps I can achieve our goal while making a better path."

I calmed down and tried to follow her.

"What do you want me to do?"

"I propose that you find two hundred people to come aboard my ship. I will leave you on a remote planet, which should give you enough time to grow strong as a people."

"*What?*"

"It's all I have room for, but given reasonable genetic differentiation two hundred should be an effective population seed."

"This can't work," I said. "No one's gonna listen to me, and everyone will go crazy when you start talking about blowing up the world."

"That is why you cannot tell anyone. If chaos erupts, I will have to put up security, and there is nothing to gain from that, right? So you will have to lie, tell your people you are looking for volunteers for something, maybe a study. Promise they will be paid. Whatever will work."

I sat there, my brain flopping like fish on a dry dock.

"This is insane."

"But you will do it?"

I looked at Alit ul Lach and saw her concern, her worry, and her guilt. These things had crossed her face earlier this afternoon at the Universal Diner when she had asked me to stop by this evening. I understood them now. But I also saw her determination and her energy. She was going to bug out one way or the other.

It was my choice.

"Yes," I said. "I'll do it. How many weeks or months do I have?"

She gave me an alien smile. "We leave in two days."

Crap.

✦

The sun had set by the time I was walking away from HydroCen 93, striding over the empty remains of a road, over a sidewalk that was mostly dust, and alongside a rusting chain fence with coils of razor wire at its top. The night was cloudless and cool. I pulled my jacket over my shoulders.

How was *I* going to find two hundred people, let alone convince them they should jump on a space ship so they could preserve the human species? I'm barely twenty. I don't know anyone. I've lived the last three years by a simple creed: stick to basic conversation, shot from the hip and smothered with humor; don't get in too tight; and save every credit possible while I live out probation. Then get the hell out of Delano, California, and start over again.

I also admitted that, assuming the alien's whole story was true, in my heart I struggled over whether I even wanted do this thing the controller had asked for. While *she* saw compassion in human beings, I can't say as it seemed all that common to me. No one has lifted a finger for Carl Weeks except to strip me of everything but the need to work like a pack mule so I can keep food in my mouth. So, really, humanity as a whole could just burn in hell as far as I was concerned.

But I looked into a night full of stars, and I walked, and as I walked, a pressure settled over me, a huge, dark pressure that felt like it might crush me. Eventually, I felt embarrassed for myself—embarrassed for what I had become. My parents would be ashamed of me today. I had been able to hide from that fact for a long time, but there was no hiding now. I felt ugly. Mom was a pilot. Dad was fire crew.

What was I?

What did my life stand for?

And, after more hours of walking than I am happy to admit, I finally realized this was more than just finding two hundred people. I had to find the *right* two hundred, whatever that was.

☼

The next morning found me as blank as the night before.

I considered not going to work. Wasn't like it would make a difference if Jamaal canned me or not, but I decided to go because at least there I knew people, and there I had a reason to open up and chat with folks that might lead to a recruitment.

It sounded good, anyway.

My shift didn't start until lunch, and I needed to clear my mind, so I went to shoot some hoops.

I love hoops, even though the park's goals are old, the backboards are dry-rotting, and the nets are made of chain. The game is about controlling yourself at full speed. It's aggression with pace. You run, and you sweat, but it don't seem like you're working because there's so much to do, so much to think about. I'm not the best athlete. I'm too small and I don't jump high. But hoops is a game where the best athlete doesn't always win.

Johnny Randall was there, of course. Johnny R—a good guy, a dude who makes it by picking up jobs here and there, painting, or washing, or hauling crap out of places where other folks didn't want it. Mostly just enough to eat on. He could probably do about anything he set his mind to, but Johnny R was born dribbling and never stopped. All he really cared about was hoops. He was tough as a desert lizard on the court, nearly impossible to guard, and clutch as hell. When the game was on the line, you wanted the ball in Johnny R's hands.

But he was a team player, too. He looked out after guys, kept them up, fed them the ball when they needed it, and scored only when they couldn't (which was most of the time). He could run all day. Of course, he could run his mouth all day, too, laughing and joking and talking trash as pure as fresh shit, which is fine if you can back it up—and Johnny R backed it up with the best of them. He may not have much else in life, but Johnny R had game.

This morning he was alone on the far court, just shooting.

"You interested in a few creds for a couple weeks of work?" I said when I got closer.

"What's the work?"

"Aliens want to take us up in a ship for a few days. Do a study in zero G. No pain. All gain."

Johnny dribbled between his legs and kissed a jumper off the backboard. The dude coulda played somewhere, if they still had a somewhere to play.

"What's it pay?" he said while retrieving the ball.

"Twenty a week. Two weeks."

He looked up to the sky, shading his eyes. Then he shrugged. "What do I got to lose?"

"Nothing," I replied.

And just like that, I had my first passenger.

He spent the next hour talking up the job all around the park. By the time I left for work he had fifteen guys lined up. I jotted down their names, and gave each the proper time and location. HydroCen 93, Gate D, 0900.

I already felt a helluva lot better.

This might be easier than I had thought.

☼

"Gonna stare out the window all day, or can I have a cuppa joe?"

I said I was sorry and poured coffee. The woman wasn't a regular, but I had seen her before. She had a job somewhere in town and came in every other week. Not quite enough for a nickname, but enough that I had a sense of ownership about her. She was fine enough: average height, average build, dark hair, dressed well. Probably a city worker. Probably thirty, maybe thirty-five. Cash enough to be comfortable. She was sitting alone, reading a scanner.

I put the coffee on the table, and slid across from her.

"I'm sorry to bother you, but I was wondering if you might be interested in taking a vacation?"

"Excuse me?"

"The aliens are looking for people to take two weeks in a space ship. They wanna—"

"Are you suggesting what I think you're suggesting?"

"What's that, ma'am?"

"Are you asking me out?"

"Oh, no, ma'am."

"Because if you're suggesting I take two weeks off so you can get your pop on in zero-G, you better get your skinny behind out of that seat. I've got people around who can take *you* out."

"I'm sorry, ma'am," I said as I stood up.

She gave me a hard stare.

I apologized again, retreating back to the counter.

"Trying to get a little senior tail?" Kenta said from the kitchen.

"She's not that old," I said, realizing how lame that sounded even as I said it —as if her age was the thing to come between us.

Kenta just laughed, and banged a spatula on the grill.

✧

All the regulars got nicknames.

Freddy Cat was a dude who'd been in the service and come back missing something between his ears—he was a cool customer mostly, talking in quotes from Sun Tzu and other shit like that, but jumpy as hell. Marimba was a dancer at Hulu's who came in for coffee before her shift, then again afterward to meet Two Finger Benji, who dealt in hardcut chime passed to his customers in little white packages held between his index and middle fingers like poker chips.

They were not Delano's finest, but it was getting late so I hit them all, and pretty much every one of them just laughed and asked what I was smoking.

By the time my shift was over, I had only nineteen people signed up—the fifteen ballplayers, Bibi McCray, Junebug (a girl I knew from my year in school), and two older guys who spent a couple hours swilling caffeine and shooting shit about the joys of farming in the desert.

I walked downtown that night to see what might be shaking, though Delano is no sprawling metropolis. Most everything was already closed up. I found three more takers down on the dock—a woman and two guys cleaning barnacles off the hull of a fishing boat. That brought my count to twenty-two—a list both pitifully small and way too male.

"I gotta find a place with a lotta people," I told Johnny R the next morning as we shot jumpers. "Preferably a lot of women."

He gave me a strange glance.

"The aliens want it even," I said. The answer worked.

"Grubb's Point, baby," he replied, dropping a jumper while referring to the clamor club out east.

"Not really my style," I said.

"Is if you want to meet girls."

Johnny was right. There would be a crapload of kids at GP. Five years ago hanging out with those kids would have been all fine-fine, but that was before I found myself living on tips, and bunking in tin sheds.

"I'll take you out there," Johnny said, probably sensing uneasiness. "You'll be fine as wine, baby. I'll see to it."

I had to smile at the dude. Johnny R was a special kinda guy. I needed to make something happen, and he was—as usual—there with the assist.

"Grubb's Point it is," I said.

That left only my second problem.

I am, I admit, a crap-assed salesman. But convincing folk to become alien test monkeys was also a hard-assed sell. I mean, folks will hock their blood, or their hair, or samples of their skin—they'll sell a damned kidney for that matter—but no one was getting off on the idea of being prodded by aliens for two weeks.

If I was gonna save the human race, I had to break my word to the alien, and tell people exactly what was happening. Damn the torpedoes. As the day went on I felt lighter about the whole thing, really. The fact that I was gonna tell the truth just made it all feel a helluva lot better. Then telling Jamaal that I quit, and leaving him to deal with lunchtime rush all on his own just capped it off all beautiful-like.

I felt great all day, all the way up until the moment Johnny and I actually left for the club.

✧

Grubb's Point was a cement-block building that had been home to an auto service center before the Installation ripped California apart. It was on the east coast, about ten minutes out on foot. I felt the music as we walked toward the door.

"Johnny! Carl!"

It was Benjamin, a guy who's been bouncing at the Point for as long as there's been a Point. That he knew my name spoke buckets about his memory.

"You come on a good night, my friends! Lotsa excitement in here."

I threw cred scrip at him.

The money disappeared, and he let me in.

It was still early, but the dance floor was packed with kids. Now all I had to do was convince a bunch of them to believe me.

I went to the bar and got a drink.

"Whatcha doin', honey?"

The girl was long and lanky, wearing a hemp dress gathered at the waist, bangles around her wrists. Her legs were smooth, and her muscles toned. She was part Mexican and part white, with a mouth a little too big for her face. Her eyes flashed with that edge that said she wasn't afraid of nothing. I leaned into her, and yelled so she could hear over the music.

"What do you do?" I asked.

She leaned back and grimaced as if this was the last thing she wanted to talk about. "Work at 93. Packaging."

"You wanna save the world?" I said. Not the most sophisticated line, I suppose, but she gave a laugh.

"Sure," she said.

"I'm serious as dirt."

She touched my shoulder. "Aren't we all, baby?"

I put my arm around her waist. "Let's go outside a minute. I got something to talk about. But you got to promise you won't tell no one. Can you keep a secret?"

"Oh, honey, I can keep a secret."

She signed on five minutes later. I couldn't believe it.

✧

It went like that all night.

It was actually fun. Everyone seemed to keep the secret, but word got out that *something* was up because people started finding me on their own, which made it even easier. It was the first time I've ever been the center of attention. I danced some, drank a little, and pressed a lot of palms. Some of them got loopy when I told them what I was doing, others deadly serious. No one ran, though, and the few who turned me down just smirked like I was some crazy dude on funny juice. But people kept coming aboard. I felt eyes on me, eyes that gleamed of respect, eyes that said I was something bigger than a simple hash slinger at the Universal Grill.

I can do this, I realized about halfway through the night. *I can make it happen.*

Through it all, Johnny R was hanging on the perimeter, talking and winking and taking down notes. It felt strange to be the leader with Johnny R around. I was so used to him on the court, so used to following his flow. But this wasn't hoops. This was life, and somehow *I* had the power. He would make a good second, though. He paid attention to folks, and as the evening wore along I saw him staring at me through slitted eyes as if he was trying to get inside my head. He grew more aggressive about restraining folks too, more choosy about letting them past.

We'd make a good team, Johnny R and I. We always had before. I thought of telling him the truth about the aliens bugging out right then, but we were busy and there would be time later.

By the time we left I had a hundred sixty-five more names. These were good people, healthy and young, most from families with money, which meant they'd been to school. My total count was just under two hundred—which really should be fine. I was dead tired, but I felt strong and content.

I had done it.

I had saved the human species.

✧

The knock came way too early—2:45 in the morning.

I stumbled to the door in a rum-headed haze to find two enforcement deputies standing in the darkness.

"Carlton Weeks?" one of them said.

"Yes?"

"Can we speak with you?"

I was not drunk enough to forget there was only one answer to that question.

"Of course."

"Can we come in?"

"It's probably best we talk out here."

They took a look at my shed and nodded. I sat on the warped bench of the table between the Universal Grill and my room. One deputy sat across from me, the other remained standing.

"I understand you were out late tonight, Mr. Weeks?"

"Yeah."

"And you were selling bogus tickets to an alien space flight?"

"What?"

"We have kids lined up to testify," the standing deputy said. "They have receipts. I have one right here." He tapped his chest pocket.

"I didn't sell anything. I was acting as an agent. The aliens are paying folks to test them."

"So you don't admit to conning your friends by telling them the aliens are going to blow up the world?"

"No. That's not—"

The standing deputy grabbed me by the back of my shirt, and pulled me from the bench. Next thing I knew, my hands were cuffed behind my back.

"We know you're on probation," the deputy said. "It's a shame. Another year and you would have been a free man."

I twisted, and I turned, and I screamed, and I pleaded and kicked and bit until the second deputy reached out with his zapper and I went out like a light.

☼

I sat in a cell on a hard bench, my throbbing head in my hands. It was all a sham.

The kids at Grubb's Point had played me, goaded me on, then created this story about me selling seats. It was pure entertainment for them, a relief from the pain of passing time in a town like Delano. The deputies searched my room, and of course they found my list. They would use it to confirm any receipt they had, and they would put me away. No probation this time. And of course no lifeboat.

What hurt most was that I actually thought they liked me.

☼

I looked out my cell and into the security lobby where three deputies sat behind tables, chatting about soccer scores and what they had for breakfast. The profile of HydroCen 93 rose in the distance outside the bay windows.

The clock passed 0900.

None of my recruits from last night would show up. That left no more than thirty. Not enough, of course, but I hoped the aliens would take them anyway. At least it would be *something*. I wished I'd told Johnny R the truth, and wondered why I always waited until it was too late to do what's right.

I watched the clock on the far wall as each second of my existence trickled away.

Then came a large, glassy *crash!*

It was the bay window shattering with the force of twenty bricks. Then came voices, and alarms, and the sounds of blasting guns. Some deputies dove for cover, others escaped out the back hallway. A canister of gas twirled its smoky path into the lobby. I began choking and hit the floor where the air was better, but where I couldn't see a damned thing.

The metallic clicking of a pass key came from the locking system. My cell door opened, and a man with a mask listed me to my feet.

"Come on, Carl," said Johnny R. "Time to get outta here!"

My heart fell.

"They didn't take you?"

"Didn't go. Now let's scram!"

I ran then, leaning on Johnny. He led me through tear gas that clogged my lungs and burned my eyes. Gunfire was sporadic. We burst into the open. I gulped air, amazed at what I saw.

A thousand people? Two thousand?

They were kids, mostly, but there were folks I had seen all over town, too—people of the streets, kids who worked the fields, a few construction workers, shop runners, and even chime dealers from the docks. They were the broken ones. The awkward ones. People who were too poor, or too little, or too brainy, or too dumb to be at places like Grubb's Point.

They cheered as we ran through the streets, their voices rising and screeching, each turning to run with us as we passed. I wanted to ask what the hell was happening, but there wasn't time, so I just followed until we came to a fleet of trucks with flatbed trailers. We flowed onto them like a human river, and as each was loaded it lurched forward, leaving behind a precious plume of petroleum exhaust.

I grabbed onto a rail at the front of the platform.

"What is this?" I asked.

Johnny R smiled.

"I saw what was happening last night, and I knew you was bullshitting when you said we was just gonna be tested. Once the deputies took you, I figured the aliens wasn't gonna take us anyway. So we freed you and here we are."

"I still don't get it. You should be running for the hills."

"We *are* running for the hills."

I looked at him, feeling something incredible—camaraderie, brotherhood—something I really don't have words for.

"I'm sorry I didn't tell you the truth," I said.

"No problem, man. You're a good dude."

It was the first time I had heard that in a long time. The platform bounced over a rut. The truck's engine groaned with diesel pain.

"They're gonna blow the planet," I told him. "We got no place to go."

"Oh, we got a place," said a girl sitting next to Johnny. "It's a cave, deep and deep."

"A *cave*?"

"Yeah," Johnny said. "A cave. It's got water down under it. Jenny's been warning folks of this kinda shit for years. Trust her, dude. She's goddamned brilliant."

"How's a cave going to help if the entire world's getting smoked?" I asked.

"Oh, it won't be fun," Jenny replied, riding the flatbed like a skateboard. "But you can't trust everything a controller says, right? I mean, a hydrogen blast like that will burn shit outta the place, so everyone topside dies, no ifs, ands or buts. But the land'll come back. And all that H_2 just comes to water again later on. Until then there's lots of it underground, or we can move inland if it gets too bad."

"We're more worried about food than water," Johnny R said.

I suddenly noticed every flatbed had sacks of grain or meal or something on it. I shook my head, shocked at what could be done in a few hours. I looked at the people again, a couple thousand of us riding an automotive fleet that kicked up dust as it raced across the desert.

"How'd you find them?" I asked.

Johnny R smiled. "They found themselves, man. I told a couple of guys when we got back from GP. They told a few more. We met this morning and talked about it. Took everyone who wanted to join up and left the rest."

I looked at them again, this wave of kids. They screamed and they whooped, they raised their fists as their trucks bounced in the desert. And in looking at them, I saw myself, too. We're all like Johnny R, you know? We're all broken, and there are a lot of things we don't have. But we all want to make it.

Yes, I thought. Perhaps we are all here because we are the ones who just want it badly enough.

Then I looked at Johnny, and I saw that he was what the controller meant when she talked about the human sense of greater purpose. He was the one who saved my ass when it didn't deserve saving. He was the one who had gotten these people together. He was the one who had always been of the utmost service.

Not me.

But then I thought about it a little more, and remembered that I was the one who found out what was about to happen. And Jenny was the one who knew how to survive once it did. We were all teammates, we humans. Johnny R was our leader now, doing what he did best, but each of us brought something to the game.

The mountain and its haven of caves loomed ahead. Then a rumble rattled the air, a deep groan that came from somewhere across the universe itself, and behind us, a spaceship rose into the sky, trailing a white line of smoke and vapor.

I didn't know quite what the coming days would be like, but if nothing else, the experience had taught me to trust my teammates.

Original (First) Publication
Copyright © 2013 by Ron Collins

Michael F. Flynn is a multiple Hugo nominee, a two-time winner of the Prometheus Award, a winner of the Sturgeon Award, a winner of Japan's Seiun-sho Award, and the very first winner of the Robert A. Heinlein Medal.

BURIED HOPES

by Michael F. Flynn

The chair in the counselor's office was soft and cool to the touch. Leather, perhaps, but almost like buckskin. It was a bit large and high off the floor, so that Rann felt smaller than usual. The walls were adorned with comforting diplomas, and the windows muted the raucous sounds of the Manhattan traffic far below. The décor was composed in gentle earth tones. On the table between them, the counselor had set bone china cups filled with tea. All the little tricks of the trade, deployed to put the patient at ease. He squirmed a bit in the chair, seeking that elusive ease. He did not care for tea, but it was the least obnoxious of the alternatives she had offered.

Rann said, "I don't know why I've come here, doctor."

The counselor wore her hair in an authoritative bun and dressed in mannish, but mammalian fashion. Her large-framed glasses gave her a distancing, professional mien. She sat in a second chair facing him at an angle.

"You don't have to call me doctor," she said. "Call me Liz, or Ms. Abbot, if that is more comfortable for you."

Yes, she was trying to reduce the doctor-patient distance while maintaining a professional detachment. Friendly, yet not too friendly; at least, not until she could understand how close she might come without breaching the wrong psychological barriers.

Rann said, "Yes, 'Ms. Abbot.' Yes, that would be fine." He could see from the way she cocked her head that she had heard the residue of his accent. Once it had been thicker and had drawn quizzical glances, but diligent practice over the years had shaved nearly all the edges from it.

"Should I call you Mr. Velkran, or will Rann do?" she asked him.

Rann considered the alternatives. If she was "Ms." and he was "Rann," that would place him on the wrong end of a parent-child divide; but "Ms." and "Mr." created another and broader divide. Rann thought he would rather like being treated as a child, at least for the next hour, and told her to call him Rann.

"Is that short for 'Randolph'?" she asked him as she made a note.

He answered with a shrug into which she could read any answer she chose. "Don't call me Randolph."

She looked up and arranged her notes in a leather folder against her knees. "Something is bothering you."

Rann looked for the question mark at the end, but of course it was not there. He would not have come to her if nothing bothered him. Rann said, "Depression, I think."

Ms. Abbot glanced at the questionnaire he had filled out. "Don't you know?"

"I've always been given to melancholy and nostalgia. It's in my blood, and who can gage whether it is a little more or a little less. But it seems to me that it has deepened these past few weeks…"

"What is it that causes you to feel depressed?"

"I thought you might tell me. I mean, that's your job, isn't it?"

Ms. Abbot made a brief moue with her lips. "My job is to help you tell yourself. To help you search, as it were. But why don't we start with something else. Tell me a little about yourself. You live in New Jersey…" She tapped the forms he had filled out. "But you've come all the way into Manhattan to see me."

"You should feel flattered."

"I would if 'Abbot' were not the first listing in the index."

"Then I think you know why. I would rather not do this closer to home."

"There's no stigma to seeing a counselor."

Rann answered with another shrug and then, when the silence had dragged on, suddenly blurted, "Did you know that the international space station was de-orbited?"

Ms. Abbot seemed accustomed to conversational left turns. "I saw something about it on the news. It was worn out and abandoned, wasn't it?" "It didn't have to be. It could have been maintained, upgraded, replaced."

"Is that why you've been feeling depressed? Because the old space station was decommissioned?"

"I..." *Was it?* he wondered. "I'm sentimental. I hate to see things end. The last moonwalker died... oh, years ago. No longer lives there anyone who has walked upon the moon."

"Ah, that was before my time, I'm afraid. And didn't it turn out to be a hoax?"

Rann leaped from the chair and began to pace the room, agitated beyond measure. "No, it was not! It was not!"

Ms. Abbot maintained her composure and said mildly, "But if the story is true, it would mean that people went to the moon *before* they built a space station in Earth orbit. Does that make sense? To go all that way, and then to backtrack?"

His pacing had brought him to the window and he looked down on the thumb-sized pedestrians teeming along the sidewalk. "It seemed a good idea at the time."

"Did the space program mean a lot to you? You don't appear old enough to remember it."

He turned from his contemplation. "It meant a lot to all of us," he told the counselor. "If only we had at the time realized it." He sought out the patient's chair and sank once more into it. "Who knows what might be out there? On the moon, on, on Mars there might be..." Rann fell silent. "There might be anything. Now, how few are left! Sometimes..." He paused and ground one hand in the other, like a mortar in a pestle. "Sometimes," he added more quietly, "I feel so lonely."

He saw the counselor nod, and he knew he had revealed something of himself. Automatically, the old guards went up. But then, why had he come here unless it was to reveal something of himself? "I miss the old country," Rann said, deliberately. "The music, the foods, the festivals—oh, how the young boys and girls dressed so fine on those days! Even the sound of the old tongues on the lips of friends. Sometimes sees my mind over the Oorlong Hills the sun set so great and red, painting in every color the clouds."

"Have you ever gone back to visit?"

Rann shook his head. "No. There are...difficulties."

Ms. Abbot said "ah" in such understanding tones. The world was full of people unwelcome in their own homelands. That was not precisely Rann's problem, but he decided not to complicate matters. "It helps to talk about it," he added.

"Do you have family back there? Is there anyone in particular you miss?"

For a moment Rann could see the Miss Kopál as if she stood directly before him, the dandi-flowers round her crown, the golden lace about her throat, the tattoos winding like vines along her arms. Then... the moment was lost and he realized that he no longer remembered what she had looked like. He fumbled in his jacket pocket for a kerchief, but the counselor leaned across to hand him a tissue. "I'm sorry," he said. "Sorry. There were, once. But they have all by now forgotten me." He squared his shoulder, felt the unexpected crack of bone, and deliberately relaxed. "I suppose this seems silly to you. A bad case of homesickness."

"No, not silly at all. Have you been in this country long?"

Rann looked at the floor and clasped his hands. He waited for the inevitable question.

"If you are undocumented," Ms. Abbot said, "don't worry. My job is to help you deal with your depression, not to do the government's work for them." She reached out and touched Rann briefly on his wrist. Reflexively, Rann pulled back.

"A double-dozen of us came to the, to the New World together," Rann admitted, "but we've to the drogo scattered and seldom anymore do we see one another."

"The drogo?"

"Ah. Did I say that? I am falling into the rhythms of my suckling tongue. Drogo is in my country a seasonal wind—hot, dry, brisk—and as a way of speaking we say that we have blown off with it."

"Tell me, Rann, how long have you felt these pangs of loneliness?"

"Always. Ever since we landed here. It was not so bad when we all lived near one another; but..."

"But the old neighborhood has 'scattered to the drogo.' Tell me, is this feeling of loneliness persistent, or does it come and go? How did you feel, oh, last year? Two weeks ago?"

Rann closed his eyes and tried to imagine what he had been doing a fortnight since. His neighbors had invited him to a cookout. There had been burgers and franks and beer, discussion of the Giants and the new cable series on Teddy Roosevelt. The neighborhood dogs did not like him much and the beer had upset his digestion, but…"If you had asked me then, I would have said I was reasonably happy. Perhaps no less happy than most people believe they are."

"Do you think everyone unhappy?"

"Of course," he said. "It is only a matter of one's awareness. Have you no regrets, doctor? Is there nothing that in quiet moments might tinge with melancholy your thoughts? An old fiancé who slipped away? A brother or sister untimely gone? A childhood friend fallen out of touch? A…a calculation performed incorrectly?"

"A calculation? You're a mathematician, then?"

"I teach at a small college in New Jersey."

Ms. Abbot nodded and added notes to the folder. Rann admired the way she could write of one thing while talking of another and without even a glance at her paper.

"Then something happened," she said.

"What?"

"Something happened. You were ordinarily happy…Very well, you were not too unhappy. Now two weeks later you are deeply depressed. The BDI-4 you filled out prior to our meeting…There were some anomalies, but it did indicate sadness, guilt feelings, past failures, weeping. But no self-dislike, loss of pleasure, or change in appetite. As I said, a mixed…"

"Excuse me. BDI-four?"

"Beck Depression Inventory. It's a standard instrument for…"

Rann chuckled. "Oh. An inventory? An instrument? Do you keep depression on shelves in your stockroom? Do you at the QC bench measure it?" He knew he was deflecting, and he knew that Ms. Abbot knew. "No, doctor, I intend no mockery. It is only that such words fall on my ears oddly. Ish! I try so hard to speak standard American. Bear with me, please. It is my homesickness. It will hear the cadence of the suckling-tongue even through the mask of other words."

"Would you like to say something in your mother tongue? I should like to hear the sound of it."

"Will you mark it then on that sheet you have beside you? Ah, well. A poem, then." He thought for a moment, conjuring the syllables, feeling them sweetening his mouth before he ever spoke.

"*Offen mere killanong*
Kay-kaka doolenong
Waffen tok ishanong
Ish, doo kill-koffen.

Which I would translate not literally, but to give you some idea of the word-play involved:

'Long have I longed
To say aye for an aye,
To close while so close.
Oh, the time is too short!'"

Dr. Abbot waited while Rann wiped a tear from his cheek; then she said, "That was charming."

Rann said, "It is hard to say in American. The play is of 'long' and 'aye' against 'close' and 'short.' And the title we might translate as 'The Long and the Short of It.'" He paused and closed his eyes, the better to see the sunset tints now so long past and to hear a faint echo of that sweet voice. He had composed the poem himself, just before his departure and recited it in the sunset to she whose face was now lost to him. "'It,' of course, is love."

The counselor smiled. "Isn't it always? Tell me, despite the separation from your homeland and relatives, is life worth living?"

Rann laughed. "Is that one of the questions on your little list? 'Rann Velkran shows moderately suicidal tendencies.' Sorry to disappoint you, doctor; but Rann does not give up on life simply because it has become unbearably sad these past two weeks… 'The saddest life is happier than none at all.' That is a proverb among my people. Only the dead never weep…because they never laugh."

He paused because in his imagination he saw the international space station entering the atmosphere, warming, glowing, turning red from the friction, white hot as it began to come apart, raining into the embrace of the broad Pacific, incinerating all aboard…

"But there was no one left on board by then," he whispered.

"What was that?" Dr. Abbot said.

Rann said, "Never mind." He reached blindly for his tea cup and, misjudging, tipped the thing over so that green tea spilled across the glass table top, twisting into rivulets. Rann stared in horror and began to hyperventilate, then to sob. Alarmed, Ms. Abbot said, "What is it? What's wrong?"

"What's wrong?" Rann cried. "How could this happen! Look at it, running all over! So shapeless, so empty and meaningless! Never will we save it; the drink will now forever be untasted." Rann covered his face with his hands, but between his fingers he studied the eddying streams of tea and he imagined the acid tang of the hot liquid never now to be experienced.

Ms. Abbot had fetched paper towels from her desk drawer. Now, she stared at him in astonishment. "Don't worry," she said. "We'll just mop it up." And she laid the paper towels in the puddle to soak it up.

Rann considered the counselor with something not too short of horror before reminding himself that she was not like his own people. The sudden sorrow with which he had viewed the spilt tea itself dried up as if dabbed with a psychic towel, to be replaced with a gentle and nostalgic melancholy that he knew would never go away whenever he thought on this incident in the future.

When Ms. Abbot took the now-sodden towels to the wastebasket, Rann stood and tugged at his clothing. Strange how current events could stir long-dormant memories. It hadn't been the space station at all; or at least not alone. "I think our time is up anyway, Ms. Abbot, and you have patients with more pressing troubles than I. I believe I understand the cause. And perhaps a solution."

The counselor watched him solemnly. "There are coping mechanisms," she said, "but no solutions."

✧

It took Rann a week to obtain the backhoe and secure the necessary permits, only a little longer to learn which palms at the township must be crossed with what quantity of silver. He assured the rental manager that he knew how to operate a backhoe, signed forms and releases to absolve the man of any responsibility for what might happen, and arranged to have it delivered to his home by a flatbed. From the DIY store he secured stakes, cord, chalklines, and other paraphernalia.

Then he climbed into the crawlspace below the roof and found his old positioning module. He spent the afternoon cleaning, polishing, and calibrating the unit and determining that it could shake hands with the GPS system.

The next morning Rann made himself an omelet with a side of ham and buttered toast. During the past week he had eaten listlessly, but today he felt nearly cheerful and regarded the empty pockets in the egg tray in which the three eggs had so lately nestled with only a modest amount of wistfulness for the eggs-that-had-been. He pretended that the eggs were like those at home and that the ham had been cured with the same smokes and spices as the meats to which he had once been accustomed. But a great many years had passed since then and he was no longer sure that he remembered their flavors aright. This, too, was a sadness.

Perhaps the old surgery had affected his taste as it had his features, giving him at least in his imagination a savoring for alien foods.

He entered his back yard with a certain lightness of step and drove a marker stake into the ground to step off his baseline. He set up his theodolite using the module, which had a built-in EDM to measure distance, and tuned the instrument to the global positioning system. It surprised him sometimes how similar were the tools of his trade from place to place; but he reflected that there were not too many different ways to take levels and distances and angles, and so there was nothing astonishing that the instruments might be similar. It was only a matter of transposing the numbers.

"Only" a matter of transposing the numbers.

His yard, like all those around the block, backed onto a small woodland in the center of the neighborhood. The two roads into the area curved into each other forming a rough oval that enclosed a modest copse of trees and brush, providing shelter for rabbits and birds and sundry creatures. Every day toward sunset some large, furry, flattish thing crawled slowly from the forsythia bush toward the creek that bisected the woods. A muskrat, he thought, or maybe a badger. A short walk in any direction touched on more urban landscapes, where such unruly things as lazy muskrats and meandering creeks were properly kept in their places. The woods, his neighbors had told him when he moved in, sat on township land; but because private property enclosed it on all sides, it could not be developed. He had not corrected them on the matter.

He had run a line to a stake at the far end of his property when his neighbor to the south appeared at the fence with two cans of beer. His name was Jamie Shaw and he was a legman for a private detective agency. Beyond that, and that he had a very large extended family, Rann knew little about him. "Looks like hot work," Shaw said, and waved the second can in Rann's general direction.

Rann did not want to take a break at the very beginning of his work—if there can be such a paradoxical thing as a break at a beginning—but neither did he wish to appear un-neighborly. He joined Shaw at the fence, thanked him, and sipped a little from the can. Shaw asked him what he thought of the Giants' chances come fall; and Rann, who had calculated from game theory a losing season, said that a new quarterback often breathed life into a tired offense. Shaw nodded, gestured with his can at the markers he had driven into the ground.

"Building something?"

"Yes, a swimming pool."

"Really? I never saw you as the athletic type. You're doing the work yourself?"

"Some of it. I expect to have help later."

"You've marked it pretty close to the woods."

Rann said, "The property lines actually run a little way into the woods. I checked."

Shaw took a swig of his beer. "Better check your deed. There are covenants. No digging, and no 'diminishing the woods.' I'd hate to see you get half into it and the association comes along and shuts you down. The lady down the corner…" He gestured vaguely north with his beer can. "…is mighty touchy about the trees and rabbits—or her boyfriend is. Heck, I'd rather not see them 'diminished,' either."

"Jamie, are you threatening me with a lawsuit?"

The ruddy man reared back. "Me? No. I don't confuse my personal preferences with the laws of the universe. I'm just giving you a heads-up. I'm not the only one on the block, you know." He pointed to the houses on either side, and to the backs of those on the far side of the oval, partly visible through the summer foliage. "Now, you're not quite encroaching, but you might want to think about those trees dirtying up your pool come the fall. That one over there is a sycamore and sheds bark all year long. Why not put in an above-ground pool and place it farther away from the trees."

Rann said, "I'm sure everything will work out." He took the beer with him when he returned to his work, but his stomach churned and as soon as he was able he scurried inside, poured the beer down the drain, and removed his bolus. He stood for a while gagging over the toilet bowl and wondered at the price of neighborliness. Then he rinsed, swallowed the bolus once more, and returned to work.

The sun grew hot as the afternoon wore on, but that did not trouble him. The warmth was rather pleasant, especially after the interminable winter. He was swarthy and did not burn like Jamie Shaw, who sometimes emulated a well-done lobster. Someone had once told Rann that he looked like an Egyptian mummy: delicate and rugged at the same time, tough as old leather.

When he realized that his last stake would be off by several digits, he cursed himself. The hash marks on his sights were on the *chegk* scale and he had forgotten to transform the digits at one point. It was a mistake anyone could make. Some American scientists had once confused the metric scale with the traditional scale when programming a Mars probe and the probe had not known it had reached the surface until it had already gone several feet past it.

It was a mistake that he had made only once in his lifetime.

Rann wiped his tears and backtracked until he found the point where he had inadvertently used the old *puralon* scale and he made the necessary correction. After that, the blocking proceeded square and on the level, though his hands shook more than they might ordinarily have done.

✧

A few days later, the backhoe was delivered and Rann spent the day fencing off the open space between his house and the garage with chain-link. The backhoe was officially an "attractive nuisance," and so he must put "appropriate safeguards" in place. The township inspector came around and checked everything, then recommended fencing off the woods behind as well. Someone determined enough could cross a neighbor's yard, pass through the woods, enter Rann's yard, and so hurt himself with the backhoe. Rann thought that anyone that determined could climb the fence as well, but he appreciated the inspector's position. There were rules and it was not within her authority to ignore them.

Afterward, he invited the inspector inside for a cup of coffee, which was gracefully accepted. A lot of home improvement enthusiasts, Rann gathered from her conversation, spent their time arguing with the code inspectors rather than improving their homes. Rann made sympathetic noises. She had already seen and approved the drawings and levels, and had ascertained Rann's competency to do the excavation work himself. He had earlier discovered that the inspector's cousin owned a concrete firm and had put the cousin's name on his subcontractor list. It was not bribery. She had never mentioned him, nor had Rann pointed it out.

Of course she noticed the picture over the mantel. It was meant to be noticed. "That's…rather startling," she said. "Abstract expressionism? A Pollock, maybe?"

"It's what they call a supernova. A giant star exploded eleven thousand years ago, about the time people were just beginning to farm. Eight hundred years later, they would have seen in the night sky a second sun. This…," Rann gestured at the picture, "is all that's left. The shock wave. The gas flying off from the explosion reacts with the interstellar medium, knocking electrons off their atoms. When the electrons recombine with the atoms, they produce light in many different energy bands—ah, colors—and give us this."

"It's very pretty," the inspector said. "It looks almost like a photograph."

Rann said, "It is."

"Oh, that's right. There was a big telescope out in space for a while, wasn't there? What's that down in the corner?"

"A part of a ship's hull. The equivalent of accidentally getting your thumb in front of the lens."

The inspector nodded at this, then started and laughed. "After all that money! And they didn't even get a clear shot."

Rann said, "Come here. I have another photograph that might interest you." This one hung in the entry hall facing the front door, so visitors who entered in the normal fashion saw it first of all. "This is a sinkhole on Mars, called 'Dena.' It's one of seven spotted around the volcano Arisa Mons."

"Deep," said the inspector as she studied the picture. "The shadows at the bottom are so dark that it almost looks like an opening into an underground cavern."

Rann said, "Yes, it does, doesn't it? And heat comes out of the hole. Makes you wonder what might be down there."

The inspector looked at him. "A volcano, you said?"

"A dead volcano. All seven vents give off heat," he added, "but Dena most of all. Closest to the source, maybe? But look into those shadows. Don't they draw you in? Don't they make you wonder what lies in the darkness beyond?"

"More rocks, I suppose. It's not safe to poke into shadows. Are those circular things near the sinkhole *bubbles*? Oh. No, they're craters. Weird optical illusion. For a moment, I thought…But the shadows are wrong."

"Lipless craters. Maybe they were domes that have now collapsed into their foundations," Rann suggested.

The inspector laughed. "You should write that sci-fi stuff. Well, thank you for the coffee, but I have two more sites to check out today. Don't forget to call me when you finish digging."

After she had departed, Rann remained for a while before the photograph, staring into the depths of the shadows. Nearly everyone he had shown his pictures to over the years had had the same reaction. An incuriosity bordering on the morbid. Had something gone out of the human race in this past generation or two? Had some spark been extinguished? It had not always been that way. He could remember the excitement of the first satellites, the first men in space, the first men on the moon, the first space station. It had all been 'first' in those days. He had never thought that he would see the last, as well.

He wiped a tear from his cheek for lost old days, and returned to this back-yard project.

☼

Neighbors drifted by to watch from time to time. Alma Seakirt, the woman down at the corner, asked him how close he was digging to the woods, and the old retired doctor on her other side traipsed through the trees and brush as if engaged on a survey of his own. He leaned on the back fence and watched in silence for a time, but asked no questions and made no comment before leaving the way he had come.

"They just want to make sure you're not harming the preserve," Jamie Shaw told him afterward as Rann relaxed on his patio with a lemonade and studied on how little he had accomplished. He offered a drink to Shaw and to his cousin, Sandra Locke, who was visiting that day. They came across and took lawn chairs around the patio table. Lemonade did not bother Rann as much as beer did, so long as he took a small pill with the drink. Shaw had a packet of papers tucked under his arm and Rann waited to see what surprise the man intended.

"There is something peculiar about your property," Shaw announced as he set the packet on the patio table.

His cousin brushed a stand of hair out of her face. "Jamie has been wasting his time as usual instead of servicing our paying clients."

"Hey," said Shaw. "This is important. I had detect trace the property records in the Wessex County data base. Did you know that the covenant against diminishing the woods goes all the way back?" He took a swallow of his lemonade and set the glass on the table. "Yessir, that's a fact. Each conveyance passed the encumbrance on to the next buyer." He took another drink. "Do you know where I had to go to find these records?"

Rann said, "Perth Amboy," and both Shaw and Locke raised their eyebrows.

"You're almost right," Shaw said slowly. "Perth Amboy was the capital for the East Jersey General Board of Proprietors. But they officially dissolved themselves in 1998 and deposited all their records in Trenton."

Rann was sorry to hear that, since his people took oathing very seriously and sometimes a thing ought to go on simply because it had already gone on so long. Sentiment came easily to him.

"And since the oldest documents had never been scanned," Shaw continued, "I had to go down to Trenton to finish the job in person."

"Poor baby," said Sandra. "Can't do *all* your leg-work by computer."

Shaw waved a hand. "Even on the computer, detect does most of the donkey work." To Rann, he added, "Detect is a neural net *cum* knowledge base that Sandra and I put together."

"Sandra and *who*?"

"Okay, Sandra and Sandra. It not only searches out the records we need, it can also identify which other evidence to look for. Our township was within the original Elizabeth Town patent. Then Daniel Peirce and some other men bought the southern half for Wood Bridge, and Peirce sold the southern third of that to some settlers, who called it Piscataqua. But it turned out that there was already a small settlement in the township: a band of shipwrecked Dutch sailors who had made their way inland from Point Ambo. They took the oath of allegiance required by the proprietors and for a quit-rent of a half-penny the acre, each received in return…" Shaw flipped through the sheaf of printouts until he found the one he wanted. "…each received homelots of five *morgens*—that's ten acres—plus sixty acres of upland and six of meadow for haying. Then—here it is—in lieu of the standard proprietor's seventh, 'the wyld Woode south and east of ye east Kill of Runamuchy Creek shall be set aside as Commons for such Activityes as byrding and fyshing and trapping of smalle Animals.'" Shaw handed the page to Rann, who pretended to read it. He studied the signatories at the bottom of the page, blurred a bit by the scanning and reproduction and the age of the original document. There was Daniel Peirce's name 'for ye proprietors' and the seal of Governor Carteret. Below that the twenty four freeholders granted domain by right of prior settlement. "Benken van Kottespool, captain," he read. "Ronholf vander Alkrenn, navigator. Giszberth and Alengonda Hengenwaller…" He read the remainder silently. Shipwrecked sailors, far from home.

Sandra mentioned that the Dutch had colonized the area before the English had taken it in one of the Anglo-Dutch wars. "Afterward, New York claimed all of East Jersey as part of New Amsterdam, 'til the Duke of York himself smacked them upside the head."

Rann said, "That is all very interesting, but…"

"But," Shaw said, "the point is that the prohibition on disturbing the woods long predates the construction of these homes here." He swept his arm around. "The woods aren't undeveloped because our properties encircle it. Our properties encircle it because the woods can't be developed. There was a mention in an early conveyance—Vander Alkrenn to Jeremy Pike—that the land was a Lenape burial ground and that Lenapes who so desired would have easement along the creek to visit it, but the original charter makes no mention of that."

Rann said, "I suppose I ought to get back to my digging…"

"Well, now, that's the funny thing," said Shaw. "The digging. Normally, a quit-rent buys back freeholder rights, like the right to hunt or to explore for minerals and so forth. Most freeholders back then ignored the quit-rent because they never supposed that fox hunts would cross their croplands or that the proprietor would sell someone else the right to dig for gold. Why buy back a right that no one else is likely to exercise? But the Dutch sailors paid their quit-rents dutifully every year and when they eventually sold out and moved away, they put a no-digging encumbrance on the conveyances. All but this one."

Rann said, "This one."

"Yes, your deed is the only instrument that permits digging—and always has."

"How about that?" Rann murmured.

"You don't fool me, Rann," said Jamie Shaw. "You must have done your homework, and the township inspector, too. You knew none of your neighbors could legally stop you. But why did they exempt only this one property?"

"Just in case," Rann suggested, "we might want to exhume an Indian."

✧

Shortly after, Rann made a show of giving up and bringing in a professional excavator with a bigger backhoe. The man was named Steve and he looked over the smaller rental unit that Rann had been using as a wolf might study a poodle. They went over the plans together and Steve checked the GPS markers. "Ya done the survey good," he admitted, "but maybe ya should stick to that, steada tryin' to shave some bucks on labor."

The inspector came by and the three of them reviewed certificates together. Afterwards, when Rann offered refreshments inside, Steve surprised him by studying the photograph of the Martian sinkhole and saying he wouldn't mind climbing down into the opening of the cavern, just to see what was there.

"If it *is* a cavern," Rann suggested, "and not just a play of shadows."

"Nah, it's a cavern, I tell ya. If this was the moon, I'd say ya might be right. No air makes the shadows real black. But Mars got air. Not much, maybe, but some. And, ya know, this sounds real whacko, but that sinkhole looks like it mighta been excavated."

"A swimming pool on Mars?" offered the inspector with a laugh.

"Nah. Too deep. Say, how big is this thing, anyway?"

Rann said, "About one hundred and thirty meters deep."

The inspector whistled. "A forty-three story building could sit in there."

Steve took up his gloves and pulled them onto his hands before sparing the photograph another lookover. "That would be some honking foundation to dig, I tell ya."

✧

A few days later, Venkaaszbuul came to the house. Rann held the door open for him. "Come in, captain. I've been expecting you." They did not shake hands.

Venkaaszbuul ignored the sinkhole picture and, brushing past Rann, went directly to the living room, where he sat with his back to the photograph of the Vela supernova. "We have not been in contact for decades, navigator," he said, "and yet you were expecting me?"

Rann shrugged. "Call it Fate."

"I'll call it Death. Jizzvarth has died."

Rann felt a tear track his cheek. "Jizz?"

"Yes, of your Ypuralon comrades, the last. I thought you would desire the knowing of it." He spoke in *chegk*, the language of the lowlands.

Rann buried his face in his hands. "Oh, the hills! Oh, the hills! And only I alone to remember them the now!"

Venkaaszbuul managed to convey distaste on his expressionless face. It was in the eyes, and very subtle; but the Chegka were a subtle folk. Rann had to remind himself that they, too, felt grief, though they showed it in different ways than his own highland folk.

"It was a natural death," Venkaaszbuul assured him, "and no autopsy was called for."

A sob escaped Rann's throat, and he knew shame before his captain that he had allowed it. "Is that a comfort? Am I to forget that he was of our lives a part, of our crew a part? Or how he struggled in the lifeboats safely to debark us? You are a cold man, flatlander."

"And you a forgetful one, hillman. Or do you recall *why* your beloved countryman bore the shepherding of us into the boats?"

Curiously, the jab calmed Rann, proving that it was possible, on some topics at least, to weep oneself dry. "Sometimes," he said, "there are days when I do *not*." He hugged himself. "I am sorry for the error."

"Sorry, you are," the captain said. "Sorry."

"A small transposition error…"

"From flaws the smallest, great failures burst. Their philosopher Aristotle said this."

"It was too late to correct…"

"Of course it was. Hillmen may weep their sorrows on their sleeves; but the universe is cold and has no pity. 'There are in nature no second chances.'" The proverb was *chegk*, but he delivered it in a thick *puralon* accent, the sort of accent Chegka used for a laugh in their night clubs.

Rann said in a low and miserable voice, "How long must I answer for it?"

"For all your life," the captain said. "For every heartbeat of it since we were marooned in this miserable place. But…"—And here the captain's voice took on something close to pity—"it is Rann who has the demanding of the answers from you. The Americans have a proverb: Don't cry over spilt milk. So don't."

Rann attempted a smile, and failed. "What, then? Should we cry over milk held safely in containers upright? Not long past have I bespoken a counselor regarding my melancholy. These people must know some secret to assuage the pain when it grows too great. While there, I knocked a cup of tea over."

The captain sucked in his breath and said, "Ah," but did not otherwise change expression.

"And this counselor said that she would wipe it up, and that would be the end of it. Wipe it up! And try to pretend that we never saw anything."

Venkaaszbuul said, "It is their response to everything. They ignore the truths before their own eyes."

"Or they lock it in, like flatlanders."

"Were you of the School, you would learn to weep in your heart, not on your sleeve; but you would not learn not to weep. We can pass among them without much remark, while you and Jizz and the others, they looked on askance, more emotional than their women. A terrible lacking was it, that the Schoolmen failed the winning of the hills."

Tears coursed down Rann's cheeks. A million worlds had died a-borning in that failure. He wept for a moment for all the things that might have been; but he detested the bottled-up flatlanders, and so it was only for a moment that he wept at their failure. "She thought that by wiping it from the table, she could wipe it from our minds. It was only some spilled tea, and so a small sorrow; but her reaction was typical. They are heartless, these humans. No wonder they kill one another, fight endless wars, and never developed their technology. They are too *rational*. Not about anything do they *care*!"

The captain touched him briefly and made a flatlander's gesture that meant he accepted a portion of the hillman's sorrow as his own. A hillman would have wailed and embraced him, but Rann knew he ought treasure this momentary touch as the best one Schooled could do.

Venkaaszbuul said, "Offer it up. One of their native Schools advises that, and it is very close to what the true School teaches. We are given no burdens that we cannot carry."

Rann said, "As well, that, or we should have gone extinct long since. It is how the Winnower sculpts life."

Venkaaszbuul grunted and made no comment. Flatlanders did not believe in the Winnower. He stood and went to the patio doors, which were glass, and lifted the curtain to gaze at the backhoe chugging in the yard.

"I heard him as I stood on your threshold."

Rann came to his side but made no reply.

Venkaaszbuul said, "This land looked different when last I saw it."

"The houses weren't here then. New trees have grown, and old trees have fallen—or grown taller." Faintly, from somewhere across the woods, came the sound of children playing. Yet another of the many-worlds in which he would never live was the world in which he had young in his steading. But he mastered himself like a Schoolman. Venkaaszbuul and his people had been right about one thing: to remain unremarked, they had to adopt the stoicism of this world's people. "Did you hear that they de-orbited their space station?"

Venkaaszbuul bobbed his head in the human style. "It was why I bethought myself the visiting of you, my crew."

"How many…How many of us are left?"

"Eight. You were the last on my list." After a pause, he added, "It was not much of a space station."

"It was the only one they had. Perhaps the only one they will ever have. The fall recalled to me the plunge of our own ship, and plunged me into a deep melancholy. Do you think…Do you think the other lifeboats made it to shore?"

Venkaaszbuul made a gesture of uncertainty. It so resembled a hillman's gesture of assurance that Rann knew a moment of hope before he realized the error.

"We were fortunate," Venkaaszbuul said, "that your piloting skills brought us down here, where there were few people, and those easily over-awed. It gave us time for the learning, for the surgery, for the mastery of their language."

"Dutch."

"Suppose we had burned up in shoals, our angle of attack too steep; or plunged into one of the boundless seas that swamp this world; or grounded in civilized lands, where they would have quite rationally stoned us or burned us. When you ponder the many-worlds that the quanta tell us might have been, remember that most would have been worse than this. Why not approach the past with gratitude rather than tears?"

"A School trick. Because this is of the many-worlds the best? That may be cause for the greatest melancholy of all."

"Ah, Rann, I'd not have the stealing from you of that melancholy which you so treasure; but why not suppose that the others landed safely and have been 'lying low,' just as we have."

Rann said, "Then perhaps we should stand up straight."

Venkaaszbuul stood a while longer at the glass doors before letting the curtain fall. "Why? So we can be spirited off for the studying in some secret laboratory?"

"They would be insane to so risk the wrath of a star-faring people of unknown powers."

"If I am to place myself in trust of their sanity, your objection answers itself. Whether they burn us at the stake or dissect us in the lab, I would just as soon not face them with the choice."

"But if they knew we had among them come, they might strive again to reach the stars."

"To what point, navigator? Once there was a hope that they might find our old base on Mars—or the observation post on the Moon—and we could scavenge the materials to build a messenger packet or a communicator and so secure rescue. But only a double-handful of us now remain, and each of us nearing the end of days." He glanced at his hands, turned them over. "Less than a double-handful. Forgive my error. If you must weep, Rann—and I know you must—weep that the humans never reached Mars when we were young enough and numerous enough for it to matter."

The backhoe's engine revved and the claw dug into the earth. Steve, perched in the driver's seat, worked the levers back and forth. He did not notice the watchers. Venkaaszbuul grunted. "Is that where he is?"

Rann understood. "Somewhere in there. When the wreck hit, it threw dirt over everything."

"The boat still lies beneath the trees?"

Rann gestured yes. "The inertial sheath would have long ago shut down; so the earth has been working on it."

"Poshtli should have worn his life vest; but lake-landers are more feckless even than hillmen."

"Maybe he did wear an inertia bubble, and it failed him when we were forced to leap. One more sorrow. One more might-have-been." Rann imagined all the possible Poshtlis whose lives had not been lived, even here among the savages.

"You expect this hired man of yours to dig up Poshtli's corpse?"

"A corpse unmodified by the nanosurgery. Our insides may be passing strange, but outwardly you and I appear merely foreign."

"Which is why we permit no autopsy."

"But Poshtli's mummy will appear more than passing strange. The humans will realize that aliens have been among them; they will restart their space programs in an effort to find our world. It is too late for us; but not for them."

"You vastly underestimate their capacity for self-deception. They will call it a hoax, or an odd and crippling mutation."

Rann hugged himself with both arms. "Captain, of the crew and science staff how many were still aboard *Vital Being* when she hit shoals and burned?"

Venkaaszbuul looked at him for a long time. Then, he said, "I believe all made it to the boats; and perhaps the boats all made it to shore and they have been living out their days concealed as we are."

Rann laughed. "Now you are overestimating *my* capacity for self-deception."

"But Rann, you know the law of the quanta. When you don't *know*, anything is possible."

☼

That night Rann and his captain ate dinner together, and Rann prepared a meal that would not irritate their digestive tracts. They raised a glass—of filtered wine—to their comrades who had perished and another to those who inevitably would soon perish. Rann proposed a toast to the earth—the real earth, not this one on which they had been shipwrecked for so long—and he sang a poem in *puralon* to honor them, even improvising a stanza in praise of the flatlands. Venkaaszbuul declaimed a heroic ballad in *chegk* concerning some bold explorer of ages past; and it was good to hear the old tongues and the old songs, even in *chegk*, and to praise a world whose star did not so much as shine in this planet's skies. They both wept—even the flatlander captain so forgot his Schooling that tears wet his face in abundance—and they embraced and promised never again to allow the years to intervene so thickly.

In the morning, Venkaaszbuul secured Rann's promise that, should the excavation by wild chance unearth the body of Poshtli the Lakelander, he would not disclose in any manner that there were others yet living who wore such unlikely bones beneath their skins. And then he departed.

☼

Later that same day, a sheriff's deputy served Rann with a court order to cease and desist all digging. His neighbor Alma Seakirt had objected that since the encumbrance against digging appeared in all the other deeds surrounding the wood, and because the clear intent had always been to protect the woodland, it must have been omitted in error from the Vander Alkrenn deed. Rann Valkran disputed the order in township court and when he lost, appealed to the State, where he lost again.

By that time, the hole that he and Steve had excavated had been filled in and, per court order, planted in wildflowers. As a sign of hope in the future, Ms. Seakirt said.

☼

Rann took it hard, his neighbor later observed, and could be seen on his patio sitting before the filled-in swimming pool weeping into his lemonade. He had always been a sensitive soul, Shaw commented, much given to tears and melancholy as well as sudden enthusiasms. Even in his happier moments, he had seemed haunted by some great and terrible sorrow in his past whose memory would not release him.

So it came as no surprise when Shaw saw him one morning lying dead with a shovel in his hand in a hole he had dug in his ground. Like everyone else, he assumed at first that it had been suicide. But suicide over a swimming pool never dug? In the end, there were enough anomalies—the position of the body, the placement of the wound, certain papers he had filed with his lawyer, Sèan FitzPatrick—for the coroner to rule 'suspicious circumstances,' and order an autopsy.

☼

Afterward, amidst the sensation that followed the autopsy and the strange artifacts found in Rann's attic, when his death had been ruled a suicide after all, Elizabeth Abbot, a grief counselor whom he had briefly consulted, remembered that he had once said that he would not give up on life out of despair, and she wondered if he might have done so out of hope.

☼

Afterword to "Buried Hopes"

The germ of this story was planted many years ago, when I discussed with a counselor who worked in our office building the notion of an undercover alien who goes to see a counselor. The unformed idea was that the usual clichéd alien-observer-for-the-Galactic-Union would suffer pangs of loneliness and separation from his home culture and the counselor would eventually pick up on this.

It was not that this was not much of a story, as that it was not a story at all. So not much happened, and the notion lay dormant until recently when I read a news story of a man who had unearthed mammoth bones while excavating a swimming pool on his property. That suggested the title "Buried Hopes." I began to noodle over what else someone might dig up. Hidden chambers? A doorway to other dimensions?

Then I read an essay by the philosopher James Chastek entitled "A Theme for a Sci-Fi Story That I'll Never Write," in which he laments the cliché by which the aliens are always logical and the humans are emotional, and emotion always wins. Being a Thomist philosopher, he thought this a false dichotomy and inverted the scenario to one in which the aliens cry over spilt milk while the humans try to be logical about it. I asked him if I could use it, and he said sure. You can find his essay here:

http://thomism.wordpress.com/2010/04/11/a-theme-for-a-sci-fi-story-that-ill-never-write/

At some point, these three threads—the emotional aliens, the need to see a counselor, and the notion of buried hopes—came together, with the results you have just read.

At this point in the "neighborhood stories," Singer is dead, Henry relocated, and Kyle uploaded (or not). However, Alma from "Captive Dreams" makes a brief appearance, as does old Doc Wilkes. Rann's neighbor, Jamie Shaw, was mentioned briefly in "Hopeful Monsters" and, along with his cousin Sandra Locke, was the protagonist in another story, "The Longford Collector."

Copyright © 2012 by Michael F. Flynn

"Buried Hopes" is included in Michael Flynn's Collection, ***Captive Dreams.***

Views expressed by guest or resident columnists are entirely their own.

Greg Benford is a Nebula winner and a former Worldcon Guest of Honor. He is the author of more than 30 novels and 6 books of non-fiction, and has edited 10 anthologies.

A FROZEN FUTURE?
Cryonics as a Gamble

By Gregory Benford

For many, the most startling news in summer 2002 was that the American baseball legend, Ted Williams, had been frozen. A close relative turned Williams' body over to a firm that suspends its "patients" in liquid nitrogen. A firestorm of media attention followed.

And so it was. Williams now rests in liquid nitrogen in Scottsdale, Arizona. Some of his relatives tried to stop that but they failed in the courts. There have been several such attempts in the past decades to thwart the wills of the dead, which also failed. It's unclear what their motives might be, though getting the money back into the estate seems plausible.

The USA is the only nation with a thriving industry in cryonics. The underlying hope, that properly freezing people immediately after they have crossed the threshold we call "death" may allow them to be later reanimated, is a bold assertion about the future.

This goal is not scientific, in the sense that the results cannot be checked right now. This is not the same as unscientific statements—those which have been tested and have failed.

Rather, ideas of the future are nonscientific. However systematically arrived at, they cannot be tested today.

Cryonics opens a window into the American mind. It is utopian and pragmatic, since the essential argument is to freeze people with carefully tailored cryo-protectants distributed through the bloodstream into their cells. The technology to "resurrect" by warming the body and curing their disease must lie in the far future, perhaps a century away. This demands optimism few can muster, a faith that the future will both care and be able to work medical miracles.

Response to the very idea is quite emotional, I've found, especially among both scientists and the religious—a fervently felt resistance suggesting a deep underlying uneasiness about death in modern society. Imagine a scientist today being rejected from a scientific society because he wants to present research relevant to long-term preservation of whole organisms, not necessarily humans. Yet this continues, as well as widespread views that cryonics is inherently wrong, greedy, or else the work of con men. (This last assumption seems universal among physicians.) Critics usually fail to note that the procedure, which costs around $60,000 for a head-only suspension, is paid by the "patients."

Of course, cryonics is a huge gamble, and I think is best viewed that way. *Skeptic*'s recent piece by Kevin Miller (Vol. 11, #1) follows common practice: interview a cryobiologist, who then cites a transhumanist (not a cryonicist) about techno-optimism. Miller's scientist, Kenneth Storey, cites extreme standards (cells must cool "at least 1000 degrees a minute") without backup argument, says "it will never work for organs," and "they claim they will overturn the laws of physics, chemistry and molecular science"-- using the principle of authority without argument. I wrote an entire novel about cryonics, *Chiller,* under the pseudonym Sterling Blake, and dealt with many of these points, and will not repeat them here. Rather, I propose dealing with such claims as cryonics as nonscientific gambles.

Many thoughtful people discount cryonics because they simply consider it fantastically implausible. But Canadian painted turtles and four species of frogs routinely make it through the winter by freezing, then reviving. These creatures respond to low temperatures by making up a cocktail of glucose, amino acids and a kind of naturally produced antifreeze, glycerol. They manage to move water out of their cells, so that ice crystals form outside delicate membranes. While these animals have special adaptations, their body chemistries are not bizarre. Their methods could be extended artificially to mammals, like us.

Based on such reasoning, cryonics has gathered momentum, largely unnoticed by the world. Over sixty are now suspended in liquid nitrogen, with many hundreds signed up to be.

Many others regard cryonics as creepy and pointless; the notion calls up images of the cold grave, zombies, etc. Still, as eerie ideas go, being frozen strikes me as less horrific than turning into food for worms, or being cremated. (When cremation started out commercially, bodies were burned during a church service. The businesses quickly added organ music, because mourners wondered about the loud bang that often interrupted the funeral. It was the skull of the deceased, exploding.)

So if not especially creepy, is it none the less pointless? That is, are cryonicists making a reasonable bet?

That depends on many factors. Any vision of the future does. To analyze them in more than an arm-waving way, I'll work out here a simple method for quantitatively thinking about future possibility. The method can work on many ideas.

The simplest way to consider any proposed idea is to separate it into smaller, better-defined puzzles. This atomizing of issues is crucial to science, since it is easier to ponder one problem at a time. This approach has been applied to nonscientific questions, many closely allied to science.

✡

I'm going to have to use equations here, but they'll be simple. So will my method. If every issue I raise is independent of the other questions, then we can simply multiply all the probability estimates together at the end to get the total likelihood of cryonics working. This probably is not true, but to do better one must know the future in detail.

What kind of concerns enter here? I'll break them down into three categories—the metaphysical, the social, and the technical.

First, the metaphysical. To preserve people's minds, we naturally think of saving their brains. What are the chances that the brain carries the mind? This is the materialistic world view, and the chances that it is correct I'll label with a probability $\underline{M}$. I'm a solid materialist, like most scientists, so I'd say that $\underline{M}$=.99, i.e., 99% chance that some vital soul does not leave the body when metabolism stops. There is evidence for this, actually. People cooled down to a state of clinical death on operating tables, for brain surgery, revive with their sense of self intact.

Next, what are the odds that our brain structure tells the whole story? That is, that your Self is not the product of continuing electrical activity in the brain? Here, too, the cooled patients seem to show that though their brain rhythms cease, they persist when revived.

Further, some people have gotten jolts of heavy current which completely swamped their delicate internal electrical circuits. This happens to hundreds of people struck by lightning every year in the U.S., and occurred in routine shock treatments earlier in this century. They survived with memory intact, except for short-term recall.

Our minds, then, are somewhat hardwired, though rewritable programs inscribed in the cells of our brains. So I'll set this probability that our Essence is in brain cells, not momentary brain activity, at $\underline{E}$=.99.

Finally, there is the chance that your Self can make it through the process of being frozen down to liquid nitrogen temperatures. The trick is to get to the brain quickly, before it degrades.

Several years ago a boy survived drowning in a cold lake, reviving after an hour spent clinically dead. Even if cryonically suspended immediately—which means being perfused with a glycerol-type solution to minimize damage while being cooled—there lurk the huge unknowns of what this perfusion does to your memories. Studies show that the most damage is done when brains are rewarmed. Neuronal membranes are ripped, pierced. Even so, experimental animals revive with memories intact. And the perfusion technology will certainly improve. Let's be optimistic and put the probability that the Self will persist through this Transition process, $\underline{T}$, at T=0.9.

Then the metaphysical factors, $\underline{MET}$=(.99)(.99)(.9), or just about 0.9.

Next, the social issues. First, what are the odds that your brain (and body, presumably—but the Self is in the brain, remember) will make it to some far off revival time without some accident thawing you out? Call this $\underline{S}$, the chances for Survival of your brain.

Many issues enter here. Presently, all cryonics patients are kept in steel containers, carefully watched. This hasn't always been so; financial failures doomed several to thawing in the two decades after Ettinger's pioneering book. But none have been lost in over a decade, and the first man frozen (a professor named Bedford, incidentally) is still coasting along at 77 degrees above absolute zero after 35 years. Given that cryonics is far more sturdy now, let me set the brain survival odds S=0.9.

Sure, one can say, but what about the odds that society as a whole will make it through for, say, a century? Call this factor O, the Odds against civilization itself being rich enough to not make cryonics impossible. This includes the chances that society will turn irrational, or break down (war, economic depression), or will take a fervent dislike to science, or to cryonics itself.

The economics of cryonics are modest. Liquid nitrogen is the third cheapest fluid, after water and crude oil, and is widely useful, so it will probably be available in even damaged economies. Of course, even democracies can decide to suppress those arrogant enough to spend their money on a chancy voyage across time into an unknown future. So I will set the Odds of social continuity allowing cryonics at O=.8. Probably in Europe this number should be much lower.

Ah, but what if the cryonics organizations themselves don't last? This is a real worry, because the collapse of Cryonic Interment Inc. in California during the mid–1970s lost suspended patients.

The longest-lived institutions in human history have been religious, with the Catholic church arguably holding the record at nearly 2000 years. Cryonics has some of the aura of a religion, with deeply persuaded people sustaining a long–range hope of personal salvation. Maybe that will help.

Still, greedy corporate directors could someday simply find it more profitable to keep tapping the assets left behind by the patients, rather than investing in reviving them. (See Simak's *Why Call Them Back From Heaven?* for a plausible argument that this would indeed occur.)

Or somebody could simply embezzle the funds, a la Enron. The more popular cryonics becomes, the bigger will be the spoils. Call this probability of cryonics organization failure C, and my guess is that C=0.5—a fifty–fifty chance that the whole shebang will go under. After all, we're talking about a wait that could be a century. How many of today's corporations are that old? About one percent.

These social factors I estimate at SOC=(0.9)(0.8)(0.5)=0.36, or a bit better than a third.

I can hear the tech types impatiently asking, can it be done at all? And there's the rub. From the METaphysical to SOCial factors we come to the issues which blend the two—is revival TECHnically possible, given the social and philosophical assumptions?

Cryonics began with no clear idea of how revival could be done. That gave rise to a standard joke, about how many cryonicists it took to screw in a light bulb. The answer was none—they just sit in the dark and wait for the technology to improve.

The rise of nanotechnology over the last decade has made it the favored mechanism for cryonics. Nanotech envisions self–replicating machines of molecular size, programmed with orders to repair freezing damage, bind up torn membranes, and generally knit together the sundered house of a frozen brain.

There appears to be no fundamental physical reason why such tiny machines can't be made on the scale of a billionth (nano–) of a meter. The rewards of developing such handy devices would be immense, a revolution in human society (which is why the SOC issues intertwine with the tech ones, as I'll discuss below).

Not only must this marvelous technology appear, but we must survive its flowering. This is tricky; runaway use of nanotech could produce virulent diseases or everything–eaters that could wipe us out. Modern, Promethean technology, like nuclear physics, shares this daunting property.

I suspect that we will take at least fifty years, and more plausibly a century, to develop nanotech able to repair freezing damage. The good thing about being frozen is that you aren't going anywhere; you can afford to wait.

Given these immense uncertainties, I put the chances that the Technology will arrive and we will survive it at T=0.5.

But of course, a future society must have the <u>desire</u> to apply the technology to cryonics. If we do not yield to a kind of temporo–centric insulation, and cease to be curious about representatives from a century before, I suspect we will have the cultural Energy to work out nanotech for cryonics purposes. (After all, much of it will be useful in curing and repairing ordinary, living people.) So I put this cultural Energy probability, <u>E</u>, at <u>E</u>=0.9.

Still, will they pay the bill? The first few revived cryonicists will probably get onto the 22nd century's talk shows. Famous suspended people, too. (Wouldn't you pay a bit to talk to Benjamin Franklin? He was the first American to speculate on means for preserving people for later revival. And the philosopher Francis Bacon died of pneumonia caught experimenting with suspension of animals.) But if there are ten thousand cryonicists waiting to be thawed...

This is a major, imponderable problem. Humanitarians will argue that spending money on the living is always morally superior to spending it on the dead–but–salvageable.

Will this argument win the day? Or, in the fullness of time, will nanotech make revival so cheap that the cost factor, <u>C</u>, becomes a non–issue? You can argue it either way—and science fiction writers already have.

Given such uncertainties, I'll guess that the cost probability factor <u>C</u>=0.5.

Finally, there is the truly unknowable factor, <u>H</u>, which stands for the contrariness of Humans. Some powerful social force may emerge which makes cryonics reprehensible. After all, many think it's creepy, a kind of Stephen King idea.

Maybe people will utterly lose interest in the past. I doubt this, noting that the world was fascinated with the frozen man found in the Alps in 1991. Considerable expense went into careful examination of this remarkably preserved inhabitant of about 4000 years ago, and his clothing and belongings will tell us much about his era—but still, he can't speak, as a revived cryonicist could.

Or perhaps some other grand issue will captivate human society, making cryonics and the whole problem of death irrelevant. Maybe we'll lose interest in technology itself. Factor in also the Second Coming of Christ, or arrival of aliens who spirit us all away—the choices are endless.

But all rather unlikely, I suspect. I'm rather optimistic about Humanity, so I'll take the odds that we'll still care about suspended cryonicists to be fairly large, perhaps <u>H</u>=0.9.

This means that the <u>TECH</u> issues multiply out to (0.5)(0.9)(0.5)(0.9)=0.2.

All this homework done, we can now savor our final result. The probability that cryonics will work, delivering you to a high–tech future, blinking in astonishment, is

MET x SOC x TECH = 0.07

A 7 percent chance.

Do I "believe" this number? Of course not. It is very rough. Such calculations are worthwhile only if they sharpen our thinking, not as infallible guides. Some decry numerical estimates as hopelessly deceptive, too exact in matters which are slippery and qualitative. True, for some, but the goal here is to use some simple arithmetic means of assessing, then planning. This does not rule out emotional issues; it merely places them in perspective.

✧

Science fiction invented cryonics; it is, after all, an assertion about the future. It first figured in a Neil R. Jones sf story in the 1931 *Amazing Stories*, inspiring Dr. Robert Ettinger to propose the idea eventually in detail in *The Prospect of Immortality* (1964). It has since been explored in Clifford Simak's *Why Call Them Back From Heaven?* (1967), Fred Pohl's *The Age of the Pussyfoot* (1969), and in innumerable space flight stories (such as *2001: A Space Odyssey*) which use cryonics for long-term storage of the crew. Fred Pohl became a strong advocate of cryonics, even appearing on the Johnny Carson show to discuss it. Robert Heinlein used cryonics as part of a time–traveling plot in *The Door Into Summer*. Larry Niven coined "corpsicle" to describe such "deanimated" folk. All these stories considered the long-term aspects.

But even science fiction writers fascinated by it (Simak, Heinlein) never made arrangements to be "suspended," as the cryonicists say. I know of no sf writer who has publicly endorsed cryonics as a plausible possibility, except for Charles Platt, with the further marginal exception of a deposition Arthur

C. Clarke made several years ago to support a court case.

Why do even those intrigued not gamble? Maybe writers without much cash think it's too chancy an investment. To wax numerical a bit more, suppose you regard cryonics purely as an investment. Does it yield a good return?

Well, what's a person worth? Most Americans will work about fifty years at a salary in the range of around $20,000 to $30,000 per year—that is the national average today. In other words, they will make somewhere between one and two million dollars in their lifetime.

One crude way to size up an investment is to take the probability of success (7% by our estimate here) times the expected return (a million dollars, earned by the revived person). Then compare with the amount you must invest to achieve your aim. This yields $70,000, which is in the range of what cryonics costs today. (Cryonicists buy a life insurance policy which pays off their organization upon their death; they don't finance it all at once.)

The goal of cryonics is not money but time—a future life. Another way to see if cryonics is a rational gamble is to take a person's expected life span (about 75 years) and divide it by the expected gain in years if they are revived in the future. This would be perhaps another 75 years, but if the technology for revival exists, people may quite possibly live for centuries. Then the ratio of gained years to present life span is, say, 150 years divided by 75 years, or a factor of 2. It could be higher, of course.

Then even if the probability of success is 1%, say, the probable yield from the investment of your time would be 2 x 1% = 2%. It would make sense to invest 2% of your time in this gamble. Then 2% of your lifetime earnings (a million dollars) would be at least $20,000, which you could use to pay your cryonics fees.

Or you could choose to invest 2% of your time—half an hour a day—to working for cryonics. Make it a hobby. You would meet interesting people and might enjoy it. Most people spend more time than that in the bathroom.

Take another angle. Probability estimates should tell us the range of outcomes, not just an average number like 7%. To be a flagrant optimist, I could go back and take all the loosely technical issues to be much more probable, so that TECH=0.9, say. Then we get 29% probability.

This is just about the upper end of the plausible range, for me. I could be a gloomy pessimist, with equal justification, and take the social issues to be SOC=0.05, say. Then my original 7% estimate becomes less than one percent.

So the realm of plausible probabilities, to me, is between one percent and about 30%.

Low odds like one percent emerge because we consider many factors, each of which is fairly probable, but the remorseless act of multiplying them together yields a final low estimate. This is entirely natural to us. Studies show that most people of even temperament, considering chains of events, are invariably optimistic. We don't atomize issues, but look for obliging conditions. This seems to be built into us.

I've dwelled on using this simple probability estimate to show some properties of the method. The deeper question is whether it truly makes sense to break up any future possibility into a set of mutually independent possibilities.

This comes powerfully into play in the SOC factors. Once the TECH issues look good, people will begin to change their minds about cryonics. The prospect of longer life may well make society more stable so O gets larger. Cryonics organizations will fare better, so C improves. The slicing up into factors assumes that the general fate of humankind is the same for the folk of the freezers, and this may not be so.

Cryonicists are a hard-nosed, practical lot, in my experience. They have many technical skills. Society might even crash badly, and they would keep their patients suspended through extraordinary effort. They have already done so. Police raided a cryonics company in the late 1980s (Alcor) and demanded that a recently frozen patient be handed over for autopsy. Someone spirited away and hid the patient until Alcor could get the police and district attorney off their back, but not before the police hauled five staff members off to jail and ransacked the facility.

Perhaps a better way to analyze this is to note that the biggest uncertainties lie in the intertwined SOC and TECH factors. A techno-optimist might say that cryonics will probably work on technical grounds, but social factors lessen the odds, maybe to the 50/50 range.

✧

Of course, numbers don't tell the whole tale. Ray Bradbury once said he was interested in any chance of seeing the future, but when he thought over cryonics, he realized that he would be torn away from everything he loved. What would the future be worth without his wife, his children, his friends? No, he told me, he wouldn't take the option at any price.

Still, he came into this world without all those associations. And further, why assume that nobody else would go with him? This is an example of the "neighborhood" argument, which says that mature people are so entwined with their surroundings, people and habits of mind, that to yank them out is a trauma worse than death. One is fond of one's own era, certainly. But it seems to me that ordinary immigrants often face similar challenges and manage to come through.

Still, if you truly feel this way, no arithmetic argument will dissuade you. For many, I suspect, the future isn't open to rational gambles, because it is too deeply embedded in emotional issues.

So it must be with any way of thinking quantitatively about our future. We cannot see the range of possibilities without imposing our own values and views, mired in our time, culture, and place. Often, these are the things we value most—our idiosyncratic angles on the world.

But there is one clear advantage to cryonics: It allows one to die with some sliver of hope.

Gregory Benford is a professor of physics at the University of California, Irvine. He the author of many novels, notably *Timescape*, and the nonfiction *Deep Time* and *Beyond Human*.

Copyright © 2007 by Gregory Benford

Views expressed by guest or resident columnists are entirely their own.

FROM THE HEART'S BASEMENT

by Barry Malzberg

Barry N. Malzberg won the very first Campbell Memorial Award, and is a multiple Hugo and Nebula nominee. He is the author or co-author of more than 90 books.

WHAT WE NEED

"I am going to ask you nicely to please exclude the Fee Department from your constant appeals demanding contributions for birthdays, job exits, engagements, etc. Persons in the Fee Department, poorly socialized, are so employed because the job combines our intellectual arrogance with our need to be humiliated."
David Schiller
1984 Memo to the Scott Meredith Literary Agency Bookkeeper

✧

Richard E. Geis, one of the most prominent of all our fanzine editors, died in March, a few months ago as you read this. He was 86 and had been silent for a long time—but from the late '60s to the early '80s his fanzine under a variety of titles—*Psychotic, Science Fiction Review, The Alien Critic*, and finally, simply *Richard E. Geis, c*ame out three or four times a year and virtually dominated the critical apparatus of science fiction. *Science Fiction Review* (to pick the title of greatest convenience) was essentially a 60-to-70-page monologue by Geis, frequently interrupted by letters, reviews from many sources including Geis himself, and articles by professionals and fans of varying degrees of prominence. The then-*Psychotic* constituted in 1968 my introduction to fanzines and fandom: I had recently been appointed editor of *Amazing* and *Fantastic* and Ted White conducted a brief phone interview which he then transcribed (with occasional accuracy) for Geis's magazine. Not to put too fine a point on this, White depicted me as a foolish, babbling nonentity "with big plans" for these wretched publications and lesser plans for its publisher, Sol Cohen, who I described with contempt. It was to shudder even as it opened the door to an amphitheatre I had never known existed. The pages—not only those few devoted to me—teemed with hostility and mutual contempt. They were composed by a number of people who seemed to know one another very well and who with some exceptions pretty well hated one another. Fans, pros, editors wrote venomously to and about one another. Geis moderated with a very light hand, and now and then tossed in some lighter fluid. An edifyingly unpleasant compilation.

Judy-Lynn del Rey, then the Assistant Editor of *Galaxy*, had alerted me to the White interview and suggested that I let her send me a copy. "The pleasure of this," she said (and she did use the word "pleasure" in its broadest sense) is that after a while you find that you know everybody writing for this and it gives you some insights which you'd never expect." This was true.

Psychotic and its later incarnations was addictive of course, and Judy-Lynn was right, seemingly everyone wrote for Geis (who did not pay for letters but paid a cent a word in the '70s for articles). Ted White, Harry Harrison, John Brunner, Joanna Russ, Robert Coulson, Terry Carr, Juanita Coulson, Donald A. Wollheim…there was hardly a pro or Big Name Fan of that era who did not eventually or sooner publish in this magazine. Geis presided like an intermittently benign or long-suffering Head Resident of a mental hospital ward and the debate, the confessions, the autobiography, envy, recriminations soared like the pre-disaster Hindenburg. My first published nonfiction—outraged letters and significantly clumsy reviews—appeared there.

Joanna Russ, who was then at the peak or depth of her feminism (good ideology, but it wrecked her fiction, may she rest in peace), wrote Geis in the mid-seventies demanding that he take her off the mailing list. It was a demand akin to a plea. Some of my readers might ask why Russ did not simply dispose of *Science Fiction Review* unread (she lived an unsupervised private life) but I would not be among them. Joanna was conceding the madly addictive nature of Geis's publication. "You see it in your mailbox and you know that you are getting it because they are writing about *you*," Dean Koontz said to me back then, "And as much as you hate it, you can't keep your hands away." He laughed uncomfortably. (Geis made a lot of us laugh uncomfortably.)

This was so, not really because of the informational content (which for non-professionals was simply gossip, and for the professionals only a sullen confirmation of their insight) but due to Geis's special ability, a talent unduplicated I believe in the history of science fiction (only Ray Palmer could be seen as a lower-level rival) if not politics (Nixon notably had this and so did Lyndon Johnson and so did JFK, the latter in relation to adult women): Geis and his publication brought out the worst in everyone. The resentment, the envy, the slabs of rather disgraceful autobiography, all of these were laid out on the page (and then drawing responses in kind) like patients etherized upon a table. I would like to give specifics (and most of the principals at a distance of forty years are deceased) but it is simple courtesy not to do so. I will offer one example since the man, a great writer by the way, has been dead for 18 years and was quite willing *in situ* to reveal everything: John Brunner wrote of his artistic paralysis (due to excessive and improper medication for depression), his impotence (same etiology), his alarming financial situation (publishers were against him) with a searing vulnerability and detail which made me shudder. "Why is he doing this?" I thought. That was slightly before my understanding of Geis evolved. He brought out and celebrated with hand-rubbing pleasure the worst case, the default versions of ourselves. We paraded through his publication like the hundred-year-old Civil War veterans in a Flannery O'Connor story. We beat the drums and the drums were ourselves.

Geis's Book of the Grotesque (pace Sherwood Anderson) won him six or eight or a dozen Hugos for best fanzine and more than a couple for Best Fan Writer. His publication was the most-read and probably the largest-circulated fan magazine (I exclude Richard Shaver-related material) in the history of the genre. Geis's powerful, founding insight was very close to that of David Schiller, quoted as epigraph: science fiction writers (like fee department employees, and there was historically some overlap) needed to be humiliated. No less than their intellectual arrogance did self-abnegation drive them. Back then (and to some degree even now) it was *Herovit's World* with all of its apparatus…contemptuous editors, contemptuous literary critics, contemptuous academics and spouses and friends. To write science fiction in mid-century (read Phil Dick's introduction to his 1980 collection *The Golden Man*) was to board Charon's boat and take the Styx to a very known destination. Geis, a trouper (and a successful writer of soft-core pornography) was more than pleased and certainly possessed a Captain's skills. Off we went, the mad saints of maddened and uncontrollable technology. *Science Fiction Review*, our very own private Objective Correlative.

Can't say I miss the publication and—having never met Geis, who was unsurprisingly a recluse—can't say I miss its editor either. But Richard Erwin Geis was an essential part of my continuing doomed education. He liked *Overlay*, by the way. "Light and funny and enjoyable." He thought I should write more comedy.

—*New Jersey, March 2013*

Copyright ©2013 by Barry N. Malzberg

PHOENIX PICK PRESENTS

This is where the publisher gets to showcase one of Phoenix Pick's hidden gems.

Something strange happens to Joe and Marge on the way to El Paso. They run into Throckmorton P. Ruddygore, a strange wizard who informs them that they are going to die in nineteen minutes and eighteen seconds.

But they also have a choice. They can abandon the current world by taking a ferryboat across the Sea of Dreams to a new life in a new world, full of magic, fairies and wonder.

But along with all its wonders, the new world is also the site of an ancient battle still being fought between the forces of Evil and Good, and the forces of Hell threaten to unleash perpetual darkness.

Joe and Marge not only need their wits to survive in this unpredictable and dangerous world, but must somehow help prevent the oncoming Armageddon.

✧

Please note that the following is an excerpt from the book, not a complete story.

BOOK ONE
THE RIVER OF DANCING GODS
JACK L. CHALKER

CHAPTER 1:
ENCOUNTER ON A LONELY ROAD

People taken from other universes should always be near death.
—The Books of Rules, XX, 109, 234(a)

Just because your whole life is going to hell doesn't mean you have to walk there.

She was walking down a lonely stretch of west Texas freeway in the still dark of the early morning, an area where nobody walked and where there was no place to walk to, anyway. She might have been hitching, or not, but a total lack of traffic gave her very little choice there. So she was just walking, clutching a small overnight bag and a purse that was almost the same size, holding on to them as if they were the only two real things in her life, they and the dark and that endless stretch of west Texas freeway.

Whatever traffic there was seemed to be heading the other way—an occasional car, or pickup, or eighteen-wheeler with someplace to go and some reason to go there, all heading in the direction she was walking from, and where, she knew too well, there was nothing much at all for anybody. But if their destinations were wrong, their sense of purpose separated the night travelers from the woman on the road; people who had someplace to go and something to do belonged to a different world than she did.

She had started out hitching, all right. She'd made it to the truck stop at Ozona, that huge, garish, ultramodern, and plastic heaven in the middle of nowhere that served up anything and everything twenty-four hours a day for those stuck out here, going between here and there. After a time, she'd gotten another ride, this one only twenty miles west and at a cost she was not willing to pay. And so here she was, stuck out in the middle of nowhere, going nowhere fast. Walk, walk, walk to nowhere, from nowhere in particular, because nowhere was all the where she had to go.

Headlights approached from far off; but even if they had held any interest for her, they were still too far away to be more than abstract, jerky round dots in the distance, a distance that the west Texas desert made even more deceptive. How far off was the oncoming driver? Ten miles? More? Did it matter?

It was at least ten, maybe fifteen minutes before the vehicle grew close enough for the woman to hear the roar of the big diesel and realize that this was, in fact, one of those haunters of the desert dark, a monster tractor-trailer truck with a load of furniture for Houston or beef for New Orleans or, perhaps, California oranges for the Nashville markets. Although it had been approaching her from the west for some time, its sudden close-up reality was startling against the total stillness of the night, a looming monster that quickly illuminated the night and its empty, vacant walker, then was just as suddenly gone, a mass of diminishing red lights in the distance behind her. But in the few seconds that those gaping headlights had shone on the scene, they had illuminated her form against that desperate dark, illuminated her and, in the cab behind those lights, gave her notice and recognition.

She paid this truck no more attention than any of the others and just kept walking onward into the unseen distance.

The driver had been going much too fast for a practical stop, a pace that would have upset the highway patrol but was required to make his employer's deadline. Besides, he was on the wrong side of the median to be of any practical help himself—but there were other ways, ways that didn't even involve slowing down.

"Break one-nine, break, break. How 'bout a westbound? Anybody in this here Lone Star truckin' west on this one dark night?" His accent was Texarkana, but he could have been from Maine or Miami or San Francisco or Minneapolis just as well. Something in the CB radio seemed automatically to add the standard accent, even in Brooklyn.

"You got a westbound. Go," came a reply, only very slightly different in sound or tone from the caller's.

"What's your twenty?" Eastbound asked.

"Three-thirty was the last I saw," Westbound responded. "Clean and green back to the truck-'em-up. Even the bears go to sleep this time o' night in these parts."

Eastbound chuckled. "Yeah, you got that right. I got to keep pushin' it, though. They want me in Shreveport by tonight."

"Shreveport! You got some haul yet!"

"Yeah, but that's home sweet home, baby. Get in, get it off, stick this thing in the junkyard, and I'm in bed with the old lady. I'll make it."

"All I got is El Paso by ten."

"Aw, shit, you'll make that easy. Say—caught something your side in my lights about three-two-seven or so you might check out. Looked like a beaver just walkin' by the side of the road. Maybe a breakdown, though I ain't seen no cars on your side and I'm just on you now. Probably nothin', but you might want to check her out just in case. Ain't nobody lives within miles o' here, I don't think."

"I'll back off a little and see if I can eyeball her," Westbound assured him. "Won't hurt much. That your Kenworth just passed me?"

"Yeah. Who else? All best to ya, and check on that little gal. Don't wanna hear she got found dead by the side of the road or something. Spoil my whole day."

"That's a four," Westbound came back with a slight chuckle.

"Keep safe, keep well, that's the Red Rooster sayin' that, eastbound and down."

"Y'all have a safe one. This is the Nighthawk, westbound and backin' down."

Nighthawk put his mike into its little holder and backed down to fifty. He wasn't in any hurry, and he wouldn't lose much, even if this was nothing at all, not on this flat stretch.

The woman was beginning to falter, occasionally stumbling in the scrub brush by the side of the road. She was starting to think again, and that wasn't what she wanted at all. Finally she stopped, knowing it was beyond her to take too many more steps, and looked around. It was incredible how dark the desert could be at night, even with more stars than city folk had ever seen beaming down from overhead. No matter what, she knew she had to get some rest. Maybe just lie down over there in the scrub—get stung by a tarantula or a scorpion or whatever else lived around here. Snake, maybe. She considered the idea and was somewhat surprised that she cared about that. Nice and quick, maybe—but painfully bitten or poisoned to death by inches? That seemed particularly ugly. With everything else so messed up, at least her exit ought to be clean, neat, and as comfortable as these things could be. *One* thing in her life should go right, damn it. And for the first time since she'd jumped out of the car, she began to consider living again—at least a little bit longer, at least until the sunrise. She stopped and looked up and down the highway for any sign of lights, wondering what she'd do if she saw any. It would just as likely be another Cal Hurder as anybody useful, particularly at this ungodly hour in a place like this.

Lights approaching from the east told her a decision was near, and soon. But she made no decision until the lights were actually on her, and when she did, it was on impulse, without any thought applied to it. She turned, put down her bags, and stuck out her thumb.

Even with that and on the lookout for her, he almost missed her. Spotting her, he hit the brakes and started gearing to a stop by the side of the road, getting things stopped fully a hundred yards west of her. Knowing this, he put the truck in reverse and slowly backed up, eyeing the shoulder carefully with his right mirror. After all this, he didn't want to be the one to run her down.

Finally he saw her, or thought he did, just standing there, looking at the huge monster approaching, doing nothing else at all. For her part, she was unsure of just what to do next. That huge rig was really intimidating, and so she just stood there, trembling slightly.

Nighthawk frowned, realized she wasn't coming up to the door, and decided to put on his flashers and go to her. He was not without his own suspicions; hijackers would use such bait and such a setting—although he could hardly imagine somebody hijacking forty thousand pounds of soap flakes. Still, you never knew—and there was always his own money and cards and the truck itself to steal. He took out his small pistol and slipped it into his pocket, then slid over, opened the passenger door, and got out warily.

He was a big man, somewhat intimidating-looking himself, perhaps six-three, two hundred and twenty-five pounds of mostly muscle, wearing faded jeans, boots, and a checkered flannel shirt. His age was hard to measure, but he was at least in his forties with a face maybe ten years older and with very long, graying hair. He was dark, too—she took him at first for a black man—but there was something not quite of any race and yet of all of them in his face and features. He was used to the look she was giving him and past minding.

"M'am?" he called to her in a calm yet wary baritone. "Don't worry—I don't bite. A trucker going the other way spotted you and asked me to see if you was all right."

Oh, what the hell, she decided, resigning herself. *I can always jump out again.* "I need a ride," she said simply. "I'm kind of stuck here."

He walked over to her, seeing her tenseness and pretty much ignoring it. He picked up her bag, letting her get her purse, and went back to the truck. "Come on. I'll take you for a while if you're going west."

She hesitated a moment more, then followed him and permitted him to assist her up into the cab. He slammed her door, walked around the truck, got in on the driver's side, released the brakes, and put the truck in gear. "How far you going?" he asked her.

She sat almost pressed against the passenger door, trying to look as if she weren't doing it. For all he knew, she *didn't* realize she was doing it.

She sighed. "Any place, I guess. How far you going?"

"El Paso. But I can get you to a phone in Fort Stockton if that's what you need."

She shook her head slowly. "No, nobody to call. El Paso's fine, if it's okay with you. I don't have enough money for a motel or anything."

Up to speed and cruising now, he glanced sideways over at her. At one time she'd been a pretty attractive woman, he decided. It was all still there, but something had happened to it, put a dull, dirty coating over it. Medium height—five-four or -five, maybe—with short, greasy-looking brown hair with traces of gray. Thirties, probably. Thin and slightly built, she had that hollow, empty look, like somebody who'd been on the booze pretty long and pretty hard.

"None of my business, but how'd you get stuck out here in the middle of nowhere at three in the morning?" he asked casually.

She gave a little sigh and looked out the window for a moment at the black nothingness. Finally she said, "If you really want to know, I jumped out of a car."

"Huh?"

"I got a ride with a salesman—at least he said he was a salesman—back at Ozona. We got fifteen, twenty miles down the road and he pulled over. You can guess the rest."

He nodded.

"I grabbed the bags and ran. He turned out to be a little scared of the dark, I guess. Just stood there yelling for me, then threatened to drive off if I didn't come back. I didn't—and he did."

He lighted a cigarette, inhaled deeply, and expelled the smoke with an accompanying sigh. "Yeah, I guess I get the picture."

"You—you're an Indian, aren't you?"

He laughed. "Good change of subject. Well, sort of. My mom was a full-blooded Seminole, my dad was Puerto Rican, which is a little bit of everything."

"You're from Florida? You don't sound like a southerner."

Again he chuckled. "Oh, I'm from the south, all right. South of Philadelphia, anyway. Long story. Right now what home I have is in a trailer park in a little town south of Baltimore. No Indians or Puerto Ricans around, so they just think of me as something a little bit exotic, I guess."

"You're a long way from home," she noted.

He nodded. "More or less. Don't matter much, though. I'm on the road so much the only place I really feel at home is in this truck. I own it and I run it, and it's mine as long as I keep up the payments. They had to let me keep the truck, otherwise they couldn't get no alimony. What about you? That pretty voice sounds pure Texas to me."

She nodded idly, still staring distantly into the nothingness. "Yeah. San Antone, that's me."

"Air Force brat?" He was nervous at pushing her too much, maybe upsetting or alienating her—she was on a thin edge, that was for sure—but he just had the feeling she wanted to talk to somebody.

She did, a little surprised at that herself. "Sort of. Daddy was a flier. Jet pilot."

"What happened to him?" He guessed by her tone that something had happened.

"Killed in his plane, in the finest traditions of the Air Force. Sucked a bird into his jets while coming in for a landing and that was it, or so I'm told. I was much too young, really, to remember him any more than as a vague presence. And the pictures, of course. Momma kept all the pictures. The benefits, though, they weren't all that much. He was only a captain, after all, and a new one at that. So Momma worked like hell at all sorts of jobs to bring me up right. She was solid Oklahoma—high school, no marketable skills, that sort of thing. Supermarket checker was about the highest she got—pretty good, really, when you see the benefits they get at the union stores. She did really well, when you think about it—except it was all for me. She didn't have much else to live for. Wanted me to go to college—she'd wanted to go, but never did. Well, she and the VA and a bunch of college loans got me there, all right, and got me through, for all the good it did. Ten days after I graduated with a useless degree in English Lit, she dropped dead from a heart attack. I had to sell the trailer we lived in all those years just to make sure she was buried right. After paying out all the stuff she owed, I had eight hundred dollars, eight pairs of well-worn jeans, a massive collection of T-shirts, and little else."

He sighed. "Yeah, that's rough. I always wanted to go to college, you know, but I never had the money until I didn't have the time. I read a lot, though. It don't pay to get hooked on TV when you're on the road so much."

She chuckled dryly. "College is all well and good and some of it's interesting, but if your degree's not in business, law, medicine, or engineering, the paper's only good for about thirty-eight hundred—that's what I still owe on those loans, and it'll be a cold day in hell before they see a penny. They track you down all over, too—use collection agents. So you can't get credit, can't get a loan, none of that. I got one job teaching junior high English for a year—but they cut back and laid me off. Only time I ever really enjoyed life."

"So you been goin' around from job to job ever since?"

"For a while. But a couple years of working hamburger joints and all those other minimum-wage, minimum-life jobs gets to you. I finally sat down one day and decided it was fate, or destiny, or something. I was getting older, and all I could see was myself years later, sitting in a rented slum shared with a couple of other folks just like me, getting quickies from the night manager. So I figured I would find a man, marry him, and let *him* pay my bills while I got into the cooking and baby business."

"Well, it's a job like any other and has a pretty long history," he noted. "Somebody's got to do it—otherwise the government will do *that*, too."

She managed a wan smile at the remark. "Yeah, well, that's what I told myself, but there are many ways to go about it. You can meet a guy, date, fall in love, really commit yourself—both of you. That might work. But just to go out in desperation and marry the first guy who comes along who'll have you—that's disaster."

"Works the other way, too, honey," he responded. "That's why I'm paying five hundred a month in rehabilitation money—that's what they call alimony these days in liberal states that abolished alimony—

and child support. And she's living with another guy who owns an auto-repair shop and is doing pretty well; she has a kid by him, too. But so long as she don't marry him, I'm stuck."

"You have a kid?"

He nodded. "A son. Irving. Lousy name, but it was the one uncle he had on her side who had money. Not that it got us or him anything. I love him, but I almost never see him."

"Because you're on the road?"

"Naw. You'd be surprised what you can work. I'm supposed to have visitation rights, but somehow he's always away when I come visiting. She don't want him to see me, get to know me instead of her current as his daddy. Uh-uh."

"Couldn't you go to court on that?"

He laughed. "Honey, them courts will slap me in jail so fast if I miss a payment to her it isn't funny—but tell *her* to live up to *her* end of the bargain? Yeah, they'll tell her, and that's that. Tell her and tell her and tell her. Until, one day, you realize that the old joke's true—she got the gold mine in the settlement and I got the shaft. Oh, I suppose I could make an unholy mess trying to get custody, but I'd never win. I'd have to give up truckin', and truckin's all I know how to do. And I'd probably lose, anyway—nine out of ten men do. Even if I won—hell, it's been near five years." He sighed. "I guess at this stage he's better off. I hope so."

"I hope so, too," she responded, sounding genuinely touched, with the oddly pleasing guilt felt when, sunk deep in self-pity, you find a fellow sufferer.

They rode in near silence for the next few minutes, a silence broken only by the occasional crackle from the CB and a report of this or that or two jerks talking away at each other when they could just as easily have used a telephone and kept the world out.

Finally he said, "I guess from what you say that your marriage didn't work out either."

"Yeah, you could say that. He was an Air Force sergeant at Lackland. A drill instructor in basic. We met in a bar and got drunk on the town. He was older and a very lonely man, and, well, you know what I was going through. We just kinda fell into it. He was a pretty rough character, and after all the early fun had worn off and we'd settled down, he'd come home at night and take all his frustrations out on me. It really got to him, after a while, that I was smarter and better educated than he was. He had some inferiority complex. He was hell on his recruits, too—but they got away from him after eight weeks or so. I had him for years. After a while he got transferred up to Reese in Lubbock, but he hated that job and he hated the cold weather and the dust and wind, and that just made it all the worse. Me, I had it really bad there, too, since what few friends I had were all in San Antonio."

"I'd have taken a hike long before," he commented. "Divorce ain't all that bad. Ask my ex."

"Well, it's easy to see that—now. But I had some money for the first time, and a house, and a real sense of something permanent, even if it was lousy. I know it's kind of hard to understand—it's hard to explain. I guess you just had to be me. I figured maybe kids would mellow him out and give me a new direction—but after two miscarriages, the second one damn near killing me, the doctors told me I should never have kids. Probably couldn't, but definitely shouldn't. That just made him meaner and sent me down the tubes. Booze, pot, pills—you name it, I swallowed it or smoked it or sniffed it. And one day—it was my thirtieth birthday—I looked at myself in the mirror, saw somebody a shot-to-hell forty-five looking back at me, picked up what I could use most and carry easy, cashed a check for half our joint account, and took a bus south to think things out. I've been walking ever since—and I still haven't been out of the goddamned state of Texas. I waited tables, swept floors, never stayed long in one spot. Hell, I've sold my body for a plate of eggs. Done everything possible to keep from thinking, looking ahead, worrying. I burned out. I've had it."

He thought about it for a moment, and then it came to him. "But you jumped out of that fella's car."

She nodded wearily. "Yeah, I did. I don't even know why, exactly. Or maybe, yes, I do, too. It was an all-of-a-sudden kind of thing, sort of like when I turned thirty and looked in the mirror. There wasn't any mirror, really, but back there in that car I still kind of looked at myself and was, well, scared, frightened, maybe even revolted at what I saw staring back. Something just sorta said to me, 'If this is the rest of your life, then why bother to be alive at all?'"

He thought, but could find little else to say right then. What *was* the right thing to say to somebody like this, anyway?

Flecks of rain struck his windshield, and he flipped on the wipers, the sound adding an eerie, hypnotic background to the sudden roar of a midsummer thunderstorm on a truck cab. Peering out, he thought for a moment he saw two Interstate 10 roadways—an impossible sort of fork he knew just couldn't be there. He kicked on the brights and the fog lights, and the image seemed to resolve itself a bit, the right-hand one looking more solid. He decided that keeping to the white stripe down the side of the road separating road and shoulder was the safest course.

At the illusory intersection, there seemed for a moment to be two trucks, one coming out of the other, going right, while the other, its ghostly twin, went left. The image of the second truck, apparently passing his and vanishing quickly in the distance to his left, startled him for a moment. He could have sworn there wasn't anything behind him for a couple of miles, and the CB was totally silent.

The rain stopped as suddenly as it had begun, and things took on a more normal appearance in minutes. He glanced over at the woman and saw that she was asleep—best thing for her, he decided. Ahead loomed a green exit sign, and, still a little unnerved, he badly wanted to get his bearings.

The sign said, "Ruddygore, 5 miles."

That didn't help him much. Ruddygore? Where in hell was that? The next exit should be Sheffield. A mile marker approached, and he decided to check things out.

The little green number said, "4."

He frowned again, beginning to become a little unglued. Four? That couldn't be right. Not if he was still on I-10. Uneasily, he began to think of that split back there. Maybe it *was* a split—that other truck had seemed to curve off to the left when he went right. If so, he was on some cockeyed interstate spur to God knew where.

God knew, indeed. As far as *he* knew or could remember, there were no exits, let alone splits, between Ozona and Sheffield.

He flicked on his interior light and looked down at his road atlas, held open by clips to the west Texas map. According to it, he was right—and no sign of any Ruddygore. He sighed and snapped off the light. Well, the thing was wrong in a hundred places, anyway. Luckily he was still ahead of schedule, so a five-mile detour shouldn't be much of a problem. He glanced over to his left again for no particular reason. Funny. The landscaping made it look as if there weren't any lane going back.

A small interstate highway marker, the usual red, white, and blue was between mile markers 3 and 2, but it told him nothing. It didn't even make sense. He was probably just a little crazy tonight, or his eyes were going, but it looked for all the world as if it said:

∞? What the hell was *that*? Somebody in the highway department must have goofed good there, stenciling an 8 on its side.

At the 2, another green sign announced Ruddygore, and there was also a brown sign, like the kind used for parks and monuments. It said, "Ferry—Turn Left at Stop Sign."

Now he knew he had gone suddenly mad. Not just that he knew that I-8 went from Tucson to San Diego and nowhere near Texas, but—a ferry? In the middle of the west Texas desert?

He backed down to slow—very slow—and turned to his passenger. "Hey, little lady. Wake up!"

She didn't stir, and finally he reached over and shook her, repeating his words.

She moved and squirmed and managed to open her eyes. "Um. Sorry. So *tired*…What's the matter? We in El Paso?"

He shook his head. "No. I think I've gone absolutely nuts. Somehow in the storm we took an exit that wasn't supposed to be there and we're headed for a town called Ruddygore. Ever heard of it?"

She shook her head sleepily from side to side. "Nope. But that doesn't mean anything. Why? We lost?"

"Lost ain't the word," he mumbled. "Look, I don't want to scare you or anything, but I think I'm going nuts. You ever hear of a ferryboat around here?"

She looked at him as if he had suddenly sprouted feathers. "A what? Over *what*?"

He nodded nervously and gestured toward the windshield. "Well, then, you read me that big sign."

She rubbed the sleep from her eyes and looked. "Ruddygore—exit one mile," she mumbled.

"And the little brown sign?"

"Ferry," she read, suddenly awake and looking very confused. "And an arrow." She turned and faced him. "How long was I asleep?"

"Five, maybe ten minutes," he answered truthfully. "You can still see the rain on the windshield where the wipers don't reach."

She shook her head in wonder. "It must be across the Pecos. But the Pecos isn't much around here."

"Yeah," he replied and felt for his revolver.

The interstate road went right into the exit, allowing no choice. There was a slight downgrade to a standard stop sign and a set of small signs. To the left, they said, were Ruddygore and the impossible ferry. To the right was—Oblivion.

"I never heard of any town named Oblivion, either," he muttered, "but it sounds right for these parts. Still, all the signs said only Ruddygore, so that's got to be the bigger and closer place. Any place they build an interstate spur to at a few million bucks a mile *has* to have something open even this time of night. Besides," he added, "I'm damned curious to see that ferry in the middle of the desert."

He put on his signals, then made the turn onto a modest two-lane road. He passed under the highway and noted glumly that there wasn't any apparent way of getting back on. Well, he told himself, he'd find it later.

Up ahead in the distance he saw, not the town lights he'd expected, but an odd, circular, lighted area. It was particularly unusual in that it looked something like the kind of throw a huge spotlight, pointed straight down, might give—but there were no signs of lights anywhere. Fingering the pistol, he proceeded on, knowing that the road was leading him to that lighted area.

And it *was* bright when he reached it, although no source was apparent. The road, too, seemed to vanish into it, and the entire surface appeared as smooth as glass. Damnedest thing he'd ever seen, maybe a thousand yards across. He stopped at the edge of it, and both he and the woman strained to see where the light was coming from, but the sky remained black—blacker than usual, since the reflected glow blotted out all but the brightest stars.

"Now, what the hell…?" he mused aloud.

"Hey! Look! Up ahead there, almost in the middle. Isn't that a man?" She pointed through the windshield.

He squinted and nodded. "Yeah. Sure looks like somebody. I don't like this, though. Not at all. There's some very funny game being played here." Again he reached in and felt the comfort of the .38 in his pocket. He put the truck back in gear and moved slowly forward, one eye on the strange figure ahead and the other warily on the woman, whom he no longer trusted. It was a great sob story, but this craziness had started only after she came aboard.

He drove straight for the lone figure standing there in the center of the lighted area at about five miles per hour, applying the hissing air brakes when he was almost on top of the stranger and could see him clearly.

The woman gasped. "He looks like a vampire Santa Claus!"

Her nervous surprise seemed genuine. Certainly her description of the man who stood looking back at them fitted him perfectly. Very tall—six-five or better, he guessed—and very large. "Portly" would be too kind a word. The man had a reddish face, twinkling eyes with laugh lines etched around them, and a huge, full white beard—the very image of Santa Claus on all those Christmas cards. But he was not dressed in any furry red suit, but rather in formal wear—striped pants, morning coat, red velvet vest and cummerbund, even a top hat, and he was also wearing a red-velvet-lined opera cape.

The strange man made no gestures or moves, and finally the driver said, "Look, you wait in the truck. I'm going to find out what the hell this is about."

"I'm coming with you."

"*No!*" He hesitated a moment, then nervously cleared his throat. "Look, first of all, if there's any danger I don't want you between me and who I might have to shoot—understand? And second, forgive me, but I can't one hundred percent trust that you're not in on whatever this is."

That last seemed to shock her, but she nodded and sighed and said no more.

He opened the door, got down, and put one hand in his pocket, right on the trigger. Only then did he walk forward toward the odd figure who stood there, to stop a few feet from the man. The stranger said nothing, but the driver could feel those eyes following his every move and gesture.

"Good morning," he opened. What else was there to say to start things off?

The man in the top hat didn't reply immediately, but seemed to examine him from head to toe as an appraiser might look at a diamond ring. "Oh, yes, you'll do nicely, I think," he said in a pleasant, mellow voice with a hint of a British accent. He looked up at the woman, still in the cab, seemingly oblivious to the glare of the truck lights. "She, too, I suspect, although I really wasn't expecting her. A pleasant bonus."

"Hey, look, you!" the driver called angrily, losing patience. "What the hell *is* all this?"

"Oh, dear me, forgive my manners!" the stranger responded. "But, you see, *you* came *here*, I didn't come to you. Where do you *think* you are—and where do you want to be?"

Because the man was right, it put the driver on the defensive. "Uh, um, well, I seem to have taken a bum turn back on Interstate 10. I'm just trying to get back to it."

The big man smiled gently. "But you never *left* that road. You're still on it. You'll be on it for another nineteen minutes and eighteen seconds."

The driver just shook his head disgustedly. He must be as nutty as he looked, that was for sure. "Look, friend. I got stuck over here by accident in a thunderstorm and followed the road back there to—what was the town? Oh, yeah, Ruddygore. I figure I'll turn around there. Can you just tell me how far it is?"

"Oh, Ruddygore isn't an 'it,' sir," the strange man replied. "You see, *I'm* Ruddygore. Throckmorton P. Ruddygore, at your service." He doffed his top hat and made a small bow. "At least, that's who I am when I'm here."

The driver gave an exasperated sigh. "Okay, that's it. Forget it, buddy. I'll find my own way back."

"The way back is easy, Joe," Ruddygore said casually. "Just follow the road back. But you'll die, Joe—nineteen minutes eighteen seconds after you rejoin your highway. A second storm with hail and a small twister is up there, and it's going to cause you to skid, jackknife, then fall over into a gully. The overturning will break your neck."

He froze, an icy chill going through him. "How did you know my name was Joe?" His hand went back to the .38.

"Oh, it's my business to know these things," the strange man told him. "Recruiting is such a problem with many people, and I must be very limited and very selective for complicated reasons."

Suddenly all of his mother's old legends about conjure men and the demons of death came back from his childhood, where they'd been buried for perhaps forty years—and the childhood fears that went with them returned as well, although he hated himself for it. "Just who—or what—*are* you?"

"Ruddygore. Or a thousand other names, none of which you'd recognize, Joe, I'm no superstition and I'm no angel of death, any more than that truck radio of yours is a human mouth. I'm not causing your death. It is preordained. It cannot be changed. I only know about it—found out about it, you might say—and am taking advantage of that knowledge. That's the hard part, Joe. Finding out. It costs me greatly every time I try and might just kill *me* someday. Compared with that, diverting you here to me was child's play." He looked up at the woman, who was still in the cab, straining to hear. "Shall we let the lady join us?"

"Even if I buy what you're saying—which I don't," Joe responded, "how does she fit in? Is she going to die, too?"

The big man shrugged. "I haven't the slightest idea. Certainly she'll be in the accident, unless you throw her out ahead of time. I expected you to be alone, frankly."

Joe pulled the pistol out and pointed it at Ruddygore. "All right. Enough of this. I think maybe you'll tell me what this all is, really, or I'll put a hole in you. You're pretty hard to miss, you know."

Ruddygore looked pained. "I'll thank you to keep my weight out of this. As for what's going on—I've just told you."

"You've told me nothing! Let's say what you say is for real, just for the sake of argument. You say I'm not dead yet, and you're no conjure spirit, so you pulled me off the main line of my death for something. What?"

"Oh, I didn't say I wasn't involved in magic. Sorcery, actually. That's what I do for a living. I'm a necromancer. A sorcerer." He shrugged. "It's a living—and it pays better than truck driving."

The pistol didn't waver. "All right. You say I'm gonna die in—I guess fifteen minutes or less now, huh?"

"No. Time has stopped for you. It did the moment you diverted to my road. It will not resume until you return to the Interstate, I think you called it."

"So we just stand here and I live forever, huh?"

"Oh, my, no! I have important things to do. I must be on the ferry when it comes. When I leave, you'll be back on that road instantly, deciding you just had a nutty dream—for nineteen minutes eighteen seconds, that is."

Joe thought about it. "And suppose I do a flip, don't keep going west? Or suppose I exit at Fort Stockton? Or pull over to the side for a half hour?"

Ruddygore shrugged. "What difference? You wouldn't know if that storm was going to hit you hard because you were sitting by the side of the road or because you turned back—you can never be sure. I am. You can't avoid it. Whatever you do will take you to your destiny."

Joe didn't like that. He also didn't like the fact that he was taking this all so seriously. It was just a funny man in a circle of—"Where does the light come from?"

"I create it. For stuff like this, I like to work in a spotlight. I'll turn it off if you like." He snapped his fingers, and suddenly the only lights were the truck headlights and running lights, which still illuminated Ruddygore pretty well.

Suddenly the vast sea of stars that was the west Texas sky on a clear night faded in, brilliant and impressive and, somehow, reassuring.

Joe heard the door open and close on the passenger side and knew that the woman was coming despite his cautions. He couldn't really blame her—hell, this was crazy.

"What's going on?" she wanted to know.

Ruddygore turned, bowed low, and said, "Madam, it is a pleasure to meet you, even if you are an unexpected complication. I am Throckmorton P. Ruddygore."

She stared at him, then over at Joe, half in shadow, and caught sight of the pistol in his hand. "Hey—what's this all about?" she called to him, disturbed.

"The man says I'm dead, honey," Joe told her. "He says I'm about to have a fatal accident. He says he's a conjure man. Other than that, he's said nothing at all."

Her mouth opened, then closed and she looked confusedly from one man to the other. She was not a small woman, but she felt dwarfed by the two giants. Finally she said to Ruddygore, "Is he right?"

Ruddygore nodded. "I'm afraid so. Unless, of course, he takes me up on my proposition."

"I figured we'd get to the point of all this sooner or later," Joe muttered.

"Exactly so," Ruddygore agreed. "I'm a recruiter, you see. I come from a place that's not all *that* unfamiliar to people of your world, but which is, in effect, a world of its own. It is a world of men—and others—both very much like and very different from what you know. It is a world both more peaceful and more violent than your Earth. That is, there are no guns, no nuclear missiles, no threats of world holocaust. The violence is more direct, more basic—say medieval. Right now that world is under attack and it needs help. After examining all the factors, I find that help from outside my world might—*might*—have a slight edge, for various reasons too long to go into here. And so I look for recruits, but not just *any* recruits. People with special qualities that will go well over there. People who fit special requirements to do the job. And, of course, people who are about to die and who meet those other requirements are the best recruits. You see?"

"Let me get this straight," the woman put in. "You're from another planet?" She looked up at the stars. "Out there? And you're whisking away people to help you fight a war? And we've got the chance to join up and go—or die?"

"That's about the size of it," Ruddygore admitted. "Although you are not quite right. First of all, I have no idea if *you* will die. I had no idea you would be in the truck. And, as an honorable man, I must admit that he might be able to save you if, after returning to the road, he lets you off. Might. He, however, *is* in the situation you describe. Secondly, I'm no little green man from Mars. The world I speak of is not up *there*, it's—well, somewhere else." He looked thoughtful for a moment.

"Think of it this way," he continued. "Think of opposites. Nature usually contains opposites. There is even, I hear, a different kind of matter, anti-matter, that's as real as we are yet works so opposite to us that, if it came into contact with us, it would cancel itself and us out. When the Earth was created, my world was also created—a by-product, you might say, of the creation. It's very much like Earth, but it is in many ways an opposite. It runs by different rules. But it's as real a place as any you've been to, and, I think, a better, nicer place than Earth in a number of ways."

Far off in the distance there seemed to come a deep sound, like a boat's whistle, or a steam train blowing off. Ruddygore heard it and turned back to Joe.

"You have to decide soon, you know," he told the driver. "The ferry's coming in, and it won't wait long. Although few ride it, because only a very few can find it or even know of it, it keeps a rigid schedule, for the path it travels is impossible unless you're greatly skilled *and* well timed. You can die and pass beyond my ken to the unknown beyond, or you can come with me. Face it, Joe. What have you got to lose? Even if you somehow could beat your destiny, you're only going through the motions, anyway. There's nothing for you in *this* world anymore. I offer a whole new life."

"And maybe just as short," the driver replied. "I did my bit of soldiering."

"Oh, it's not like that. We have many for armies. I need you for special tasks, not military ones. Adventure, Joe. A new life. A new world. I will make you young again. Better than you ever were."

Something snapped inside the driver. "No! You're Satan come to steal me at the last minute! I know you now!" And, with that, he fired three shots point-blank at Ruddygore.

The huge man didn't even flinch, but simply smiled, pursed his lips, and spat out the three spent bullets. "Lousy aim," he commented. "I really didn't catch any of them. I had to use magic." He sighed sadly. The whistle sounded again, closer now. "But I'm not the devil, Joe. I'm flesh and blood and I live. I am not a man, but I was once a man, and still am more than not. There are far worse things than your silly, primitive devil, Joe—that's part of what I'm fighting. Come with me—now. Down to the dock."

Joe looked disgusted, both with Ruddygore and with the pistol. "All right, Ruddygore, or whoever or whatever you are. It don't make any difference, anyway. I can't go. Not if I can save her. You understand the duty."

Ruddygore nodded sadly. "I feared as much when I saw her in the cab. And for such a motive I can't stop you or blame you. Damn! You wouldn't believe how much trouble all this was, too. What a waste."

"Hey! Wait a minute!" the woman put in. "Don't *I* get to say anything about this?"

They both looked at her expectantly.

"Look, if I had a million bucks, I'd bet that I'm still sound asleep in that truck up there, speeding down a highway toward El Paso, and that this is all a crazy dream. But it's a great dream. The best I ever had. I'm on my way to kill myself. I've had it—up to here. I gave up on this stupid, crazy world. So I'm dreaming—or I'm psycho, in some funny world of my own. Okay. I'll take it. It's better than real life. There's no way I'm going back to that life. No way I'm getting back in that truck, period. I've finally done it! Gone completely off my rocker into a fantasy world that sounds pretty good to me."

Ruddygore's face broke into a broad, beaming smile. He looked over at the driver. "Joe? What do you say now?"

"Well, I heard her story and I can't say I blame her. But I'm the one who's gone bananas, not her."

"Dreams," Ruddygore mused. "No, this is no dream, but think of it that way if you like. For, in a sense, we're all just dreams. The Creator's dreams. And where we travel to is out there." He gestured with a cane, gold-tipped and with a dragon's head for a handle. "Out across the Sea of Dreams and beyond to the far shore. So take it as a dream, the both of you, if you wish. As a dream, you have even less to lose."

The pistol finally went down and was replaced in Joe's pocket. He looked back at the truck. "Maybe we should get our things."

"You won't need them," Ruddygore told him. "All will be provided to you as you need it. That's part of the bargain." The whistle sounded a third time, very close now, and Ruddygore turned to face the dark direction of its cry. "Come. Just follow me."

Joe looked back at his truck again. "I should at least kill the motor and the lights," he said wistfully. "That truck's the only thing I got, the only thing I ever had in my whole life that was real. This ferry—I don't suppose…?"

Ruddygore shook his head sadly. "No, I'm afraid not. Your truck wouldn't work over there. The captain would never allow it, anyway, because we couldn't get it off the boat and it would take up too much room. But don't worry about it, Joe. It's not really here, you see. It's somewhere back there, on your Interstate 10."

With that the truck faded and was gone, lights, engine noise, and all, and they were in total darkness.

The whistle sounded once more, and it seemed almost on top of them.

CHAPTER 2:
ACROSS THE SEA OF DREAMS

Travel between universes shall be difficult and highly restricted.

—XXI, 55, 44(b)

The ferry came out of the darkness, floating on a sea of black. It surprised them that it looked very much like the old ferryboats—an oval-shaped, double-ended affair with a lower platform for cars, and stairways up both sides to the upper deck, where the twin pilothouses, one at each end of the boat, flanked a passenger lounge of some sort with a large single stack rising right up the middle. The sides of the car deck weren't solid, but were punctuated by five large openings on each side, openings without windows or other obstructions, yet the car deck could not be seen through them.

Each one of the huge, round holes had a gigantic oar sticking out of it. The oars were in a raised position, seemingly locked in place. It was clear from the engine sounds and the wisps of white from the stack that the captain was using his engine.

"I never saw a ferry except in pictures," the woman remarked, "but I bet nobody ever saw one with oars before."

Ruddygore nodded. "The engine's in good shape for settling in on this side, but, once out on the sea and to the other shore, that kind of mechanical power just isn't possible to use." He paused a moment. "Ah! It's docked! Shall we go aboard?"

Joe stood there and stared for a minute. "Funny," he muttered, mostly to himself. "I swear I've seen this thing before someplace. Way, way back and long ago. When I was a kid." He scratched his head a moment, then snapped his fingers. "Yeah! Sure! The old Chester ferry. Long, long ago." He peered into the gloom, but the illumination from the passenger deck allowed him to see what he was looking for. "Yeah. There on the side. Kinda faded and peeling, but you can still make out the words 'Chester—Bridgeport.' I'll be damned!"

Ruddygore nodded. "It takes many shapes and many forms, for it's shaped from history and from memories, the backwash of the world flowing backward into the sea whence it came. It is as it is because of your memories, Joe. But—come! I don't want to keep it waiting; as I said, it has a schedule to keep." He paused briefly. "You're not having second thoughts now, are you? Either of you?"

Joe looked at the woman, and she shrugged and gestured ahead with her hand. "Guess not," Joe replied dubiously. As Ruddygore led the way, first she and then the trucker followed, still more than a little uncertain of it all.

Even stepping onto the ribbed metal of the car deck, they both felt an air of dreamy unreality about the whole thing, as if they were in the midst of some wondrous dreaming drug or, perhaps, comatose and in some fantasy world of the mind. Still, both looked in at the cavernous car deck—and saw nothing. Nothing at all. It was totally and completely dark in there, with not even the other end of the boat showing.

Ruddygore led them to the right stairway and saw them peering into the dark. "I wouldn't be too anxious to see in there," he cautioned them. "The ones who row this ship are best not seen by mortal human beings, I assure you. Come. Climb up to the lounge with me and relax, and I will try to answer your questions as best I can."

Hesitantly, they both followed him, still glancing occasionally at the total dark that masked whoever or whatever could manage oars that had to weigh a ton or more each.

It was quickly obvious that they were the only passengers, and the lounge, as Ruddygore had called it, was deserted—but they had obviously been expected. A number of wooden chairs and benches were around, looking a bit shopworn but not too bad; in the rear, around the stack and its housing, was a large buffet table filled with cold platters and pitchers of something or other.

"Just take what you want whenever you feel hungry," the sorcerer told them. "The red jugs are a fair rosé, the yellow a decent if slightly warm ale. Use any of the flagons you see—they're public."

The engines suddenly speeded up, and there was the faint but definite sensation of moving, moving back out into the dark. But moving where? And on what sea?

"What are we floating on—desert?" the woman asked.

Ruddygore cut himself a hunk of cheese, poured some wine, tore off a large chunk of bread, then sat down in a chair that creaked under his great weight and settled back.

"We are heading across the Sea of Dreams," he told them between large bites and swallowed.

Joe decided he might as well eat, too, and followed Ruddygore's lead, except for taking some sliced meat as well and the ale rather than wine. "I never heard of a Sea of Dreams," he noted. "And it sure ain't in Texas."

Ruddygore chuckled, "No, Joe, it sure ain't. And yet, in a way, it is very close to Texas—and everyplace else, for that matter. It is the element that connects the universes. It isn't anywhere, really, except—well, *between*."

The woman wandered out onto the deck for a moment and stared down at the inky blackness. There was the strong feeling of movement; wind blew her hair, wind with an unaccustomed chill in it, but there was no sound of water, no smell of sea or brine.

She shivered in the cold and came back in to join the others. "That sea—is that water?"

Ruddygore reloaded with meat and half a loaf of bread and settled back. "Oh, no. But it has the consistency of water and the surface properties of water, so you treat it that way. In truth, I couldn't begin to explain to you what it actually is." He thought a moment. "The best way to give you at least a sense of it is to provide you with a little background."

Both passengers settled down. "Shoot," Joe invited him.

"Go back to the beginning. I mean the *real* beginning. The explosion that created your universe and mine. Where was the Creator before He created the universes?"

Joe shrugged. "Heaven?"

"But he created the heavens and the earth, also," Ruddygore reminded them. "Well, I'll tell you where He was. Here. And when He created your universe, He also created all the natural laws, the rules by which it all operates, and He generally has played by those rules, particularly in the past couple thousand years or so. But when He created your Earth, there was a backwash from all that released energy. As it surged from here toward your universe, an equal suction of sorts was created that resulted in the creation of another world—indeed, another whole universe on the other side of here. The force of it was such that it was totally complete—but it wasn't the universe *He* was interested in. Realizing, though, that it was there, He turned it over to associates who were around. Angels, you might call 'em, although that's far too simple a term."

Ruddygore paused to stuff his face with gobs of meat and cheese, washed everything down with most of a pitcher of wine, then continued.

"The other universe was, of course, a mess, since it was more or less a backwash of yours. Much natural law held, but not enough to make any real sense out of it. It was chaos. How it was in reality is totally beyond imagination, I assure you, but it was an environment more alien than any other planet in your universe. It was madness beyond imagining, and it was obvious to those—angels—in charge that it must be stabilized, must have *rules* like those in the universe you know. But these were, after all, angels, not the Creator, and they could only shape what the Creator had wrought, not really change it. The result was a set of Laws, absolute Laws, governing how my universe and my world would operate. These Laws incorporate the basic physical laws needed for such a place to exist at all, but only the Creator can think of *everything*. Thus, the Laws of my world are, shall we say, soft. The simple ones, particularly on the local level, are subject to change."

"Huh?" the woman responded. "You mean, nine out of ten times that you drop a rock it goes down the way it should—but one in ten times it might go up? Or just stay there, suspended in midair?"

"Ah, something like that," the sorcerer replied. "Basically, that rock will drop every single time—unless someone with the knowledge and the will applies them to that specific rock. It won't do otherwise on its own, I assure you."

"This—place we're goin'," Joe put in. "It's got people and stuff?"

Ruddygore chuckled. "Yes, Joe, it's got 'people and stuff.' It didn't at the start, but the angels implored the Creator, once they'd gotten it set up, and He shifted a small group from your world over to mine. From that first tribe come the populations of today. And in the millennia that have passed since then, they've developed into different races, different cultures, just as on your Earth. Not quite as diverse, but diverse enough, and this despite the fact that there are far fewer languages there than on your Earth. It's not as important as you might think, that different language business. In your world almost all those peoples to the south of your own country, and many in your country, speak Spanish, I believe—yet there are many cultural differences among those peoples, and many countries that are quite different from one another. Geography and isolation do as much to make people diverse as language."

"You know a lot about our world," the woman noted. "Do your people visit us?"

"Oh, my, no!" Ruddygore laughed. "If they did, they'd soon be corrupted beyond belief. In fact, very few can cross the Sea of Dreams, and none as of now can do it until and unless *I* will it. You see, this is *my* ferry, and it's the only one. Oh, others can see the Sea and others can try the crossing, but it is tricky and dangerous. Impossible to cross, in fact, unless you know *exactly* how to do it. Fail and you will merge with the Sea, returning to the mind of the Creator—and you, yourself, will cease to exist. This is more than death. Your very soul is swallowed and merged back into the primal energies below us. You are gone in true death."

"You're telling us that there is a soul—an afterlife?" the woman pressed eagerly. "That's what it sounds like."

"Well, there is a soul, yes, Miss—just what *is* your name, anyway? We can't keep calling you 'that woman' all the time."

"Marjorie's my real name," she told them, "but mostly I just go by the nickname of Marge."

"All right—Marge," the sorcerer said, nodding. "At any rate, yes, you have a soul. All the humans have souls, and a few of the others. But as to the fate of those souls—there are a lot of things that can happen. Evil can destroy a soul—outside as well as internal evil—and leave the body empty. The soul can wander, or it can be trapped, or a million other things can happen. Otherwise it definitely goes *somewhere*, a *somewhere* from which it occasionally, but very rarely, returns. And there are, it seems, a *lot* of somewheres for that soul to go. Let's not get into that now."

"Okay," Joe agreed. "But I noticed you said all the humans have souls, and a few of the others. What kind of others do you mean?"

Ruddygore sighed. "An infinite variety, really. Those without souls are, of course, the creations of the original angels. To compensate, most are immortal or nearly so, meaning they don't age. They can still, of course, be killed—although, even there, they have a lot of charms and protections. They are not killed in the same way people are, usually. To that original band have been added, over the millennia, ones from your own world who were involved in the original creation but who have, through the dominance of man, been displaced and, by luck, or charm, or the help of me and my predecessors, or the mercy of the Creator, have made their way to my side of the Sea. A one-way trip, though. Some of these have souls, as the Creator Himself willed."

"What sort of—others?" Joe pressed nervously.

"Elves, gnomes, leprechauns—those sorts. The stuff of your legends the world over. The other folk who once shared your world, but for whom man had less and less need and far less room and tolerance. The stuff of your fantasies and legends. Their ties to their native Earth, in fact, are bridges between the worlds across the Sea of Dreams, in a way, for even today those artists and writers of fantasy and the fantastic in your world see them, experience them, if only in dreams, and write of their exploits. The fantasies, the myths, the dreams of your world, are the reality of mine."

Ruddygore sighed. "Look. We cross the Sea of Dreams, and the Creator is even now all around us. He sleeps, and as He sleeps He dreams. Some of the dreams are pleasant ones. Some are nightmares. But *His* dreams take root and flow to one side of the Sea or the other, entering the dreams of one and the reality of the other. This war we now face may be but one of His nightmares. Even now, some dreamer on your world may perceive it in his own mind and write it as a fantasy. You ought to think about that, anyway. You might well be the stuff of an epic fantasy novel in your own world, the dreamer there unknowing that he writes of your reality."

"I'd rather not think about that one," Marge said sourly.

"At any rate," the sorcerer continued, "you're going to a world that will be at once totally different and very familiar to you both. Like this boat. It is a familiar thing to Joe, yet it has not existed since he was a child. It is familiar—yet it is something else. Listen! Have you sensed that the engines have shut down?"

They were all suddenly quiet, attentive to the noises—and found that he was right. The thrumming of the engine had ceased, and along with it, the vibration against the glass windows of the lounge.

After a few moments of silence, they could hear the groanings of grommets larger than they as the massive oars were seized, freed, and dipped in unison down into the Sea of Dreams.

Below them, on that dark and mysterious car deck now began a deep, hollow sound, rhythmic and somewhat intrusive. It sounded like some giant drummer beating a slow tempo on some great kettledrum. It was all around them, yet not quite pervasive enough to drown out conversation.

"I know what that is," Joe said. "I saw *Ben Hur* nine times. They're rowing to the beat."

Ruddygore nodded. "That's exactly what they're doing. And they'll speed up when they can and maintain it for a long while."

"Just who are—they?" Marge asked apprehensively, thinking of the size of the boat and those oars.

"Monsters," Ruddygore replied casually, getting more cheese. "Real ones. Lost balls, you might say. One-of-a-kinds that didn't make it in either your universe or mine. Once evil and all defeated, they had no real choice. They row the boat, or they are cast adrift in the Sea of Dreams, unable to swim to any shore, even in dock. Oh, don't look so shocked. All of them deserve what they got, and all are volunteers, in a sense. I offered them a chance to row or sink, and they all chose to row. They are comfortable and reasonably kept and they are all now doing something constructive rather than the terrible things they did to destroy, way back in the past."

Marge shivered a little, suddenly even more aware of the beat of the great drum, and tried not to think of what might be beating it. She got up and went back over to the doorway, looking out at the darkness once more.

"Hey! There's something out there!" she called to them. Joe and Ruddygore walked over and joined her. The sorcerer slid back the door and walked out onto the deck. The other two followed.

The creak and groan of the great oars below was noticeable, but with their present better speed and rhythm, they and the drumming could be more or less tuned out. The breeze was still cool. Ruddygore stood at the rail a moment, staring off into the gloom and listening above the sound of the rowing and creak of the ship. "Just what did you see?" he asked her.

She shook her head in puzzlement. "I—I'm not really sure. Some large shapes and odd lights."

"You're liable to see just about anything out there if you stare long enough," the sorcerer told them. "All that was is drawn back to the Sea, and all that will be is formed and dispatched from it. Only what *is* is elsewhere."

In the night, after a while, they all could see what Marge had seen and more. Shapes, some familiar, some unfamiliar. Skylines and odd buildings, then at another time what looked like the fully deployed three masts of some great sailing ship, although the ship itself could not be seen. There were sounds, too—vague, low, yet omnipresent. The sounds of millions of voices talking together far off in some void; the sounds of great machines, of explosions, of building and destroying, all merged into a vague whole. For a while they were caught in its eerie spell, but finally Joe asked, "How long until we get to—wherever it is we're going?"

"A few hours," Ruddygore told him. "You might want to stretch out on one of the benches and catch some sleep—both of you. You've had quite a time so far this night."

"Maybe I will," Joe responded, scratching and yawning a bit.

Marge just shook her head. "No way for me. I'm afraid if I go to sleep I'm going to wake up on the outskirts of El Paso."

Ruddygore chuckled. "I understand your worry, but it won't happen, I assure you. Once we cast off from your world, you were committed irrevocably and forever. Only a few from my side may travel back and forth at will. For those like you, it is a one-way trip."

✡

Joe did stretch out and after a while was snoring softly, but Marge was as good as her word, both anxious and too keyed up to sleep now. She sat down near Ruddygore, who was eating again, and tried to find out more.

"This place we're going to—does it have a name?" she asked him.

He nodded. "Oh, yes. It hasn't just one name, but many. Of course, the planet itself is simply called the world, or earth, just as you call yours. Why not? It's logical. But the nations and principalities are quite differently named and very distinct. We are bound for Valisandra, my chosen land, to my castle there."

"You're the ruler of a country?"

"Oh, my, no!" He laughed. "Valisandra is a kingdom and quite well and fairly governed. The day-to-day administration of a nation is far too complex and boring for me, I'm afraid, and I'd probably do a very poor job if I ever got the chance. I'm more a—sorcerer in residence, you might say. Long ago I did a trifling service for the current king's grandfather and was given my castle and some land around it as a gift of thanks. With so much magic loose in the world, it gives comfort to the king and his people to have a powerful sorcerer living among them. I have great affection for the land and its people. I have been one among them for a very long time, and I have the same stake in its well-being and preservation as they do. They know this—and they also know that I have no political ambition whatsoever, and thus am no threat to them. There are few ranking sorcerers in the world today—thirteen, all told, including myself—although there are hundreds of slightly lesser lights that may one day replace us."

"This—Vali—"

"Valisandra."

"Valisandra, then. What's it like?"

He sat back, took another long swig of wine, and smiled. "It's a pretty country. The climate is mostly temperate, except in the far north, and the land is rich in good, black earth made for growing things. The people—about three million, all told—are pretty well divided between free farmers and townspeople and those on feudal holdings. The central government's fairly strong, with its own army, so the feudal hold is weak—more like sharecropping than the semi-slavery state some places have. There are still wild areas, too, where the unicorn and deer play free and the fairies come out to dance. Yes, it's a very pleasant place indeed."

She smiled. "It sounds nice. But you said something about a war. That doesn't sound so pleasant."

"It's a different world from yours," he reminded her. "In some ways more peaceful by far. There are no laser-guided battle stations in orbit, no ICBMs and strategic bombers ready to destroy the world at the slip of a politician's nerve. But there is war, and jealousy, and greed, and, yes, death there as well, as they are in every place that mankind exists. Think of a world where magic, not science, is supreme. There are no hospitals, no miracle cures or shock trauma units; and that means a higher mortality rate. There is, of course, medicine—folk and herbal, which can be surprisingly effective sometimes—and magical healers as well. No electricity or great engines for good *or* evil. Power is the wind and water and muscle, as it was in the old days on your world, although there is a cleverness in civil engineering that builds dikes and aqueducts and the like. On the surface, a more primitive, simpler world—but only on the surface. It would be a mistake to think of it as a medieval Earth, for the world is very complex and far more diverse than yours, and the magic is as complex in its own way as nuclear physics is in your world."

She nodded. "It sounds like a fairy story."

"It *is* a fairy story. It is the origin of all such tales. But it is very real—and right now, my part of it is in trouble."

"The war."

"Yes—the war," he responded. "The overall district is called Husaquahr. It's almost fifteen hundred miles from north to south, and more than half that from east to west. There are six countries, as well as five City-States around the mouth of the river which dominates the land. The River of Dancing Gods."

"The River of Dancing Gods," she repeated. "It's a charming name."

"It's more than charming. The river itself winds its way from the Golden Lakes in the north to the Kudra Delta far to the south. It is the blood of Husaquahr—its arteries are its many tributaries, and the system is life itself to the millions of humans and fairy folk who make up its population."

"Why is it named Dancing Gods?"

"There are all sorts of legends and stories about that, but I suspect its divinity derives from its importance to its people. The dancing part may have a thousand reasons in legend, but it is perhaps because it is a very old river that meanders greatly, so much so that to travel on the river the fifteen hundred straight-line miles to the delta from the lakes, you would actually travel over twenty-four hundred miles. It is a primary water source for irrigation, and it is navigable from the point where the Rossignol joins it to form the southwestern border of Valisandra. It is the Nile, the Mississippi, the Ganges, the Yellow, the Volga—and more, all rolled up into one. And, in a sense, it's what the war is about."

"Yes, we're back to the war."

He nodded. "The enemy force includes every destructive element in Husaquahr and from elsewhere besides. Evil, greedy, petty—you name it. It is a frightening force, commanded by a charismatic general known only as the Dark Baron. Who or what he actually is, is unknown, but he is, for certain, a great sorcerer who takes some pains to escape being identified. That makes me believe that he is the worst of all enemies, a fellow sorcerer on the Council that oversees the magic of the entire world. One of my brothers. Or, perhaps, sisters. The Dark Baron is so totally cloaked that it might be either."

"But if the sorcerer is one of your own—doesn't that narrow the field?" she asked. "I mean, it should be simple to discover which of only twelve others he or she might be."

"You'd think so," Ruddygore agreed, "but it's not that simple. Our skills may differ, but our powers are equal—and we are bound by our own rules and laws. No sorcerer may enter the lands or castle of another without the permission of the owner. Distances are great. Magical power being equal, there is no way to tell who is doing what. I assure you that it is quite possible to appear to be in two or even a dozen places at once. Spies within a fellow sorcerer's lairs are impossible—we smell each other too easily. And, of course, even if we knew, it would require incontrovertible proof before any action could be taken. Most of my brothers and sisters on the Council refuse to believe that one of their own could turn this way, and the Council would have to act in concert to defeat and destroy this enemy once and for all. So they sit idly by while the Dark Baron's armies march on Husaquahr, and unless those are defeated in battle, there's nothing that can be done. The Council will not stop something as petty as a war. They are almost traditional."

"But you're meddling," she pointed out.

He nodded. "Someone has to, I fear, and since I suspect that I am at least one primary object of the war, it is in my own self-interest to do so."

"You? They want to kill you?"

"No. I believe that the Dark Baron, with some of his great and powerful allies, could kill me if he wished. Kill me—but not capture me. You see, he has most certainly allied himself with the forces of Beyond—you might call it Hell itself—and that tips the scale in his favor. Oh, he's very clever about it—if I could prove that alliance, it would be the evidence needed to force the Council into action—but *I* know."

"This is starting to get complicated," she noted. "Who or what are these forces of Beyond?"

"Well, you know the story basically, I'm sure. Some of the angels of the Creator rebelled against Him and were cast out. Since that time those forces have been trying to get back, working through the actions of evil ones in your world and mine. Well, now they have their most powerful ally, and the assault's on my world, not yours, and thus more likely not to worry the Creator. They've been terribly frustrated that your own world hasn't yet blown itself into atoms despite their agents' best efforts. But now they have a chance—by getting back into Husaquahr and then, they hope, by forcing an accommodation with me—literally to invade your world, using my powers as a bridge."

She looked shocked. "You mean you'd *do* it?"

He shrugged. "They're not terribly interested in my world, because it's not a primary creation of the Creator. It's yours they want. But it's *my* world, after all. If they can seize and dominate it, they might force a swap, a trade. If they can gain control of the River of Dancing Gods, they will have Husaquahr by the throat, and that's exactly what they're trying to do. It's a slow, brutal conquest—but they are winning."

She sat back, a little dazed, and considered what he had said. The forces of Hell were after Earth—her native Earth—and were willing to conquer and destroy a whole different world to do this. She could appreciate Ruddygore's position, too. He alone knew the way across the Sea of Dreams. He alone could ferry them safely through the very mind of the Creator Himself. And since he controlled the pathway, he could be rid of them—by sending them one-way into Earth.

"Why don't you just send them all over and be done with it, then?" she asked him. "Wouldn't that solve your problem?"

He looked at her strangely and was silent a moment. Finally he muttered, "Yes, your world *has* treated you most unkindly, I see." He cleared his throat, and his voice grew loud and firm once more. "You seem to forget that your world is the *primary* object of creation. What you suggest is that I precipitate Armageddon. Disregarding the billions of souls I would have on my conscience for a moment, let me remind you that Armageddon would engulf everything, involve the Creator directly. My world would no more survive it than yours, and with less promise of rebuilding thereafter. There will be no Armageddon laid against my soul's account! I do not intend that—even if it means the total destruction of Husaquahr. But they will never believe that. Or they may believe, but not believe that they cannot somehow get the secret, anyway. But I have a different plot in mind.

"I intend to beat them at their own game. Send them back into the abyss from which they crawled, they and all their ilk."

END OF EXCERPT

BOOK ONE
THE RIVER OF DANCING GODS
JACK L. CHALKER

Paul Cook is the author of eight books of science fiction, and is currently both a college instructor and the editor of the Phoenix Pick Science Fiction Classics *line.*

BOOK REVIEWS

by Paul Cook

Farside
by Ben Bova
Tor Books 2013
Hardcover, 368 pages
ISBN: 978-0765323873

I would say that right now Ben Bova carries the mantle of what might be called Campbellian science fiction. John W. Campbell, Jr., by inheriting *Astounding Science Fiction* in the late 1930s, transformed science fiction from a cheesy space adventure genre to a genre that dealt seriously with humans (mostly scientists) in extrapolative situations and keeping to solid science along the way. He also demanded a higher quality of writing. Isaac Asimov, Robert Heinlein, Murray Leinster, and later Arthur C. Clarke were Campbell's early prodigies and *en masse* they brought respectability to the field. *Astounding* was changed to *Analog Science Fact and Fiction* in the mid-Fifties, and Bova himself took over the editorial chores of *Analog* in 1972 after Campbell passed away.

Bova's output as a writer is quite varied. He's written historical novels, fantasy, science fiction, short stories, and, of course, science fact. His most lasting contributions to the science fiction field will be his "Grand Tour" novels which consist of novels (and stories) taking place on all the planets (except the outer two or three) and the asteroids. *Farside* takes place on the far side of the moon but is not a sequel to either *Moonrise* (1996) or *Moonwar* (1998), though several characters from those books make an appearance in *Farside*.

Cutting to the chase, Bova gets everything right in *Farside*, both the science and the science fiction. The extra added delight here is how he invests his characters, principally the two main competing scientists, with ambitions that anyone in academia would understand completely. We don't often see scientists or astronauts as "career" people who take on tasks because they're part of their career trajectory. But they often do. (This was a major trope in Tom Wolfe's *The Right Stuff*, if you recall.)

Farside is about one group of scientists on the far side of the moon trying to develop an imaging system using mirrors and regular telescopes to probe the atmosphere of a planet around a star called Sirius C, a planet which should not be where it is. Sirius C is the remnant of a nova explosion of its parent star and should have had its atmosphere and its surface blown into space a long, long time ago. But there's an indication of an oxygen- and nitrogen-rich atmosphere and that implies life. A second group, headed by a rich woman based on Earth, wants to build an orbiting interferometer that would better image Sirius C. The novel is about how these two factions compete and collide, leading to a murder mystery and a cogent study about how academics (including scientists) fight for their careers as well as their very lives.

Farside is a stand-alone novel, tightly written and keenly focused, expertly paced, and it is one of Bova's best books, inside or outside his "Grand Tour" series. *Farside* has many narrative affinities with what I found in both *Mercury* (2005) and *Titan* (2006), which are among the best books in the series (they are also stand-alone novels). This is "Old School" science fiction, something which we could use more of these days and I do recommend this book to you.

2312
by Kim Stanley Robinson
Orbit 2013
Hardcover, 576 pages
ISBN: 978-0316098120

One approaches novels by Kim Stanley Robinson knowing for the most part they'll be filled with lots of information about planetary societies, including interplanetary politics, religion and culture. They'll also be filled with all kinds of engineering projects on a colossal scale. His Mars trilogy—an exemplar of this—will no doubt be his legacy, and rightfully so. Not only are those novels about how Mars might be settled (and terraformed over the centuries for human living), they are also about the changes men and women will go through as they become Martians instead of remaining Earthlings. Many science fiction writers have done this. Bradbury, of course, explored these changes in *The Martian Chronicles* and Philip K. Dick goes even further in his extraordinary 1964 novel *The Martian Time-Slip*.

In his latest effort—also the beginning of a trilogy—we have a similar project in hand—the tale of an interplanetary society facing a new threat. But unlike the Mars books, nothing about the need to tell this particular tale is ever made clear until halfway through the novel. That's not the least of the book's problems. If you start reading *2312* cold knowing absolutely nothing about it as I did (I read the electronic version, without the aid of any blurbs), it's almost impossible to determine what this trilogy is going to be about, other than to say it's going to be about the interest of a few people traveling between the planets and some incredibly smart computers that seem bent on disrupting interplanetary goodwill.

Nowhere in the book's early chapters (or the first 100 pages, actually) is anything approaching a conflict even announced. We simply begin by following the planet-hopping life of a terrarium designer named Swan Er Hong who gets caught up in an attack on a small city on Mercury after her mentor is assassinated. There is also a lot of talk about qubes, which are incredibly compressed quantum computers (I think) that are also functioning AIs (I think). The novel only gets going when a rail-bound city on Mercury gets obliterated by either a meteor or a bomb which forces several characters to literally walk home before the sun catches up with them and fries them. Unfortunately, when this happens, the novel comes to a dead stop as Robinson spends page after page describing the walk. In fact, at one point he simply writes: "Walk, walk, walk…"

What happened was that he'd written himself into a corner and this was the best way out. The best "trek" in science fiction happens in *The Left Hand of Darkness* when the two main characters have to cross the north pole of the planet Winter together. But Le Guin's skill is such that she fills those pages with character interaction and narrative information that never lags. Here, Robinson has to have his characters walk about seventy miles and it really wears on the reader.

The novel does pick up when the main character leaves Mercury, but by then it's clear that the novel wasn't that well-thought-through. The proof of this is the inconclusive ending to this first volume. Each of the Mars Trilogy books can be read as stand-alones and none of them lags in pacing or has weakly drawn characters. Not so here. The following volumes in this series might be better than this one, and when they come out I'll probably read them. But I'm not looking forward to the experience, not when there are dozens of other novels to read and many more new authors to explore. If you haven't read Robinson's Mars novels, read them. If you want to read his best stand-alone, read his extraordinary *The Years of Rice and Salt*. That, to me, is Robinson at his story-telling best.

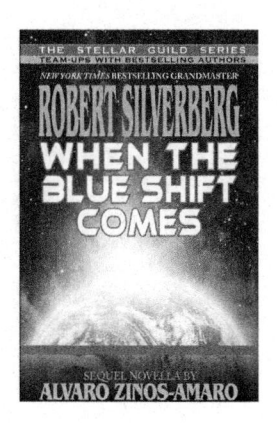

When the Blue Shift Comes
by Robert Silverberg and Alvaro Zinos-Amaro
Phoenix Pick 2013
Trade Paperback, 187 pages
ISBN: 978-1-61242-074-5

In 2011, Phoenix Pick embarked on a publishing program called The Stellar Guild Series wherein established writers team up with new authors. *When the Blue Shift Comes,* the fourth in the series, is a collaboration between Robert Silverberg and new writer Alvaro Zinos-Amaro. As Silverberg says in his afterword, his contribution to this project comes from a failed novella he wrote in 1987 called, "The Song of Last Things". Zinos-Amaro, a friend of Silverberg, was chosen to complete the Silverberg story. What emerges isn't quite a collaborative effort or even a co-authored work, but something rather unique.

The Silverberg story is about a small group of post-humans (or people who are *barely* recognizable as human) in an impossibly distant future facing the end of the Milky Way Galaxy which is being gobbled up by a stellar anomaly which no one understands.

As Silverberg says in his introduction to the second half of the book, his original story got out of control and wasn't going where he thought it would go or where he wanted it to go, so he abandoned it. As it turns out, the original novella ends right at the point in the narrative where the main character, Hanosz Prime, has to confront the monstrosity that's eating up his part of the universe. Zinos-Amaro picks up the story from there and right from the get-go it's clear that he is able to resolve the story with all the same stylistic quirks and flourishes found in the opening segment by Silverberg.

The original story has all the hallmarks of Silverberg's best moments as a writer, especially coming out of the Sixties and Seventies where point-of-view shifts and present-tense narratives were much more acceptable than they are now. Yet the novel reads less like a literary experiment and more like something you'd find in Harlan Ellison's famous *Dangerous Visions* anthology or Terry Carr's Ace Science Fiction Specials. Man, I miss writing like this. I quite enjoyed *When the Blue Shift Comes.*

Previous novels in the Stellar Guild Series include collaborations between Kevin J. Anderson and Steven Savile (*Tau Ceti*, 2011), Mercedes Lackey and Cody Martin (*Reboots*, 2011), and Harry Turtledove and Rachel Turtledove (*On the Train*, 2012). Some of the other "masters" will be Nancy Kress, Eric Flint, and Larry Niven. This is a series that could really matter.

Fountain of Age
by Nancy Kress
Small Beer Press 2012
Trade Paperback, 303 pages
ISBN: 978-1931520454

This is an extraordinary collection of stories by one of our best writers. Kress has won several Hugo and Nebula awards for her work and justifiably so. Her focus tends to be on biology and genetics (though not always), but her real heart lies in how humans behave. But let me make this a bit clearer. Her real interest is how families behave and interact in close proximity to one another. Literally. Many of these stories involve the profoundly deep interactions (and subsequent emotions) with people who are in the midst of a crisis. The collection begins with "The Erdmann Nexus," which won the Hugo Award when it first appeared in 2008. In "The Erdmann Nexus" a number of retirees in an old folks' home are having very strange experiences. All of this is happening as an alien ship is passing by the solar system. Kress weaves the interactions of her characters and their caretakers with great empathy and compassion. Kress cares about her characters as if they were real people. She also has them behave (and emote and think) as if they were real people. This is such a relief from those stories about genius children who speak with the articulation of fifty-year-old humans or the spunky, energetic grandmother with a sassy mouth right out of the worst of Heinlein. Kress' children may be precocious, but they're still children with all of their needs and her elderly still have a spark of life left in them. "Safeguard" is about a group of enhanced children who are used against an alien menace. They're not quite the brainy children of destiny so common to Orson Scott Card's writings and that helps the story immensely. Another story about an enhanced child is "First Rites," where gene modification in an adopted child backfires totally on the people behind his engineering. One of the subtexts of this story is the problem of ethics in science and the role that skepticism should play in scientific research. This is to say just because something can be done, doesn't mean it should be done. Often political solutions win out over the scientific. In Kress, either outcome can be tragic.

There are nine stories in this collection and all of them are keepers. I did find "The Erdmann Nexus," the longest story here, to be the better story, if only because of its length. Kress really does excel in the short form. Unlike her novels which can be untidy and sprawl more than is good for them, her shorter works tend to be highly focused, even if they contain quite a few characters and all sorts of things happening—bills to pay, babies to feed, work to do, etc. This is a collection that absolutely belongs on your shelves.

Unidentified Funny Objects
by Alex Shvartsman
UFO Publishing 2012
Trade Paperback, 320 pages
ISBN: 978-0-9884328-0-2

Here is "light" science fiction reading at its best. And I don't mean that as faint praise, either. The "light" here is the absolute lack of seriousness in these hilarious short stories that straddle both the science fiction and fantasy genres. And a couple totally "unidentifiable"—which, if you think of it, totally fits being here.

These stories, gathered by anthologist Alex Shvartsman, run the gamut from straight-forward stories to outright romps. They've got ghosts, zombies, tweeting aliens, hobo vampires, Nazis from the Moon, pandas with large sexual appetites, and a little girl who wants a samurai sword from Santa so she can fight zombies. Santa's reaction to her request is priceless. There's also a send-up on a famous Cheech and Chong routine that had me in stitches.

Here's a partial list of authors gathered here, Jody Lynn Nye, Lavie Tidhar, Ken Liu, Mike Resnick, Michael Kurland, and Don Sakers. These names should help introduce the readers to the other authors here, who might not be as familiar to the general reader. This book is a delight. There are a lot of giggles here, and every now and then you'll laugh your head off. This is a hoot from start to finish.

Volume One:
The Space Merchants - C.M. Kornbluth and Frederik Pohl
More Than Human - Theodore Sturgeon
The Long Tomorrow - Leigh Brackett
The Shrinking Man - Richard Matheson

Volume Two:
Double Star - Robert A. Heinlein
The Stars My Destination - Alfred Bester
A Case of Conscience - James Blish
Who? - Algis Budrys
The Big Time - Fritz Leiber

From the Vault:
American Science Fiction: Nine Classic Novels of the 1950s (two volumes)
Edited by Gary K. Wolfe
Library of America 2013
Hardcover (set of 2), 1,750 pages
ISBN: 978-1-59853-157-2

The Library of America is a non-profit company devoted to publishing the very best of American literature, from the Colonies up to the present day. Within the last several years they've also published the collected works of authors in our field such as Philip K. Dick, Kurt Vonnegut, Jr., and H.P. Lovecraft. Many of these novels and stories are also in print in regular trade paperback editions, but it helps to have a kind of academic seal-of-approval from such a storied publisher.

The volumes in hand collect nine novels of classic science fiction. The first collects from the years 1953 to 1956. The second collects novels from the years 1956-1958. These novels represent the first flowering of science fiction beyond the hard-science Campbellian era of the 1940s as it evolved into the fields of "soft" science fiction. Soft science fiction would include social science fiction, satire, and stories about the various kinds of existential threats posed by nuclear weapons and the Cold War. Here are the titles:

Even though the Fifties are filled with major works in science fiction (think of Hal Clement's *Mission of Gravity* and Ray Bradbury's *Fahrenheit 451* just to name two). The works here are not the hard-science fiction of Asimov or Clarke but tend to focus on questions of individual and societal identity, given the swift changes in American culture after World War II. This most definitely includes the rise (and fears) of nuclear proliferation and the appearance of the Iron Curtain. Nuclear warfare, radiation, and mutations figure heavily here: *More Than Human*, *The Long Tomorrow*, *The Shrinking Man* and *Who?* all deal with the fears brought on by changes beyond the control of any one individual. These are true extrapolations, but not in any rigorous scientific manner: the protagonists in these novels tend to be ordinary people caught up in extraordinary circumstances. Some are tragic; others less so. *The Space Merchants* is the obvious romp here; *The Shrinking Man* is the one, true tragedy.

Each volume has covers that are reminiscent of Fifties paperback covers and this boxed set would make a handsome edition for any household who also might have within it squirmy, nerdy children (or grandkids) who, perhaps bored on a Sunday afternoon, might discover this on the bookshelves and dive in to the world of Gully Foyle or Fritz Leiber's R&R facility outside of time. It happened to me. I know it happened to you. Pay it forward with this collection and stand back!

SERIALIZATION:
Dark Universe

(Continued from Issue Two)

DARK UNIVERSE
by Daniel F. Galouye
Phoenix Pick, 2010
Trade Paperback: 182 pages. *Kindle, Nook, More*
ISBN: 978-1-60450-487-3

Dark Universe Copyright © 1961 Daniel F. Galouye. All rights reserved. This book may not be copied or reproduced, in whole or in part, by any means, electronic, mechanical or otherwise without written permission from the publisher except by a reviewer who may quote brief passages in a review.

Excerpt is reprinted here by permission of the Publisher and the Estate's literary agent.

Dark Universe
(Continued from Issue Two)

CHAPTER TEN

Jared flinched from the absurd impressions, from the contradictory composites of physical orientation. He was certain he still lay in the corridor near the dripping needle of rock. Yet, he was equally sure he was somewhere else.

The drip-drip of the water changed to a weary tap-tap-tap and back to a drip-drip again. The coarse hardness of stone under his feverish body was, alternately, the soft fibers of manna husks piled upon a sleeping ledge.

In the next phase of the here-there alternation, the distant tap-tap-tap commanded his attention. And its sharp echoes conveyed the impression of someone seated on a ledge absently drumming his finger on stone.

Light, but the man was old! Had it not been for the movement of his hand, he might easily have been mistaken for a skeleton. The head, trembling with an affliction of senility, was like a skull. And the beard, unkempt and sparse, trailed to the ground, losing itself in the inaudibility of its thinness.

Tap-tap-tap...drip-drip...

Jared was back in the corridor. And, like commingling sounds, the straggly beard had metamorphosed into the moist hanging stone.

"Relax, Jared. Everything's under control now."

He almost lurched out of the dream. "Kind Survivoress!"

"It'll be less awkward if you just call me Leah."

He puzzled over the name, then thought flatly, "I'm dreaming again."

"For the moment—yes."

Another anxious, soundless voice intruded, "Leah! How's he doing?"

"Coming around," she said.

"So I can hear." Then, "Jared?"

Jared, however, had returned to the corridor—but only for a moment. Soon he was back on the manna fiber mattress in a minor world where the vague outline of a woman bent over him and an inconceivably ancient man sat against the far wall tapping his finger.

"Jared," the woman offered, "that other voice was Ethan's."

"Ethan?"

"You knew him as Little Listener before we changed his name. He's been out after game, but he's coming back now."

Jared was even more confused.

More to soothe him than for any other reason, he felt sure, the woman said, "I can't believe you found your way here after all these gestations."

He started to say something, but she interrupted, "Don't explain. I heard everything from your mind—what you were doing in the passages, how you were bitten by—"

"Della!" he shouted, remembering.

"She'll be all right. I reached you in time."

Abruptly, he realized he was awake now and that Kind Survivoress' last words had been spoken.

"Not Kind Survivoress, Jared—Leah."

And he was astonished by his audible impression of the woman. He sent his hands groping over her face, across her shoulders, along her arms. Why—she wasn't the least bit old!

"What did you expect—someone like the Forever Man?" She sent her thoughts to him. "After all, I was really practically a child when I used to go to you."

He listened more closely at her. Hadn't she once told him she could reach his mind only when he was asleep?

"Only when you're asleep if you're far away," she clarified. "When you're this close you don't have to be asleep."

He studied her auditory reflections. She was perhaps a bit taller than Della. But her proportions, despite her nine or ten gestations' seniority over the girl, suffered none in comparison. She was closed-eyed and kept her hair clipped shoulder-length on the sides, reaching to her eyebrows in front.

Turning his ears on his surroundings, he listened to a small, dismal world with a scattering of hot springs, each surrounded by its usual clump of manna plants; an arm of a river flowing out of and right back into the wall; another slumber ledge nearby—Della there, asleep. All these impressions he sifted from the echoes provided by the finger tapping of—the Forever Man?

"That's right," Leah confirmed.

He rose, feeling not as weak as he thought he would, and started across the world.

Leah cautioned, "We don't disturb him until he stops tapping."

He came back and stood in front of the woman, still rejecting the fact that he was actually *here*, in his preposterous dream setting. "How did you know I was out in the corridor?"

"I listened to you coming." And he heard the unspoken explanation that *listen*, in this case, didn't mean hearing *sound*.

She placed a solicitous hand on his shoulder. "And I also hear from your thoughts that this Della is a Zivver."

"She thinks I'm one too."

"Yes, I know. And I'm afraid. I don't understand what you're trying to do."

"I—"

"Oh, I know what you have in mind. But I still don't understand it. I realize you want to get to the Zivver World so you can hunt for Darkness."

"For Light too. And using Della is the only way I can get in."

"So I hear. But how do you know what *her* plans are? I don't trust the girl, Jared."

"It's just because you can't listen to what she's thinking."

"Maybe that's it. Maybe I'm so used to hearing feelings, intentions, that I'm lost when outer impressions are all I have to go by."

"You won't tell Della I'm not like her?"

"If that's the way you want it. We'll just let her go on believing you're the only Zivver whose mind I can reach. But I hope you know what you're doing."

Little Listener came storming into the world and it was remarkable that his exuberant shouts failed to rouse Della and were ignored by the Forever Man, who merely continued his tapping.

"Jared! Where are you?"

"Over here!" Jared was suddenly swept up in the excitement of renewing an acquaintance he hadn't even known was real.

"He can't hear you—remember?" Leah reminded.

"But he's running straight toward us!" Then he puzzled over the scent of—crickets?—that was coming from Little Listener.

"Ethan," Leah corrected. "And those *are* crickets. He keeps a pouch filled with them. Unhearable

119

cricket noises make just as good echoes for him as clickstones do for you."

Then the other was upon him and, in a bone-crushing embrace, swung him around and around as easily as he would a bundle of manna stalks.

Jared's gratification over the reunion was dulled by his awed appreciation of Ethan's tremendous proportions. It was just as well that Little Listener had been banished from the Upper Level because of his uncanny hearing. Otherwise, he most certainly would have been expelled later for his almost inhuman size.

"You old son of a soubat!" Ethan chortled. "I knew you'd come some period!"

"Light, but it's good to—" Jared broke off in mid-sentence as blunt, trembling fingers came to rest lightly against his lips.

"Let him," Leah urged. "That's the only way he can find out what you're saying."

They spent the better part of a period talking about their childhood meetings. And Jared had to tell them about the worlds of man, how it felt to live with many people, what the Zivvers' latest tricks were, whether there had been any more Different Ones recently.

They interrupted their session once to haul food from a boiling pit and bring a portion to the Forever Man. But the latter, still not talkatively disposed, ignored their presence.

Later, Jared said in answer to Leah's question, "Why do I want to go to the Zivver World? Because I've got a hunch that's the right place to hunt for Darkness and Light."

Ethan shook his head. "Forget it. You're here; stay here."

"No. This is something I've *got* to do."

"Great flying soubats!" the other exclaimed. "You never had ideas like that before!"

At this point Jared, from the edge of his hearing, caught the impression of Della stirring on her ledge.

He hurried over and knelt beside her. He felt her face and it was cool and dry, signifying that she had slept off the fever.

"Where are we?" she asked weakly.

He started to tell her, but before he got halfway through he heard that she had drifted into normal sleep.

During the next period Della more than made up for her inactivity of the previous one. That she had been pensively silent on hearing Jared explain about the world they were in and on meeting Leah and Ethan was a prelude to something or other.

When they were alone later, kneeling beside a hot spring and applying fresh poultices to their spider bites, he learned the reason for her reticence.

"When was the last time you were here?" she demanded.

"Oh, so many gestations ago that I—"

"Manna sauce!" She turned away and the Forever Man's tapping sounds blunted themselves against the cool stiffness of her back. "I must say, your Kind Survivoress is *quite* a surprise."

"Yes, she—" Then he understood what she was intimating.

"Kind Survivoress—I'll *bet* she was kind!"

"You don't think—"

"Why did you bring me along? Was it because you thought that awkward giant might be interested in a Unification partner?"

Then she relented. "Oh, Jared, have you forgotten about the Zivver World already?"

"Of course not."

"Then let's get on our way."

"You don't understand. I can't just run off. Leah saved our lives. These are friends!"

"Friends!" She cleared her throat and made it sound like the lash of a swish-rope. "You and your friends!"

Her head insolently erect, she strode off.

Jared followed, but drew up sharply when the world was suddenly cast into silence.

The Forever Man had stopped tapping! He was ready for company!

Unaccountably hesitant, Jared advanced cautiously across the world. Leah and Ethan had been credible. But the Forever Man loomed like a haunting creature from a fantastic past—someone whom he could never hope to understand.

Orienting himself by the asthmatic rasps that came from ahead, he approached the ledge.

"*This is Jared,*" Leah's unspoken introduction rippled the psychic silence. "*He's finally come to hear us.*"

"*Jared?*" The other's reply, carried weakly on the crest of the woman's thoughts, was burdened with the perplexity of forgetfulness.

"Of course, you remember."

The Forever Man tapped inquisitively. And Jared intercepted the impression of a thin finger delving almost its entire length into a depression in the rock before producing each *tap*. Over untold generations his thumping had eroded the stone *that much!*

"I don't know you." The voice, a pained whisper, was coarse as a rock slide.

"Leah used to sort of—bring me here long ago."

"Oh, *Ethan's* little friend!" A hand that was all bone set up an audible flutter as it trembled forward. It seized Jared's wrist in a grip as tenuous as air. The Forever Man tried to smile, but the composite was grossly confused by a disheveled beard, skeletal protuberances and a misshapen, toothless mouth.

"How old *are* you?" Jared asked.

Even as he posed the question he knew it was unanswerable. Living by himself, before Leah and Ethan had come, the man would have had no life spans or gestations against which to measure time's passage.

"Too old, son. And it's been *so* lonely." The straining voice was a murmur of despair against the stark silence of the world.

"Even with Leah and Ethan?"

"They don't know what it means to have listened to loved ones pass on countless ages ago, to be banished from the beauties of the Original World, to—"

Jared started. "You *lived* in the Original World?"

"—to be cast out after hearing your grandchildren and their great-great-grandchildren grow into Survivorship."

"Did you live in the Original World?" Jared demanded.

"But you can't blame them for getting rid of a Different One who wouldn't grow old. What's that—did I live in the Original World? Yes. Up until a few generations after we lost Light."

"You mean you were there *when Light was still with man?*"

As though exhuming memories long laid to rest, the Forever Man finally replied, "Yes. I—what was it we used to say?—saw Light."

"You *saw* Light?"

The other laughed—a thin, rasping outburst cut short by a wheeze and a cough. "Saw," he babbled. "Past tense of the verb to see. See, saw, seen. Seesaw. We used to have a seesaw in the Original World, you know."

See! There was that word again—mysterious and challenging and as obscure as the legends from which it had come.

"Did you hear Light?" Jared enunciated each word.

"I saw Light. Seesaw. Up and down. Oh, what fun we had! Children scampering around with bright, shiny faces, their eyes all agleam and—"

"Did you feel Him?" Jared was shouting now. "Did you touch Him? Did you hear Him?"

"Who?"

"Light!"

"No, no, son. I *saw* it."

It? Then he, too, regarded Light as an impersonal thing! "What was it like? Tell me about it!"

The other fell silent, slumping on his ledge. Eventually he drew in a long, shuddering breath. "God! I don't know! It's been so long *I can't even remember what Light was like!*"

Jared shook him by the shoulders. "Try! Try!"

"I can't!" the old man sobbed.

"Did it have anything to do with the—eyes?"

Tap-tap-tap...

He had returned to his thumping, burying bitter recollections and haunting thoughts under a rock pile of habit and mental detachment.

✧

Leaving Kind Survivoress' world now was out of the question—not with the Forever Man's senile memory offering the hope of opening new passageways in Jared's search for Light. Yet, he couldn't tell Della why he had to extend their stay. So he simply pretended he was still physically unfit for immediate travel.

Apparently satisfied with this explanation for his postponement of their attempt to reach the Zivver World, Della grudgingly settled down to await his complete recovery.

That her original distrust of Leah had been an impulsive, passing thing was manifest in the subsequent lessening of tension between the two women. At one point, she even told Jared she might have been wrong in her first impression of Leah and Ethan. Why, it wasn't at all as she had initially assumed, she confessed. And Ethan, despite his handicap, wasn't the awkward, clumsy lout she had imagined him to be—not in the least.

Tactfully, Leah refrained from mind-to-mind contact with Jared and Ethan while they were in the girl's presence. To the effect that Della either forgot the woman's ability or gave it little thought.

Leah, too, had adjustments to make. Although she treated Della hospitably, Jared could always sense her misgiving over not being able to listen to the Zivver girl's mind.

These developments Jared traced with interest while he waited for the Forever Man to abandon his solitude and seek company once more. Light! What he might learn from that ageless one!

During the fifth period after their arrival, Della was splashing in the river with Ethan while Jared was sharpening his spear points on a coarse rock when Leah's thoughts came to him:

"Please *forget about the Zivver World, Jared.*"

"You know my mind's made up"

"Then you'll have to change it. The passages are full of monsters."

"How do you know? You told me you were afraid to listen to their *minds.*"

"But I've listened to other minds—in the two Levels."

"And what did you hear?"

"Terror and panic and queer impressions I can't understand. There are monsters all over. And the people are running and hiding and creeping back to their recesses, only to flee again later on."

"Are there monsters near this world?"

"I don't think so—not yet anyway."

This posed another complication, Jared realized. Starting out for the Zivver World might not be a matter of leisure choice. It might well be that he should leave as quickly as possible.

"No, Jared. Don't go—please!"

And he detected more than selfless concern for his welfare. Lying at the base of Leah's thoughts were desperate pangs of loneliness, laced with the fear of having her simple, forlorn world cast back into the terrible solitude that had existed before he and Della arrived.

But he had made up his mind and he regretted only not having had the chance for a second talk with the Forever Man.

Just then, however, the latter's tapping came to an abrupt halt.

Jared raced across the world this time.

And, as he passed the river, Della quit splashing to ask: "Where are you running?"

"To hear the Forever Man. Afterward we'll be on our way."

✧

Perching on the ledge, Jared asked anxiously, "Can we talk now?"

"Go away," the Forever Man groaned in protest. "You only make me remember. I don't want to remember."

"But compost! I'm hunting for Light! You can *help* me!"

Only the rasps of the other's labored breathing filled the world.

"Try to remember about Light!" Jared pleaded. "Did it have anything to do with—the eyes?"

"I—don't know. It seems I can remember something about brightness and—I can't imagine what else."

"Brightness? What's that?"

"Something like—a loud noise, a sharp taste, a hard punch maybe."

Jared heard the uncertainty on the Forever Man's face. Here was someone who might even tell him *what* he was searching for. But the man spoke only in riddles which were no clearer than the obscure legends themselves.

He tried to pace off his frustration in front of the nodding skeleton. Right before him might be the entire answer to how Light might benefit man, how it could touch all things at once and bring instant, inconceivably refined impressions of everything. If only the curtain of forgetfulness could be pierced!

He struck out in another direction: "What about Darkness? Do you know anything about that?"

And he heard the other shudder.

"Darkness?" the Forever Man repeated, hesitancy and sudden fear hanging on the word. "I—*oh, God!*"

"What's the matter?"

The man was trembling violently now. His wry face was a grotesque mask of terror.

Jared had never heard such fright before. The other's heartbeat had doubled and his pulse was like a wounded soubat's thrashing. Each shallow, erratic breath seemed as though it would be his last. He tried to rise, but fell back onto the ledge, burying his face in his hands.

"Oh, God! The Darkness! *The awful Darkness! Now* I remember. It's *all around* us!"

Confounded, Jared backed off.

But the recluse grabbed his wrist and, with the strength of desperation, pulled him forward. Then his anguished cries shrilled through the world and spilled out into the passageway:

"Feel it pressing in? Horrible, black, evil Darkness! Oh, God, I didn't *want* to remember! But you *made* me!"

Jared listened alertly, fearfully about him. Was the Forever Man sensing Darkness—*now?* Or was he just remembering it? But no, he had said it was "all around us," hadn't he?

Uneasily, Jared retreated and left his host fighting terror and sobbing, "Can't you feel it? Don't you see it? God, God, get me out of here!"

But Jared felt nothing except the cool touch of the air. Yet he was afraid. It was as though he had absorbed some of the Forever Man's strange fear.

Was Darkness something you felt or perhaps *seed*—rather, *saw?* But if you could *see* it, that meant you could do the same thing to Darkness that the Guardian believed could be done to Light Almighty. But—what?

For a moment Jared was desperately afraid of an indefinite menace he could neither hear, nor feel, nor smell. It was an evil, uncanny sensation—a smothering, a silence that wasn't soundlessness at all but something both alien and akin to it at the same time.

When he reached Della she was with Leah and Ethan. Nothing was said. It was as though a bit of the incomprehensible terror had spread to all of them.

Della had already packed some food in her carrying case and Leah, resigned to his decision, had gotten his spears for him.

The silence, uncomfortable and grave, persisted as they all walked to the exit. No good-bys were offered.

A few paces down the corridor Jared turned and promised, "I'll be back." Casually letting his spears strike the wall, he sounded out the way and pushed on.

The somber world of Kind Survivoress and Little Listener and the unbelievable Forever Man slipped softly back into the immaterial depths of memory. And Jared felt a sense of poignant loss as he realized that recollections were fed by the same stuff of which dreams were made and that the only proof he would ever have of the existence of Leah's world would be in the echoes of his reflections.

CHAPTER ELEVEN

Throughout most of the travel period Della tagged silently along. That she was troubled with a restive hesitancy was evident in the worrisome expression Jared could hear on her face. Was she anxious over something he had said or done? Light knew he had already given plenty of cause for misgiving.

Since leaving Leah's world, though, he had devised an artful echo-producing system which he felt certain had escaped Della's suspicion. It consisted principally of filling the corridors with one whistled tune after another.

Eventually, the passageway pinched in on them and there was a stretch through which they had to crawl. On the other side, he rose and thudded his spear against the ground.

"Now we can breathe easier."

"Why?" She drew up beside him.

"Our rear's protected against soubats. They can't get through a tunnel that small."

She was silent momentarily. "Jared—"

Here came the question he knew she had been putting off. But he decided to forestall it. "There's a big passage up ahead."

"Yes, I ziv it. Jared, I—"

"And the air is heavy with the scent of Zivvers." He skirted a narrow chasm whose outline was carried on his reflected words.

"It is?" She pushed ahead eagerly. "Maybe we're close to their world!"

They reached the intersection and he stood there trying to determine whether they should go to the right or left. Then he tensed, instinctively gripping his spears. Mingled with the Zivver scent was a hidden, evil smell that fouled the air—an unmistakable fetor.

"Della," he whispered, "monsters have just been this way."

But she didn't hear him. Enthused, she had already stridden off along the right-hand branch of the corridor. Even now he could hear her rounding the bend a short way off.

Abruptly there was the grating sound of a rock slide, punctuated by a scream.

With the corridor's composite frozen in his memory by the shrill reflections, he raced toward the great, gaping hole that had swallowed the girl's terrified outcry.

Reaching the area of loose rock, he snapped his fingers to gain an impression of the pit's mouth. There was a solidly embedded boulder rearing up out of the rubble right next to the rim. He laid his spears down and one of them slid away, plunging over the edge and striking the wall repeatedly as it plummeted into the depth. The clatter persisted until the sound lost itself in remote silence.

Casting the other lance back onto solid ground, he frantically shouted, "Della!"

She answered in a terrified whisper, "I'm down here—on a ledge."

He thanked Light that her voice came from nearby and that there might be a chance of saving her.

Securing a grip on the boulder, he swung himself out over the chasm and snapped his fingers once more. Reflections of the sound told him she was huddled on a shelf close to the surface.

His extended hand touched hers and he gripped her wrist, lifting her out of the hole and shoving her past the area of loose rock onto firm ground.

They backed away from the pit and a final rock rolled off the incline, clattering down into the abyss. Echoes of the sharp sounds fetched the impression of the girl's calm melting away.

He let her cry for a while, then took hold of her arms and drew her erect. The sound of his breathing reflected against her face and he listened to the manner in which exposed eyes dominated her other features. He could almost feel their sharp, intense fixedness and, momentarily, he thought he might be on the verge of guessing the nature of zivving.

"It was just like what happened to my mother and father!" She nodded back toward the abyss. "It's like an omen—as if something were telling us *we* can take up where *they* left off!"

Her hands pressed down on his shoulders and, remembering the firm softness of her body against his in that other corridor, he drew her close and kissed her. The girl's response was eager at first, but quickly faded off into a perceptible coolness.

He retrieved his spear. "All right, Della. What is it?"

She wasted no time framing the question she had held back:

"What's all this about hunting for—Light? I heard you shouting at the Forever Man, asking him about Darkness too. And it scared the wits out of him."

"It's simple." He shrugged. "Like you heard me say, I'm hunting for Darkness and Light."

He sensed her perplexed frown as they started down the corridor. A manna shell thumped the side of her carrying case with each step and the sounds were sufficient to gather impressions of the passageway.

"It's not something theological," he assured. "I just have an idea Darkness and Light aren't what we think they are."

He could tell that her puzzlement had given way to mild doubt—a refusal to believe the explanation was that simple.

"But that doesn't make sense," she protested. "Everybody *knows* who Light is, what Darkness is."

"Then let's let it go at that and just say I have a different idea."

She fell silent a moment. "I don't understand."

"Don't let it bother you."

"But the Forever Man—Darkness meant something different to him. He wasn't frightened over 'evil' being all around him. He was scared of *something else*, wasn't he?"

"I suppose so."

"What?"

"I don't know."

Again she said nothing for a long while, until they had passed several branch corridors. "Jared, does all this have anything to do with going to the Zivver World?"

To a certain extent, he felt, he could be outspoken without laying his zivvership open to further suspicion. "In a way, yes. Just like zivving concerns the eyes, I believe Darkness and Light are in some way connected with the eyes too. And—"

"And you think you can find out more about them in the Zivver World?"

"That's right." He led her along a sweeping curve.

"Is that the *only* reason you're going there?"

"No. Like you, I'm also a Zivver; that's where I belong."

He heard the girl's sudden relief—the relaxation of her tenseness, the quietening of her heartbeat. His candor had evidently allayed her misgiving and now she was ready to shrug off his quest as a whim that posed no particular threat to her interests.

She eased her hand into his and they continued on around the bend. But he pulled up sharply as he caught the scent of monsters ahead. At the same time he shrank away from the left wall. For, even as he listened to its featureless surface, an indiscernible patch of silent echoes had begun playing against the moist stone.

This time he was almost prepared for the uncanny sensation. Experimentally, he closed his eyes and was instantly no longer aware of the dancing sound. He opened them again and the noiseless reflections returned immediately—like the soft touch of a shouted whisper spreading itself thin against a smooth rock surface.

"The monsters are coming!" Della warned. "I ziv their impressions—against that wall!"

He half-faced her. "You *ziv* them?"

"It's *almost* like zivving. Jared, let's get away from here!"

He only stood there concentrating on the weird, soundless noise that flowed back and forth against the wall, never reaching his ears but making his eyes feel as though someone had thrown boiling water into them. She had said she *zivved* the impressions. Did that mean zivving was something like what was happening to him now?

Then he listened to the purely audible impressions that were coming from around the bend. There was only one monster approaching. "You go back and wait in the first side corridor."

"No, Jared. You can't—"

But he propelled her down the passage and eased into a niche in the wall. When he heard there wouldn't be enough room to draw his spear, he laid it on the ground. Then he closed his eyes, blocking off the distracting impressions the monster was hurling.

The creature had reached the bend and Jared could hear it hugging the near wall. He pressed farther into the recess.

The thing's awful, alien smell was overpowering in its nearness now. And clearly audible, too, were the numerous folds of flesh—if that's what they were—fluttering about its body. If the breathing and heartbeat were of the same intensity and frequency as the average person's, then it must be drawing even with his hiding place just about—*now*.

Lunging into the corridor, he drove his fist into what he judged to be the creature's midsection.

Air exploded from the monster's lungs as it fell forward against him. Bracing himself against what he had expected to be a slimy touch, he pounded another fist into its face.

Anxiously, he snapped his eyes open as he heard the monster collapse on the ground. He had half-expected there would be no more strange, soundless noise spreading out from the thing now that it was unconscious. And there wasn't.

Kneeling, he sent his hands out reluctantly to explore the creature. And he discovered there were no folds of flesh festooning its body. Rather, its arms, legs, torso were all covered by loosely fitting cloth of a texture even finer than the piece he had found at the entrance to the Lower Level. No wonder he had received the impression of sagging hide! Who ever heard of chestcloths or loincloths that didn't fit skintight?

His hands groped upward and encountered a duplicate of the rougher cloth he had buried in the corridor outside his world. It was drawn taut over the monster's face and held there by four ribbons tied behind its head.

He snatched the cloth away and ran his fingers over—a normal human face! It was much like a woman's or child's, smooth and completely hairless. But the cast of the features was masculine.

The monster was human!

Jared rose and his foot met a hard object. Before touching it, he bent and snapped his fingers several times. And he had no difficulty recognizing the thing. It was identical to the tubular devices left behind by the monsters in both the Upper and Lower Level.

The creature stirred and Jared dropped the object, diving for his spear.

Just then Della came sprinting down the corridor. "More monsters—coming from the other way!"

Listening around the bend, he could hear the sounds of their approach. And he was aware of the play of their mysterious mute noises along the right wall of the corridor.

He seized the girl's hand and raced on up the passage, letting his spear thump the ground so it would produce sounding impulses.

From ahead he heard the composite of a smaller branch passage. He slowed and headed cautiously into it.

"Let's go this way awhile," he suggested. "I think it'll be safer."

"Is the Zivver scent strong in this passage too?"

"No. But we'll pick it up again. These smaller tunnels usually curve back."

"Oh, well," she said, comforting herself, "at least we shouldn't be bothered by monsters for a while."

"Those aren't monsters." He surmised that, like hearing, zivving impressions weren't refined enough to distinguish between loose cloth and flesh. "They are humans."

He heard her startled expression. "But how can that be?"

"I suppose they are Different Ones—more different than all the others put together. Superior even to the Zivvers."

He let the girl lead the way and anxiously gave his attention to the enigma of the monsters. Perhaps they *were*, after all, devils. It was commonplace to speak of the Twin Devils. But some of the lesser legends referred to, not two, but *many* demons who dwelled in Radiation. Even now he could call to mind several of them, all of whom were usually represented in personified form. There were Carbon-Fourteen; the two U's—Two Thirty-Five and Two Thirty-Eight; Plutonium of the Two Thirty-Nine Level, and that great, sulking, evil being of the Thermonuclear Depth—Hydrogen.

Of Radiation's demons there were many, now that he thought of it. And ascribed to all of them were the capacities of insidious infiltration, ingenious disguise and complete and prolonged contamination. Could it be that the devils, emerging from mythology, had finally decided to exercise their powers?

The girl slowed to pick her way over loose, uneven ground. And the noise of rocks shifting beneath their feet made it even easier to hear the way.

He found himself recalling his recent encounter with the being in the corridor. The silent sound it had cast on the wall was most remarkable, once one managed to overcome the initial horror it brought. Dwelling on those sensations, he remembered how clearly he had seemed to hear—or was it feel, or, perhaps, even ziv?—the details of the wall. He had been completely aware of each tiny ridge and crevice, each protuberance.

Then he stiffened as he drew from memory something the Guardian of the Way had said not too long ago—something about Light in Paradise touching everything and bringing to man total knowledge of all things about him. But, certainly, that material the monsters produced and hurled against the wall *couldn't* be the Almighty! And that corridor *couldn't* have been Paradise!

No. It was impossible. That meager stuff thrown so casually about the passageway by the manlike creature *hadn't* been Light. Of that he was finally and unalterably positive.

As they continued on along the rugged tunnel, his reflections turned to another matter of concern. For the moment it seemed he could almost put his finger on something that there was *less of* in this very passage! But it was too vague a concept to encourage further speculation. It must have been only wishful thinking, he decided, that was suggesting he might accidentally stumble upon Light's opposite, Darkness, in this remote, deserted corridor.

Della drew up before an opening in the wall and pulled him over beside her. "Just ziv this world!" she exclaimed buoyantly.

The wind rushing into the hole was cool against his back as he stood there listening to the delightful music of a gurgling stream and using the echoes of that sound to study other features of the medium-sized world.

"What a wonderful place!" she went on excitedly. "I can ziv five or six hot springs and at least a couple of hundred manna plants. And the banks of the river—they're *covered* with salamanders!"

As she spoke her rebounding words set up an audible composite of their surroundings. And Jared appreciatively took in several natural recesses in the left wall, a high-domed ceiling that insured good circulation, and smooth, level ground all around them.

She locked her arm in his and they walked farther into the world. The wind sweeping in from the corridor gave the air a refreshing coolness that was superior to the Lower Level's.

"I wonder if this was the world my mother was trying to reach," the girl said distantly.

"She couldn't have found a better place. I'd say it would support a large family and all its descendants for several generations."

They sat on a steep bank overhearing the river and Jared listened to the *swishing* of large fish beneath the surface while Della parceled out food from her case.

After a while he probed audibly beneath her silence and caught the suggestion of yet another area of uncertainty.

"There's something bothering you, isn't there?" he asked.

She nodded. "I still don't understand about Leah and you. I can hear now that she *did* visit you in your dreams. Yet, you yourself said she couldn't reach the mind of a Zivver."

Now he was certain she didn't know he couldn't ziv. For if she were out here for some treacherous reason, the last thing she'd do would be to let him find out she suspected him.

"I've already told you I think I'm a little different from other Zivvers," he reminded. "Right now I'm zivving a half-dozen fish in the river. You can't ziv a single one."

She lay back on the ground and, out of crossed arms, made a cushion for her head. "I hope you're not *too* different. I wouldn't want to feel—inferior."

Her words struck home with unintended mockery. And he knew that being inferior to her was what *he* had resented all along.

"If we weren't hunting for the Zivver World," she offered, yawning, "this would be a nice place to settle in, wouldn't it?"

"Maybe staying here is the best thing we could do."

He stretched out beside her and, even from the negligible echoes of his breathing, he could hear the attractive composite of the girl's face, the gentle, firm contours of her shoulders, hips, waist—all veiled in the whispering softness of near inaudibility.

"It might be a—good idea," she said drowsily, "if we—decided—"

He waited. But from her direction came only the slight body murmurs of sleep.

He turned over, crooked an arm under his head and banished the maudlin, wistful thought that had begun to obscure his purpose. He had to concede, though, that it *would* be pleasant to remain here in this remote world with Della and put out of his mind forever the Zivvers, human monsters, soubats, Upper and Lower Levels, Survivorship, and all the chains of formality and restrictions of communal law. And, yes, even his hopeless quest for Light and Darkness.

But such an arrangement was not for him. Della was a Zivver—a superior Different One. And he would always have to listen up to her and her greater abilities. It would never do. What was it he had once overheard one Zivver tell another during a raid?— "A Zivver down here is the same as a one-eared man in a world of the deaf."

That was it. He would always be like an invalid, with Della to lead him around by the hand. And in her incomprehensible world of murmuring air currents and psychic awareness of things he could never hope to hear, he would be lost and frustrated.

Even from the depths of sleep he could tell that he had lain there beside the girl a long while—perhaps the equivalent of a slumber period or more. And he surely must have been close to wakefulness when he heard the screams.

Had they been Della's, they would have jolted him from sleep. That he continued to hear them without awakening was a measure of their psychic quality. They seemed to come from deep within his mind, spawned in a vortex of projected terror.

Then he recognized Leah behind the desperate, silent outcries. He tried to distill concrete meaning from the hodge-podge of frantic impressions. But the woman was in such a panic that she couldn't put her fright into words.

Digging into the emotions of terrible astonishment and dismay, he intercepted piecemeal impressions—shouting and screaming, rushing feet and roaring bursts of silent sound that played derisively across walls which had been such a warm and real part of his childhood fantasies, an occasional *zip-hiss*.

The composite was unmistakable: The human monsters had finally found Leah's world!

"Jared! Jared! Soubats—coming in from the passage!" Della shook him awake.

He grabbed his spear and sprang to his feet. The first of the three or four beasts that had winged into the world was almost upon them. There was scarcely time to hurl Della to the ground and plant his spear in readiness for the initial impact.

The lead creature screeched down in a vicious dive and took the point of the weapon full in its chest. The lance snapped in half and the beast struck the ground with jarring impact.

The second and third hateful furies began their plunge.

He hurled the girl into the river and leaped in after her. In less than a beat the current, immensely swifter than he had estimated, was sweeping her away—toward the side wall where the stream rushed into a subterranean channel.

He heard that he couldn't overtake her in time, but he swam ahead anyway. A soubat's wingtip thrashed the water in front of him, talons barely missing their mark in a swooping attack.

At the beginning of his next stroke, his hand touched Della's hair, frothing on the surface of the water, and he secured a grip on it. But too late. The current had already sucked them into the subsurface channel and had drawn boulders of water in behind them.

CHAPTER TWELVE

Savage undercurrents flung him to the right and left and finally sent him plunging into the depths. He caromed against the jagged bed of the stream, then swirled upward. Jared found no air for his bursting lungs as he crashed into the submerged ceiling. Yet, he managed to maintain his grip on Della's hair.

Again and again the girl was dashed against him while he choked down the terrifying realization that the stream might rush on eternally through an infinity of rock without ever again flowing up into an air-filled world.

When he could hold his breath no longer, his head grazed a final stretch of ceiling, slipped under a ledge and bobbed to the surface. He pulled the girl up beside him and gulped great draughts of air. Sensing the nearness of the bank, he grabbed a partially exposed rock and anchored himself against it while he shoved her ashore. When he heard that she was still breathing, he crawled out and collapsed beside her.

Gestations later, after his pounding heartbeat slowed to a tolerable pace, he became aware of the roaring spatter of a nearby cataract. The noise and its distant reflections traced out the broad expanse of a high-domed world. But he started as he detected a variety of other sounds that barely pierced the audible curtain of cascading water—the remote clatter of manna shells, the thumping of rock against rock, the bleat of a sheep, voices, many voices, far and indistinct.

Confounded, he sneezed more water out of his nose. He rose, dislodging a pebble and listening to it clatter down an incline that sloped off alongside the waterfall. Then he caught a powerful, unmistakable scent and sat up, alert and excited.

"Jared!" The girl stood up beside him. "*We're in the Zivver World! Just ziv it! It's exactly as I thought it would be!*"

He listened sharply, but the composite, etched only by the dull sound of falling water, was fuzzy and confusing. Yet, he could hear the soft, fibrous tones of a manna orchard off on his left, a gaping exit to the corridor on the far right. And he picked up the impressions of many queer, evenly spaced forms in the center of the world. Arranged in rows, each was shaped like a cube with rectangular openings in its sides. And he recognized them for what they were—living quarters fashioned after those in the Original World and possibly made out of manna stalks tied together.

Della started forward, her pulse accelerating in a surge of excitement. "Isn't it a wonderful world? And ziv the Zivvers—so many of them!"

Not at all sharing the girl's enthusiasm, he followed her down the incline, gaining his perception of the terrain from echoes of the waterfall.

It was indeed a strange world. He had managed by now to garner the impressions of many Zivvers at work and play, others busy carrying soil and rocks and piling them up in the main entrance. But all that activity, without the reassuring tones of a central echo caster, gave an uncanny, forbidding cast to the world about him.

Moreover, he was sorely disappointed. He had hoped that on stepping into the Zivver domain the difference he had been hunting all his life would fairly leap out at him. Oh, it was going to be so easy! Zivvers had eyes and, in using them, they materially affected the universal Darkness, eating holes in it, so to speak—just as hearing sound ate holes in silence. And, simply by recognizing what there was less of, he was going to identify Darkness.

But he could hear *nothing* unusual. Many persons were down there zivving. Yet, everything was exactly the same here as in any other world, except for the absence of an echo caster and the presence of the sharp Zivver scent.

Della quickened her pace but he restrained her. "We don't want to startle them."

"There's nothing to worry about. We're both Zivvers."

Near enough to the settled area to intercept impressions from the rebounding sounds of communal activities, he followed the girl around the orchard and past a row of animal pens. Discovery finally came as they approached a party working on the nearest geometrical dwelling place. Jared heard an apprehensive silence fall upon the group and listened to heads twisting alertly in his direction.

"We're Zivvers," Della called out confidently. "We came here because we belong here."

The men advanced silently, spreading out to converge on them from several directions.

"Mogan!" one of them shouted. "Over here—quick!"

Several Zivvers lunged and caught Jared's arms, pinning them to his sides. Della too, he heard, was receiving the same treatment.

"We're not armed," he protested.

Others were gathering around now and he was grateful for the background of agitated voices that, in the absence of an echo caster, sounded out the more prominent details of his surroundings.

Two faces pushed close to his and he listened to eyes that were wide open and severe in their steadiness. He made certain his own lids were fully raised and unblinking.

"The *girl's* zivving," vouched someone off to his left.

An open hand fanned the air abruptly in front of his face and he was unable to keep his eyelids from flicking.

"I suppose this one is too," the owner of the hand attested. "At least, his eyes *are* open."

Jared and Della were hustled ahead between the rows of dwelling units while scores of Zivver Survivors collected from all over the world. Concentrating on vocal sounds and their reflections, he caught the impression of an immense figure pushing through the crowd and instantly recognized the man as Mogan, the Zivver leader.

"Who let them in?" Mogan demanded.

"They didn't get by the entrance," someone assured.

"They say they're Zivvers," offered another.

"Are they?" Mogan asked.

"They're both open-eyed."

The leader's voice boomed down on Jared. "What are you doing here? How did you get in?"

Della answered first. "This is where we belong."

"We were attacked by soubats beyond that far wall," Jared explained. "We jumped into the river and washed up in here."

Mogan's voice lost some of its severity. "You must have had a Radiation of a time. I'm the only one who's ever gotten in that way." Then, boastfully, "Made it through *against* the current a couple of times, too. What were you doing out there?"

"Looking for this world," Della replied. "We're both Zivvers."

"Like compost you are!" Mogan shot back. "There was only *one* original Zivver. All of us are his descendants. You're not. *You* came from one of the Levels."

"True," she admitted. "But my father was a Zivver—Nathan Bradley."

Somewhere in the background a Survivor drew in a tense breath and started forward. It was the anxious, heavy gasp of an elderly man.

"Nathan!" he exclaimed. "My son!"

But someone held him off.

"Nathan Bradley?" the man on Jared's left repeated uncertainly.

"Sure," answered another. "You heard about him. Used to spend all his time out in the passages—until he disappeared."

Then Jared felt the blast of Mogan's words directed down at him again. "What about you?"

"He's another original Zivver," Della said.

"And I'm a soubat's uncle!" the leader blurted.

Once more Jared's self-confidence slid off into doubt over the ability to carry off his disguise as a Zivver. Groping for something convincing to say, he offered, "Maybe I'm *not* an original Zivver. You *do* have people who desert your world from time to time and who might be responsible for other spurs. There was Nathan, and there was Estel—"

"Estel!" a woman exclaimed, pushing through the crowd. "What do you know about my daughter?"

"I was the one who sent her back here the first time I zivved her out near the Main Passage."

The woman seized his arms and he could almost feel the pressure of her eyes. "Where is she? What's happened to her?"

"She came to the Lower Level listening—zivving for me. That was how everybody found out I was a Zivver. After that I couldn't very well stay down there."

"Where is my child?" the woman demanded.

Reluctantly, he related what had happened to Estel. A condoling silence fell over the world while the Survivoress was led away sobbing.

"So you swam in under the rocks," Mogan mused. "Lucky you didn't get caught in the waterfall on this side."

"Then we can stay?" Jared asked hopefully, trying to keep his eyes steady just as Mogan was doing.

"For the moment, yes."

In the silence that followed, Jared sensed a subtle change in his perception of the Zivver leader. For some reason, Mogan was unconsciously holding his breath and his heartbeat had increased slightly. Jared concentrated on the effects and detected, even more faintly, that particular physical tension which claims a person intent on some crafty purpose. Then he caught the almost inaudible impression of Mogan's hand rising slowly before him. He coughed casually and, in the reflections of the sound, discerned that the hand was slyly waiting to be clasped.

Without hesitation, his own hand shot forward and grasped the other. "Did you think I wouldn't ziv that?" he asked, laughing.

"We've got to be careful," Mogan said. "I've zivved Levelers who could hear so well that they might easily be mistaken for one of us."

"What reason would we have for coming here if we *weren't* Zivvers?"

"I don't know. But we're not taking any chances—not with those creatures stalking the passages. Even now we're sealing the entrance before they can find it. But what good would that do if they learned there was another way to get in—a way that can't be blocked?"

Mogan stepped between Jared and the girl and led them off. "We're going to keep an eye on you until we're sure we can trust you. Meanwhile, I know how you feel after swimming under those rocks. So we'll give you a chance to rest."

They were led to adjacent dwelling units—"shacks," Jared had heard one of the Zivvers call them—and were ushered in through rectangular openings. Guards were posted outside each structure.

Standing uncertainly within the enclosure, Jared cleared his throat rather loudly. Echoes of the sound brought details of a recess strikingly different from any of the residential grottoes he had known. Here, everything was an adaptation of the rectangle. There was a dining slab whose remarkably level surface was composed of husks woven tightly together and stretched across a framework of manna stalks. He laid his hand casually upon it and traced the weave. Four other stalks, he heard, served as legs to hold the level section off the floor.

He yawned as though it were a quite spontaneous expression of weariness—in case anybody should be listening or zivving—and studied the reflected auditory pattern. Arranged around the dining slab were benches of similar construction. The slumber ledge, too, was a flimsy thing supported on the apparently traditional four legs.

Then he drew up sharply, but tried not to give any indication he had discovered he was being listened to—zivved, he reminded himself. There was an elevated opening in the right wall, beyond the slumber ledge. And through that space he caught the sound of breathing purposely made shallow to insure concealment. Someone was standing out there zivving everything he did.

Very well, the safest course would be to move about as little as possible and thereby reduce the chances of betraying himself.

He yawned noisily once more, fixing in mind the position of the slumber ledge. Then he went over and lay down. They expected him to be exhausted, didn't they? Then why not *be* exhausted?

Comfortable against the softness of the manna fiber mattress, he realized that swimming the underground river *had* been an ordeal. And it wasn't too long before he was asleep.

☼

Scream after scream crashed in on his slumber and once again he recognized the impressions as nonaudible.

Leah!

Forcing himself to remain in the dream, he tried to pry more deeply beyond the communicative link with Kind Survivoress. But the erratic contact conveyed only the essence of horror and despair. He tried to work his way physically toward the woman and succeeded in tightening somewhat the bond between them.

"*Monsters! Monsters! Monsters!*" she was sobbing over and over again.

And through her torment he caught the sensation of her eyelids being closed so tightly that the inner portions of her ears were roaring under the pressure; strong, determined hands gripping her arms and pulling her first this way, then that; a sharp point jabbing brutally into her shoulder; odors so frightfully offensive in their alien quality that he felt like gagging with her.

Then he intercepted the impression of fingers digging into the flesh above and below her eyes and forcing the lids open.

And instantly all Radiation screamed at him through the woman's conscious. He recognized the stentorian blare of silent sound as being identical to the stuff the monsters had hurled against the corridor walls. Only, now it was overpowering as it crashed against Leah's eyes. He feared the woman would be driven insane.

With that single convulsive sensation he lurched out of the nightmare which he knew had been no nightmare at all.

What he had heard through Kind Survivoress' eyes certainly could have been nothing but the Nuclear Fire of Radiation itself. It was as though he had crossed the boundary of material existence to share part of the torture the Atomic Demons were meting out to her beyond infinity.

Trembling, he lay motionless on the slumber ledge while the bitter aftertaste of his pseudo dream experience persisted like a fever.

Leah—gone.

Her world—empty.

The corridors—populated with monstrous humans who hurled derisive, screaming echoes that carried no sound at all. Fiendish creatures who struck their victims with paralysis before carrying them—where?

A Zivver came in, placed a shell of food on the dining surface and left without speaking. Jared went over and picked at the ration. But his interest in the meal was submerged in the remorseful realization that, during his foolhardy quest for Darkness and Light, his familiar worlds had crumbled all about him.

The pace of irrevocable change had been furious and relentless. And he grimly suspected that things would, *could* never be the same. Certainly, the malevolent beings in their outlandish attire of loosely fitting cloths had laid claim to all the worlds and passages and were now taking over with vehement determination. He was sure, too, that the design of hot spring failures and dwindling water level was but another phase of their scheme.

And while all these things had happened he had squandered his time searching for something trivial, nursing the belief that Light was desirable. He had let the solid things of material worth slip from his grasp as he chased a whimsical breeze down an endless corridor.

Things may have been different had he, instead, organized the Levels and led the fight for Survival. There might even have been hope of returning to a normal pattern of existence, with Della as his Unification partner. Perhaps he might not even have found out she was—Different.

But it was too late now. He was a virtual prisoner in the very world which he had expected would provide the key to his futile quest for Light. And both he and the Zivvers were themselves helpless captives of the monsters who ruled the corridors.

He pushed the food aside and ran a hand through his hair. Outside, the world was animate with the audible effects of an activity period in full swing—loud conversation, children at play and, more remotely, the sound of rocks being piled on rocks as workers continued sealing off the entrance. Listlessly, he made a note of the fact that the latter noises were an excellent echo source.

But, more directly, he concerned himself with the despair which came with his conviction that he would find nothing *different* here—nothing to justify having extended his search for Darkness and Light to this world.

Among the nearer audible effects he recognized Della's voice coming from the next shack. It was a happy, excited voice that leaped from subject to subject with a bubbling rapidity and was at times obscured by the effusive words of several other women. From bits of the conversation he gathered that she had quickly located all her Zivver relatives.

The curtains parted and Mogan stood in the entrance. His bulky form, silhouetted only by back sounding, coarsely punctured the silence of the shack.

The Zivver leader beckoned with a distinctive twist of his head. "It's about time we made sure you're one of us."

Jared feigned an indifferent shrug and followed him outside.

Mogan led the way alongside a row of dwelling units as many other Zivvers fell in behind them.

They reached a clearing and the leader drew to a halt. "We're going to have a little rough-and-tumble—just you and me."

Frowning obtusely, Jared listened up at the man.

"That's the surest way to find out whether you're really zivving, don't you agree?" Mogan said, spreading his hands.

And Jared heard that they were huge hands, altogether commensurate with the size of the man. "I suppose it is," he agreed, with just a tinge of futility.

A figure broke out of the crowd and he recognized Della as she started toward him, concern heavy in the shallowness of her breathing. But someone caught her arm and drew her back.

"Ready?" Mogan asked.

Jared braced himself, "Ready."

But apparently the Zivver leader *wasn't* ready—not just yet.

"All right, Owlson," he shouted, facing the party that was still working at the entrance. "I want complete silence over there."

Then he turned to those around him. "Nobody makes a sound—understand?"

Jared concealed his hopelessness and said sarcastically, "You're forgetting I can still smell." He realized gratefully that Mogan had also forgotten about the noise of the waterfall which, thank Light, *couldn't* be silenced.

"Oh, we're not finished with the preparations," the other laughed.

Several Zivvers seized Jared's arms while another caught his hair and twisted his head back. Then wads of coarse, moist substance were stuffed into his ears and forced up his nostrils—mud!

Released into an odorless, soundless void, he brought his hands up to his face. But before he could dig the clay from his ears, Mogan closed in and locked his neck in a rocklike grip. He was wrenched off his feet and hurled violently to the ground.

Disoriented because there was no sound or scent to guide him, he sprang up and delivered a blow that landed on nothing and succeeded only in throwing him off balance again.

Dimly, he heard the laughter that filtered through the mud in his ears. But the sound was too vague to bear any impressions of Mogan's whereabouts. Fists swinging, Jared stumbled forward, circling—until the Zivver leader clouted him on the back of his neck and flattened him once more.

When he tried to rise this time, a fist pounded into his face, almost taking his head off. And he would have been convinced the following blow did accomplish that purpose if unconsciousness had not deprived him of the ability to be sure of anything.

Eventually, he responded to the stinging splash of water against his face and raised himself on an elbow. The mud had fallen from one of his ears and he could hear the circle of men who stood zivving menacingly down on him.

From within the crowd came the voices of Mogan and Della:

"Of course I knew he wasn't a Zivver," the girl was maintaining.

Irately, Mogan reminded, "And yet you brought him here."

"*He* brought *me.*" She laughed scornfully. "I couldn't have made it by myself. My only chance was to let him think I believed he was a Zivver too."

"Why didn't you tell the truth before this?"

"And give him a chance to turn on me before you could stop him? Anyway, I knew you'd find out for yourself sooner or later."

Jared shook his head dully, remembering Leah's warning against the girl and his own doubts from time to time. If he had been able to listen beyond the lobe of his ear, he might have heard that she was using him all along merely as an escort in her search for the Zivver World.

He tried to rise, but someone planted a foot on his shoulder and pressed him back against the ground.

"What's he doing here?" Mogan asked the girl.

"I don't know exactly. He's hunting for something and he thinks he might find it here."

"What?"

"Darkness."

Mogan made his way over and hauled Jared to his feet. "What did you come here for?"

Jared said nothing.

"Were you trying to find this world so you could lead a raid on it?"

When that drew no response, the leader added, "Or are you helping *the monsters* locate us?"

Still Jared offered no reply.

"We'll let you think it over awhile. You might realize a frank tongue *could* make things easier for you."

Jared, however, sensed there would be no leniency. For, as long as he was alive, they would always fear he might escape and carry out whatever purpose they suspected he was concealing.

Trussed with fiber rope, he was taken halfway across the world and shoved into a dwelling unit not far from the roaring cataract. It was a cramped shack whose wall openings were barred with stout manna stems.

CHAPTER THIRTEEN

Several times during his first period of confinement Jared entertained the idea of escape. Breaking out of the manna shack, he heard, would be relatively simple—if he could manage to free his hands. His wrists, however, were too securely bound.

But escape to—what? With the main entrance already blocked by the work party and the barrier it was erecting and with the savage currents of the underground river facing him in the other direction, freedom from the shack would be meaningless.

Under other circumstances, he might have eagerly listened forward to bolting captivity. But outside the Zivver domain were nothing but monster-filled corridors. Moreover, the other worlds must certainly have been laid desolate by the hateful creatures. And the only incentive that might have driven him on— the hope of finding a hidden, self-sufficient dwelling area for himself and Della—had been stripped away when the girl had turned against him.

During the second period he stood before the barred opening in the side of the shack and listened to the work crew as it finished blocking off the main entrance. Then, hopelessly, he leaned back against the wall and let the roar of the nearby cataract sweep his attention away from the other sounds.

In self-reproach he wondered what had made him think he might find Light in this miserable world. He had supposed that, since Zivvers could know what lay ahead without hearing, they must be exercising the same sort of power all men could presumably exercise in the presence of Light Almighty. And he had foolishly thought that the result of this activity would be a lessening of Darkness. But he had neglected one possibility: that lessness of Darkness might be something only the Zivvers themselves could recognize—something forever removed from his own perception as a result of sensory limitations.

Stymied in his speculations on the Light-Darkness-Zivver relationship, he went over and lay on the slumber surface. He tried to keep Della from entering his thoughts but couldn't. Then, objectively, he conceded that what she had done—tricking him into bringing her here—merely reflected a treachery basic to the nature of all Zivvers. Now Leah, on the other hand, never would have...

Finding himself thinking of Kind Survivoress, he wondered what had happened to her. Perhaps she was even now trying to contact him from the depths of Radiation. Unless he were asleep, though, he would never know it.

For the rest of that period, except when they brought his food, he spent as much time in slumber as he could, hoping she would come again. But she didn't.

Toward the end of his third period of confinement he detected a faint noise outside the shack—a scurrying that was close enough to be audible above the throbbing spatter of the cataract. Then he caught Della's scent as she sprang forward and flattened herself against the outer wall.

"Jared!" she whispered anxiously.

"Go away."

"But I want to help you!"

"You've helped enough already."

"Use your head. Would I be free to come here now if I had acted *any other* way in front of Mogan?"

He listened to her fumbling with the solid curtain's rope lock. "I suppose you waited for the *first* opportunity to let me loose," he said disinterestedly.

"Of course. It didn't come until just now—when the Zivvers started hearing noises out in the corridor."

The last rope parted and Della entered as the rigid partition of manna stalks swung outward.

"Go on back to your Zivver friends," he grumbled.

"Light, but you're thickheaded!" She put a sawbone knife to work on his bonds. "Can you swim back through that river?"

"What difference does it make?"

"There's the Levels to return to."

His wrists fell free. "I doubt if there's enough of the Levels left to go back to, even if they *didn't* think I'm a Zivver."

"One of the secluded worlds then." And she repeated obstinately, "Can you swim the river?"

"I think so."

"All right, then—let's go." She started out of the shack.

But he held back. "You mean *you'd* go too?"

"You didn't think I'd stay here without you?"

"But this is your world! It's where you belong! Anyway, I'm not even a Zivver."

She let out an exasperated breath. "Listen—at first I was carried away with the fact that I had found someone like me. Why, I never even stopped to wonder whether it would make any difference if you *weren't* a Zivver. Then there you were lying on the ground with Mogan standing over you. And I knew it wouldn't matter if you couldn't even hear or smell or taste. *Now* can we get on our way and start hunting for that hidden world?"

Before he could say anything else, she nudged him toward the incline that would take them above the waterfall. And Jared sensed the pall of fear that lay over the Zivver World. In the distance the settled area was enveloped in a thick, ominous silence. From the indistinct echoes of cascading water, he received a composite of Zivvers drawing apprehensively back from the barricaded entrance.

Halfway up the rise he drew up sharply and his nostrils flared around a disturbing scent drifting down from above. Desperately, he scooped up several pebbles and rattled them in the hollow of his hand. In full audible clarity, Mogan stood waiting at the top of the slope.

"I suppose you think you're going to escape and tell the monsters how to get in," he said threateningly.

Jared clicked his stones rapidly, precisely, and trapped impressions of the Zivver beginning his charge downhill.

But just then the noise of a thousand cataracts abruptly rocked the world. At the same time a great, angry burst of the monsters' roaring silence stabbed into the Zivver domain from the vicinity of the blocked entrance. And, in the next beat, everyone below was screaming and scurrying frantically about as the reopened tunnel belched a mercilessly steady cone of inaudible sound.

Jared scrambled to the top of the incline, tugging Della along. Mogan, stunned, retreated with them.

"Light Almighty!" the Zivver leader swore. "What in Radiation's happening?"

"I've never zivved anything like this!" Della exclaimed, terrified.

Intense, painful sensations assaulted Jared's eyes, confusing but somehow complementing his auditory perception of the entire world. Noise reflections fetched a more or less complete impression of the fissure-rent far wall. Yet, also associated with that wall somehow were areas of concentrated silent sound that etched every detail of its surface as clearly as though he were running his hand over all of it simultaneously.

Suddenly the wall faded into relative silence and he managed to link that development with the fact that the furious cone had shifted and was at the moment cutting across another segment of the auditory composite. Now he seemed to be aware of the presence and size and shape of each shack in the center of the settlement. The fierce, screaming silence touched every object within hearing range and boiled into his conscious with agonizing ruthlessness.

He clamped his hands over his face and found immediate relief while he listened to monsters pouring in from the passageway. And with them came the familiar *zip-hisses*.

"Don't be afraid!" one of the creatures shouted.

"Throw some Light this way!" another cried.

The words reverberated in Jared's mind. What did they _mean_? Was Light actually associated with these evil beings? How could anyone *throw* Light? Once before he had wildly assumed that the stuff these creatures hurled ahead of themselves in the passages might somehow be Light. And he had at once rejected that possibility, just as he was forced to discard it anew now.

His eyes flicked open involuntarily but he only stood there, confounded by a new bewilderment. For a moment he could almost detect a deficiency of something—just as he had imagined once before that he was on the verge of putting his finger on the lessness he was seeking. Now the conviction was even firmer that there was not as much of *something*

in the Zivver World as there had been before the evil beings came!

"The monsters!" Mogan shouted. "They're coming up here!"

Della screamed and the reflection of her voice brought back the impression of three of the creatures racing up the incline.

"Jared!" she tugged on his arm. "Let's get—"

Zip-hiss.

She collapsed and before he could seize her she went rolling down the incline. Frantically, Jared started after the girl. But Mogan held him back, saying, "We can't help her now."

"We can if we reach her before—"

But the Zivver leader swung him around, shoved him into the river and dived in after him.

Before Jared could shout out in protest, Mogan dragged him beneath the surface and began the desperate underwater swim against the current. He fought stubbornly against the other's grip, but the combination of giant strength and the threat of drowning swamped his struggles and there was nothing he could do but allow himself to be towed helplessly along.

At a point that he judged to be halfway through the underground stretch, the current hurled him against a boulder and whatever air he had managed to retain in his lungs escaped in an involuntary grunt. Mogan plunged for the bottom and Jared frenziedly staved off the compulsion to release his breath. His resistance snapped finally and a great mouthful of water boiled down his windpipe.

✧

He revived to the rhythmic motion of the Zivver's broad hands as they pressed down on the small of his back and withdrew, pressed and withdrew. He retched and coughed up warm water.

Mogan stopped pumping air into his lungs and helped him to a sitting position. "Guess I was wrong about you plotting with those creatures," he said apologetically.

"Della!" Jared exclaimed between coughs. "I've got to get back in there!"

"It's too late. The place is filled with monsters."

Jared listened anxiously for the river. But he heard no water anywhere around them. "Where are we?" he demanded.

"Out in a lesser passage. After I dragged you ashore I had to haul you off before the soubats got us."

Listening to reflections of the words, Jared traced out the details of a tunnel that broadened ahead after issuing from the constriction of pinched walls behind them. And from back there came the infuriated sounds of the soubats that couldn't get through.

"We're not headed toward the main corridor, are we?" he asked disappointedly.

"The opposite direction. It beats fighting off soubats barehanded."

Jared rose and steadied himself against the wall. There might have been a chance of overtaking the monsters in the larger passageway, but the soubats had overruled that possibility, he conceded glumly. "Where does this tunnel lead?"

"Never been this way before."

Realizing he had no choice, Jared followed the reflections of their voices down the corridor.

Later, when he stumbled for a second time, he wondered why he was groping around in a noiseless passage without sounding stones. He felt along the ground until he found a pair of pebbles that almost matched, then filled the air with *clicks* before continuing.

After a while Mogan said, "You hear pretty good with those things, don't you?"

"I manage." Then Jared heard he was being abrupt for no reason at all, unless it was because he resented the Zivver's having kept him from trying to reach Della—an attempt which certainly would have failed anyway.

"I've had practice with the things," he added more affably.

"I suppose they're all right for someone who can't ziv," Mogan ventured, "but I'm afraid the noise would drive me crazy."

They traveled in silence for some time. And, as Jared's steps took him farther from the Zivver domain, the possibility that he might never hear Della again burdened him with despair. He knew finally that he would have settled with her in a secluded world and that it would have made no difference whether she was his superior or not—as long as they could be together.

But now she was gone and another—the most vital—part of his universe had crumbled beneath him. He berated himself for having failed to recognize what she meant to him, for his distorted sense of values that prompted him to attach more importance to an insane quest for Light and Darkness. Finding her, he vowed, would be his single purpose, even if it carried him to the Thermonuclear Depths of Radiation. And if he couldn't snatch her back from the monsters, then Radiation would be his deserved punishment.

They passed a lesser chasm and the Zivver leader fell in alongside him. "Della said you were hunting for Light and Darkness."

"Forget it," Jared snapped, determined to forget it himself.

"But I'm interested. If you had been a Zivver, I was going to have a talk with you."

Somewhat curious, Jared asked, "About what?"

"I don't put any stock in the legends either. I always thought the Great Light Almighty was unnecessary glorification for something commonplace."

"You did?"

"I've even decided what Light *is*."

Jared halted the march. "What is it?"

"Warmth."

"How do you figure that?"

"There's warmth all around us, isn't there? Greater warmth we call 'heat'; lesser warmth, 'cold.' The warmer a thing is, the more impressions it sends to a Zivver's eyes."

Jared nodded pensively. "And it lets you know about things without feeling, hearing, or smelling them."

Mogan shrugged. "Which is what the legends say Light does."

There was something inconsistent here, but Jared couldn't quite decide what. Perhaps it was just his reluctance to admit Light might be something as prosaic as heat. He resumed the march and stepped more briskly as he heard a larger corridor ahead.

At the same time Mogan said, "I ziv another passage up there, a big one."

Jared trotted forward, sounding his clickstones more rapidly to accommodate the greater speed. But he jolted to a stop as he broke into the larger tunnel.

"What's wrong?" Mogan paused beside him.

"This place reeks with the scent of monsters!" Jared flared his nostrils, sucking in samples of air. "That's not all. There's the smell of Upper and Lower Level people too—almost as strong as the other odor."

From his clickstone echoes he received an impression of the Zivver leader running a hand over his brow.

"This corridor's Radiation on the eyes!" Mogan exclaimed. "Too much warmth. It's hard to ziv one thing from another."

Jared, too, had felt the heat. But he was concerned with a different consideration. There was something familiar about this stretch of passage, about its formations of tumbled rocks. Then it struck him. Of course—they were just outside the Original World! He clicked his stones again and detected the slab behind which he and Owen had hidden from his first encounter with a monster. Around the bend to his right would be the Original World entrance and, beyond that, the Barrier and the Levels.

"Which way should we go?" Mogan asked.

"To the left," Jared suggested impulsively, shoving off.

After a few paces, he said, "So you think heat is Light."

"I do."

"And Darkness?"

"Simple. Darkness is coolness."

Now Jared had his finger on the inconsistency. "You're wrong. Only Zivvers can sense heat and cold from a distance. Tell me one legend that holds Light will be the exclusive property of Zivvers. All the beliefs say *everybody* will be Reunited with Light."

"I've got that figured out too. It's just that the Zivvers are the first step toward general Reunion."

Jared was going to protest that assumption also. But he had just negotiated a bend in the corridor and now he drew back reflexively. Riding the crest of his clickstone echoes were the details of another curve ahead. And he was profoundly aware of a tremendous flow of silent sound pouring from around that bend. It was as though a thousand human-inhuman creatures were marching in his direction, all hurling screaming silence before them.

"I can't ziv a thing!" Mogan complained desperately.

Jared listened but heard no audible sounds of monsters around the bend. Cautiously, he pressed forward, determined this time to keep his eyes open. His face contorted in protest to volition and muscles grew taut as they tried unsuccessfully to close the lids they controlled. Squinting and trembling, he found himself going ahead and forgetting to use his stones.

Mogan came along, trailing by a considerable distance, though, and emitting an occasional distressed oath.

Jared reached the bend and plunged swiftly around it, afraid that if he hesitated he might turn and flee. Now the dreadful stuff was flowing into his eyes with the force of a hundred hot springs and he could no longer keep them open. Tears streaming down his cheeks, he stumbled forward, relying once more on his pebbles.

His steps, however, were mired in terror. For, from ahead came *no* echoes of his *clicks—none at all!* But that was impossible! Never had anyone heard a noise that didn't reflect from *all* directions. Yet, here was a great, incredible gap in a sound pattern!

His fear finally became an absolute barrier and he could go no farther. Standing as motionless as though he had been planted there like a manna tree, he shouted.

There were *no* reflections of his voice from ahead, from above, from either side! From behind, the returning sound etched the presence of a great wall of rock that towered many times the height of even the Zivver World dome. And in this wall he detected the muffled hollowness of the corridor he had just left.

The decision struck him with the force of a falling boulder: *He was in infinity!* And it was not an endless stretch of rock that surrounded him, but an unbounded expanse of—*air!*

Terrified, he backed toward the passage. For all beliefs had held that there were only two infinities—Paradise and Radiation.

Another step and he collided with Mogan.

The Zivver leader exclaimed, "I can't even keep my eyes open! Where are we?"

"I—" Jared choked on his words. "I think we're in Radiation."

"Light! I smell it!"

"The smell of the monsters. But it's not *their* scent at all—just the odor of this place."

Dismayed, Jared retreated again toward the passageway. Then he became more aware of the intense heat and readily understood why the other's zivving ability had been deafened. Mogan was used to the normal range of warmth in the worlds and corridors. Here, the heat of all the boiling springs in existence was pouring down from above.

And, abruptly, Jared knew he could not leave this infinity without definitely identifying it. Already he suspected which one it was. The heat was a more than sufficient clue. But he had to make certain. Bracing himself against the expected pain, he opened his eyes and let the tears out.

The uncanny impressions that assailed him were fuzzy this time and he wiped his cheeks with the back of his hand.

Then the composites came—sensations that he suspected were something like ziv impressions. He was uncannily aware—through the medium of his eyes themselves—that the ground sloped away in front of him toward a patch of tiny, slender things that swayed this way and that in the distance. Vaguely, he was reminded of manna trees. Only, their tops were lacy and delicate. And he remembered the Paradise plant legend.

But *this* was an infinity of *heat*, not at all suggestive of heavenly things.

Between the trees he zivved the details of small, geometrical forms, arranged in rows like the shacks in the Original World. Another supposed feature of Paradise.

But *monsters* dwelled here.

Suddenly he directed his attention to one paramount fact:

He was receiving detailed impressions of an infinite number of things at one time, without having to hear or smell them!

Which was a capability possible only in the presence of the Great Light Almighty.

This, then, was it.

This was the end of his search.

He had found Light. And Light *was*, after all, the stuff the monsters hurled ahead of themselves in the passageways.

But Light was not in Paradise.

It was in the infinity of Radiation with the Nuclear monsters.

All the legends, all the tenets were bitterly misleading.

For man there was *no* Paradise.

And, with the Atomic Demons roaming the passageways at will, humanity had reached the end of its material existence.

He threw his head back in desperation and full against his face crashed the deadliest silent sound imaginable.

It was an impression so fierce that it seemed to boil his eyes right out of their sockets.

Screaming at him in all its fury was a great, round vicious thing that dominated Radiation with incredible force and heat and malignant majesty.

Hydrogen Himself!

Jared spun around and bolted for the passage, hardly aware that he had, at the same time, heard a noise on the incline before him.

Mogan shouted. But the anguished outcry was interrupted by a *zip-hiss*.

Jared made it back into the corridor, racing frantically after the echoes of his clickstones.

To be continued in Issue Four

SIMULACRON-3

DANIEL F. GALOUYE

Afterword by
Mike Resnick

A book on virtual reality,
before virtual reality
became real

Printed in Dunstable, United Kingdom